D1505457

The Preserve

The Preserve

A Novel

Steve Anderson

Skyhorse Publishing

First Edition

This is a work of fiction. Names, places, characters, and incidents are either the products of the author's imagination or are used fictitiously.

Skyhorse Publishing books may be purchased in bulk at special discounts for sales promotion, corporate gifts, fund-raising, or educational purposes. Special editions can also be created to specifications. For details, contact the Special Sales Department, Skyhorse Publishing, 307 West 36th Street, 11th Floor, New York, NY 10018 or info@skyhorsepublishing.com.

Skyhorse® and Skyhorse Publishing® are registered trademarks of Skyhorse Publishing, Inc.®, a Delaware corporation.

Visit our website at www.skyhorsepublishing.com.
Visit the author at www.stephenfanderson.com.

10 9 8 7 6 5 4 3 2 1

Library of Congress Cataloging-in-Publication Data is available on file.
Library of Congress Control Number: 2019945270

Jacket design by Erin Seaward-Hiatt
Jacket photograph: iStockphoto

Print ISBN: 978-1-5107-4209-3
Ebook ISBN: 978-1-5107-4210-9

Printed in the United States of America.

AUTHOR'S NOTE

Before and during World War II, the Imperial Japanese conquered and subjugated Asia without mercy. They also plundered it. It is said that the Japanese military even enlisted yakuza gangsters to help move vast stocks of gold and riches to occupied islands such as the Philippines, where the spoils were stored in secret caverns.

After the bloody and chaotic Pacific War, US General Douglas MacArthur reigned as Supreme Commander of all Asia from his exalted HQ in Tokyo. "Never before in the history of the United States had such enormous and absolute power been placed in the hands of a single individual," said William Sebald, the postwar ambassador to Japan.

MacArthur would also inherit that secret mother lode of plundered fortune.

This is where our story begins.

The gambit was now set. The generalissimo and soon other cunning operators would maneuver to exploit the undisclosed spoils for their clandestine special projects, using dogma and deceit, the flag and anti-Communism as their sharply honed instruments.

And in 1948, with MacArthur at peak strength and popularity, it was also the perfect opportunity for certain powerful interests back home, from America's castles of industry and finance and inevitably Washington, DC, to co-opt the whole enterprise for a devious plot. If successful, the bold move would block the march of progress and restore their ambitions of greatness, profit, and total authority once and for all.

To prevail, all they needed was a desperate fall guy.

1.

Wendell Lett had tried to catch up on his sleep but only ended up in another nightmare episode. He had been crying and gasping and he might've shouted something, his throat raw, his eyeballs stinging. Hopefully no one heard him.

He sat up on his bed. The breeze from the ceiling fan, its wicker blades driven by a belt, led him to see the bouquet on the dresser, yellow hibiscus. He breathed in its sweet, fresh scent.

For a troubled war veteran, a room all to one's self could be the harshest prison. Lett's combat fatigue hounded him from the war, unrelenting, damning him. But he figured there was hope for him yet. They had offered him a cure, so of course he'd taken the deal. The alternative, an Army stockade, would only accelerate his deadly affliction.

They had sent him to the US Territory of Hawaii. He was on the Big Island, rugged and volcanic and remote—on the map he'd seen that the other Hawaiian isles could easily fit inside the Big Island, including Oahu. As his eyes adjusted to the dim afternoon light, he saw that the leis and coconuts on the curtains matched the bedspread. The wall calendar promoting Dole Pineapple Juice was open to February 1948. If only he had some of that nectar to wash away the rum on his tongue, stale and slathered on like rubber cement. The bottle on the nightstand read, Tanduay Rhum, Manila, Philippines. It came from the Far East. Or was that now the West from here?

He'd been here two days. They'd sent him two continents away from rural Belgium, where he was living with his wife, Heloise, and their toddler, Holger Thomas. His sickness was destroying him, his family, and her love for him. He had to do something, anything—so he had.

They'd given him three days' leave before he was to hold up his end of the deal. Tomorrow, he was to report to a classified facility south of here code-named The Preserve, where they would hold up their end. They had him on a short leash, sure they did. Yet his billet was pleasant. The vast two-story house had untold bedrooms and multiple bathrooms and a second stairway for the help, surely once a home of the landowning class, but like many residences here it also had a metal roof and mismatched black lava stones for a foundation. It stood inside a grove of scraggly trees right on the ocean, edging the black rocks along the surf. A short stroll north up the main road was the town of Kailua, which locals simply called Kona Town, as it was the hub of the Kona Coast. Kona Town had the fancy Kona Inn with its peaked red roofs and groomed lawns, where all the officers drank and touring big shots stayed. But the pale man in plain clothes who had met Lett at the steamer dock two days ago advised him to stay away from town, which was fine with Lett, especially with the storms that had come and gone and might come again.

The thought of more stormy weather and a short leash made him reach for that bottle of Filipino rum, but it was empty. He so missed Heloise, her knowing fortitude. He missed his boy with his light bulb of a forehead and smile that came at the oddest times, just when he needed it.

Tomorrow couldn't come soon enough. Luckily his billet had its own bar, just downstairs. He wasn't supposed to discuss his posting, let alone his cure, but someone in the know might be willing to chat, maybe a duty officer just off shift. He sat on the edge of the bed and buttoned up the shirt of the summer service uniform they'd issued him, his only possession here apart from toiletries and his classified travel passes. The last rank he wore up on the line back in 1944 was sergeant. Here they'd issued him no stripes, no insignia at all. Such was the deal. He stood and found his new brown GI shoes he'd kicked off, stepped into them, and made for the door.

The bar was in a corner of the house, replacing what had likely been a prosperous man's den. It opened out to the broad rear porch via big folding louvered doors. A sign read, OFF LIMITS. The bar seemed only to serve those staying at the billet, mostly men wearing anything from khaki to civvies to aloha shirts. Lett assumed that all of them had something to do with The Preserve, because none wore insignia or had to show a pass or give a name. He shuffled into the compact main room. It was dead at this hour, no tables occupied. The warbles of a ukulele tune flowed from a radio behind the bar. Japanese war prizes such as rising sun flags and officer swords hung on the walls, and glossy little Asian idols stood next to the bottles of whisky and rye and more of that Filipino rum. The decor was exotic to Lett but not surprising, since the liberated Philippine Islands and defeated Japan were the big ports of call across the vast Pacific. This half of the earth was now ruled by General Douglas MacArthur from his HQ in Tokyo—Supreme Commander for the Allied Powers in the Pacific. Every newspaper Lett saw here had MacArthur on the front page daily. That alone was another universe compared to Allied-occupied Europe.

He made straight for that open porch facing the sea, what they called a lanai here, and plopped down on a low bamboo stool with a little matching table, off on his own, facing those scraggly trees on either side and a couple palms for show, and that jagged black lava rock that lay everywhere, not surprising since the Big Island provided the bedrock for its two massive volcanoes. At first Lett was surprised to discover that there was no beach. The water washed right up onto that black rock that had been there so long a whole species of small black crabs had developed to match. He liked to peer out and spot them but couldn't find any today. It was this no-good weather. The midday heat had dispersed, replaced by dense layers of more dark clouds pushing in from the sea.

The barman waddled out, a tubby Polynesian fellow. Lett ordered a double rye on the rocks and waited.

A crash made him start. It was the ocean. Crashing waves were more than enough to trigger one of his episodes, though it could be anything, anyone. His ghosts roamed everywhere. They infiltrated all, twisting time like an old rope, the stray filaments falling away.

He eyed the waves out there darkening and rising, the cool

breeze chilling his sweat. He needed that drink, now. He started shaking and oscillating inside, starting from low in his gut. So he hunkered down on his stool, pressing his tightening ass onto it, and peered around to make sure no one was onto him. Still the barman hadn't come. His right leg started hammering up and down like a telegraph key sounding out a desperate plea. He pressed his hand on it, and when that didn't work, his tight fist.

Thundering sounds found him from the distance, and the shrieks of sea birds were like screams inside his head.

The barman set down Lett's drink on the edge of the table, keeping a wider berth this time. Lett sucked it back in one gulp, shouted for another. The rush of booze helped a moment. He wiped sweat from his eye sockets and glared at the horizon, at the sea rising and falling like mountains breaking apart.

The thundering screaming in his head became trees exploding from the top down. It was the Ardennes Forest. It was the Battle of the Bulge all over again. He could smell the damp tree sap, the metallic air, the fresh splitting wood, the blood.

Every electric impulse inside him told him to hit the deck, to press his body to the floor and pull on his helmet, but he didn't have a head cover. "I'm done for, finished," he muttered. *He needed better cover, a good hole sheltered with logs. This old house was going to come right down on top of him when the artillery shells came whizzing in.*

Where was that second drink? No one came. He kept his trembling hand out for another, held on tight to the table with the other hand. Still no one came.

The hot metal ripped trees and men to shreds and those human shreds did worse to other men. Lett groaned. "Oh, God, no . . ."

***

Sometime later, a hand was holding Lett's. He wasn't sure for how long. The hand was warm. It was soft. It placed his now calm hand back onto his lap.

His eyes found her.

A young woman stood before him holding his rye, smiling. She placed it in the dead center of the little table like hitting a bull's-eye. Something about the precision of that helped bring him back even more.

"Thanks," he muttered and sat up, staring at her. She was local, or at least Hawaiian. He'd seen her here before. He added a smile for her.

"You had the rye, yeah?" she said and sauntered off, her low hips swaying. Lett watched her go. She had dark skin with faint pockmarks on her cheeks, narrow oval eyes, and long black hair swinging loose. At first glance she looked more Polynesian given her browned curves, but her individual features were sharper, as if Japanese. It depended on the angle. She could've pulled off a kimono or a grass skirt, but she was wearing a utilitarian dress of mauve, a little pocket on one breast, a bigger pocket on a hip, with a built-in belt.

A flash of shame shot through him. If Heloise saw him eyeing a girl like this, she would whack him so hard he could only hope he had a head cover. He sipped at his second rye and tried to relax. He exhaled and stretched out his legs and rested a heel on the other stool. The waves still rumbled out there and the sky dimmed the light between the trees, but maybe he was going to ride this out after all.

The local girl was now sitting at the bar. She gave him a sidelong look. She came back over with a drink.

"I'll just nurse this one I have," Lett said, "but thanks."

"Eh? Look here, bub, I'm not the help."

"No? Oh, but I . . ." The barman was gone, the bar unmanned. The drink was hers. "My mistake, sorry."

Her lips made a sound like a balloon letting out. "Forget it. Happens all the time to us locals."

"What happened to our barman? He scared of a little weather?"

She chuckled. "He scared of you—he won't come out of the back. He almost called the MPs. But 'calm down,' I told him, said that you're okay. You okay, yeah?"

"I am. Thank you. Would you like a seat?" Lett lowered his heel from the stool.

She looked around, then shrugged and sat with him, setting out a pack of Chesterfields and a shiny lighter Lett couldn't take his eyes off. It was gold and etched with Chinese characters and a snakelike dragon spitting fire. He didn't even smoke but it made him want to light up.

"Snazzy lighter," he said.

She looked around again, stretching her proportionally thick and yet somehow petite neck. "Mahalo."

"Where'd you get it?"

"Honolulu." Her fingertips neared the lighter.

"Chinatown?"

"Something like that."

"From China, though?" Lett said. "Originally, I mean."

"From a friend." She shook her head and finally lit up a cigarette. "You know what, army guy? Maybe you not so *lolo* after all."

"*Lolo?*"

"Crazy man. But possessed, like. That's what barman says. Me, I think otherwise. Plenty mainland haoles, they don't notice details like you."

"I'll take that as a compliment. So, is your friend in Chinatown?"

Her eyes narrowed. "Some haoles, maybe they ask too many questions."

"Oh. Okay, fair enough."

They sipped. She stared out at the stormy water. She stole another sidelong glance at him.

He wondered what he saw. When he made his deal to come here, the men in new suits who arranged it had showed him two photos. He hardly recognized himself in either. In one, he was twenty-one with a soft face with curly hair clinging to his forehead despite his somewhat squared head and jaw. He hadn't yet seen combat. The second photo was recent, and though he was still only twenty-five, his face was skewed and screwed up as if he'd been holding his breath far too long. It might as well have been taken in a funhouse mirror.

She said, "You saw plenty bad things in the war, yeah?"

"Guilty," he said.

"I seen you around here," she said.

"I've seen you, too."

She smiled. "Kanani is the name."

"I know—I mean, I heard it around here before." Lett repeated it anyway: "Ka-na-ni."

She smiled wider.

"My name is Wendell," he told her. "Wendell Lett."

"Wendell? Ho, I like that name plenty." She waved a hand, inexplicably. "Where you from, Wendell Lett?"

He'd just told her his name, so why not where he came from? He'd be sure not to mention The Preserve. "Ohio, originally. But I was an orphan."

"I'm sorry."

"Forget it. All in the past." He didn't add that his parents were long dead: his mother a basket case from overwork and dear old dad an alcoholic. He wasn't sure how much more to tell her about his purpose here, as the pale man who met him at the steamer dock already warned him. Other facts were plenty damning. He had deserted during the war, though he wasn't ashamed of it. He'd served on the front lines more than honorably, yet they pushed him to the point of cracking. The Preserve would keep him away from the possibility of a life sentence in military jail or worse. He wasn't sure what duty would come after they cured him, and they weren't telling. Though it was conceivable they would have him serve as some sort of clandestine instructor—that or they might want to interview him in depth about his experiences. He had kept assuring himself of this.

"I meant, what base you come from?" she said.

She was facing him, closer now, and Lett smelled the red plumeria in her hair. A breeze blew in and he could smell her too, clean and fresh like that flower just plucked, dew still on it.

"I, uh, came from the European Theater," was all he said.

A boom rattled the bar, and another.

Lett started.

It was those waves again. Then the rain came, lashing like gravel on metal, like tank tracks squealing. The wind hurled the rain around, and foaming surf smashed at the black rocks.

He grabbed at the table's edges again. She held his shoulders with her lovely brown hands. Something soft had fallen across his shoulder. Her silky black hair. That flower.

"Easy, Joe, easy," she whispered, "going stay all right," and she sung something to him in Hawaiian, and he loosened up inside.

He lifted his head, pushed back his imaginary helmet, and stared into her eyes to help make it go away for good. "Thank you," he said.

The barman showed his face behind the bar, peeking out from the back room. "Miss Kanani, try come speak one second?"

Kanani rolled her eyes for Lett. She patted him on the knee. "I'll be right back."

She and barman met at the bar, leaning into either side of it, the barman waving arms. They were speaking Hawaiian Pidgin English.

"No call da MPs, yeah?" she said. "All *pau*. We talk story, he calm down already. Mo better."

"Not *pau*. I no went call before, but auwe! He *lolo*, dat army guy. Just now I see. He going bust up joint, and me? Dey cut neck. So he gotta go."

Just then three puffed-up types with sergeant stripes lumbered in. They took a table by turning the chairs backward and wrapping their legs around them, their eyes bloodshot and bulging. Lett already had them figured—three Joes on a bender ignoring yet another OFF LIMITS sign.

Kanani and the barman kept arguing. The sergeants laughed and slapped their table and the stench of stale whisky in sour stomachs hit Lett when the wind shifted.

And the weather would not let up. Lett lowered his head, took deep breaths. But it was no good. All light dimmed. A sharp headache came, like his skull splitting, making him drool. He shut his eyes to fight it, and rubbed at his temples, and wished he'd asked Kanani for a warm rag, a cold cloth, a baseball bat between the eyeballs, anything.

"Speaka da English," one of the sergeants shouted toward the bar, and his buddies roared with laughter.

"Please one moment, sirs," the barman told them.

These aren't sirs. They surely never served in the war from the looks of them, all plump forearms, pink cheeks, and soft jaws.

More dark clouds hovered, swirling over the two palm trees as if ready to suck them up whole, the fronds slapping around. The ocean spilled forth, exploding white on the black rocks.

Gotta keep moving, Lett told himself, repeating their old maxim from the front line, *Always keep moving, don't bunch up. Stop and you're cornered. Keep your eyes open.*

"Buncha savages," one sergeant said, and Kanani started backing away from the bar.

"You there, sweetie," another sergeant said to her. "Why don't you climb up this here palm tree and fetch me a coconut," and the third made monkey sounds, and—

Lett's head jerked up. The gears inside him launched, found their cogs, and meshed, the torque steeling him. Mechanically, he stood.

The three sergeants stiffened.

"Lay off these people," Lett said to them.

The three stood, trying to clench those soft jaws but they just didn't have the chops for it.

Lett lunged.

All went dim and blurred, yet he sensed his efficient movements, the pivoting and striking. Screams followed. Metal filled the air like shrapnel, but the metal was fear and it wasn't his.

Lett heard a voice: "Stop! Stop it!"

The darkness in his head cleared out. He was standing over two of the sergeants who lay on their backs, the table and chairs upended. One had blood streaming from his nose and his chin quivered. The other was curled up in a ball. The third had pressed his back to the farthest wall, the pink drained from his face.

Lett whipped around.

The barman had vanished again. But Kanani was peering at him with, to his wonder, a calm look of understanding.

"Let me help you," she whispered to him.

"Das enough! I going call da MPs," the barman yelled from in back.

Lett started for the exit. *Gotta keep moving. Stop and you're cornered.*

Kanani came after him, pushing chairs clear. She grabbed his arm. "Come on."

Lett spun around. "Where to?"

"Where else? The Preserve."

2.

Out they rushed, and Kanani led Lett over a short coastal wall and along a narrow beach.

Lett snapped up Kanani's arm, but gently. "Wait a second. How do you know about The Preserve?"

"Because they're expecting me there. How you think?"

"You?"

She pushed at him. "Yes, me. Why you think I was in that bar if I wasn't the help?"

"Oh, all right. But, I'm not due till tomorrow."

"Me neither," Kanani said, and marched on ahead.

Soon the sand gave way to more of those slick, jagged formations of black lava rock and they tiptoed across them, keeping one eye on the calming waves. Without shoes, Lett's feet would've been ground beef. Small black crabs jumped out of his way.

"So, we're not going to The Preserve?" he asked.

"Not yet. We gotta get you calmed down. You can't be back there when MPs come. Ho ka! You really bust 'em up. Quite the warrior, aren't you? Those lugs had no chance."

"Well, I just can't stomach MPs," Lett muttered.

The rain had stopped. The wind dwindled to a welcome breeze. Kanani's shortcut had delivered them farther down the main road, Alii Drive. They were heading south. Lett's simple black-face Elgin watch read six o'clock—the sun would be setting within the hour. As they walked, Lett sorted things out inside his head as best as he could like he always did after an incident, reordering the chronology, separating flashback and daytime nightmare from reality. He rechecked his hands. His knuckles ached but there was no blood or swelling. He'd been swift and effective. At least those sergeants weren't carrying weapons and trying to use them—he could've separated those goofs from their guns in seconds flat and might even have used one on them. He hadn't held a gun since the war. He had vowed never to pick one up again, and his new masters here had, thank God, not issued him one when he arrived on the steamer.

His legs had felt light and strong from the adrenaline, but now they were tiring. Once they were a good distance down the road from the billet, a couple hundred yards maybe, Kanani stepped into the cover of trees and faced him with her arms crossed, but not as if mad. From the look on her face, it was more like she'd just eaten a good meal.

A few yards farther along she reached into a hibiscus hedge and dragged out a large English safety bicycle from the days of the Hawaiian Kingdom, it seemed.

"How far we going?" Lett said. "Pretty much all I've got is here on my person apart from a toothbrush."

"Just down the road. And I got one for you."

Lett took the heavy bicycle from her and sat on the hard leather saddle. "Here, get on the handlebars."

Kanani's handlebar ride lasted about ten yards before Lett started wobbling. Kanani had leaned back, her hair brushing his lap, framed inside his arms, and it was all too much. Just as he imagined his dead friends all too clearly, or saw himself killing someone again and again, he sometimes also visualized bearable things, lovely things worth living for. Intensely. It was the sole wonder of his affliction. So he had imagined what might come next with Kanani—and careened right off the shoulder and spilled them both into the soft crabgrass.

Kanani only laughed. But he walked the bicycle for her instead after that. She watched him in the dimming light, walking backward, her feet finding her way along the shoulder as if she were strolling forward.

"Kanani's a lovely name," he blurted. "What's it mean?"

Her face nuzzled her neck like a girl blushing. "The 'pretty one.'"

"Mahalo," Lett said. "That's your word for thanks, right? For getting me out of there."

"It is. Don't mention it."

They walked on, in the middle of the empty road now. They heard crickets chirping and the honk of an island animal. "Check 'em out," Kanani said. "Dat one nēnē bird."

"Adorable. Sounds like a goose with a cold," Lett said, smiling.

Kanani punched him in the arm. "Nēnē, dey rare now."

"Careful. You're slipping into that Pidgin you speak," Lett said.

A grin stretched across her face and she wagged a finger at him. "Right, you're correct. I normally speak like you haole folks. We learned it in school—English Standard School. I make my voice all nasally like you. I prefer Pidgin, but I better talk like you. No want sound stupid, yeah? Local kids like to pick out American first names. Joey, Freddy. Susy. Plenty haole-fied."

"You don't have a name in mind?"

She shook her head. "Kanani stay my name."

Lett wondered if they should part ways. A special truck would transport him to The Preserve from town if he wanted—it left every morning from the billet. Yet they kept slogging along, which felt all too natural to the old dogface under Lett's skin.

"You can see why I need The Preserve," he said. "It's my noggin. They told me they can fix what's wrong in my head."

"They did? They said that?"

"Sure. They're working on a new therapy. They want to try it on me."

"Oh." She walked a few more paces, nodding along to them as if searching for the right response. "Well, The Preserve, it's also a training camp. But you probably know that."

"Sure," Lett said. He didn't know that, or anything really. He only knew they could help him. He felt a twitch of unease in his gut but told himself not to worry about it.

"I got lucky. It's not easy for a local to get a post like that," she said. "No more tough streets of Honolulu for me. Maybe they'll send me to Tokyo, on assignment."

"You mean, like an agent of some sort?" Lett's twitch had turned into a rumble, like a sour stomach.

"Maybe. We'll see."

"This have anything to do with that gold lighter—with that person who gave it to you?"

She turned and stared, her teeth shining in the light. But she wasn't grinning this time.

***

Full darkness came fast. Alii Drive straightened out and stayed inland, the roadsides overgrown. Any lights were dim and sparse.

Kanani slowed her pace. "Follow close," she whispered and led Lett and her bicycle to a clearing on the inland side. A faded sign read KAPU. She flashed her lighter around. The clearing held a clapboard bungalow, a chicken coop, two old cars sinking into the ground, a stone barbecue, and various chairs and tables that had been tossed about during the storms. Palm trees and tall bushes leaned into the clearing, swaying and shimmying, the branches and leaves drooping and dripping and feeding, below them, the many giant ferns and shrubs of budding red flowers. It was just the sort of dead-end yard Lett would never have entered alone on patrol. Too much had to be checked out.

Kanani took the bicycle from him and walked it into the middle of the clearing. He halted close to a tree, his fingers clamping the wet bark. "Is someone home?" he whispered.

"Just us," she whispered back.

"What does *kapu* mean?"

"Taboo. No trespass. But we're okay."

Lett detached himself from the tree and tiptoed toward her. She leaned the bicycle up against the few front steps of the bungalow and climbed them on tiptoes. He stood down below, staring up at her.

"Why we still whispering?" she said, adding a giggle.

"Hell if I know."

She let her hands slap at her sides. She stepped back down and stood on the bottom step, eye-to-eye with him. "You're really aching, aren't you?"

He nodded. She reached out and touched his chin. He let her, watched her, his mouth open. He smiled. What a dummy. Say something. She opened her mouth and her teeth glistened again in the dark. It made him look down, at her brown legs, just a glance. She noticed, of course. And she said, from deep within her compact little chest, "Okay den. Are you coming, army guy, or you going?"

***

Lett heard her but couldn't answer. His throat had tightened up from gasping, from screaming inside and nothing coming out, and his eyeballs burned.

"You had a nightmare," Kanani repeated in the dark, her voice thin from sleep.

It was the middle of the night. They each had a quilted mattress on the floor of the bungalow, taking up most of the sparse bedroom. The bed quilts were a Japanese roll-up she called a futon. He'd kept on his GI-issue olive drab boxers and singlet. Kanani had given him a thin sheet for a cover. She had on a simple white nightgown, no sheet. He had tried not to look at her like that and was grateful there was no moonlight. They'd had a belt of rum, and the day caught up with them. Dead tired, they had gone right to sleep.

And then Lett was seeing people killed and killing and being killed. His friends, so many. The little German girl. Children. Too many. Dogs. He saw all their bulging white eyeballs, heard their individual muffled screams, felt their distended hearts swelling his. It kept coming at him, a crashing wave. He had to fight his way through it, flailing, punching, shooting. In the nightmare he kept killing just to make it all stop. Then he didn't want it to stop.

"They made me do things I never wanted to do," he muttered after a while, after his cold sweat had dried. "But you know the real sick part? Sometimes I think about doing those things again, what it would be like. Like what I did back there in that bar, but worse. I almost . . . look forward to it. That's what they did to me. I'm not broke—I'm retooled, see. They put a lever inside me. A gear. It can be turned on, activated."

"It's just the night talking," Kanani said. "They're gonna cure you. You said so yourself. And I'll make sure that they do. Okay?"

"All right."

The nightmares didn't return that night. Lett woke in the early morning light. Kanani was snoring a modest rumble-growl, like a well-fed cat. He rolled off the mattress with care. The galley kitchen had a dented metal percolator sitting on the stove. In the nearly empty cupboard, he found a couple mugs and a can of joe that probably dated back to FDR's first term.

He found other things while wandering the bungalow. In addition to double-door locks, strips of folded paper were wedged in the back door and faint threads hung off the window latches, all to warn against intruders having entered while she was out.

The kettle water rumbled and bubbled, and he whisked the perc off the burner. He took his hot joe out the front door and sat on the top step of the bungalow, its pink paint faded and peeling. Silly birds yelped from unknown perches. A tiny gecko stared back at him from the side of the railing. The clearing sparkled now, as if the branches and bushes were laced with garland and the furry moss on the yard debris were dotted with sequins. He even spotted a tree swing.

He was going to The Preserve today, he remembered. His cure could finally begin.

Soft footsteps, a yawn. Kanani wandered out in her nightgown. She sat next to him, rubbing at his shoulder, and sipped from his coffee. She spat it out over the railing.

"Tell it to the proprietor," Lett said, adding a smile.

She shoved him. He tossed the coffee over the railing. They laughed at that and breathed in the fresh air.

"I didn't know you had much crime here," he said, referring to her door locks and window snares. "With all your tripwires, you would've done well up on the line."

"Plenty things you don't know about this place," Kanani said.

"This isn't your house, is it?"

She pulled her knees up to her chest. She shook her head.

"That's what I thought. It's more like your hidey-hole—"

Kanani shot up. "Wait. Hear that?"

Something flashed by, out on the road. Kanani jumped down and kicked dirt over the tossed coffee, wiped her feet on the edge of the bottom step, grabbed him and his mug, and pulled him inside.

They watched, crouching at the corners of the one front-facing window. A black sedan had passed and turned around. It rolled to a stop, blocking the entrance to the clearing, about thirty yards away. It was a '41 Packard Clipper with four doors, sloped rear end, and bright whitewall tires that were still rare because of war shortages. Its chrome gleamed out in the sun on the road.

Lett looked to Kanani. She was nodding, counting off the number of passengers. Three.

One tall and thick man in an oversize suit stepped out, taking his time, looking around. He circled the car and gazed down the road, as if waiting for another car, perhaps, that or making sure the coast was clear for an assault. The gears of caution kicked into motion inside Lett, and his fear dissipated as his senses intensified. His eyesight sharpened, every sparkle, color, edge, and curve imprinted in his memory. The man had darker skin. Lett first thought he had gloves on but then realized that tattoos covered his hands. The man walked around the clearing. He used hand signals to speak with the two silhouettes inside the car. No tourist gestured like that. A man like this had only one reason to wear a suit jacket here, and it wasn't to block the wind.

"Frankie?" Kanani muttered.

"You know him?"

Kanani lowered her head. She nodded at the floorboards.

"You don't want to see him?"

She shook her head.

"Then don't," Lett said.

She grinned at him. The grin spread and kept going.

"I mean it," he added.

"Get dressed," she blurted.

He dressed in seconds flat as if a Tiger II tank were coming down the road. She pulled on an aloha shirt with the sleeves rolled up and new cuffed dungarees, grabbing rubber thong sandals and an aloha-print carpetbag as she went, the floorboards somehow making no sound.

She gestured at the back door. Lett squatted there, waited for her signal. She peered out, pulled the door open just enough for them to slip out, then pushed the door shut behind them.

The bungalow blocked any view of them from the road or clearing. But they faced a tangled wall of bushes and knobby trees and flowers with leaves longer and broader than anything in Europe.

"Follow close," she whispered like a squad leader, and took off.

***

Farther down Alii Drive stood a quaint little church not much bigger than a shed. It had white wood siding, teal trim, and a corrugated roof, and it looked out over a small rocky inlet. St. Peter's Catholic Church by the Sea, it read on a gable above the door. Lett and Kanani were still panting, hands on their hips. Sea birds landed to watch them inhale the brackish sea air.

The door was open. Kanani went inside. Lett followed, and they wandered around the twelve blue pews, Lett squinting at the gloss white paint and altar window brighter than outside. Kanani placed her carpetbag on the last pew and they met there. She only now slid her feet into her rubber sandals, what she called "slippahs."

"You know your terrain," he said to her.

"You kept up."

Sweat was rolling down her face. Back behind the bungalow he'd seen no hole in that wall of green flora, but she shot right through one, darting this way and that through more holes and passages in the foliage, and he matched her steps as best as he could. The greenery soon became a grove of knotty dry trees so dense they had to turn sideways to get through. She'd held his hand to guide him. Her breath was hot and metallic from a fear she hadn't shown before.

"A church, that's the last place anyone expects to find me," she said, adding a chuckle.

She sat on the edge of the nearest pew, wiping the sweat off her face.

Lett sat with her, facing her. Their knees were touching. A cool breeze was floating in through the doorway and it danced in her hair. He let the wonder overwhelm him like it should have last night in the bungalow. He imagined her pulling herself onto his lap, and her tongue finding his, and her sweat would come rolling back, and it would've tasted sweet.

She smiled. They held hands, and she pulled him to her.

"I'm married," he muttered. He showed her the silver ring on his finger.

"Ho ka, what dis?" she said in Pidgin. "Us island folks, no wear ring when marry."

They laughed. She added a bittersweet smile. But their smiles faded, and Kanani eventually pulled herself away, mercifully so because he wasn't finding the willpower.

Kanani stared out the window at the water. Clearly, she was considering something she hadn't before.

"Who's Frankie?" Lett said.

She ignored him.

"You weren't expecting him."

"Uh-uh, no sir. Luckily, *mokes* like them don't know Big Island better than one haole."

"So they're from Honolulu, too?"

Again she ignored him, still looking out.

He stared down at the plank floor; the wood was bare unlike the rest of the little church. Maybe Frankie was just an ex-boyfriend. Maybe the guy couldn't give her up. Or maybe it was worse. Lett shook his head. And here he was thinking he was the only one with a past.

"We're heading for The Preserve," he said eventually. "Right? So whoever was in that Packard will not be there. No sentry worth his salt is letting in the likes of them."

Kanani showed him a pout. "Oh, Wendell Lett. You really haven't been in the Territory long, have you?"

3.

Lett and Kanani kept moving, on foot, heading inland and uphill. "Mauka," Kanani called it, "up mountain." They weren't about to backtrack to Kona Town for the daily transport to The Preserve. It was only about ten miles to the camp's location, Kanani told him, but roads narrowed and twisted and ended dead, and they had some rock walls to hop and No Trespassing signs to ignore.

As they walked along, Lett congratulated himself for not acting, once again, on his wonder-filled urges back in that little chapel.

"I feel bad about that church," Kanani told him as they trudged up a pitted old road.

"You're Catholic?"

She gave him a look Hawaiians called da stink eye. "That church is on top of a sacred Hawaiian site. It's desecration."

"Kapu," Lett said.

She nodded.

Lett knew what was coming next.

"Tell me about your wife," Kanani said.

"If I tell you about her, I have to tell you something else: I was a deserter."

"You? Private Bust-em-up? I don't believe it."

He told Kanani how he had walked away from battle in December of 1944. Thousands of Americans had, but no one ever talked about it. Since then he'd been living under the bogus identity of one John Macklin, discharged US veteran.

"By October of '44 I had reached my limit in combat, constantly on the line for months, still running patrols after every other good GI I knew was either dead or cracked or both. I was all outta change, believe me."

They kept walking as he spoke. Kanani kept throwing him sidelong glances.

"Heloise is her name. Heloise was the one who'd truly saved me from the war," he said. She had urged him to desert. He and Heloise, and later their young son, were living in her small Belgian town of Stromville near the Ardennes Forest. But things were not going well. "We've drifted apart. Because of the way I am. She doesn't even know where I am right now."

"It's not your fault," Kanani said.

"That's what Heloise used to say. And then she stopped saying it."

Higher, on the Belt Road, they stopped for a quick breakfast in a diner that was little more than an open shack with ceiling fans, open to the road on one side, on the other a lanai overlooking the lush Kona countryside descending to the ocean miles below. They sat in a corner, both facing out. Kanani seemed even more alert now that Lett had confided in her. She didn't talk with the few locals but kept watch behind a *Hilo Tribune-Herald* with headlines about the growing threat of Communism in Asia and the martial genius of one General Douglas MacArthur. Kanani had scrambled eggs, rice, and toast; Lett, eggs and toast, papaya, Portuguese sausage. He gulped down the good coffee.

Kanani kept staring at him. "So how did they catch you?"

Lett sighed. "They didn't. I turned myself in."

Kanani jerked forward. "You what?"

The war had hounded him. It started out as night terrors or reactions to certain sounds or smells. Then it brought fits of fury, a blood rush to the head he couldn't control. He would black out, not remember a thing. He'd lash out at Heloise. He couldn't keep a job. His poor French didn't help. Who was this odd, halting, broken-down American? To keep things under some control, he'd move with a mechanical sort of vacancy. "The nightmares, the episodes, the incidents—it was all getting to be too much as it was, and living as a deserter was only making it worse. Something had to give. Heloise agreed."

"You're even braver than I thought."

"Well, I had no choice. Cutting a deal was the only card I had left. During the Battle of the Bulge, intelligence section had used me for special operations behind the lines. They had found out I had some German, from back in Ohio; a German-speaking Mennonite orphanage had taken me in as a boy. The operations were all classified. I was never to speak of it."

Kanani pushed back her hair. "You figured you could make that work for you."

"I figured they at least owed me something." He said good-bye to Heloise and his boy, no tears this time—there had already been too many shed. He crossed over into occupied Germany, found the first US headquarters he could find in the US Zone. They left him in a cell to stew. He told them his whole story. Criminal Investigations Division passed him to Counterintelligence Corps, who passed him to the men in new suits who had the two photos of him. "I had their attention, you see, because there was this one intelligence officer I knew from the war. A Captain Charles Selfer. The captain is probably the whole reason I ended up how I am. He was the one running me on those missions—before I deserted, that is. But, Selfer was also your rear-line climber type. If anyone had pull, could push papers, it was him."

"You asked for him by name? Auwe!" Kanani waved her hand again, but this time it was as if she'd touched a hot plate. "But it was classified. You could be in a prison."

"I would've been anyway. Deserters were getting nabbed all the time. And I was a head case to boot. Word was getting around about what they did with the likes of us. A stockade on its own was a sanatorium, brimming with killers and crazies and hopeless cases. Other inmates were just silent, staring into walls, curled up, stuttering sleepwalkers. On the other hand, there were treatment centers. Hospitals you never leave, wards that stay locked up. Outdated therapies. Drugs that made you dumb. Lobotomies. That was the good old Veterans Administration for you—still doing its part for the war effort . . ."

"So this Captain Selfer," Kanani said, "he made you the offer."

"Not directly, no. The men in suits had been in contact with him—the good captain was now in Washington, DC, of course, true to form. They spoke for him. Told me a new intelligence group was forming. The suits told me they could offer me a new cure in a secret facility. I was a perfect candidate. Or, I was also a candidate for a court martial. And that was that. Selfer should've been the last person I wanted to see, but he ended up my only hope. Bremen to Boston by ship, then an unmarked C-47 to San Francisco riding with the type of soldiers who don't wear insignia. From there it was a merchant marine steamer. I had a cabin all to myself."

"I seen my share of deserters before. But you're one hot potato." Kanani was staring at him in a new way, one that made her face harden. "You have a boy, you said."

"I do. Holger Thomas is his name. He thinks I'm off being a sailor." Lett added a sad chuckle at that.

"And where is this Captain Selfer now?" Kanani said.

"Oh, they tell me he's going to meet me here. At The Preserve. Transferring to where the action is. Which should be interesting. We haven't seen each other since the war."

***

The vegetation thickened, rampant bushes, giant ferns, spikey ohia blossoms like little red porcupines. The roads cutting through became ruts, and it was hard to tell if the surface was old cracking asphalt or just lava rock. Kanani was right about all the locals' warning signs. Every private property they approached seemed to have them. Do Not Enter, Private Road, Keep Out, Kapu. Kanani joked about them. And the higher they went, the more short rock walls they encountered. Kanani hopped those easily, kept going; Lett followed. The air grew cooler and the clouds loomed lower, nearly a fog.

Lett was the one showing her sidelong glances now.

"You're not going to let me off the hook, are you?" she said.

"Why you think I told you all about me?"

She pushed at his shoulder. "You're good at this."

"Whenever you're ready, I'm all ears."

"Okay, okay." Off a dirt road she found a path and a wooden gate, pushed it open. They followed more paths past more short lava rock walls. She pointed out macadamia trees and little vegetable gardens, yet another chicken coop. The farm sat on an incline. They passed donkeys that stared back and Hawaiian Japanese children who stopped playing—Kanani whispered something to them in Japanese and they smiled and ran off. Lett spotted faded Japanese writing on a shack. The scene probably would've scared the hell out of a GI vet from the Pacific, but he found it exotic. She gestured toward rows of trees in the distance and various structures of graying wood. "There's the *kuriba*," she said, "oh, and the *hoshidana*. The mill and the dryer. Dis one coffee farm, Wendell. Family *kine*."

They huddled inside the ruins of a stone house. "This was a tenant farmer's once," Kanani said. "The Ushidas are nice. My mother knew them. They'll leave us alone."

The kids brought them a small basket of macadamia nuts and ran off again for good. Kanani pulled a canteen of water from her carpetbag.

"Where you want to start?" Lett said. "With Frankie, or that bungalow? Maybe the gold lighter?"

She pushed at him again.

"You have your own angle," Lett said. "Am I right?"

"Right. Us Hawaiians, we're all citizens of the Territory of Hawaii. Right after Pearl Harbor, we were living under martial law all the way until October of '44. US Military Government, you call it. My full name is Kanani Alana, sure, but my mother's maiden name? Ogawa. So maybe you see where this is going, Wendell. My Japanese mother, Yoko, she came to Hawaii as what they called a 'picture bride'—she was ordered from a photo by a white factory manager on Oahu. That man, he abused her before hightailing it for the mainland, never to return. Leaving Mother to fend for herself. She ended up working on plantations with other Japanese, here on Big Island mostly."

"Thus, the Japanese I heard," Lett said.

"Dat my other Pidgin," Kanani said. "I spent half my childhood here on Big Island. Partly grew up on a plantation. So did Faddah— my father, I mean. Joey 'The Pug' Alana. Now he was a native Hawaiian. Mother and Faddah and me, we were always outsiders, a mixed-race family. The Japanese families were ashamed for Mother and the native Hawaiians thought my faddah was crazy. Then he got into trouble organizing workers, and we had to flee the planta- tion. For Honolulu. He worked on the docks and became a union organizer there. But then the war came. The Military Government, they detained Mother on account of her Japanese connections, not to mention those relatives back in the old country who liked to carry swords and swagger around and command those planes bombing Pearl Harbor and raise children who kamikaze American ships. So, Faddah, he saved my mother from detention camp—she could've been shipped off to somewhere cold on the mainland like Oregon or Idaho, penned in like so many chickens with all the *kotonks* thinking they better than the *bulaheads*."

"*Bulaheads?*" Lett said.

"Japanese American from Hawaii. *Kotonks*, they're the Japanese from the US. They talk like you, they look at us like you."

"What about you? They didn't detain you? The Military Government?"

"No."

"Your father helped you, too?"

"Of course. He my faddah."

"How did he do it?"

"Same as with Mother. Faddah got her released owing to his contacts—as a local labor official, he was helping to make sure the islands had enough workers despite all the martial law and security measures. Because Military Government was soon realizing that if they tried locking up all the Japanese Americans, the economy would've fallen apart. But, he also had to keep doing things they wanted so that Mother could stay free. Way I figure it, the Military Government really only wanted to put the screws on my faddah, to show him who was really the boss man. Faddah, see, he was becoming a big organizer by then. ILWU. On the dock, and the sugar and pineapple plantations, too. Employers, politicians, the military were always looking for bust him up. So, he cooperated. He advised certain union radical guys to stand down." Kanani grunted at that. "But it was really for us."

"Now here you are getting posted to The Preserve. Like I said—you must have your own angle."

Kanani stared at Lett with one eye, like a person watching a bull that got free of a pen. "You one interrogator during the war or what?"

"Something like that. I told you what I was."

Kanani lowered her head. "I worked for the Military Government, too. All right? Cooperated, more like. During the war, certain intelligence officers started threatening me, bullying me, making me spy on friends. Like they did with Faddah—they said they would start leaning on my family if I didn't play along. And they'd go after me, too—they could prosecute me as an accomplice."

"To what?"

Her eyes widened. She released a sigh. "Well, to gambling and prostitution rings, and that was just the start."

"Were you an accomplice?"

"It's not like you think. We're only a US territory. In your country, on the mainland, you might call things I did 'organized crime.' That's what *they* called it. But we never saw it that way, and the territory law you haoles brought here never see it that way before the war, either. We always had prostitution and gambling. Boogie houses, chicken fights, any *kine*. And all that, ho, it was both legal and tolerated, even into the war. Then everything changed. Everything was criminalized only in '44 when martial law ended. So at first they threaten me 'cause I was a so-called Jap, and then because I was a criminal? You guys, you always changing the rules."

"Let's get one thing straight: *They* are not me," Lett said. "Boogie houses?"

"Mainland folks call them brothels."

"Ah. You still haven't mentioned that Frankie fellow."

Kanani kicked at a stone. "Okay, okay. His real name is Francisco

Baptiste. I know Frankie from around Honolulu, Hotel Street mostly. Most think Frankie is native Hawaiian but he's mostly Flip. Filipino, that is. His growing-up faddah used to beat him, really bust him up. One day his faddah disappears fishing, and no one missed the bastard. I'm guessing Frankie was on the boat with him, if you know what I mean. Frankie, he's the new type of big kahuna *moke*. They're starting to form gangs. We never had gangs before the Military Government crackdown, never needed them. Soon we won't know what to do without them. Now, Frankie started as a bouncer on Hotel Street, but wasn't *lolo* like some *mokes*—he wasn't slow or dumb. He ended up the top muscle for the *kine* locals who never went to jail because others were sent to go there in their place. Frankie didn't stick to one boss, though. He was known for protecting certain people, but some say he also killed people he once protected, mainlanders even. I heard he was an archery champ and a kid chess master before he became a local champ boxer. Which sounds like Frankie. The man might be too smart for his own good."

"Or at least for staying loyal. Back up. So, what was he doing at our bungalow?"

"I don't know. But he's not the *kine* you should have to answer to, not on general principle."

"Whose bungalow was that?"

Kanani growled. "It's a friend's place."

"He? She?"

Kanani blew air out one side of her mouth. "Her name's Mae. Miss Mae. Frankie must want something from her. Information probably."

"Where's she from? Look at me. Come on. We're almost done."

"Chinatown . . . Okay, China, originally. She fled because of the war."

"And she's the one who gave you that lighter."

Kanani shot up on her haunches, pointing at Lett. "She was a friend. She confided in me. She's the one who gave me a job. She was a mama-san, on Hotel Street . . ." She lowered back down and stared at the rocky earth between her feet. "She was also the one who set me up doing work on the side, for you Americans. But later she made it easier for me, got them to lay off. She knew some of your big kahunas, see. During the war we had your military intelligence here like I said, but also the CID and CIC you mentioned and especially something called the OSS. Those boys, they liked my style."

"Style?"

"In Honolulu, Chinatown side, there's always plenty talk story going around in a boogie house. Never hurt that I passed them a tip now and then. You know, for the 'war effort.' And, these intelligence contacts of mine? They know how to flatter. Along the way, they led me to believe I was in training to become a secret agent. They kept telling me I was good at spying. They kept saying they were going to send me to the Philippines or even Japan because my looks let me fit in anywhere."

"It never happened."

Kanani snorted. "They just used me as their ears. They probably had a good laugh about it. Then they all headed home, and now there's a new gang in town. What? Don't look at me like that."

"What way's that?"

"You think I'm a *wahine ho'okamakama*."

"Says you. Suppose you tell me in English."

"Whore. Prostitute. Brothel girl."

"Well, were you?"

"When was I younger, briefly, but I moved up real fast. I told you. Assisting da management *kine*. Mama-san."

"Where is this Miss Mae now?"

"I don't know. She knew lots more about China and Japan and the wartime this and that than she told me. Talk about a past." An old ashen-colored donkey sidled close. Kanani looked away from it and whispered, "Between you and me? I think she was a double agent—Japanese, Chinese, the Americans."

"That's a triple agent."

"See. You smart. Word is, she cut a deal with the Americans, and they're giving her a new life. Last time I talked to her, she told me she could get me this posting to The Preserve. Gave me a phone number, and that was that. Bless her heart."

"What about your family?"

"What about them? I have relatives on Big Island. They knew me as a little girl, when I used to sing about liberating Hawaii, just like Faddah. I know where to go if I need them here."

"I mean your parents."

Kanani glared at Lett. "I haven't spoken to Mother in years. She's still not happy with me for Hotel Street. It was 'below me,' she said. But I was getting into trouble and it was a good way out." She paused and looked away, as if finding the right words, and Lett caught her wiping the glisten of a tear from the corner of her eye. "Faddah, he must not be happy, either."

"Must not?"

"He's dead. Last year. Organizing. They say it was an accident. Crushed. Crates fell. But you know crates don't just go tumbling down on their own. Mother, she's still in mourning, I bet. And she probably blames me for that, too." Kanani dropped back against the stone wall, letting her head roll around wearily like a GI coming off a patrol that went on far too long.

"I'm sorry. I think I get your angle now: You're going to show them. Every last one of them. Make them all pay if you can help it."

Kanani pulled out the gold dragon lighter, as if on instinct, like a good luck charm. She even rubbed it. "That's right. Just the way I like it."

4.

Gotta keep moving. Always keep moving, don't bunch up. Stop and you're cornered. Keep your eyes open.

Kanani was tugging on Lett's shoulder.

Lett jerked up. They were riding in the bed of an old jalopy pickup. It had approached behind them as they trudged a long narrow high road heading straight up mountain. Kanani had said the pots and pails hanging off it usually meant the pickup was coffee pickers, but it wasn't. The windows were rolled down. The driver wore khaki without insignia, had hard dark balls for eyes. Big cast-iron pots surrounded them in back as the truck jostled along, then the pots were clanking and clunking and combining with the squeaking squealing undercarriage, and to Lett all the clatter became halftracks full of SS troops flanking their line, then a King Tiger tank rolling over him in his forward hole, helmets colliding, the heads inside already dead.

Kanani yanked him back down as if he might jump out any moment. "You were muttering something. Your face is plenty pale."

"Nothing, it's nothing. I'm all right."

Lett wasn't all right. He was getting that old feeling. Why on Earth was he going in like this, without a lick of intelligence? Sending himself into unscouted terrain. Trusting in Captain Charles Selfer? He had invoked the dreaded name himself. What a fool . . .

The jalopy pickup neared a side road, gears grinding. An arched gate like the entrance to a ranch stood over the road. A sign read: Krieger Land Preserve.

Lett and Kanani traded glances, neither speaking.

They passed through the gate. The elevation kept rising above South Kona and the denser growth persisted, branches entwining, massive shiny fronds mixing with reddish leaves. Kanani eyed the jarring terrain, their distance from the sea growing ever higher, and she bounded from one side of the truck bed to the other like a dog unsure. The rise of a volcano showed above treetops.

"Mauna Loa?" Lett said.

Kanani nodded. "At some point, all this green is gonna stop and it turns into lava fields, and plenty of it too, just open and barren country."

"I don't think we're going that far."

"Other side of Mauna Loa is Kilauea Military Camp. They held Japanese after Pearl Harbor. My mother got the lock-up there."

"How long?"

"Few months. Then she got Oahu, Sand Island Camp. Fences, barbwire everywhere. Haole guards with bayonets, even in the bathroom. No dignity. Faddah got her out, sure he did. But life was never the same after." Kanani scowled at Lett. She spat into the road.

"You'll show them," he told her. "You'll show all of them."

"And you, too. You gotta make this work for you, Wendell."

The road evened out, the truck puttering and gurgling. The greenery was still dense but the trees lining the road were drier, with knotty and gnarled trunks—like the knuckles of the shrunken dead, Lett couldn't help thinking. They slowed. Lett and Kanani faced forward to look around the cab. Up ahead, a barricade stood across the dark, lava-dirt road. It was just an unpainted log. An unarmed sentry in khaki with no insignia appeared from the trees and lifted the primitive gate.

Kanani grinned at Lett. Lett had to make himself grin back.

"Go for broke!" Kanani said.

"Go for broke."

***

The newly built hut was a single-room job, like a barracks office. No one was there. A metal desk stood in the middle, matte green. Three metal armchairs and a small table occupied another corner, but Lett and Kanani had opted for the two metal chairs at the desk. The hut occupied a tidy square of a clearing carved out of the high forest growth like a shaved patch on a head of matted hair. The patrol vehicle disguised as a local jalopy pickup had dropped them off, and the driver told them to go wait inside. And there they sat. It was so quiet they could still hear insects buzzing outside.

They saw no signs, not even warnings. Lett had never seen a camp without official notices. Sweat rolled down his sides and dampened his waistband. Kanani reached over and wiped the sweat on his jaw.

"What the hell is this?" she whispered.

"Must be some kind of holding area."

Lett could smell the fresh wood of the raised foundation and the framing around them and the siding, none of it painted or stained yet. Once his sweat dried, something about the stark arrangement started appealing to him. Nail heads were spaced neatly and still shining. The metal blinds were three-fourths closed—all equally turned—to let in just enough light. And that utilitarian furniture. Everything was spick-and-span. He hoped this meant this camp was all business despite the lack of warning signs, and that appealed to him even more so and deep down, like the first warm rush of a field hospital morphine—drip, drip, drip. It should've sent him running for cover. He should've felt the jolts running through his right leg, and his leg should've been rapping away at the floorboards like a sewing machine needle at top speed.

"Know who came up with that saying?" Kanani said.

"What saying?"

"'Go for broke.' Us Hawaiians."

Then, footsteps sounded on the porch. The door opened. In strode a man who pivoted to face Lett jauntily, like a gent holding a top hat and cane. He wore the same summer khaki without insignia, but it fit him like a wealthy tourist's casual wear. This was not buffoonish. This was not glib.

Lett had to look away a moment. He felt his joints firm up. He noticed his hands had clawed. Kanani saw it, too. He pressed them flat to his thighs and held his chin higher.

The man had not yet smiled, though his easy good looks and a hint of dimples promised that he would any second.

"Captain Selfer?" Lett said.

"It is I. Welcome back, soldier. Though, it's lieutenant colonel now," Selfer said to Lett. He glanced down at his unadorned lapels. "Not that anyone's counting here."

Two whole ranks in under three years? The man must hold the record in the high jump.

"Well? Here we are," Selfer continued. "They told you I'd meet you here, correct?"

"Yes. Correct."

Kanani shot Lett an urgent look.

Lett said to Selfer, "This is Kanani Alana."

"Yes, I know," Selfer said. "How do you do?"

Kanani only nodded.

"Thank you," Lett added to Selfer. "I really need to thank you for this."

He and Kanani joined Charlie Selfer over in the metal arm-chairs in the corner only after he gestured for them to do so. He still sounded like a dashing man in a movie, though not as much as Lett had remembered. Selfer always seemed to resemble certain things more than he ever actually was certain things, Lett recalled. He looked the type to wear a pencil-thin mustache yet still didn't; people only remembered him that way after the fact, after he'd plied you with his smooth talk. At least he was wearing less hair tonic than during the war, Lett noticed.

Once Kanani sat down, Selfer said to her, "Oh, dear, would you mind cracking a couple blinds, maybe a window or two?"

"I don't see why I'd mind, no."

Selfer watched Lett as Kanani turned the blinds to half open on each window—on each opposing wall. Lett eyed Selfer as Kanani pushed up the rear window a few fingers and cracked the front door for the slight breeze that came through.

"Lovely," Selfer said. He lit up a Camel.

"It's not exactly 'soldier' anymore," Lett said to Selfer.

"Say again?" Selfer said.

"When you welcomed me back just now. You said 'soldier.'"

"It's only an expression. Care for a smoke?"

"Still don't smoke, but thanks."

"Why, not even one fortifying cigar?"

Lett just shook his head, he and Selfer still eyeing each other, Selfer crossing his legs, Lett bolt upright with his palms pressed to his thighs. The metal armchair was new and stiff, did not creak. Selfer stood and offered Kanani a cigarette as she came over.

"I'd take one of your cigars just the same," she said.

Selfer smirked, a thin crimson line to match his raised eyebrow and imagined pencil mustache. "Say, there's a lady who knows the score," he said to Lett through a chiming chuckle as he opened a silver case that probably belonged, Lett figured, to some captured high German official who resorted to hanging himself after one Captain Selfer had extracted all the finest intelligence from the man with only sterling words and promises.

Kanani plucked a thin brown cigar from the case. She started to pull her gold lighter out but clamped her fist around it, concealing it, and tucked it away. She waited for Selfer's light.

"Thank you, sir," she said, batting eyelashes.

"Do enjoy. They're Filipino."

Selfer sat back and crossed his legs, wiped any ashes away, though there were none, then crushed his cigarette in the beanbag ashtray on the small table between them. He kept his limpid gray corneas on Lett. Kanani might as well have been out scrubbing the porch.

He said, "Miss Alana, could you please wait outside? Someone is coming for you now. You two will need to be separated."

Lett and Kanani exchanged glances.

"Oh, it's nothing to worry about," Selfer added. "It's just for now. Standard operating procedure. They'll check you in, confirm you're on the roster, the usual rigamarole."

Kanani shrugged. She kept her cigar lit. "You're gonna do great," she said to Lett. "Bust 'em up."

"Thank you. You too. See you soon."

After Kanani left, Selfer showed Lett a sideways grin. "You two aren't . . . are you?" He wagged fingers.

"What? No."

The warm rumble in Lett's gut burned white hot. He remembered all too clearly that Selfer was the whole goddamn reason he was here in the first place. In Captain Charlie Selfer's first mission for him, he and two other GIs were to cross the German border disguised as German soldiers and reconnoiter enemy strength along the Ardennes line. They ended up in bombed-out Cologne. There a German girl recognized Lett and his team as American spies. But she was alone on the rubble street. She screamed and tried to run, and she would've given them away. It was war. Lett strangled her. He didn't think, just did it, mechanical. He and his sorry crew somehow found their way back over the lines. Yet Selfer didn't want to hear the truth Lett had to report—that the Germans were amassing an invading counterattack force. This horror didn't fit the popular intelligence reports already making the rounds that Selfer had crafted. So it was all for nothing. A poor girl suffocated for a damn report that did not fit. And Lett had nightmares about that girl ever since.

Lett glared at his GI shoes. They should just get to the point. He was a deserter once, and Selfer, once again, had him right where he wanted him.

But Selfer owed him. Selfer owed him the cure.

Lett's heat made the sweat return, trickling down his spine. He grabbed at the chair arms, focusing on a knot in the floorboards, the spot evenly spaced between his planted feet. He did this when he expected a blood rush to the head and a firefight inside his skull.

"Hey, relax. That chair's not made of needles," Selfer said.

"It's no featherbed," Lett said.

Selfer held onto his smile. He held out his hands. "What can I tell you? Ask away."

"What about Washington, DC? Wasn't that always your goal? I'd have figured you for a natural."

"Oh, I gave DC a go. All of three months. Then I got the call.

You see, I want to be my own man." Selfer's curling mouth had taken a straight line.

Lett wasn't buying it. "You just like things hotter. Wilder. That Washington pond is too big and all the fish, as well. The Pacific's just about right for a big swimmer like you." Something made Lett refrain from calling him a shark.

"Let's just say that I don't suffer mediocrity. And I don't think you do, either. In any case, you're in no position to be casting stones. You could still have bars blocking your way."

"So why am I not in a stockade? Or made an example, Eddie Slovik-style? So I turned myself in. Big deal. You could've claimed you found me—gained you a whole basket of brownie points."

Selfer sighed. "I told you, from that very first day—you're special. I mean, look what you did to those halfwit blotto sergeants back at your billet." He added a happy shake of his head.

"They all right?"

"They'll live. They shouldn't have been in an off-limits bar. You were defending your post. There was no need to run."

Lett glared at Selfer.

"Okay, maybe there was," Selfer said. "I understand. But we will fix that. You only need to listen to me. That's all." He added a smile. "I knew that I'd find you again. But I didn't have to in the end, did I? Because you came asking. For me."

The very sight of Selfer should've done Lett in. But the man had said it himself: Lett had asked for him, by name. He had practically pleaded for Selfer, even though the last time he saw the captain during the war, at the height of the bloody Bulge, he had promised the man, *I will head back out there for whatever you cooked up because I have no choice. But I won't kill for the likes of you. Not anymore.*

"All you ever had to do was ask, Lett. Just tell me the truth. Tell me what you wish."

"I just want to be cured of it," Lett said finally. "Of what they did to me. What you did to me."

Selfer let out a long, reedy sigh. He looked around the room. His eyes landed back on Lett. "Let me admit something to you," he said. "No one knows this: My father was a simple con man. A city sparrow turned slicker, sure, but a sharpie just the same. That was me, what I was becoming. Where I was headed. Because that, in a nutshell, is Washington, DC. But things are different here. We're all looking for a new start."

Lett opened his mouth, but nothing more came out.

Selfer inserted in its place, "You remember that very last thing you said to me? At the command post? Before I sent you back out?"

"I won't kill for you," Lett muttered.

"Yes. You also mentioned the Golden Rule. The old 'Do Unto Others.' And I told you that I know it well," Selfer said. "Here— on the cusp of the Orient where we've now ended up, me and you—they have the good rule, too. Confucius. Laozi. 'Regard your neighbor's gain as your own gain, and your neighbor's loss as your own loss.' You see, I believe in reciprocity. Lett, listen to me. I want to help. I will help. But you have to come and meet me halfway."

Tears had run down Lett's cheeks. He only now noticed them, already cooling. He leaned forward, his hands hanging off the insides of his knees.

Selfer had scooted closer, also leaning forward, elbows on his knees, speaking low. "I couldn't believe it when they told me, I truly couldn't. You wanted me to keep you out of a stockade. Me. I was the one you called for."

More tears came, splashing hot on Lett's wrists, blurring his view of the floorboards. All he could do was shake his head.

"You've had certain troubles. The war returns inside your head. You are not well. Then I read reports that you have voiced threats to people. Very important people. I'm told there are reports of you claiming you wanted to kill Ike Eisenhower, even President Truman. Good Lord, Lett."

Had he done that? Was it on the boat, or sooner? In Belgium? He did have blackouts. Blackouts were always worse than benders. Blackouts brought out matters a man could never take back.

"But, you know something?" Selfer continued. "I know better. I know plenty better. Because I know you. I know what I saw in you and still do."

Lett had stopped shaking his head.

Selfer whispered now. "You're not just any man, despite your afflictions, your demons. You have special skills. They can take you places. Better places." He patted Lett on his right knee, held it there a moment. "We'll keep you out of a hospital. You'll be undergoing certain treatments here."

"I see," Lett muttered but had no clue what he was supposed to be seeing.

"Now, I have to admit—I have a stake in this, too. Your failure could reflect on me. Understand? I brought you onboard, touting you as a prime candidate for our duty roster. My hero from the European Theater. So, your success . . . well, it will happen."

"What is this place exactly?" Lett said.

"It's a training camp. For a new intelligence agency. It's all hush-hush. I don't know that much myself."

"What's your role?"

"Well, I'm like the camp manager, for now. More administrative than tactical. Expecting to move up soon, so we'll see. Not the snazziest post but it was a way in the door. But never mind that. What matters for you is you. Now, their training for you, it goes far beyond anything you've had before. What anyone has."

"I just want to be cured of this. Goddamn it . . ."

"I can cure you. We can. Do you have to make me confess it? I don't like what the war made you do—what I made you do. There, I said it."

Lett stared. He wiped at his face.

"The first step of treatment is therapy. I'm told there will be a method of talking things out. There will come medication. You'll feel cured. After that comes another step. We will retrain you. And then you will help us. You'll be fulfilling your end of your bargain—the one you yourself asked for."

Part of Lett wanted a blackout now, but one wouldn't come. "I'm not reenlisting," he said. "Not a chance. Not as a regular Joe."

Selfer smiled. "Come now. Do you think that's what this is? We are far above a regular post. This is a duty, surely, but it's not serving those same old forces who put you in a hole in Northern Europe."

"I don't know what that means. I don't know what any of this means."

"You will. And you'll know soon."

They sat there a long while. Lett wasn't sure how long. What he experienced wasn't a blackout. It was more like a meditation. They were two monastics. The next thing Lett knew, Selfer was walking him to the door with one arm around him, his fingers splayed across his back to cradle his ribs. Selfer opened the door all the way with the other hand, and the light streamed in, and more breeze along with it, drying any tracks of his tears left. This helped Lett take a long, deep breath to compose himself. He was glad that Kanani didn't have to see him like this. They stepped out onto the porch.

"How would you like to get a letter to your wife?" Selfer said.

Lett whipped around. "You can do that?"

"Sure. And no one else needs to know." Selfer patted his shoulder. "Just me and you."

"Okay. All right. Thank you."

Selfer rocked on his heels like a family man in gray flannel waiting for his train home to the suburbs. Lett strode to the other end of the porch, stepped down onto the barren clearing and looked both ways, then peered into the greenery surrounding them. He spotted a trail leading off into the forest. He looked back up to the porch.

Selfer was looking down on him, sizing him up in a way that Lett had never seen before. Lett almost thought he saw worry in Selfer's softening eyes.

"Why don't you go and take a stroll into camp?" Selfer said. "Take that trail there."

"Really?" Lett tried to make it sound casual, but his eyes had widened and his joints firmed up again. "I . . . I haven't been anywhere near a real military post in a very long time—except as a prisoner, that is."

"It's all right. Besides, this is more of an intelligence operation, less military. You can't stray. There's a perimeter fence, and the sentries. The trail is clearly marked. Look for the sign reading Quarters. Take your time. Someone will find you, check you in, get you to your billet."

"If you say so."

"I do indeed. Consider it your first test. I'll come find you when you're done—on the other side, as it were."

5.

Lett followed the trail. Dense foliage on both sides kept him walled in, and it was nearly a tunnel with the branches stretching overhead. Insects hummed; a strong wind swished between branches, leaves, fronds. He heard other sounds coming his way, but they were muffled. At a fork in the path, he saw the sign that read QUARTERS. Another sign read TRAINING GROUND. That trail led to the left. Despite Selfer's instructions, he started to follow it out of curiosity, but then he spotted, through the bushes, the whole works—an obstacle course, dummies for bayoneting, a platform for something, perhaps parachuting, or for sniping? Farther away, in a distant clearing, he heard the muffled pops and ripples of weapons firing.

Despite Selfer assurances, he realized that this was the first time he'd been on a training base since the war. His pulse raced. He was sweating again, despite the cooler air this high up, and it coated his neck and he wiped at it. He backtracked; took the trail he should've taken.

The stronger wind brought a sudden rain that washed out all sound. He stopped and stood under a large frond a moment until the rain faded to a blanket mist. Less than ten minutes had gone by, but it seemed like an age by the time he reached the end of the trail.

He crouched behind a large fern at the trailhead and looked out. The clearing resembled the one he and Kanani first entered in the disguised pickup, but it was larger—about one football field wide and long. It held six newly built bungalows, three on each side, separated by a wide lane down the middle. At the opposite end, the clearing made a hard right and continued like an L, and down that way Lett saw some olive drab tents blending in with the tree line.

His chest had tightened. His leg quivered but he squeezed his thigh till it stopped. His senses amplified from his old caution.

Every sparkle, color, edge, and curve etched in his mind. This kind of caution shouldn't have been necessary here, but he welcomed it as the finest quirk there ever was. It had saved his ass so many times. On the front lines in France and Belgium, he didn't see quaint junctions and lush forests—using his etching eyes, he had carved out enemy snipers focusing, machine guns targeting, the artillery aiming. Caution was his rabbit's foot. Caution was God.

He peered farther. Just above the horizon of treetops he spied the tip of a water tower, and a guard tower, maybe two, which likely meant more. That meant barbed-wire fences somewhere, a sentry hut. He focused now on the people passing between the bungalows, coming back out after the rain, bearing folders, gathered in small groups chatting—not that many, maybe ten. But there were probably double that, unseen in the bungalows. A few were women. The people wore a mix of fatigues and khaki summer dresses, but some had on casual civvies, modest aloha shirts and pallid flower dresses. Still no one carried insignia and no one had any weapons, to his relief.

He straightened up, took a deep breath, and stepped out into the clearing, keeping it casual, even sinking his hands in his pockets, though caution was telling him to keep crouching with his arms cocked and hands clenched at the ready. Caution was steel cables pulling on him. Caution wanted a gun in his clawed fingers, even though he'd sworn off weapons. A man and woman passed—the man smoking a pipe, the woman wearing a WAC garrison cap. Lett smiled at them and the steel cables gave him some slack and he strolled onward, right down the midway. At the far end of the clearing stood a cluster of signs on a pole.

Keep going. Gotta keep moving, always. Lett walked on. Inside the foliage on the trail, under the large fern, the dripping and rustling had dampened outside sound. But here out in the open, all sounds came roaring back.

He heard something new, growing stronger, faster. It was a hammering-ripping sound like some gargantuan zipper, and it wouldn't let up. What if it came closer?

Machine gun, MG 42. Coming right for him.

Lett crouched.

A thunking sound boxed his ears.

Enemy artillery. Their 88 guns wrecked whole ridges, a valley.

He shot off, moved on. A trash barrel stood a few yards away, his only cover. He hugged it, burying his shoulder into it. He smelled something; his nostrils snorted like a pig's. It was bitter. It might be something burning, rubber maybe.

This was France. He was up on the line, a town called Mettcourt. Buildings loomed on either side, about to spit fire.

"Mettcourt, fug it," he muttered. "Only one way outta this town."

The smell turned sour, then fetid in a way that burned the nostrils, so Lett clamped a hand over them. Dead enemy left out in the open. They gave off a different rot because of what they wore, decomposing along with their skin and meat and insides.

Then they weren't so dead. Figures passed, rushing along just out of eyeshot.

The Krauts, they had a flank on him.

Lett had no weapon. Nothing. Not even a trench knife. "Goddamn," he muttered and rose onto his haunches. He made for the closest edge of the clearing. Cover.

A shape rose out of the dense foliage as if formed from it. Arms flailing, knees high. The man was sopping, his loose wet uniform hanging off him like animal pelts, his balding head slick and his white eyes wild.

He was coming right for Lett. Lett saw he had a gun—*a Kraut luger.*

Lett froze. The man kept coming.

"Run! Run for your fugging lives!" the man screamed. "They're everywhere, see, in the trees, the caves—those deep dark caves, everywhere we go!"

Lett crouched. "Hands up," he ordered.

But the man still kept coming. Saliva squirted from between his front teeth. "You gotta help me, Mac, you gotta. They're coming and we gotta run, me and you!"

The gears inside Lett launched and found their cogs and meshed, the torque steeling him. Mechanically he stood, becoming twice as large as he was, his muscles like stones. He lunged, kicked at a knee and chopped at the man's neck and kept coming. The man slipped, landing on his back. Lett grabbed the Luger. The man held up his hands. Lett brought the Luger down on the man's forehead, clunking on bone.

The man wheezed underneath him, blood leaking out his nostrils, streaming over his face.

"Do it," he muttered to Lett, "just go and do it, why don't you? Do me the goddamn favor."

Lett eased off.

The people came outside, rushing from doorways, turning his way.

"Get inside! Find cover!" Lett shouted at them. The man below him was crying now. Lett shot up, pressed onward. He felt the people stopping to watch him, many lining up like it was a gauntlet he had to run in a witch-burning medieval hamlet at the height of the Inquisition, but these people wore khaki and prints instead of rags and vestments, had clipboards instead of scrolls, all the judgers that ever were now. All of time was combining, the cruelest centuries blending, piling on him to halt him right here. But he kept moving. *Gotta keep moving.*

As he ran, he saw the white helmets of MPs and their black armbands. They had batons, pistols, rifles. "Hey! There he is."

He looked like a deserter. He was a deserter.

He saw more of the tree line ahead and kept sprinting, he was going to make it.

"Ow . . ."

He felt a twinge in his back, then a prick, then it was red hot and spreading, flowing through him like lava itself, hotter, heavier. He kept running but his legs were concrete, and his lungs wouldn't pump, and he was staggering, stomping his feet like some drunken bandleader, the world spinning and he spinning in the other direction. The double spinning locked the world in place, two gears synchronizing, a brake slamming. A trap door opened. Lett was falling, plummeting, deep into the earth and more hot lava found him, submerging him, scorching and suffocating him at once.

All went black.

6.

Kanani tapped the jade cigarette holder against the shiny rim of the gold ashtray. They had left her Camels, as many packs as she wanted, along with more of those Filipino cigars. She was reclining on a chaise, in her living room. That high *makamaka* of a colonel by the name of Charlie Selfer had released her into The Preserve, which left that poor cracked-up GI Wendell Lett all on his own. A friendly haole lady in a WAC outfit with no insignia had appeared from nowhere and walked her along the trails to the nice DeSoto convertible waiting for her, the driver just as handsome. That had been the first surprise. She took the backseat, why not? Then the handsome haole was driving her down a paved road lined with pruned shrubs and clipped grass and palm trees planted in patterns—like one upscale country club. A fancy house loomed, what driver called the Main House. They passed that. Instead they ensconced her in this bungalow nearby.

This was another kind of surprise. Her new place had red felt wallpaper and plush rugs and beaded lamps and upholstered chairs, fringe and all. The separate bedroom had a four-poster bed as fluffy as a bunny.

She couldn't get too comfortable. She needed to stay wary. She'd come here for one thing only: to find their treasure and take it from them. There was almost certainly gold somewhere here or would be soon. Miss Mae had told her about it. Miss Mae had given her the gold lighter. Miss Mae knew everything. She wasn't just a mama-san. She'd been the mistress of at least one bigshot American who passed through Honolulu.

The ashtray was yet another strong confirmation that she was getting closer, somehow. It had dragons on it, hand-painted in gold over a red background, and turquoise inside. Did they even know it was a tea bowl, not an ashtray, and probably worth a pretty penny?

She lifted it, looked underneath. The calligraphy looked like ancient Chinese to her. So, it had to be worth a mint. *This is quite promising,* she reminded herself. It all fit the situation unfolding. Her instincts told her to pocket the thing, but she couldn't.

She had to learn more. She had to bide her time.

If she only knew where Miss Mae had gone. Miss Mae had disappeared. Kanani hoped Mae had taken a deal from the Americans, for working with them. Maybe she'd end up on the mainland. Maybe they'd give her a Chinese restaurant in some cold, gray city. That made her laugh. But that also wasn't Mae's style. She knew too much. What she revealed to Kanani was only the tip of the volcano. And Mae had seemed scared, and hurried, and that wasn't like someone who had probably been a double if not triple agent and always seemed to know how to choose a winner.

On their way up mountain, that poor Wendell Lett had started to figure out her true angle. He was smart, that one, and a cutie-pie, too. "You're going to show them," he'd said. "Make them all pay if you can help it." But he didn't know the half of it.

Wendell had helped save her from Frankie's questions if not the strong arm, and she would never forget that.

She had asked around and heard he'd had an episode, a setback. That hurt her heart. She hoped that Wendell was already getting the treatment he so dearly needed and wasn't just speeding up his own demise instead. She should've warned him better. Everything here served the pursuit of gaining intelligence and exploiting it. She'd never meant to string along that unhappy haole and certainly didn't want to make him think they were going to have sex. But then what did he do? He went and turned adorable enough to offer her a bicycle ride. She wasn't one *kola*—some oversexed *tita*—despite what a man might imagine on account of her previous profession. In the end, flirting with Wendell had seemed the only gesture that could calm the man. She was glad she didn't go any further. She had to admit that she might've liked it— maybe a bit too much.

She was liking too many things for her own good. Take this little place—it was finer than any she'd lived in and smelled nice too, seemingly smoked through with the potpourri of island flowers. This was surely one of the nicest places she might ever have sex in. She thought about that sometimes, all the boys she'd been with in that one Hotel Street boogie house alone. How many now dead local boys and haoles alike had she given herself to? Their bodies decomposing or buried all over Asia, on this or that island. So many thousands left to rot by that so-called military genius and kahuna number one, Douglas MacArthur. Their soul spirits visiting one another and plaguing the survivors like Wendell Lett, men wracked with guilt and nightmares and a desperate need to break free.

She needed to stay wary. She had so much to stay on top of. Miss Mae might've told her about the gold, but she never told her how it was coming in or how she could get at it.

And then there was Frankie. Frankie from her wild young days before the war. Like her and Miss Mae, Frankie had been working his own angle with the Americans, strong-arming folks mostly, and he was paid well for it. He had his reasons. Playing the goon and sometimes even the slick guy let him find out about this or that good thing. It was he, stoned on rum and probably *pakalolo*, who first told her about a rumor of gold and treasures. But he could never find it on Oahu. He wondered if it was on another island. And so did she. On her own. She kept prying, spying. Frankie would ask her about it. But she always told him she'd given up on pipe dreams, pots of gold at ends of rainbows. It was scary. Frankie was gaining power all the time and had started a little ring. He kept bugging her to tell him. They would make a deal, share in it. She would only laugh at him and bide her time. Until Miss Mae confided in her. Mae had told her about The Preserve—that it might be key. Frankie meanwhile had been keeping his evil prying stink eye on Miss Mae. At least Frankie hadn't made it up here. He'd come looking for Mae at her little place on the Big Island and found no one, thanks to Wendell's help. It did worry her that he knew about her place at all, but what could she do? With any luck, Frankie was back in Honolulu and figuring a different angle.

Hopefully, Mae would show up after all. Kanani hadn't told a soul that Mae had gotten a telegram to her before she disappeared, telling her that she would find Kanani at The Preserve if she could, most likely arriving via a ship putting into Hilo on the other side of the island.

Meanwhile, Kanani knew she had to bide her time even more. She could easily imagine what her new duty was. All they had to do was come and confirm it. Another boogie house wasn't exactly the posting she wanted, but it was the end goal that counted. She would just have to make this joint work for her. And they had left her the jade cigarette holder, so why not use that, too?

She leaned back on the chaise with its gold legs, wondering now if they might be real gold, as well. She sat up and tried to budge the chaise with her hips and it didn't move, not one inch. She chuckled at that, wondering if they even knew it was gold. She took a drag of her Camel and blew it toward the ceiling fan and her mind drifted back to Wendell. She hoped Wendell wasn't wrong in the head for good, like a big fight was too much for him. That army guy had that stare. He was seeing spirits of the dead. And he'd killed folks. That was why his stare went on so much longer, not to mention his leg wanting to hop around like a fish out of water. Still, if she had to, she was ready to chance him anyway.

She shook off that daunting thought with a yawn and a stretch, gazing around at the late afternoon sun doing its wonders on the room through the sheer lace curtains, twinkling this and that. She liked how her bungalow was secluded inside a grove, camouflaged. The grove sat on a rise. From the little lanai, she could see through to the Main House and just make out the sea, far on the horizon.

She wasn't dumb. She knew. They were buttering up a pig before the big luau roast. But who was the pig, and who was the roaster exactly? The notion made her hungry . . .

The doorbell rang. DeSoto? It was about time for that handsome driver to bring her another tray of food. She was calling him DeSoto. He did most whatever she requested. She should ask him to rub her feet. She would teach the likes of him. There had to be thousands of his *kine* on the mainland. All she had to do was throw some act or talk story real sweet. She chuckled at that, then checked her casual coolness. She had to remember to be on her strong toes.

"It's open," she shouted across the room and sat up, smoothing out the skirt of her floral aloha dress. It was a cute number but a little loud, the type haole officers brought back to the mainland for their wives and girlfriends, yet it was the least frilly and skimpy of all the dresses they had put in her closet.

"DeSoto? What did I say, eh? You come right in."

Only it wasn't DeSoto. Striding in was that high *makamaka* himself, Charlie Selfer.

She sprung off the chaise, slipped her feet into Oriental house slippers, and planted herself in the middle of the room.

Selfer had her food tray, silver dome and all. He wore civilian clothes—a tawny linen suit, open collar white shirt, white sandals. Not many haoles could pull off that look, but he carried it like a bouquet of plumerias.

"Please, no need to get up," he said. "I'll put it down right here."

She stepped back as he set the tray on the little table beside the chaise, crowding out her Camel smoldering in the ashtray. She couldn't help noticing that he added the slightest bow.

"Where's that DeSoto boy?" she said.

Selfer laughed. "Even buck privates get time off now and then."

She felt for the chaise behind her and sat on the edge, eyeing the silver dome.

"It's Spam with poi," Selfer said.

She rolled her eyes.

"Only kidding," he said through another laugh. "Mahi-mahi, sticky rice, coconut pudding." He nodded at the room. "Nice digs."

"Snazzy. Only thing missing is the opium pipe."

"I'll take that as a confirmation," Selfer said, losing the smile. He lowered himself into the armchair at his heels without so much as a glance at it. "Are you going to eat?" he added.

"You planning on watching me?" she said.

"The food can wait, then. I won't take up too much of your time."

She picked up the jade cigarette holder and got the Camel glowing again.

Selfer, eyeing her, said, "So, your father is native Hawaiian. Joey 'The Pug' Alana."

"*Was.*"

"Indeed. I'm sorry."

"Is this supposed to be the small talk story?" Kanani blew smoke toward the ceiling. "I'm not fooled by this, you know."

"Oh? Go on."

"All this splendor you show me. Throwing da act. Sailor guys in Honolulu Chinatown get the same treatment but it's plenty liquor, flower behind an ear, one skimpy silky bodice."

"And then?"

"Next thing they know they're out on their *popos* in a Hotel Street gutter."

"Undoubtedly. But you, my dear, are not a sailor."

It was how you received the act they were throwing, Kanani reminded herself. First came the luxury. Then came the sweet talk. "Well, I'm no admiral either, bruddah," she said.

Selfer sat up, rested his elbows on the chair arms, and produced a Chesterfield he didn't light. "I apologize for being short with you before. With Wendell Lett. I needed to talk to him."

"You treated me like the help." Kanani shrugged. "That's nothing new."

Selfer held a hand to his heart. "May I never do it again, dear."

Oh, Selfer was good. He was plenty smoother than the white men in their starched collars. A smoothie like him makes you figure you're in it together and for keeps. Sure, she saw right through Selfer. For keeps lasted only until you lost. All the same, she started thinking there might be a way to make this rapport they had work for her. First she had to find out who he worked for exactly, and what they had in store for her.

"You know about me, about my past, during the war, yeah?" she said. He nodded. "So where are the guys I used to work for in Honolulu?" She hadn't yet seen one face from the old days.

"The CIC? Most have relocated or are relocating. There was also the OSS around these parts, I believe. It doesn't matter. You're with us now."

"And who are you exactly, mister?"

"We're so fresh and new we don't have a name."

"Maybe you could try one out for size."

"Some call us The Directorate. But that's a placeholder."

"So, who's your big kahuna?"

"Why, that's a droll way of putting it."

"I don't mean it that way. To us the word means priest and wizard and chief and so on. You might be a type of kahuna here, who knows. But I'm asking about the kahuna of you."

"My big chief? I can't tell you. This is S.O.P., I'm afraid."

"Standard Operating Procedure. Then what's your S.O.P. gonna mean for me exactly?"

"Your food is getting cold," Selfer said.

"Maybe I like it cold. Go ahead—chance 'em."

Selfer nodded. "Very well. We would like you to comfort certain important persons who might stay here or pass through. Right here, in this exact quarters."

Bingo. Just as she suspected.

Many men would've looked away presenting such a notion, but Selfer kept his eyes right on hers. "Not necessarily you personally. At a future point, if things work out, we might bring in other women who are capable of operating in such a capacity."

Kanani shot him a sideways glance, then she stood up and paced the room, though there suddenly wasn't much of this bungalow to go around. There was only that one bedroom, the bathroom, and a combination kitchenette and dressing room along the back end that was cordoned off with an exquisite Chinese folding screen, also of great value. It had to be.

Despite the game at hand, she was on the right track—and how. Her plan was the only way for a woman to become her own person, to be free from the leash of the man and the haole land grabber. Independent means. That was what Miss Mae had. What her mother never had.

"These are our terms," Selfer said. "Besides, you were the one who wanted in here."

"You don't have to tell me," was all she said.

"Oh, and, no visitors just yet," Selfer added. "Only the ones we say."

She was pacing the whole room. He watched her. She passed through behind the partition and glanced out a window, where she saw nothing but sun and green and that fine DeSoto convertible, which, she realized, must be Selfer's personal car. For her, it was just a loaner.

"I got one question," she said. "This house isn't big enough for me, not if it's going to be the boogie *kine*, too. Not if other girls coming, going."

Selfer nodded, so she came around and stood before him.

"No, it's probably not," he said.

"Seems like that Main House over there has more room," she said, batting eyelashes.

"First, you prove yourself. And then? Well, we shall see, won't we?"

"See what?"

"Easy, easy. You just got here. For now, you assume more of a forward operating position. Along the way, there might be a special assignment or two."

"Ah. There it is. Let me guess: you like me playing the gal who's such a good listener."

"As I say—droll. You don't wish such special treatment?"

Kanani lowered her cigarette holder. "There's only one problem. Maybe I've seen this picture show already."

"Not quite like this you haven't. Any other girls—women— might be capable of comfort, but not of listening correctly. You can. It's a proven fact."

"Ho, careful there. 'Comfort women,' that's what the nasty Imperial Japanese Army used to call them."

"How soon we forget," Selfer said.

Kanani glared at him. "What are you paying me, eh? Let's talk about that."

Selfer chuckled. "You know how this works. You can move up, out of the bordello."

"Boogie house, we call 'em."

"As you like. And, you control all tips."

"Hallelujah," she said.

"Is there not a Hawaiian word for that?"

"Oh, sure. But you wouldn't like the sound of it."

"I think I like your style, Miss Ogawa."

Kanani gave a little bow. "Try call me Miss Alana," she said with a thicker accent. She blew out more smoke. If she gave it any more of an angle it would be blowing right up his behind. Still, she figured she had to feel things out a little. She shrugged and added, "Anything's better than Honolulu. Things were worse enough during the war. The haole policeman, they tolerated boogie houses but only in the way they liked. Police Chief, he set all the rules—'Ten Commandments,' we called them. You like me to recite them for you?"

"It's okay, I already heard—"

"We couldn't even use our own beaches, on our own island, and all because we made your sailors and soldiers feel good before going off to die." And she was one of the lucky ones working for a good mama-san. Kanani made sure not to mention Miss Mae by name. Still, she wondered if he'd ever heard of her. She might have to find out eventually.

She added a little grunt.

Selfer's expression had not changed as she spoke. He crossed his legs. "By the by, don't you have another question for me?"

"What *kine?*"

"About Wendell Lett. About how he is."

She didn't want to seem too close to anyone. When push came to shove, they could use anyone as weight against her and vice versa. Besides, how could she ever tell Wendell about this? A good man like that was only going to be disappointed in her—he and her faddah would have gotten along well that way. She made herself shrug. "I'm sure he's all right," she said.

"Wendell hit a snag, truth be told. Didn't exactly pass his first test here. But, the treatment's already helping, I'm sure."

"Swell," was all she said, "that's just swell." She took a long, worried drag of her Camel, but it was already out.

7.

When Lett woke, he was lying on a bunk. It had a thin, clean mattress on crisscrossed metal slats. The room was narrow, with gray concrete walls and caged light bulbs and no windows. Ventilation came down from a square grate in the low ceiling. The steel door to his room was left open. He could go out and walk down the short corridor, which had no windows, either. Three other steel doors had been left open, too, showing rooms like his but vacant. One end of the corridor had a connecting door, more like a submarine hatch with bolts and a wheel handle. That was shut. He had tried the wheel, but it did not budge. The other end of the corridor was just more gray concrete wall.

He was wearing a US Army medical corps robe of blue corduroy. Someone must've put that on him. His unadorned summer uniform had been hung on the one hook on the wall, his brown GI shoes shined and set on the floor, and the meager contents of his pockets stacked on a metal chair. He wasn't hungry. He felt rested. His face had no beard stubble that he could feel, but there was no mirror to check. He sat up a few times, then lay back again and closed his eyes. Something made him flinch, like a person does right before sleep. He thought he'd heard a man screaming, far away, muffled. He told himself that the scream was only in his head.

Later, he heard a squeak of the wheel on the hatch down the corridor. Then came footsteps, measured but not marching. Lett had left his door open. He stood, brushed his bed cover taut, planted his feet in the middle of the floor.

Two men approached, athletic types with angular faces, their expressions relaxed. They wore Army coveralls like mechanics or tankers, but their khaki was spotless, with creases even. They looked inside the room.

"Afternoon," one said.

"Gentlemen," Lett said.

The two stayed out in the corridor. A third man approached the door, his head down, still reading from a clipboard. He wore a white coat, like a doctor. It looked Government Issue, but it lacked insignia. His thick, dark hair had a perfect part. As he turned into the doorway and stepped inside, he looked up. His gray eyes showed a metallic sharpness.

"Time to get cracking," he said, "or a man's not really hacking."

Lett didn't know if it was supposed to be a saying or a proverb or what. He just smiled and nodded.

The man strode in and smiled back and seemed to gain inches in height doing so. "No saluting here," he said as if reading Lett's mind.

"Good to know, sir, as I hadn't received any instruction—"

"No sirs, either, son. We're all in this together."

Though he'd called Lett "son," he couldn't have been more than forty. He nodded around the room, and his long, practically rectangular face and thin mustache loomed over Lett.

"And welcome, I should add," he said in a more patient voice that reminded Lett of a small-town grocer. Of Ohio. He hadn't thought about Ohio in such a long time.

The man stepped even closer, the clipboard held behind his back. "I'm Lansdale. Edward Lansdale." He was holding out his other hand.

Lett shook it. "A doctor?"

Lansdale tugged at his white coat. "Oh, this? Of sorts. Though as I said, we don't bother with titles here, rank and degrees and so forth. It's more about what a man can achieve."

Lett tensed up.

"Relax, take it easy," Lansdale said. "Questions? Fire away."

"How long have I been here?"

"Not long. A few hours. It's night now."

"Where are we? Underground?"

"Good. That's good." Lansdale pivoted on a heel, looked around again. "It's a tunnel system, right under camp. Just yards from where you blacked out."

"No kidding."

"Why, sure. It's from the war. Was supposed to be a top-secret hole-up should the Japs invade—Japanese I mean—but now we get to inherit it. Pretty ideal."

"How far does it go?"

"Oh, not far. Far enough. Links up with some of these lava caves they have here if you head inland, but I can assure you that's not in our plan for you. Don't worry." He added a flash of a grin that was more like a sneer. "This is just for your own safety, and that of others, until you get up to speed."

"Who was that man I attacked? Or he attacked me. I . . . I'm not sure."

Lansdale flashed the sneer-grin again. "It was both. It was really something, you two going at it like that, like two stray cats. He's a Marine, that one. Also having the treatment. More on that later."

"Is he all right?"

"Of course. He's been through worse."

"Are you here for the cure?"

"The cure? Ah. Yes. But it's for you, you see, not me."

"Is this part of the VA?" Lett asked. "Is this a VA program?"

"A what?"

"Veterans Administration."

"Oh, right. No, no. You can put that notion right out of your head. Ours is a special project." Lansdale smiled and swung his clipboard around and tapped at it. "As I said, let's get cracking."

***

"One thing war taught me was that we are all ants," Lett said, letting the words form and flow before he could think them. "Just ants. We are all ants and we are done for, sooner than later. It's as if we are crossing, say, a fast boulevard of heavy vehicles, and it's all in deep fog, and the noise is so deafening that you couldn't have seen that giant truck coming, crushing you like you're that ant, flattened by people and forces that don't even know it or care. And even if you make it across that hopeless divide, you're still heading for a cliff deeper than the Grand Canyon, so deep that the best binoculars a unit could obtain by hook or by crook could not penetrate that abyss, so deep that as you fall you lose all sense of time. You are neither here nor there. You're just facing it, see, forever, back against the wall, all out of change . . ."

"I see," Lansdale said. He sat next to Lett, who lay on his bunk, his head resting atop two pillows. This was their second morning session, two days later. In their sessions, Lansdale called Lett's talk "free association." Lett welcomed talking for once. Simply jawing on was the whole point of their sessions. Lansdale sat in a simple metal chair, but he made it seem as cozy as an upholstered armchair by the way he rested his long torso.

Lansdale had told him the way the treatment would proceed. There were three stages: talk, medication, and training. "You see, our treatment here results in the full confrontation of what's troubling you. First, you're talking it out, then you're helping things along with revolutionary new medication, then, and only then, you're 'replacing' your problem areas with a fresh new duty that retrains your ability to cope by reinforcing your latest deeds. You will own your combat fatigue and thereby destroy it. We rebuild you, you see. You see?"

"Training, duty?" Lett had said. "That implies an assignment at some point."

"That's good. Yes. If we have a specific need, yes. Training is where you begin to reacquaint the new you with the world, working matters out, and an assignment—or assignments, I should say— would be where you finally act things out so as to understand and confirm that you are, indeed, cured. Make sense?"

It had. So Lett talked and talked and now he was talking some more. He let out a big sigh, and another. He interlocked his fingers on his stomach, then let them relax.

Lansdale said, "Our aim is to get you to the point where you feel like the one driving that big truck, instead of feeling like that lousy ant."

Lett said, "But, I have to stay alert. The distractions will fool a guy. Trick you. There are so many triggers out there. Weather, smiles, sudden pops, people simply screwing up. So much can trigger it. But then there are other tricksters beyond the real and the triggers. Nightmares. Hallucinations. You cannot let down your guard, even when you think you are dreaming or even dreaming of dreaming. Because then you're dead, too. You just focus on the mission at hand, but go about this deliberately, trusting no one. That's all you do. It's mechanical, and you let the machine inside sync its gears. That's how I found the peace and calm to operate. I let the machine inside me take over. I didn't concern myself with who or what flipped the switch. All of which, of course, is a hell of a problem in peacetime."

Lansdale was nodding. He picked up his clipboard, glanced at it, set it down. "That is how you 'survived' in the field. You might call it 'operate,' but it's really performing at the highest levels of confidence despite all odds stacked against you—it's what made you perform so ably on your missions. You possess what few do. You don't crack. You're the perfect engine."

"Oh, I come close to cracking, Doc. I come close. But it's *after*. After is the problem."

"Which is what we are here for. And we are making progress, don't you agree?"

Lett had to admit it. Call it what Lansdale may, call it whatever the headshrinkers preached, but just talking it out like this seemed to work wonders.

Along the way, Lett asked more questions of Lansdale. Lett wondered what intelligence agency ran the camp. Lansdale hesitated at first, just staring. "I can't tell you much, but . . . Well, we work in conjunction with SCAP, but we're really becoming our own autonomous group. That's our aim. Driving that big truck, if you will."

"SCAP?"

"Supreme Commander for the Allied Powers in the Pacific— MacArthur's boys in Tokyo. It doesn't hurt to tell you. During the war, you had the OSS and the MIS and later the CIG and what have you, but now there's a need for a new, prevailing agency. Because of the Red Menace, you see—this Cold War of ours could get hot any time, especially in Asia. Now, there's another new gang calling themselves the CIA. They want to absorb us all, but we'll see. We might well end up on top. If we can help it. Don't make the claim if you don't got the aim!"

Lett was getting as used as he could to Lansdale's impromptu slogans. He had learned just to nod and smile, as if Lansdale had offered words both profound and entertaining. But he couldn't just laugh. It wasn't a joke. Just laughing made Lansdale glower and leave the room, which he did once, and he took too long to come back. As Lansdale came and went, Lett noticed he had the slightest stoop, and his left arm tended to dangle with his left hand twisting slightly. At first Lett thought this pointed to a disability. That was far off the mark. It was just Lansdale. He had his own way.

"I can't believe you had me sent here from halfway around the world," Lett asked at one point.

"That was Colonel Selfer's doing, getting the ball rolling. But it was your own keen initiative that started it. You're quite the go-getter! As far as transport goes, well, we do that all the time. No matter if it's for the right goal or for the right man. The right man is so hard to find, especially one who's been proven in the field. And you're definitely the right man."

"What's an intelligence agency doing in the healing business? I mean, this isn't part of a VA program, yet you want to cure combat fatigue?"

Lansdale grinned and kept grinning, showing Lett plenty of yellow teeth. He held up a finger. "We want to understand better how men reason, and don't reason. Isn't that what intelligence is all about? Yes? Yes. Besides, it gives our new agency a damn fine edge. Because it's the future. Strike that—you're the future!"

At one point, Lett gestured at the two men in coveralls out in the corridor and asked Lansdale, "Do they need to be here?"

Lansdale shrugged.

"When they first came?" Lett said. "By the looks of them I was a little worried you were going to replace my carburetor or tinker with my ticker or something worse."

"Say no more," Lansdale said, and the men only ever returned to bring him his chow.

***

The talking therapy went on for a couple more days, but that stage was ending, Lansdale told Lett. They were moving him to the second stage: the medication. At intervals over the next two days, Lansdale would inject him with a shot of a clear solution. The glass syringe was too wide for Lett's taste and the metal ends too stout. After the prick, it stung a little for fifteen seconds or so. But Lansdale knew how to find a vein. Lett didn't feel much different after. His head was clear, yet he felt relaxed, and talking came easier—he could still talk all he wanted if he wished. It certainly helped that Lansdale administered the dose himself, not some lug in an orderly smock. They were hunkering down here on this tropical island and just taking it easy. He felt free and easy. He might as well be swinging in a hammock in the breeze between palm trees. He didn't even need a drink of that rum from the Philippines.

"Hey, I was just thinking: They got a hammock up there somewhere?"

Lansdale chuckled. "I'm sure they do. If not, I'm sure they can set one up for you."

He had asked about Kanani. Lansdale told him she was doing fine and getting trained, and Lett didn't worry about her. He felt so good about everything. He was being given a new lease, really. That was the way he was looking at it.

Lett didn't care if Lansdale was a doctor or not. He just liked calling him "Doc" now and then. It fit. Lansdale didn't tell Lett what the shot was; Lansdale only said that it contained a "revolutionary light sedative," and that it was confidential information. It was best for the cure, and he cautioned Lett not to swap too many treatment stories with the other subjects because every cure was different. That was fine with Lett—all he knew was he wasn't feeling any adverse side effects. In fact, he welcomed the way he was breathing easier and talking things out and learning things and knowing matters. His treatment could've ended up much worse for him. Electric shock. Lobotomy. A dark cooler that no one ever came to release him from.

Once Lansdale felt Lett was ready, he broke down the incident on his first day and helped Lett understand his episode. That gargantuan zipper Lett heard was no MG 42 but just a dumbo recruit gone a little too happy with a jackhammer—they were still building here in camp, after all. The thunks Lett heard? Not enemy artillery of course. Just a motorized pile driver. Meanwhile, a crew had been burning trash and it had old tires in it. And no bodies were decomposing, for that matter. Some goldbricker hadn't sorted the barrels of trash, which happened to contain carcasses of small island animals, which mixed up with the rest of it, and when the breeze carried that smell it was just horrid. So Lett got a whiff at just the wrong time.

"You triggered it all," Lett protested, tightening up.

Lansdale clucked his tongue, a *tsk-tsk* sound. "No, that we did not. Now, I know what you're thinking. I can see it on your face. That you had failed. It had been your first test, certainly, but don't think that you had failed it. You can only learn from this."

Lett nodded along, loosening up again. "What about the incoming? The attacker, I mean."

"That was fantastic. As I said. You really walloped him. Nice job."

"Oh. I didn't mean to."

"But you did—you did. You really impressed us with it."

"That wasn't my intention. You said he was a Marine."

"Yes. Jock Quinn. Unfortunate." Lansdale added one of those sneers of his and wiped at his mustache. "He'd been undergoing his own treatment. But he managed to go off on his own for a while. That was him finding his way back. The rain didn't help. You didn't. And that was no German Luger pistol in his hand, son, just a lava rock."

"Aw. Gee. I hope I get to tell him sorry."

"You will. Now, those MPs you saw were actually there, and they were armed as it happens, which was regrettably the first weapons here that you'd seen—and it didn't help one iota that MPs present a trauma for you owing to your war service."

No one had ever called his deserting a service before. He had served heroically, after all. Lett told himself this was progress, too. "What about my back, Doc? I took one in the back."

"You did indeed, Wendell." By the end of the first day, Lansdale had taken to calling him by his first name. "I must apologize for that. Certain sentries had been trying out a new tranquilizer gun, and one got a little eager with the clumsy thing."

"A dart gun?" Lett remembered his muscles had gone weak and he could not breathe and he'd dropped.

"I'm afraid so, yes." Lansdale added a shake of his head. "It was curare. Our weapons team was working on something new."

"You were experimenting with me?"

"No, it's not like that."

"Tranquilizers are for animals. I'm not some animal, Doc."

"No. Of course not. In point of fact? I'll have you know that I investigated all of this personally and have passed my recommendations on to Lieutenant Colonel Selfer. All appropriated parties are being reprimanded."

At the end of that day, Lansdale assured Lett that the third stage, his training, would begin once they determined that he was ready. Lett's development would be "cultivated until it met a certain standard."

"This is the whole point of the cure, after all," Lansdale told him.

"What's the training?" Lett asked. "The assignment."

"Well, that's up to us," Lansdale said. "And, it will depend on how you respond from here on out."

And then, Lansdale stopped visiting Lett.

8.

Without Lansdale, Lett didn't get his injection. Without that syringe, Lett didn't seem to be able to find those profound and illuminating thoughts he was voicing before when "associating free," as Lansdale called it. Staying calm wasn't as easy, either. He worried that the nightmares or an incident would come any moment. Even the slightest muffled sound through the ventilation grate could set him back. He needed to keep his treatment going.

Lett wasn't sure how much time had passed exactly, but he figured it had been a day. The minutes wore on, becoming hours. He didn't know when it was daylight exactly, let alone the position of the sun. The two guards in coveralls returned but only to bring him his food. Other than that, Lett paced and he stewed.

He banged on the hatch of his room until the two guards opened up. He repeatedly demanded to see Lansdale. The two told him that Lansdale had other business and had instructed that he stay put.

He stewed more, paced more. He hung up his blue corduroy robe and made sure he was fully dressed, ready to go. He reasoned things out in his metal chair, facing the wall as if it were a chalkboard, the gray paint blurring into options, acceptable losses, lesser evils. Again, he banged on the door, this time with a more measured pace that brought the two guards back sooner.

"I would like to speak to Lieutenant Colonel Selfer," he told them in an equally measured tone. "I'm a patient, not a prisoner."

They exchanged the briefest glances. "We'll see what we can do," they said at nearly the same time.

The two guards came back a couple hours later and, to Lett's full surprise, announced that Selfer himself had authorized his release. They escorted him out, taking him along more corridors like his and through connecting hatches, then finally to a narrow metal stairwell painted the same gray as the concrete walls. The stairwell shaft rose straight up. At the top landing waited a large hatch with an oversize handle. Lett stepped outside and saw that the hatch was built into a rectangular steel housing inside the forest, its olive drab paint blending in with the thick greenery. He could see from the sun that it was late afternoon. A short trail delivered him to a clearing that neighbored the one where he'd lost his marbles.

There a clerk gave him a small bungalow of his own. Lett noticed, meanwhile, that he was feeling none of the effects he'd felt the first time out here. The clerk advised him to remain at his quarters until called for. He shouldn't have visitors just yet, and he shouldn't try visiting others, any offices, or even the mess hall just yet—these were Selfer's strict instructions. They brought him his meals, good chow and lots of it, too, with fresh coconut on the side and the best coffee he'd ever tasted. Yet another day passed. He was growing jumpy again, and itchy, so much so that he kept unbuttoning his shirt and trousers to check for ants. He started walking laps around his bungalow and pounded out a little path. While he was circling the bungalow, the man who brought him food offered to put up a hammock for him.

"I don't care about a hammock!" Lett shouted back.

When he wasn't pacing, he was sitting on the edge of the porch, very much like he had as a boy, keeping lookout for a nondescript sedan to pull up after he'd been directed to wait outside his latest foster home, only to be taken away to another, and another, until he started thinking maybe he was better off in that Mennonite orphanage. And then he had started thinking that maybe he didn't need another of their homes or institutions or even a high school like the regular kids from regular homes had—that maybe what he really needed was to strike out on his own, and for good, and so he would dream of hopping on a train or fighting in Spain or later of a room in a boarding house that he could call his very own while he saved for night school. And then the war came. At least the Army would want him, or so Lett thought. Only death and desertion wanted him in the end. That thought made him want to pull up all the planks off the bungalow porch and smash them over a rock and light the fragments and splinters into a bonfire before ripping off the plain fatigues they'd given them and tossing them on the fire.

He wasn't done. He had more in him. He needed more.

Selfer had promised to get a letter to Heloise. He needed that, too. That had to be done.

He walked more laps around his bungalow, his fists balling up. Then he shot inside, grabbed the letter he'd written, came back out, and bounded down the middle lane of the clearing. He made his way through camp using various trails and cut-throughs, the clearings he passed like so many compartments, drawers, cells. He followed the signs. A longer, bending trail through forest delivered him to the area holding what was called the Main House—Lansdale had mentioned it in their conversations as being Selfer's quarters. It stood on a ridge, open to a horizon made up of three layers—the green island coastline, the gray-blue sea, the azure sky spotted with white puffs.

The well-groomed house grounds resembled those of an upscale country club, with shrubs like sculptures and a lawn like a putting green and palm trees in rows like giant sentries. He'd expected to find guards. He saw no one, not even a gardener. In the circular driveway before the house stood a couple brand-new jeeps and gleaming postwar sedans, a DeSoto convertible, a Chrysler four-door. The Main House wasn't that imposing in itself—a ranch style in an L shape with white walls and a modest swimming pool nestled in the L's angle. Not quite modern but with clean lines, one of those homes owned by people who made it rich at a rapid rate and liked to pretend they were still homespun and ordered out of the Sears catalog.

A small and elderly Hawaiian woman opened the front door. "Aloha. Have appointment?" she said smiling.

"Yes." Lett tried to add a smile but couldn't quite force one out.

"Try wait, please." She pressed the door almost shut, leaving it cracked.

Lett could hear peals of men laughing and boasting from some-where inside. He kept his fists stuffed in his pockets, shifting his feet, teeth grinding.

"You come, please." Lett followed the woman down a hall, pass-ing open rooms lined with the house's many windows. Through the glass panes and their reflections, Lett could see men in civilian clothes going out the back way, strolling by the pool, still laughing and slapping one another's shoulders.

The woman left Lett in a main room. The low-slung rafters and columns were carved with decorative curves in the Polynesian style. Various objects stood on shelves, miniature pagodas and Buddha figurines of gold—Lett wondered if the glimmer was the real thing. A bar had more of that Filipino rum—cases of it stacked as if just delivered. The center of the living room, he now saw, had a sunken circular area. He figured it was supposed to look modern, but it only reminded him of a field latrine. His intestines quivered a little.

Charlie Selfer marched in. He was wearing civvies: a shirt with a tastefully faint Hawaiian print of palm trees on white, light gray linen trousers, white leather sandals. "What are you doing?" he barked.

"Thanks for releasing me."

Selfer sighed, shrugged. "Look, don't mention it. I mean, really don't. Lansdale won't like it. But I'll explain it to him. He shouldn't just leave you hanging like that."

"That's just it—the doc, I mean Lansdale, he's gone AWOL."

"You're not supposed to be here," was all Selfer said. "I have work."

"I need to talk. Please."

Selfer sighed again. He gestured Lett down into the sunken area, which held high-back rattan chairs, and dropped into a chair with a squeak of grinding wicker. Lett did the same.

"I want the next stage," Lett said. "I want some duty. I'm ready."

Selfer just stared at Lett, a long while. "I have to believe you really mean it," he said finally. "We all have to believe."

"What do you want? A thanks? You're the one who caused all

of it. You." Lett shot up out of the chair, then dropped back down. "I had to kill a little German girl," he muttered. "In Cologne. All on account of you."

Selfer shook his head, but it wasn't in denial. They sat in silence a moment, grasping at the wicker chair arms.

"So help me," Lett said, in a whisper.

"I don't . . . have the authority," Selfer said. "Only Lansdale does for that. I was already pushing it by releasing you."

"Where is he?"

"I don't know. On business." Selfer shook his head again.

"I can show you I'm ready for more," Lett said. "Remember you promised I could get a letter to my wife, to Heloise?"

"I did. The offer stands. Is she still your wife? I never asked you."

"It's a good question. We're separated."

"Oh. I'm sorry."

"Does anyone else know about her?" Lett said.

"Here?" Selfer said. "No. This one is just between us."

"Okay," Lett said. He pulled out the letter he'd grabbed from inside his bungalow. He held it out for Selfer. Selfer unfolded it and read:

My Love,

I hope with all my might that you receive this letter. It probably took some time getting to you. I'm well and safe. I can't tell you where I am, but as you may have guessed I'm receiving the cure to my problem.

I should've listened to you and never should've ever returned to the front line. If I hadn't, I never would've seen the things I had, nor done them, nor become this shell of a man with a mechanical beast living inside him. They wrecked me just like you said. The warmongers, the opportunists, they use men like me like matches for cigarettes.

You were also right to make me leave you and go find a cure for it.

I'm part of a special classified program that promises a solution. By participating, I won't have to go to prison. I'm putting all my

faith in it, and in the people running things. It's my only hope. I'm
getting good help so far. In fact, it's much warmer here than home.
That's all I can say about things. But I take them all as a good sign.

You won't hear from me again, not until I'm healed for good.
That could take some time.

I remain strong just thinking of how strong you are. Hug our
good boy for me and tell him I love him and that I'll see him again
one day, provided that I beat this thing.

Destroy this letter as soon as you read it.

Je t'embrasse,
W. L.

Back in Belgium he had tried to work odd jobs away from
people, helping out foresters and farmers mostly. Sometimes he
would go berserk. The forests were never kind to him. Farms could
bring smells that provoked. Worse than that, he trusted no one. He
couldn't. He didn't even trust Heloise anymore. He hated that about
himself. And he didn't want to pass this on to his boy. He himself
never had a father to speak of, but having none was probably better than a paranoid father who haunted a boy and plagued a man.
Supposing he did that to Holger Thomas? Kept scaring the good
boy with his erratic behaviors. Heloise could only explain it away for
so long. Supposing his boy tried to live up to things that could not
and should not be lived up to, not ever, the weight of centuries of
war and hate delivered down his throat like so much cod-liver oil till
he choked? Lett wanted to return a good father or not at all.

As Selfer read the letter, his eyebrows raised. When he finished,
he held up the page like a winning ticket, then he folded and slid it
into his trouser pocket. "The warmonger line is a little rich but, hey,
you're entitled."

"Believe me now?" Lett said.

Selfer smiled. "Okay, Lett, okay. I'll have this sent off pronto, on
the QT."

"Then what?"

"Then, I'll look into getting you to the next stage. I'll do what I can, that is."

"Thank you." Lett took a deep breath, his lungs opening up.

"It's the least I can do. Considering."

"There's another thing," Lett said. "I haven't had my shot."

"What?"

"The second stage—medication. Lansdale dropped it, discontinued it, something."

"Oh," Selfer said. He paused a moment, staring into the carpet.

"I know I'm not supposed to discuss it, but I figured you knew."

"Sure, sure. But, isn't that half the point of a dosage—so that you don't require it eventually?"

"It was helping. I really think it was. What if my condition comes back, but worse? Who says it can't continue?"

Selfer nodded. "Well, I suppose we could reintroduce your dosage. Maybe just not so much. I'll check with Lansdale. Anything that is helping should be considered and reconsidered . . . This is a work in progress, after all."

"Thank you. Again. Never thought I'd say that to you."

"Don't get your hopes up too much," Selfer added.

"You mentioned not having the authority. What does that mean exactly?"

Selfer pursed his lips. They threatened to form a pout. "It's just that . . . Lansdale, well, he outranks me. I know we don't talk about rank and so forth much here, but the fact is that he does prevail. I'm . . . Like I told you before, I'm more like the manager here than a commander. Sort of a caretaker with pull."

"So, you don't create any orders?"

Selfer looked up at Lett with sad eyes. "I barely give them."

"So who does? Lansdale only?"

Selfer looked around, even though they were clearly alone. He crossed his legs one way, then the other. He lit a cigarette. "Lansdale has been reporting to SCAP, GHQ, Tokyo, The Dai Ichi. Got me? Whatever you want to call MacArthur now. But there's also others. Some of them pass through here."

"Like those ones out by the pool."

"Some, yes. A new combined intelligence agency is being established, I'm hearing, and it should prove more powerful than any organ that came before." Selfer looked at his watch. "But this is all I can tell you. Understand? Mum's the word."

"Of course," Lett said and tried to make it sound earnest. But he was left with the awkward feeling that Lansdale had earlier confided in him just as much or more than he had in Selfer, possibly. He certainly wasn't going to tell Selfer that. He buried the thought away.

Selfer watched his cigarette burn down. "You're doing so well. I'm proud of you, you know. I do admire your gung-ho way."

"I'd just like to get cracking, as Lansdale puts it."

"Certainly. Now, if you'll excuse me. I have another meeting to arrange." As Selfer stood, Lett noticed he had actual wrinkles despite his smooth skin. Crow's feet. They bore the slight greasiness of sweat. He touched Lett on his forearm. "You're part of something big," he added, "and at the vanguard, as well. Remember that."

"Something I can take back with me?" Lett said, repeating Selfer's assurance to him back in the darkest days in the Battle of the Bulge. Selfer was already calling him a hero then. What a word that was.

Selfer ignored the remark. Lett wondered if the man even remembered it.

"I'll do what I can," Selfer repeated absently and nodded to his words. He lit another cigarette. He hadn't offered one to Lett. This might've been the first time Lett ever saw Selfer's slick manners slip—not that Lett would've accepted. Selfer certainly had things on his mind. Maybe he did have a lot riding on his so-called hero from the European Theater.

"But, if we move too fast," Selfer said, "or push things too hard—don't say I didn't warn you."

"Consider me warned. And ready."

"Fine." Selfer turned to step out of their pit.

"One more thing, if I may," Lett said. "Where is Kanani?"

"Who? Oh, yes." Selfer smiled wide, and the wrinkles smoothed out. "Miss Kanani Alana has been given good duty. She's still here. Doing more than fine. Now there's one who needs no cure. I dare say that she's the remedy."

9

Two days later, something like normalcy had set in. The clerk had told Lett that he still had to remain in his quarters as much as possible. Now, however, he could visit the mess hall and take short walks, though only out in the clearings. Not too many trails for Lett just yet. And he should still avoid visiting any offices, at least until Lansdale returned. This was all on Selfer and Lansdale's orders, the clerk had been sure to remind him.

So, on his second afternoon, Lett again found himself roaming the same turf. This let him reassess and retrain his senses. The main clearing where he'd failed his test was one football field wide and long, he confirmed again. It held those six new bungalows, three to a side, separated by a middle lane. At the opposite end, the clearing turned like an L, leading to olive drab tents that were quickly surrendering ground to the wooden frames of more low huts.

This was the fourth time he'd passed through. He still felt no ill effects. He peered farther again and just above the treetops spied the tip of that water tower and the guard tower, just like before. The people passing were likewise unchanged, still wearing a mix of fatigues and khaki, aloha shirts and flower dresses. Still no weapons that he could see.

None of his senses let him down. As he strolled, all he smelled now was barbecue smoke wafting through camp from the mess, though it was interspersed with something pungent, possibly from fermentation or a rotting plant. And he heard an occasional rooster crowing. It was colder up here than he'd recalled, with more wind. Then again, they were closer inland to the two volcanoes that dominated the center of the island.

He recalled something Kanani had said on their way up to The Preserve. "At some point, all this green is gonna stop and it turns into lava fields, and plenty of it too, just open and barren country."

Kanani. She was the real reason he was out here by this point. He was hoping to catch her out, and he bet that she was doing the same. So he kept showing himself.

He noticed other things. The equipment and gear and matériel were a mix from all branches, with even some British equipment thrown in. And the kitchen items weren't military grade but commercial. The sum of it all was decidedly not Government Issue but a surplus haul, as would be procured for some private foreign legion. An espionage operation, maybe. Mercenaries even. So Lett imagined. He tried not to think too much about that. Selfer had openly stated that this was more an intelligence outfit than a military post, after all. For him, the cure was what mattered.

He strolled on, skirting the dense line of jungle foliage that held the camp's many trails. He brushed large ferns and giant fronds, the greens occasionally dotted with the bright-purple pink of bougainvillea and slick, leather-like leaves tinged rust-red.

He turned into the next clearing. Along the wall of jungle green, he spotted a floral dress—a woman sitting on a bench.

Kanani.

The aloha dress looked adorable on her, but it was a little too colorful, like something a tour guide might wear, and he wondered if they'd asked her to wear it—that or they limited her wardrobe. Her hair now had a little wave to the bangs, and she wore yellow plastic-frame sunglasses with a slight uplift at the outside corners, like a cat's eyes.

He crept up from the side, keeping to the shadows along the backsides of the tents.

She sat upright, on the edge of the bench as if on lookout, her back not touching the backrest. Looking for him?

She kept her eyes behind those big sunglasses.

Her outfit had disarmed Lett a little. He couldn't help a smile.

Then she turned those sunglasses his way.

He smiled bigger; she smiled back and rose to hug him.

"Aloha," Lett said. "You just come from the mainland, doll?"

She gave him a little thump on the chest. "Don't ask."

"Well, finally—it's about time we get to see each other."

"It sure is. Sit, sit." She found her perch. He joined her, just like on the pew in that little old Kona church. She pulled her sunglasses down.

"You doing okay?" she said.

"I am. I can actually say so. I think treatment is helping. You?"

A group of people passed, just beyond the tents. A doctor's coat. He and Kanani paused. She slid her sunglasses back on.

"They set me up in my own bungalow," Lett said eventually.

"Me too."

"Though I don't know what comes next. Not exactly."

"Me neither."

"I'm not supposed to have visitors yet," Lett said. "But who knows?"

"Same with me, more or less," Kanani said. "That will change . . ."

It seemed to Lett that her eyes were avoiding him, even under those sunglasses. He thought of what he could ask her, what she could tell him.

"We should tell each other everything," he blurted.

"Yes. Look out for each other. Same as before."

"All that we can, that is. Some things being classified."

"Right. You smart, Wendell."

"Well?"

"Oh. I met Jock," she said, adding another smile. "Ho! Just like a Marine guy."

"Who?" He recalled Lansdale saying the name. Jock was the Marine he'd fought. "Ah, right."

"He's okay. You didn't hurt him any more than he hurt himself. You two will be all right. I like him. You'll like him."

"I'm going to take your word for it," Lett said. "Listen, when should me and you see each other, you think?" But then he saw it. Them.

Two MPs passed, in the far distance. Lett turned his back to them, breathing deep. Kanani waited it out.

"The Preserve has a bar," she said.

"I saw it."

"They're giving me work there when I'm not, uh, training."

Lett wanted to ask her what she was training for, but of course she couldn't say anything about that. She certainly wouldn't ask him. As a local on the inside, she was probably on thinner ice than he was. "I'm guessing I won't see you there much," he said. "You'll be busy. And too many mucky-mucks, I suppose."

She gave a little shrug. "It's something, Wendell."

Lett nodded. "The clerk says I'll be getting work in the kitchen. Kitchen Patrol," he added with a chuckle.

"KP?" Kanani snorted. "You don't deserve that."

"It's just to fill the hours, in between."

Kanani sat up a little taller. Half of one eye appeared out the side of her yellow sunglass frames.

"It's Selfer," she whispered.

Lett didn't turn around. "Oh. Well, it's okay. We're just chatting. Right?"

"Right, yes." She rushed to say, "I'm glad you're doing all right."

"Me too. And you too—"

"Kids? Hope I'm not interrupting . . ."

Lett whipped around. Selfer was tiptoeing up to them like the manager of a dime-a-dance hall forced to check on a patron. He wore the same tame aloha shirt, linen trousers, and sandals as the other day, and Lett wondered if it was the only such outfit he had.

Lett stood.

"Hello again," Kanani said, already standing.

"Hello there," Selfer said around Lett's shoulder.

"Well, I must be going," Kanani said, "you two always have so much to talk about," and added a wink at Lett. "Aloha." She turned on her heel, and Lett and Selfer watched her go.

Selfer patted Lett on the shoulder, and Lett turned to look at him. The man had a grin on, Lett saw, and it was real.

"What is it?" he said.

"You did it."

"I did?"

"Uh-huh. You passed the test! That's what Lansdale said on the horn."

"He's not here, not back? Wait, what test?"

"Not yet he's not, no. So. When I tried explaining to him why I took the liberty of releasing you, I have to confess that I was a little worried. But he wasn't disturbed a bit. He was delighted! The thing is, you took the initiative. That was the test! That was why he made sure you knew about the Main House. You weren't going to just stew down there. You needed to act."

"I guess I did, in my own way."

Selfer's grin had faded. It was still a smile, though he seemed to be holding it there so it wouldn't drop. He said, "Do you know what this means? Lansdale told me, Lett. You've made it to stage three. Congrats and bravo, you did it! You're ready for your first assignment."

10.

A few days later, Lett still hadn't had any episodes. When the duty clerk finally told him to report for transport in the morning for his first assignment, he had expected to find a GI troop truck. But a civilian Chevy was waiting at the front gate on the south end of camp. The one-and-a-half-ton job had rounded fenders and matte blue paint that didn't flash in the sun, and a logo of the Krieger Coffee Plantation on the side. The five men assigned to it gathered around but not too close, and Lett wondered if there had been some kind of snafu.

Then a man in new fatigues bounded up to join the group, his shoulders swinging around.

Lett got that feeling, his warning lever clicking in. The man had his back to Lett, but the Joe's way was familiar. Lett stepped close to the opposite side of the truck bed, keeping an eye.

The man's balding head had a sturdy shape to it, the sun glistening on its hard angles. Lett saw the longish curls around the sides. The man turned Lett's way, and Lett saw a gauze bandage between his eyebrows and plenty of black and blue and cuts for decoration. The others were eyeing Lett and the man, stepping back too now, and Lett had to nip this thing in the bud and fast before they all had to climb up and cram in.

"It's you?" he said.

The man held up his big mitts for hands. "Do I know you, bub?"

"We got off on the right foot," Lett said, smiling, but the man didn't get the joke. "I apologize," Lett added. "I owe you a drink, owe you an explanation, one dogface to another."

"I ain't no Army doggie." The man patted at his chest. "I'm all gyrene."

Some Marines in the Pacific called themselves that, Lett had heard. He said, "Sure you are, Marine. Sorry."

"These here Army fatigues are just what they gave me. This Army crap." The Marine tugged at his khaki shirt and spat. "But what am I gonna do?"

The other four had left Lett and the Marine all alone near the back of the truck, where there was lots of open ground just in case. Lett couldn't remember the Marine's full name. Jock something. He said, "You don't remember? You came out of the bushes . . . Your face—I did that to you."

The Marine only stared. He raised a mitt to scratch at his head.

"I wasn't in my right mind," Lett said, smiling again, "me and you both, I hear."

The Marine glared. "You!"

Lett told himself not to resist. He stepped backward, out into the open ground, and kept his arms fixed to his sides. Let the Marine have his do.

The Marine lunged. Lett flinched, closed his eyes.

The Marine hugged him, patted him on the shoulders, and took a step back to have a good look at him. "I should thank you. You saved me from my own self. Who knows what I woulda done?"

"Really?"

"Why, sure." The Marine grinned. "Hey, come off it, why the sour puss? We're all right."

"We are?"

"We're just gung-ho, me and you. My name's Jock, Jock Quinn. Sure we are. Tell you what—after this duty, you buy me a drink, looks like you're the one could need one or four. You like rum? They got the good stuff here from the Philippines."

The pickup bed was staked like a fence but had a canvas pulled over it, which, Lett had to concede, did not seem to serve any purpose on a clear and fair island day other than to conceal them. The six of them climbed up and in, ready to ride on plank benches. Jock Quinn planted himself next to Lett and kept grinning and shaking his head at Lett as if he'd just discovered they were from the same hometown. The truck pulled out, the canvas top flapping in their ears, their shoulders banging into each other's, the foul blue exhaust peppering their nostrils as they stared into battered floorboards stained through with dried mud. Lett could have been riding into any meat grinder from Normandy to the Ardennes, one of those rare short hops to the next red-hot situation. It could have been the very morning that Captain Selfer of Military Intelligence had sent them over the enemy lines with no hope in hell let alone a whisper of a prayer. When they first rolled away, the gears grinding and the springs clanging along the jagged roadway, Lett had squeezed his eyes shut, ready to lower his head between his knees. But, then, miles passed and nothing happened. He could breathe. He could perceive his actual surroundings. He could gauge how much time had elapsed exactly, having counted off the seconds and then minutes in his head, and then confirming it by checking his watch.

The current circumstances could've triggered one of his episodes, plainly. This disguised truck, having to face Jock, the jostling ride—something should've gotten his leg twitching at the very least. But Selfer had also gotten the okay from Lansdale to put him back on his regular shots. Selfer had even given him a handy little travel pouch with vials of the stuff that he could inject himself, so Lett had poked himself in the latrine before reporting to the truck.

It turned out to be a lovely morning, all blue sky, just enough breeze. The other four included a boy-faced former paratrooper, two local Hawaiian vets from the looks of them, and one grizzled gooney bird dogface—most of them likely a year or two younger than he and Jock, though only the younger local looked it. They talked among themselves.

Jock talked to Lett. Jock was from a coastal town in Oregon: Coos Bay. He thought volunteering to fight would beat working in the mill. Jock said he knew a Marine from Ohio like Lett who bought it on Okinawa, mortar hit his hole, they never found one shred of him. Lett knew a guy from Oregon who took a direct tree burst in the Hürtgen Forest, and Jock joked that the man was probably a logger, the way this world worked, and indeed he was. They didn't laugh, though.

"How did you get the special invite?" Lett asked Jock. "It's not like they looked you up at the Royal Hawaiian."

"Oh, no. My trouble first started finding me in Manila. Leave wasn't helping me, see. I'd roam the countryside on benders. Then we got transferred. It was here in Hawaii Territory where they found me. Honolulu. I was hunkered down in Schofield Barracks stockade, starting to worry they were going to throw me in the sort of hospital you don't get out of. The VA. You hear stories."

"I heard them," Lett said. "But now look at us, me and you. We're doing well enough." He added a slap on Jock's shoulder.

"We sure are."

They were doing so well that they compared their memories of the different ways the putrefying enemy dead reeked, the German as opposed to the Japanese because of their different gear, and then it was how dogfaces in the ETO smelled versus gyrenes in the Pacific, wool versus twill. It was quite the icebreaker.

"We on da Belt Road," the soldier at the tailgate said, the local Hawaiian kid. Lett could tell they had headed south. The old highway ran along the coast, and long stretches of black lava rock fields replaced the barren, wind-swept rises of shrubs and boulders and scrubby grass. The black rock spread down to the water, jagged and punctuated with holes and crevices. "Heading for da big volcano," the kid added, though no one was asking. "Mauna Loa."

Seeing all the rock didn't seem to help Jock's mood. His right foot started tapping.

"We're going around the other side," said the other Hawaiian. He had a Japanese face but sounded as American as Gary Cooper. Lett wondered if he was *kotonk* instead of *bulahead* but wasn't about to ask.

A couple hours later, lush greenery gave way to open expanses and the wide ocean to their right. A few cars and pickups passed them. Shacks and bungalows appeared here and there. They were entering a community. "Next stop: Hilo Side," said the local kid.

They shifted in their seats. All had surely entered the edges of a town before a battle, and all knew what it meant. It could change a life forever, not to mention who a person was.

"What I don't get," grunted the ex-paratrooper. "Why didn't they issue us weapons?"

Lett had been wondering the same, since they were riding like a patrol after all. He could figure why. They didn't want anyone jumping ship on this, their first outing—it might be an assignment, but it was still a test. Lett was relieved not to be carrying.

Soon his lungs started constricting, which let him know they were close. And the more they constricted, the more he wanted a weapon. He recalled what he'd told Kanani about his wartime nightmares. He had kept killing just to make it all stop. Then he didn't want it to stop. And sometimes he thought about doing those things again, and about what it would be like. What weapons he would use. He almost looked forward to it. *I'm not broke—I'm retooled*, he'd confessed to her. *They put a lever inside me. A gear. It can be turned on, activated.*

He thought about his various weapons. It had been so long since he'd wanted to. He told himself it was okay, healthy, part of the process. He liked his M1 carbine the best because it was so light strapped on his shoulder, so forgiving yet compliant in his grasp. His fingertips still knew that wood grip and now they tingled with that feeling. He broke the rifle down in his mind. He sighted it. Then he made himself stop. In his head he put the rifle down. And suddenly his head ached a little and he had to stand for a moment in the truck, his hands hanging off the canvas roof supports above like a prisoner in some medieval torture restraint, hovering over the guys. They told him to quit staring and they jabbed him and joked, "If you got to take a shit, bub, why not just hang it off the back?"

***

Hilo Town had been softened up and good. Their eyes widened at all the devastation. One bridge was out and debris had been piled up. Yet other objects had been swept around as if shoved there by giant hands. Whole bungalows and shacks pressed into one another, some slanting, none with any foundation. A train caboose lay stuffed under the sharply leaning second story of a clapboard building bearing the remnant of a sign that read CHOP SUEY. Cars, trucks, and even boats lay in heaps like toys, some upside down. The buttressed span of a railroad bridge stood forlorn on flat, dry lowland, looking like a skeleton of a hill.

Lett whistled under his breath, but only to disguise the briny taste in his mouth and the stomach reverberations like writhing worms from the old dogface dread that always returned at sights like this. He thought about taking another dose, even though he'd already taken one today. He wondered how he would explain his taking his shot to the rest of them. Call it insulin maybe. Penicillin would do, but he'd have to come up with a story there, too. Mostly, he didn't want the team to think him a weak number—it would only make them worry. So, he didn't take the second dose. And yet, no episode followed his briny taste and wormy stomach.

Then they saw that the devastation wasn't from a bombardment of any kind. Nothing looked scorched or shredded with shrapnel. Low areas closer to the water's edge looked to have been streets before they became swamps, the rocks and debris and trees in piles there, too. This destruction had hit a while ago, and their trained eyes picked out details that proved it. The rebuilding far outnumbered the debris, for example. Cranes rose closer to a modest main street where the downtown met the beach. Fresh plywood waited on flatbeds, paving crews were patching cracked roads, and the tang of tar filled their noses.

"You guys really don't know?" said the local kid in the know. "Tsunami."

"Why should they know?" said the Japanese-looking one.

"I'm not following," Lett said.

"Tsunami means a tidal wave, see? Hit Hilo a year or so ago. Still mopping up."

Before the center of town, they took a bumping cracked side road heading straight for the water, for the wharf area. A water tower loomed, and Lett couldn't help but scan it for snipers or forward observers, and he wasn't the only vet doing so. They could hear the ocean crashing against rocks. The driver was barking into a portable radio. At the south end of the wharf they passed between tall storage tanks, which the local kid said were full of molasses. "Well, I'll be," ex-paratrooper blurted.

"Reckon they're fixing to put us on a boat," gooney bird dogface said. He had faint burn scars down one side of his face and neck. "Don't like the looks of this, not one bit."

"Pipe down," Jock said. "They see you spooked, it makes us all look the worse for wear."

"I'm all right," the man muttered.

"Of course you are. We all are. Ain't we?" Jock was glaring at all their faces now, for sure confirmation, making each man look him in the eye. He suddenly became the exemplary Marine squad leader from the pictures, a little too much *Guadalcanal Diary* for Lett. But it was working. The men sat up straight. Lett could see himself going on patrol with him, he had to admit, and he didn't imagine such a thing lightly.

"You bet we are," someone said. Heads nodded and at one another. "Gung-ho."

"Now remember," Lett heard himself declare, "they send us out as a team, don't bunch up, but stay in sight of the pack just the same, and keep it moving. Got it?"

They all nodded at Lett. Jock added a proud lift of the chin.

Next thing they knew they were jumping out the back, squinting at the bright sky. Those tall molasses tanks kept their area secluded, cutting them off from the rest of the wharf. A modest wooden dock held what looked like a large fishing boat, a trawler, towering over its mooring, even though it sat low in the water. Lett imagined the vessel smashing its berth with the slightest big wave.

The rest happened fast. Men disguised as stevedores appeared from between two of those huge tanks and ordered them around. They issued them submachine guns—newer, smaller M3s, called "grease guns" in the ETO. This made Lett wince. He expected worse feelings to hit him. But none did. His head didn't even ache. And, he had no choice. On top of that he'd never used an M3, had never been trained on one. He didn't need to be, as it turned out, for the weapon wasn't loaded. Though that didn't stop a couple of the guys from clicking out the magazine and pushing it in again, again and again, and Lett recalled that the first M3s had given dogfaces troubles up on the line. The gun was light in his hands, which he had to admit he liked. Then he and Jock were handed black MP armbands and those white helmets that MPs wore. The others weren't given any. Lett wondered if he and Jock had been selected for some reason or if they simply didn't have enough to go around. Either way, Lett didn't contradict orders, even though he wanted to toss the MP gear back in their faces. It had been an MP who shot him in the back in Belgium, after all.

The men dressed as stevedores ordered them to guard the road in and the perimeter, which was only a half circle about the area of a baseball field, all hemmed in by those molasses tanks. Their MP role was just for show, Lett told himself, in case anyone got near.

From the boat came wooden crates the size of larger foot lockers, maybe four feet long, each marked RHUM and THE PHILIPPINES and FRAGILE. Two unmarked deuce-and-a-half trucks were waiting ready, two-and-a-half tons and six wheels each. The stevedores used a winch and a standard flat cart with four wheels to unload the cargo, but at one point the winch jammed. Then the cart broke under the weight of only a couple crates, busting the axle. They had to wait around for the fix.

A tractor arrived with a bigger flatbed cart that could hold a tank. Snafu solved.

Once the cargo was offloaded, about five men strode off the boat and down the gangway. Some might have been important figures. A couple were Asian, one likely Japanese, the other a Filipino, possibly. All wore civvies, but Lett could picture any of them in officer's uniforms from the swagger they had. They swaggered into four waiting sedans. But the sedans didn't leave. Lett and Jock shrugged at each other.

Edward Lansdale strode off the boat, down the gangway. Then another sedan pulled up: four doors, sloped rear end, whitewalls, and plenty of chrome. Lett stiffened. It was a 1941 Packard Clipper.

Lansdale met the car, opened the back door. And out stepped a large, darker man. The man had taken off the jacket of his oversize suit, which revealed a holster. His sleeves were rolled up, too, which revealed ornate island warrior tattoos spreading from his hands up his arms.

Frankie.

11.

Lett and his team got Spam and rice, water, and coffee. Afterward, Lett ducked into a wharf outhouse that smelled like the inside of a dead man. He produced his syringe and shot up in there. Just in case. He didn't want what he'd seen to haunt him on the way back and get up on top of him when he needed it least. Any weakness was a blind spot.

What was Frankie doing there? Lett wondered what to tell Kanani. His mission was hush-hush of course. He'd seen her around camp a couple times since reuniting with her on that park bench, but they were kept so busy and were among so many others that he barely had time for small talk let alone for sharing telltale details. Apart from that, he'd mostly kept to himself at his bungalow, not wanting to make any false moves before his first assignment of the third stage.

Another thing rattled him. Lansdale had simply ignored him, all of them. He hadn't shown the team the slightest nod. It was as if he'd never spent time underground with Lett, talking things out like they did. Lansdale had just shaken Frankie's big tattooed hand and ducked into the Packard.

And then, the question lingered: what was in those trucks?

The entire operation had lasted a couple hours. Lett and the other four climbed back into their truck. They followed the two loaded and unmarked deuce-and-a-half trucks, but at a distance. The sedans traveled up front, led by the Packard with Lansdale and Frankie inside. They, too, traveled at a distance ahead. This was clearly intentional, so as not to resemble a column. The team had to keep their M3 guns, and Lett and Jock Quinn the MP garb.

On the way back, the few clouds had cleared out and the sun was high and hot. A couple of the team complained about the heat under the canopy. This led to Jock the Marine complaining, again, about having to wear what were clearly inferior Army fatigues and gear.

"Just what you'd expect from Dugout Doug," Jock muttered.

He told Lett about the Pacific grunts' derisive nickname for their wartime Supreme Commander, Douglas MacArthur. The name came from Dugout Doug's so-called prowess at retreating but also from reports that he hid out in tunnels when the Japanese overran Corregidor in the Philippines in '42. An Army man, the great general didn't want to help the Marines stranded above when it came down to it. A couple of the others overheard and nodded solemnly.

Then they sang songs, Jock leading the Pacific Theater guys in a ballad that had many names, from "Bless 'em All" to "The Long and the Short and the Tall" to their own version: "Fuck 'em All." Their suitably crude and defiant lines called out MacArthur for abandoning them wholesale. But it really told most all generals and lords and masters just where to stuff their brass and gold and shiny medals— if they and their fellow Marines were doomed to bite the dust, then they'd do so in any damned way they pleased.

Lett offered up the version he knew from the ETO, which had plenty more to do with women than bossmen, and they sang that one, too. They laughed and slapped shoulders and someone should've had a bottle. After that, they quieted down as if drunk from that make-believe bottle, deep in the memories and nightmares such a song brought.

Lett found himself talking with Jock as if he were Lansdale himself right here next to him. He free-associated about everything from the slaughter in the Normandy hedgerows to the tree bursts in the Ardennes. Jock launched into a story of his own about fighting the Japanese in caves. They smoked them out with whatever they had, grenades, flame throwers, phosphorous.

"Half the time they came running out melting. We'd just stand back, let 'em pass till they dropped. What are we supposed to do, huh? What? They don't want to give up."

"Nothing you can do," Lett said.

A silence crept in, their knees bumping as they rode along.

Eventually, Jock told Lett that some of the more certifiable grunts had stripped the dead of medals and guns and gold teeth while they were still smoking, still bleeding out. Jock was shaking his head.

"Only tell me if you want to," Lett said.

Jock's eyes screwed up. After another half mile or so he said, his voice clogging in his throat, "Babies. Babies . . . On one island, Saipan, it was all just caves and tunnels. Some of them opened onto high cliffs. Well, then the civilians come out. Apparently the Emperor told them we Yankees were coming to kill them all, better off going to their kind of heaven after going out with a big bang . . ." He was glaring at his knuckles as if checking for shaking. "So you had civilians running out, Japanese, women, elderly. Some of the younger women clutching babies. Screaming at us. Some had explosives rigged on 'em, see. Some didn't go off. Others only partly. Bad powder, my guess? I don't know. Ah, fuck, Lett, I don't know. Some of us started picking them off, but most of us just took cover till they passed by and on they went, here they come, no one wanting to touch them. Or their babies. I tried. I tried, Lett. Goddamn it, I done tried. She . . . She . . ."

"It's okay. You're all right."

"I thought I had her. She slipped by me anyways. What was she supposed to do, huh? Here I was this Yankee killer carrying a big ole fugging Thompson gun, probably had blood on my face or teeth for all I know. I thought maybe I'd grab the baby from her, little thing, little white face, big eyes. She . . . She was just saving her little girl, you know? So, on she went. Well, right at the edge of the cliff, one of her shoes came off. Looked like a slipper. I kept that little slipper for a good long while. It was all chewed up from all the lava rock on that goddamn fugging rock of an island." Jock shook his head again. After another half mile he said, "It was only the staff at camp who convinced me to get rid of it finally."

"Lansdale?" Lett said.

"Very same." Jock kept shaking his head. His hands had retreated to under his thighs.

Lett glanced around. The ex-paratrooper had wet eyes and the gooney bird dogface was burying his hands the same as Jock. They rode a while in silence.

"That's what their leaders done to those people," he said. "What they put in their heads."

"What they do to all of us," Lett said.

"What? No, siree. Our leaders never do that. We're different."

"Sure, we are. Sure." *We just do it in different ways*, Lett couldn't help thinking, and suddenly his leg wanted to start hammering too, and he wanted to jab himself with one of those shots of his again. He felt at the pouch in his daypack.

After a few miles, Jock apologized for ambushing Lett when he first arrived at The Preserve. "It was bad timing. I was coming from a test and not in such a good way, neither."

"A test?"

"Sure. Part of my cure."

They weren't supposed to discuss their individual cures much, but Lett wasn't going to argue. Because talking like this seemed to be helping Jock, too. The road had swung low through the south coast, and they were riding along another unending expanse of that black lava flow, the road running right over it. Jock stared at the rock, all thousand yards of it. Lett eyed him in case he got spooked again. Jock wiped at his eyes, but it was only perspiration. Then a grin stretched across his face, and the gaps between his teeth seemed to widen. "Know how they tested me? They left me out on that vast lava slope at the base of the volcano, just left me there."

"That's rough."

"Sure. Sure was. They left me in a cave to start. Now, I start hearing and smelling things, the likes of which you can't even imagine—or maybe you can on account of what I told you where I served. Then I see things too, but I wasn't sure if they were real. Nip infantry. Women. Bayonets. Fire. Babies. Cliffs that weren't there, even. Hot blood on my face that I had to wipe out of my eyes but it's just the sweat. But, you know what, Lett?" Jock's teeth seemed to widen out even more.

"What?"

"I think it worked. After I came at you, I mean. It finally made me confront what ails me. They said that really cures you up. And I do think it did."

"Did Lansdale say so?"

"The very same. Now look at us. Now it's on to the next stage."

"You are doing better," Lett said. "I can see it. I didn't know you before, but . . ."

"You wouldn't have recognized me."

"Same goes for me."

They traded a grunt and a chuckle.

"I'm getting by, Lett. Getting by best I can. You?"

"I have to say that I am," Lett said. "Say, just wondering, they give you a dose when they treat you?"

"What? Nah, I ain't had no VD since '45 . . ."

"No, not that kind of shot." Lett recalled what Lansdale had said about confidential information. What if this was another test? He lowered his voice even more. "I just heard that some guys were getting shots, is all."

"Nope, no sir," Jock said. "Besides, I don't take to needles well . . . Weird word, 'dose.' It can mean the cure and the disease."

"I suppose so," Lett said.

He leaned close to Jock, their ears brushing. "Listen: what do you make of what happened today?"

"Why they used us, you mean? They coulda used anyone. Nah, that was another test. Lansdale wanted to see if we could protect him. And we passed it flying."

"But we were there for show, too. But for who? The town people?"

"Town people know better to stay clear," Jock said.

"Supposing it was to show those types coming off the boat."

"The Oriental-looking ones maybe. They did have at least one Nip. Jap, I mean. Sorry, not supposed to call 'em that anymore. At least one Japanese."

"Yeah, that's what I thought, too."

Jock stared ahead. They had cleared the black rock again,

heading inland and uphill, the brown scrub along the road giving way to green foliage.

"What do you want?" Lett said. "From The Preserve, I mean."

"Ain't it clear, doggie? I want back in."

"Reenlistment?"

Jock nodded. "I'm a career Marine, way I see it. My family, we've been in the military in one form or another going back to the War of 1812. Not even coming out West could stop us."

That's no reason, Lett thought. *That's just a treadmill.*

Jock patted at his chest. "There'll be another war someday, and they will need me."

"Oh, you bet they will."

Jock's grin vanished. "I'm not just fodder, Lett. Not me. I survived the Big One. And you did, too."

"Tell it to the officers in that song you were just singing."

"Yeah, yeah. I get you. But I figure I got clout now."

Sometime later the truck started rolling ever slower, and it jostled them, and gears moaned. They were heading higher uphill. They were nearing The Preserve, finally.

The local kid at the tailgate kept peeking out the canopy. "Hey, they all gone," he said finally and looked forward out the other side to confirm it.

"How so?" Lett said.

"Those two trucks, the sedans, they all went take one side road somewhere. Just us now."

Lett looked around. The others were sleeping, heads bobbing, the ex-paratrooper slumbering down the middle of the truck bed at their toes.

Lett leaned close to Jock again. "What do you think is in those crates?"

Jock shrugged. "Who knows. Most fellas didn't notice."

"Well, I noticed."

Jock started. He grabbed Lett by the forearm. "Now hold up. What do you think'll happen if you keep asking that question?"

"So you didn't think it?"

"Nope. No."

"You didn't notice that a sturdy cart like the one they had buckled under and right away? And how low that boat was sitting in the water? How those two deuce-and-a-halfs kept straining at every hill, making us have to drop back to a crawl so it don't look like we're with them in our disguise truck?"

Gold, Lett thought, but he didn't say it. He finally let himself form the dirty word in his mind. *And Frankie, and . . . Kanani.* And what about her friend, Miss Mae?

"Sure I did, but I ain't making no conclusions," Jock said. "Look. The war is won and we're the ones what won it. This is a whole new world we're living in. Now, if a man has his head on straight, why, sky's the limit."

Lett sure hoped that was true. Because the opposite was a dark cave, deeper into the center of the earth. "You know something? You're right. Thanks for straightening me out."

"The pleasure is all mine," Jock replied, letting it go, and the grin was back for good. "You'll be all right. I saw you back there. You were liking it, and well and good, too. Cradling that eensy grease gun like a newborn lamb, you were."

12.

Jock had a point, Lett had to admit. He truly had been cradling that M3 gun like it was a newborn lamb. He had indeed liked performing the first assignment they had given him. He could've stood there all day guarding that perimeter.

He thought this as he sat on the tiny lanai of his tiny bungalow in The Preserve, another just-built square of plywood and corrugated metal that still smelled of both. But this one wasn't too sparse. It had just enough room for two Adirondack chairs on either side of the front door. Inside, it had rattan chairs with cushions, a kitchenette, and a two-chair chromium dining set. The walls were painted a cool green, and there was a jute rug to boot. It had a separate bathroom with tub. All that was missing were the pipe and slippers.

He unbuttoned his shirt a couple more buttons and stretched out his legs until the heels of his bare feet rested on the edge of the lanai, letting the plank dig into his skin a little. This was the first period of serenity he could remember. The damaged man that he'd become could still appreciate the simple clarity of a clear duty, especially one that wasn't about to get a man killed, or anything like that. A duty like that took all the stress of deciding away. Let someone else choose what he was to do, where to stand, how long. Who to be. Sometimes he could understand the career military mindset, how a guy like Jock could want that.

All was so orderly here, so secure. His bungalow stood along a line of six others, a miniature suburban street inserted smack dab in the middle of high Kona forest. The Preserve had so much land to spare up here, they might as well be in Timbuktu. No one could see them except from a low-flying plane—of which Lett had seen not one—and he wondered if even their air space was off-limits.

He smelled more pork roasting from the next clearing over where they did a lot of the cooking for mess hall. He heard the breeze rustle through the foliage, finding its way to him where it tickled his forehead and toes.

Then a shiver ran up his legs, torso, neck.

He thought about the two shots he'd taken while on assignment, and how Selfer had supplied him with it only after he'd begged Selfer to bother Lansdale for it, and this made him shrink inside a little. He was starting to depend on the dose, to look forward to it, even to that little prick on his skin and the sting along his vein. How long would that last? Was that the only reason why he felt so serene here on his porch? The treatment had to work in the long run. They didn't call it a cure for nothing.

Still, he wondered if he shouldn't be feeling more uneasy. Jock had a point, sure. He could've stood guard there all day—if not for some of the things he'd seen at that Hilo dock surrounded by molasses tanks. He still didn't know how he was going to tell Kanani about Frankie. Or should he? But they owed each other. He couldn't deny that she'd probably saved his ass back in that Kona billet bar. And he'd been the one who convinced her to dodge Frankie, after all.

And then there was Lansdale. Ignoring him like he had? What kind of treatment was that? Lett told himself it was only the man's professional demeanor and reminded himself not to take it personally. He was far from the only person Lansdale was responsible for here.

A woman was walking up his lane of bungalows, darker skin, her black hair pulled back under a khaki Army bucket hat with the brim flipped up in front, what they called a Daisy Mae. She wore an aloha shirt with rolled-up sleeves and cuffed dungarees and her rubber slippahs.

Kanani.

Lett sat up and fought the urge to run to her. Again he thought of that load they'd guarded, and how it had to be gold. He'd somehow been able to avoid her for the couple days since he'd been back—that way he wouldn't have to tell her about what he'd seen. He also knew that it was only a matter of time before she'd simply come find him at his bungalow. Meanwhile, he kept expecting, worrying even, that he would see Frankie in all his dark tattooed glory striding around the camp. Yet the man had not showed here. His assignment had been in Hilo, all the way over on the other side of the island—Hawaii's biggest island by far. It was nowhere near The Preserve. Maybe that was the last time he'd ever see Frankie.

Now he couldn't help it: he walked down the two steps to Kanani. She grinned and pushed back the brim farther and showed him all of her face. Something still made him hold back. He kissed her on the cheek, just a brush. She looked to her feet as if embarrassed, and sure enough when she looked up again, she was blushing.

She would want him to tell her. So he just had to.

She laughed and pushed at his chest and prodded him back up the stairs. "Like one plantation around here," she joked, looking back down the lane of bungalows.

They sat in the chairs and caught up. Lett now had regular KP duty to fill time until the next assignment, but at least he was serving food in the mess instead of doing the dirty prep and cleanup. Kanani had her work in the bar as a hostess and bartender and waitress when need be, always with a flower behind her ear. She sold cigarettes on the side and no one blinked an eye.

"I haven't seen you," she said.

"We have such different schedules," he said.

"They put me in a bungalow too, you know. Over by the Main House."

She'd mentioned it when they were first reunited. She hadn't told him it was by the Main House, but then again, he hadn't asked. "Sounds nice," he said.

She peered out. "Your lane, it's mostly deserted. So many empty bungalows."

"Others must be out on assignment, that or they're still being tested. I haven't met many. Most have kept to themselves, and I can't say I blame them."

Kanani didn't respond. She smoked one of those Filipino cigars. She didn't use the gold lighter this time, but a GI-issue Zippo. Then the rum came out—that same Filipino trademark.

And Kanani kept giving him that sidelong glance of hers.

Lett was getting that old bad feeling, just a whiff of it, like a light sunburn heating his skin even here in the shade.

She pushed back her khaki bucket hat. "Okay den," she said.

"Okay what?"

"We're gonna talk things over before dat rum goes for broke on you."

Lett sat up. He had sunglasses on. He pulled them off.

"No. Keep them on. And keep the drink. Looks natural."

"Okay. Wait, why? You think someone's watching maybe?"

She shrugged. "I just like to be sure." They were drinking from metal cups. She took a long sip of her drink. "I can tell something's on your mind."

"You can?"

"Hilo Side," she said. "You were there. I heard you and a crew were there."

"I was, yes." Lett tightened up inside. Of course she could tell.

"So, is this why you're avoiding me? You're in on it?"

"Avoiding you? Hold on. In on what?" Lett set down his drink. He shifted in his seat, but an Adirondack chair only had one position—sunk down.

He sighed. He started to tell her. They were there to guard a shipment, from a boat—an unmarked trawler, with men disguised as stevedores. The heavy load busted a cart's axle, so it took longer. A group got off the boat and were the kind that didn't bother with stevedore denim.

She leaned forward, held up a hand. "Was Miss Mae there?"

"No. I'm sorry. I saw no women getting off."

Kanani sighed. "Who was it?"

"Some men. Looked like important persons. Not all American though. Some Asian looking. Japanese, Filipino, maybe Chinese, not sure. They got in sedans. They drove with us, along with those other trucks carrying the load."

Kanani's chair jumped closer with a thump. "Who else was there? Tell me. I can see it on your face."

Lett paused to look around. He didn't know why he needed to, but his leg told him to. "Lansdale," he said.

She stared, blank-faced.

"You don't know him?"

She shook her head, her eyes darting.

That surprised Lett enough to make him take another drink. He told her about Lansdale, what he looked like. He didn't have to tell her that she probably would know him in due time. He had been getting the feeling that Lansdale touched everything here eventually. "Well, he was on the boat, but I don't know if it was just for a meeting or what. He might've been on board longer. He'd been gone at least a week."

"Okay, okay," Kanani said. She sipped the rum.

"I'm not in on anything," Lett said. "Except getting cured."

"I know. I just wanted to feel things out, keep you on your toes."

He thought of Frankie now and what a thug like that could be doing here even if it was on the other side of the island, and the whiff of heat on his skin filled his head, rushing his brain. He sucked down his drink and wanted to kick it out into the trees. Darker thoughts found him and clawed him, and he didn't know what hole they had crawled up from.

"My shot," he barked at her.

"Your what?"

"I need my shot. There's a syringe."

"Oh. You need it? Where?"

"Inside. Little pouch."

She rushed inside to get it for him, and he pressed his back to the chair until she fetched his pouch and returned and opened it and—

"I do it myself," he barked again. "It's mine."

She backed away, holding up a hand.

He inserted the needle, letting it sting a little, taking a deep breath.

He had his strength back instantly. Clarity. Serenity. He pushed himself out of the chair, drew in a deep fresh breath, and sat down on the steps, letting his hands hang off his knees.

Kanani joined him there.

"I guess I'm not supposed to tell you about this medication they're giving me, but we go back." He now realized telling her was a good way to stall, to avoid the subject of gold, of Frankie even, and added a smile that he wanted to wipe off his face immediately. He told her the dose was helping him. She wanted to know what it was, but he couldn't tell her—they wouldn't tell him.

"I see," she said.

"Thanks," he said.

"Doing better?"

"Yes. I'm okay now. You just got me thinking, is all."

"You can say that again."

"Sorry I barked at you."

"Forget it."

They sat there a minute. He could feel her eyeing him. She'd gone quiet. Her face had lost some color. She grabbed his wrist.

"Now, that's quite enough stalling," she said.

Lett looked her in the eyes. He sighed again. "There was another sedan, Kanani. A '41 Packard."

She closed her eyes. Her head dropped between her legs. She moaned. Her head might've been spinning. Lett held a hand ready above her in case he had to hold her head up while she vomited. But she only muttered something in Pidgin and glared at the lava earth.

Kanani stayed on Lett's porch. She didn't say much. Lett brought her water, refilled her rum, lit her a cigar from her GI Zippo.

"But you haven't seen him around here?" she said after a while. "Right? Only on Hilo Side. Not in The Preserve itself?"

"Frankie? No. I've been keeping my eye out."

"Why didn't you tell me?"

"I haven't seen you."

"You've been avoiding me," she said.

"*You've* been avoiding *me*," he said.

She ignored him.

"Have you seen your friend Miss Mae here?" he said.

Kanani only shook her head. Lett gave her time. He refilled his rum. Eventually, she sighed. "They have a brothel here," she said. "Well, okay, not so much a brothel but a bungalow they have set aside. Near the Main House."

"The same place you live."

She nodded.

"Is it for anyone?"

"No. I think just for important visitors."

Lett thought of those men coming off the boat in Hilo and swaggering into fancy sedans. "You work there."

"Uh-huh. Your friend Selfer gave me the duty."

"Of course. I bet he really smoothed it over."

"Oh, he's one smoothie. One sharpie, too. He says I'll run the show. Won't have to do all the dirty work." Kanani added a bitter chuckle. "It's why I never invited you, I guess."

"Don't beat yourself up. I understand. They want to see what we can do, is all. Each of us in our own way."

Kanani looked away, toward the tops of the palms and crooked trees. "Where did it go?"

"What, the shipment? Here, basically," Lett said. He wasn't going to lie. She perked up, so he continued. "We followed the trucks back this way, but they turned off close to camp. I didn't see where. We were crammed in the back."

Kanani's mouth formed an O. She tapped at her chin. "They got some *kine* underground complex here. Right? Tunnels at the very least."

"Yes. I've been down there. It's where I started my treatment. They have rooms. I came out a stairway, just a hatch above ground like a pillbox."

"They must have several ways in. There must be other entrances, exits, depending on your clearance." Kanani nodded at that. "They could even stretch on into island, into caves."

Lett didn't like the thought of all those tunnels merging into earthen caverns, leading ever deeper inland, a maze without a map. He buried the sickening thought away like he'd done so many times before, but another one came rushing up at him from the deepest caverns of his memory: the sight of a dead boy near the front in France. A team of GIs was pulling his bloated little body from a well. Why the damn well? Was he trying to save himself? Use it for cover? Lett would never know. He shook off the memory, took a deep breath.

He searched his mind for something he could know. There was one thing, he now realized. He recalled his first, gut reaction in Hilo when he noticed how heavy that load was. *Gold*, he'd thought, a dirty word. And then *Frankie, and . . . Kanani.* They'd come to him like links in a chain, the chain now attached to an orb he was polishing in his mind. It was blurry at first, but he kept polishing, slowly, all without looking at it. Without looking at Kanani, either. Then he looked. It was crystal goddamn clear.

He was glaring at Kanani.

She jerked her head back. "What? You're scaring me."

"Aren't you forgetting something?"

"Eh? No, no, I'm not."

"You never asked me what the cargo is. The shipment to Hilo. Because you know. It's gold, isn't it? Gold that broke a sturdy loading cart. That's your angle. You get in here, nab some, get out again, you're gone. Your friend Miss Mae tipped you off to it."

She held up her hands. She made that sound she did with her lips, like a balloon sputtering air.

"But now Frankie is after it, too," Lett said.

She stared at the treetops a while. She pulled out her gold lighter finally and flipped it between fingers. "I'm afraid it's more than that, Wendell. There's always more to it with Frankie. He must be after everything, here to win the whole pot, or he wouldn't be here at all."

13.

Kanani had seen a man wearing a kimono before, but that outfit was the plain male version. This getup before her now was a shiny garment, pink and blue and floral all over. Kanani had also seen men in makeup. In a certain haunt of Honolulu, down a narrow alley lined with wooden fire escapes, one could find nice and fun fellows wearing a little rouge or lipstick or mascara even. But those guys were never this guy. This guy's face had a stark white base with red lipstick and red-and-black highlighting around the eyes. The red circles on his cheeks were supposed to be blush, she guessed. And the black geisha wig he'd slapped onto his head was such a cheapie.

She could stare at him like this because the man was out cold, his head turned her way. He lay on the chaise in the boogie house where Selfer had set her up. He was still breathing, luckily, hot air pulsing from his nostrils. It reeked like the whisky they were drinking.

He had showed up, alone, and his faint knock on the door proved to be the only formality he'd shown. He was smoking one of those Filipino cigars and was already drunk. She had widened her smile and bowed and ushered him in with a sweeping gesture. Once inside, he had kicked his thick sandals off and plopped into the chairs. He kept grunting at her. He was no *bulahead* and certainly no *kotonk*—the guy was straight Japanese, and straight off the boat or plane. But she was guessing it was the boat arriving Hilo Side that Wendell Lett told her about.

He was talking story in Japanese. She didn't know near enough Japanese words for that. Then he barked at her in Korean, and then it was broken Chinese. She only offered him coy giggles, all the while thinking of China and what the Japanese Army did to the poor people there, and it gave her shudders like ice sliding down her neck.

Miss Mae had told her about the Rape of Nanking, the mass raping, the mass murder. More "comfort women" forced into slavery.

All the more reason to make this goon tell her what he knew. But she had to be careful. It was that Edward Lansdale who sent this important person to her—the man Wendell had told her about, and the man who got into that shiny Packard with Frankie.

That morning, the man called Lansdale had cornered her in camp. He was wearing Army khaki without insignia and sunglasses the whole time. He didn't introduce himself, but she knew it was Edward Lansdale. He was all thin mustache and long face with a sneer trying hard to be a grin. Lansdale told her that they were having a going-away party this evening at the Main House.

"At some point, likely after, a certain guest of ours will be coming to see you. Aren't you delighted? He asks for 'comfort,' as he puts it. He likes to drink, and drink he does. Give him this serum." Lansdale held out a fist.

She opened her hand. He set a small vial of brown glass into her palm. No one had asked her to do anything like this. It was just chatting and sweet-talking before. Her pulse raced.

"Relax, honey," Lansdale said. "It's only a . . . let's call it a type of truth serum. It loosens him up. He won't remember."

"Oh." She closed her hand, turned it, slid the vial between two fingers.

"There you go. Beginner's magic trick. No one's the wiser. Then? Candy from a baby. He's our friend now, sure he is, but he's playing hard to get. Hoping to retain his value. So he just needs a little extra special coaxing."

Lansdale gave her vague instructions: She was to get him talking about what he called the "location." They needed the location. She thought of asking Lansdale about Frankie, but the act Lansdale was throwing hinted at some real dark mojo. This was the real reason her pulse was racing. She wondered if Wendell had noticed the depth of the darkness. She certainly wasn't going to ask this Lansdale about Miss Mae either, in case she showed up.

Never speak till you know the score.

"I'll do my best, sir," she had said.

Lansdale was still sneer-grinning, showing her all his teeth. "Simply believe that you can," he'd chirped, "and you're halfway there to be sure!"

When Selfer first set her up here, he had told her this or that important person might want her dressing up geisha, some of them being in Asia too long and going native. You never knew what they might want. So they had all the props here in a footlocker. They even had the opium, fancy pipe and all.

Who knew that this Japanese goon would have geisha as *his* angle? She had showed the getup to him, and he put it on with little help from her. He had her rub his feet before slipping his toes into his geisha zori, and his face started to scrunch up with an anticipation of desire, and she was starting to worry a little about what came next.

As it turned out, the man's needs were simple. She was to sit on the floor cross-legged and watch him please himself in his geisha getup. Which was a relief to her, plenty *lolo* though it was, he in his makeup while dipping his fingers into the folds of that kimono and pulling it out. She did her best not to laugh. The wig fell off as he bobbed up and down, and he let it fall and she saw his shaved head had a bump or two that weren't natural. That kept her from laughing for good. So too did his wide jaw, his scar tissue for cheeks, the fat lips, and those steel eyes. His grimace seemed to be daring her to laugh, at which point who knew what manner of blow or weapon would find her. So she kept her face a curiously sensual mask.

You like geisha, Tojo? I'll watch you be geisha. Then you give me the gold.

She had to get to the gold before Frankie. Who cared what he did after?

The Japanese goon uttered a soft honk, which sounded like a nēnē bird, and this almost sparked a laugh from her belly, but she choked it back down by clearing her throat. To keep any laughs away she thought of a dead nēnē she'd seen on one of the camp paths, just a baby male with little black head and bill and legs and feet. Poor thing. And so rare now, what with the haoles and Asians bringing so many predators to the islands for so long. Some unlucky nēnēs couldn't fly properly. It must have been lost up here in the forest. She then thought of its mother looking for it all day and night. So, she ended up setting it alongside the path in case her *makuahine* was still looking. The next day she returned and found it still there—but gone to heaven. She buried it just among the trees, wondering how many sentries or staffers or important visitors strolled on by it without even a care. They could all go to hell.

"Ohhhh," the geisha man grunted in conclusion.

She handed him another handkerchief. She didn't want to have to clean that kimono.

Then she served him another whisky, this one nice and special with ice, soda water, lime.

But extra special, too.

The prospect of serving up that extra-special whisky to her geisha goon had made her sweat between and under her breasts. But it had proved so easy. All she needed to do was turn her back to him while he wiped up and dump the serum right in, lots of soda and lime in a big glass. He had chugged it right down. Apparently, the Japanese man trusted his new masters. He certainly had no choice on account of recent history. The next thing she knew, the tough guy was smoking *pakalolo* in a skinny, neatly rolled reefer he brought with him. He had made her smoke some and she'd held it in her mouth, pretending to inhale it. And then, he was giggling.

And now here he was, just lying there passed out with his head turned her way, that hot whisky reek pumping out of him. He made that honking sound again, apparently dreaming of jacking off in a geisha getup while he was at it.

She rolled her eyes.

Then the Japanese goon's face went slack. Kanani sat up, took notice. What if she hadn't given him enough? Or too much? They needed this man for information, because he, by the looks of him, had surely extracted his share of information from others during the war. He was a thug, a gangster. *Yakuza* was a word she'd heard used for Japanese *mokes* like this.

Now he released a long hiss. His eyes popped open. They were glazed over, tilting around. They found the ceiling fan, and finally her. She let him stare. He kept staring, in wonder it seemed, his mouth curling up in a smile.

"How you feeling?" she said.

"Pretty . . . pretty lady."

"Mahalo."

They exchanged a few embarrassed smiles, his white face flushing a horrid salmon color.

"You like me?" she said.

"Ah. Oh, yes."

"That makes me happy."

"I happy," he said.

"Good . . ." She leaned forward, holding his hand, her other hand on his thigh. "So, you were saying? Something about a certain location."

He beamed. "Location!"

She nodded. "Yes, the same place your good friends here asked you about. You really, really like to tell me." She kept nodding. It couldn't hurt.

He nodded. His eyes turned hard, though, and it brought her sweat back. It was night outside by now. Where would she run if she had to? What would she shout? Why hadn't she asked that creepily cheerful Lansdale if they were going to post guards outside, just in case. She could slap herself now. She just had to assume, hope, stay wary.

"You should tell me," she added. "That makes me happy, too."

He released a happy groan and was grinning again. His English improved suddenly. He rambled on about glory, about his military days and many gangster triumphs, some of these two one in the same, it seemed. He boasted of running the show in China, which he called Manchukuo. "Special units," he said. "We eliminated so many, we showed them," he blathered on. Then he made sliced motions with an imaginary sword that was all too real. She was sure he had been in Nanking. It was just as she thought. But it was all hemming and hawing.

Then he said, "You are not my wife?"

"What? No, dear."

"Where is she, eh?"

"She's back home? That's my guess."

"Oh," he said.

She rubbed at his thigh and squeezed his hand, wide and full of knuckles, all rough skin. "Now, like you were saying—you like to give me that location."

He nodded. "San Mariel," he whispered.

"What's that?" She'd heard the name but had to be sure.

He opened his mouth to repeat it, but instead said, "Cagayan Valley."

"Cagayan Valley. I see. Where's that?"

"Cagayan Valley in the Philippines."

"Philippines?"

"Oo," he said, nodding, the two Os pronounced like *Oh-Oh*, then he clicked his mouth shut and wiped at his lips.

Oo meant yes in Filipino. She'd heard it on the plantation. She'd heard Frankie say it.

"*Mabuti*," he added, which meant good.

That was it. Her job was done. She was only supposed to extract the name of the location. She was supposed to stop there. But the stuff in his drink was still working away. He stared at the ceiling fan, losing himself in its turns. He started talking to it, in a mix of Japanese and English.

"That big old mango tree, at base of hill. It all covered . . ." His mouth hung open.

Covered up? She waited it out.

"Beware!" he snapped.

She started.

His eyes darted. "Many traps. Many! All deadly. All dead . . ."

What was she going to do, not listen?

"Find him," he muttered.

"Find who?" she whispered.

"De Garza. He the one."

"He's the one how?"

He shook his head. Sneered at the fan blades whirring. "Golden Lily," he muttered eventually.

What was that? Was that his name for her or something else? She stared, willing him to say more.

He patted at his chest and looked at it with a gentle expectation, as if a carnation should've been pinned there.

"Whose name is that?" she asked.

"No who—what. But . . . *Hindi na.*"

No. No longer. "What is covered up?"

He beamed up at her. His eyes elsewhere, beyond those fan blades.

"You thinking of your wife? Your children?"

"You my wife," he said. His eyes seemed to float in their sockets, and they were like glass balls on ocean. Empty. Going.

"Sure. That's right. Sure I am," she whispered.

His eyes found their way back to her. "You're my gold," he said.

"Yes. Go on."

He told her, in fragments, but just as she'd hoped, about the Japanese plundering golden treasures and fine objects in China. The scheme went back decades. He was like an art dealer on his death bed, recounting his greatest sales and acquisitions.

"Good contract," he sputtered, "so very good. General Yamashita."

Kanani could feel her blood racing through her body, in her wrists, up her neck. "Where?" she demanded. "Where exactly?"

He jolted. His head jerked her way.

"Is it here? Right here?" she growled. "No? You understand?" She tried in her clunky Japanese, "Where here on island? Where exactly? Tunnels, lava tubes, what?"

"You!" he shouted. "You not my wife. My wife dead. Bombings. My son."

"No. *Hindi.* No . . . *Ee-eh.*"

"Do you know how many wives I kill? My unit. My crew?" His hands clawed up.

She shook her head, the blood rushing to her head with panic. They had that opium here, pipe and all. Maybe she could load him one, maybe—

"Children? You have?" he demanded.

"Me? No, I—"

He tore at his kimono as if looking for a wound. He pulled it down and sat up, half naked now, the veins in his neck throbbing. Glaring at her.

You come at me, Geisha-san, I bust you up, she thought. But she knew she'd go down fighting all too fast against a tough like this, just a black crab facing a shotgun.

He wiped at his mouth. He made fists. He stood up, planting one foot down, then the other, his eyes straining to focus on her.

"You tell me," he growled in English, "who are you? Or I kill you."

His hands clawed, one clenched around an imaginary sword handle, the other pointing as if wielding a pistol.

She had a whisky bottle, somewhere behind her.

"Please don't," she said, stalling.

"Or maybe I have Frankie do it?"

She recoiled. "Who? I don't . . ." She could feel the bottle behind her, on the counter.

He laughed. "He Hawaiian like you. But, oh, he good. Man, he good. Frankie, he like blood flowing . . . Maybe he like it more than gold."

She turned and grabbed the bottle.

He bounded after her. She could've bashed it over his head. She handed it to him.

He grabbed the bottle with both hands and chugged the last few fingers of whisky left. He threw it against the wall, and it clunked away, somehow not breaking.

She handed him the bottle of rum now, the Filipino rum. He grabbed that with both hands and chugged, backing up to the edge of the chaise. Panting. He groaned and leaned forward. She snatched the bottle from his hands right as he vomited out onto the floor with a loud slap. She stepped back, the sour stench filling her nose.

He grabbed the bottle from her, chugged some more. He positioned himself in the middle of the room, his toes mixing with the vomit, but he held his ground, feet wide apart.

"Gold!" he screamed at her. "There. We have it. They have it."

"San Mariel," she said in a calming monotone. "Cagayan Valley?"

"Yes, yes."

"But here, too? Under us? Or near?"

His head was rolling around like a coconut dropped into a bowl, and she couldn't tell if he was confirming it or not.

"No? Yes? That a yes?"

His face screwed up, and his mouth stretched open wide as if yawning. Then that coarse mug of his slackened with one big sigh that sent more acrid vapors her way. "You take me there, please? Take me home, mother," he muttered and took another chug, and the bottle slipped from his fingers and hit the floor with a crack, splitting in two, splashing vomit.

He swayed and pivoted and his eyes rolled back and fluttered and he dropped, his forehead hitting the rug as he went down. *Thunk.*

She checked the Japanese thug's pulse as he lay there half on the rug, half in his own vomit. He was still alive. She couldn't lift him. She opened the windows to flush out the stink. She tried to lift him again, heaving and hoing, and almost threw her back out. Eventually a couple guard types from the Main House came over, followed by Lansdale.

Lansdale took her out on the lanai. As she reported to him, she could only see his silhouette in the darkness, which helped her tell it to him the way she did. She mentioned her mark wanting the kimono, but neither of them laughed about it—to Lansdale it was surely just useful information, another weak point. She told him about his drinking hard, but they knew that already. The *pakalolo* didn't surprise Lansdale—they probably gave him the reefer themselves to keep him good and loose. The dose from the vial worked like a charm, she reported. She sweet-talked him and went for broke. Eventually their Japanese visitor told her a location.

"San Mariel," she stated. "Cagayan Valley."

Lansdale's eyes flashed, just a half second. "Are you sure?"

She shrugged. "That's for you to decide, sir. I only know that this was his answer."

Lansdale's shadow seemed to grow and move closer, though he hadn't budged. "Good, good. How did you ask it?"

"I just asked. He was good and loose, just like you said. So I went for broke, see. I had him confirm in different ways. At one point he said it was the Philippines, and in that valley."

Lansdale was nodding along.

"He said one other thing," she added.

"Go on."

"A name. I don't know if it means anything."

"In what context?"

"No context. He just blurted it out. He was muttering at that point. That serum, it was wrestling with the hooch and the reefer."

"I see. So, what was it?"

"The name was de Garza, Grazza, something like that." She had to give up the name. Just in case. It would prove her worth, giving them something extra.

"Did he say anything else useful? Anything at all."

"No. At that point he was plenty stoned. He was thinking I was his wife, then his mommy." She shook her head at the notion.

The two guards passed them carrying the Japanese thug away, one at each end.

"Where they taking him anyways?" she asked Lansdale.

"Back to his room, in the Main House. He's flying out pronto. He's gonna have a heck of a hangover."

"I hope so," Kanani said, "and with plenty of blackout."

"Now don't you worry," Lansdale said. "It's just like I told you: He won't remember anything. It's amnestic, that stuff."

Kanani shuddered anyway, and it made her shoulders quiver.

"I would hate to see that one getting ahold of a sword or pistol. Because I think he's used both of those plenty."

Lansdale stared over her, at the doorway, nodding as if thinking over what she said.

"Got one pig shitting on fence," she added, "take plenty white-washing for make dat fence look mo nice."

Lansdale nodded at that. His teeth shined. "To grasp what you know and what you do not know, that is true knowledge," he replied, this being another of his sayings or proverbs or whatever it was he liked to spew. Wendell had told her to watch out for these, but she still didn't know what it was supposed to mean or what to say.

"All righty," she said.

"You went did good, wahine," Lansdale said.

"Please don't do that, mister."

"Do what?" Lansdale added a spurt of a laugh.

"Try talking Pidgin. Only make one haole sound dumb."

"Ah." Lansdale tapped at his temple. "Will do."

And he left her standing on the boogie bungalow lanai. He blended into the night. And she would have to go back inside and clean up the whole damn stinking mess. She didn't even want to fathom what the Americans were doing working with a monster like that Japanese thug. That was Lansdale's racket, and possibly Charlie Selfer's, but she only hoped it wouldn't end up Wendell Lett's problem.

14.

A couple weeks into his treatment and just days after his first assignment, Lett had gotten the call—his next assignment. His cure could continue. They traveled straight from the Big Island in a Catalina flying boat, taking off from the water down in a cove along the South Kona shore. Deploying by airplane sounded first-rate, but it ended up like being inside a submarine, a tight-as-hell mess of erratically placed seats and bunks with thin padding. They had to watch their heads and elbows and toes because of all the bolts and brackets left where wartime equipment used to be—machine guns, old navigation equipment. Jock loved finally getting a ride in a floating plane, but his excitement cooled once they took off and the giant metal tube of a fuselage rattled and shook and dipped and shifted and kept at it after they rose to altitude. It had blister windows that bulged out, but looking over the vast sea below and seeing only nothingness until the horizon didn't help a man cope. They were a six-man team again, a few from the group that did the job in Hilo, a couple new ones. The fragility of the ride didn't help any of them want to get to know one another any better. It wasn't like a game of craps or cards would last anyway on account of the droning racket alone.

They landed on Guam first, for refueling, and they were only allowed to get off long enough to stretch their legs and walk around the plane. At some point—hours, maybe a day after their first lift-off—Jock was rocking Lett awake for landing. They touched down on water and floated into another cove, but this inlet was far across the Pacific from the one they had left.

They were now in the Philippines.

A pontoon boat was waiting, and it took them ashore. A few men joined them there, "in-country" as they called it—two more Americans looking as GI-issue as they come, and a couple Filipinos

for translating, guiding, and what have you. After coffee and Spam-
and-egg sandwiches and a half hour of shut-eye on solid land, they
all piled into the two waiting troop trucks. Then they rode south on a
narrow highway that bordered swamplands and curved along water-
ways of brown water lined with lush greenery wanting to overgrow
to the opposite bank. Longboats rode the water; the men in them
stooped. It was even more humid than in the Territory of Hawaii.

They drove for hours, Lett nodding off half the time, as did the
rest of them, leaning into one another. Sometimes he looked out
the truck. They passed little villages they called barrios. Churches
were in the Spanish style, more or less, but of red brick with white
rounded columns. The poverty looked as bad as he'd seen anywhere,
even in war. Boys sat up in trees for no reason he could make out.
People, most of them barefoot, fetched their water from puddles.
Ramshackle huts were slapped together from who knew what—corrugated metal, wood flats, pallets, leather, tarp sheets, all of it held
together with rope and tar and mud and a whole lot of worry. Fences
were just the thickest sticks people could find. Then came more of
those vast swamplands along their waterway road, which Jock told
him were for rice, and sure enough, rice farmers were standing out
in the water tending to their crops. The wind smelled sweet, but it
wasn't from flowers or anything Lett could recall from Hawaii. It
had more of a spice or tang to it.

Lett wished he could've said good-bye to Kanani before he left.
He would've warned her not to do anything stupid. He wondered
how it was going in that boogie house they had her running. She
must be let down by the duty, but if anyone could make it work, it
was her. He only wished he didn't know about the gold.

He couldn't have told her where he was heading exactly because
he didn't know himself. The vast countryside had opened around
them. Hours into the journey, as the sun lowered, green mountain
ranges rose higher and tighter on either side. "I know where we
are," Jock told Lett. "This here is all one vast valley. Cagayan Valley.
Luzon. North of Bambang, then there's Manila south of that. To the
west you got your Cordillera Range. You know they still got tribes

up there wearing loin cloths? East, you got the Sierra Madre, high as hell . . ."

Lett was hardly listening. He worried about Kanani now—because her goal, clearly, was getting at that gold. It was her way out of this world. How many had thought the same? Misled themselves? He knew what it was like to mislead oneself. Once upon a time, an eager orphan had believed that serving in battle would transform him into his own man, dependent no more.

***

The giant beast stared at Lett with its mammoth horns that curved rearward as they tapered and swooped upward at the sharp tips, like bicycle handlebars sculpted by some Baroque master. The blackish brown beast faced Lett, its legs planted like posts, its elongated ears extending parallel to those horns. And it kept staring at Lett.

Lett was guarding a modest courtyard with the others. They had slept through the darkness and were woken at dawn. The sun was only now rising above the treetops of the hills. Lett manned one solitary corner of the courtyard, and the beast stood its own ground in the low grass between the courtyard and a line of jungle foliage. It kept its black eyes on Lett, and he couldn't help staring back.

He thought it was a water buffalo and Jock had called it an Oriental cow, but another man told him, "They call it a carabao here. It's the national animal—their bald eagle."

And that horned beast wouldn't stop staring. Lett would shift his view from time to time, since he was watching the perimeter after all. But every time he turned back around, the beast was still eyeballing him. He wondered if the animal had any idea he was carrying a weapon. They had rifles this time, not submachine guns. He had an M1 carbine, his trusty favorite from the war, light on his shoulder, his thumb tucked under the strap of Army-green webbing. This time their weapons were loaded. Lett didn't like the idea—not at all. He'd practically started when they issued him ammo to load and told him to show the ones who hadn't handled an M1, yet he couldn't help but assume the role. He'd done it so often. It didn't make him jitter or act out or black out, and to his surprise, it calmed him so much that he forgot all about taking his dose.

The courtyard had uneven paving stones, pocked and cracking, the seams growing weeds. It didn't seem like a place intended for an official meeting. It had one narrow road in, lined with lush green ridges on either side. A dilapidated sign read Cagayan Mining Company. The building facing the courtyard was nondescript, two stories, stucco. A few low Quonset huts stood beyond, and a warehouse of rusting corrugated metal. Four heavy cargo trucks waited there, two of them weighted down, the tires close to fenders, their loads covered in canvas. The two other trucks stood empty, standing tall.

Kanani would want to know about it. Lett still didn't want to know about it. He just wanted to get the assignment over with. An hour into the guarding, he was growing restless. What the hell were they even watching for? And why had they brought them all the way here? Still no one told them. It grew more humid, and the light M1 weighed heavier on his shoulder than it should have been. If he grew jittery and felt like shooting up a dose—it was quite all right under the circumstances, he assured himself.

Jock was the next man over, tens of yards away. They had two other sentries on the opposite corners of the square, a couple down the road, and two more at the entrance, as well as men on the rooftops.

The next time Lett turned around, the carabao was gone. He hadn't even heard it.

Jock's head rose, and Lett saw billows of dust rise from far down the narrow entrance road. They straightened up. A sedan was coming, a prewar Dodge but in fine shape. It passed through the courtyard and rolled to a stop before the two-story building.

An Army captain in summer dress stepped out from the front seat of the car and came around to meet the two men exiting the rear seats. The two were Japanese in civvies, but they rose from the car glaring at the scene around them and assumed that erect stance of military men—or at least proud men. Two more Americans in summer dress came out to meet the car: an Army colonel and a captain. Seeing the two American officers, the Japanese men's shoulders dropped, and they pulled off their hats and held them in their hands before them and their heads went down as the two Americans addressed them on the front steps. Within that minute, the Japanese visitors went from looking like thugs to royalty and then back down to prisoners. Their American masters waved them inside, and the two shuffled along like donkeys dragging a load.

Lett wondered whose staff the officers in khaki were. They wore actual insignia, but Lett was too far away to make out any more than rank. He saw Jock show him a little shrug from across the way.

Then he heard a strange thrashing sound, coming closer, underscored by a droning noise. It was coming from the sky. Coming right at them.

Lett crouched. The rest did, too. He wondered if his friend the carabao had heard it. He must have thought it was a giant insect. It looked like a massive dragonfly.

It was a helicopter. Lett had heard of them but had only seen a couple in pictures and a newsreel once. It was the Sikorsky model, he believed—Army olive drab with a stout nose of glass panels. The thrashing became thumping as it hovered over them, the palms and branches flapping and waving all around, the dirt and dust swirling below.

They stayed in a crouch as it set down, hands over their eyes until those giant revolving rotors slowed and relaxed, sagging as they stopped.

One of the officers from inside ran up crouching and set down a little stepstool before the helicopter's side door. The door slid open. The officer gestured to help a man out but was dismissed as the man shook him off and bounded down the craft's built-in stair, skipping over the stepstool and hitting the earth in stride. He was a tall man in all khaki: his loose wrinkled trousers pulled up high, open collar shirt, his ornately embroidered officer's cap cocked a little, but his aviator sunglasses set straight ahead.

General Douglas MacArthur? It had to be. The officer jogged alongside him, shaking his hand without breaking stride, and the two bounded up the stairs into the main building.

***

Once the general made his entrance, Lett and half his team were assigned to watch over the building while the others got a rest. Lett patrolled closer to the building over the next couple hours. He constantly passed the half-open windows. He could see the main room. It had sofas, and all who'd arrived were gathered there, the staffers speaking to the Japanese, the Japanese speaking to MacArthur, MacArthur speaking to all.

The next time Lett passed, he had to halt a step. He saw that the important Japanese visitor who'd disembarked in Hilo was there—he had a scar and a block of a head with dents like in an old helmet—but he also saw a man he knew. The man now wore the blue uniform of the newly independent United States Air Force and the gold oak leaf of a major.

Lansdale. It was Edward Lansdale. It had to be him. There was that long, squared-off face and that thin mustache. Something made Lett wince, and it took him a moment to realize it. Lansdale's smile looked more like a grimace to him now, and each time Lett passed the window it started to look more creepy-crawly in that newly created uniform. Yet it seemed to work for the men in the room, whom Lett could hear laughing at Lansdale's every word, even the Japanese and once or twice MacArthur.

Lett was seeing Lansdale in a new light. But it had been slowly dawning on him, he now understood, like the sun not yet up over the horizon. Now it was out in the open, casting its harsh rays. Lett's wince became a shiver. Ever since Hilo, he had started to mistrust Lansdale.

While Lett couldn't make out exact conversations, he could tell the talk was turning serious and focused. This wasn't a negotiation, but rather a hammering-out. Maps lay on a coffee table at one point.

It reminded Lett of one of his many prepatrol meetings up on the line: these men had done this before and knew what did and did not work. At one point they ate, and the aromas of grilled meats and fresh fruit drilled a hole in Lett's gut.

On one pass, Lett saw MacArthur and Lansdale alone in a suite room. They were standing over a table, poring over another map, the general nodding, Lansdale pointing out this and that. Finally, on Lett's last pass, Lansdale was given a hearty slap on the shoulder from the general himself.

Lansdale, the Air Force major, wore no doctor's insignia. Lett felt embarrassed for ever having called Lansdale "Doc" back at The Preserve. And just because he was wearing a white coat? Lansdale never said he was or wasn't a doctor. He'd only let Lett think what he wanted to think. And yet Lett couldn't deny it had helped with his cure.

Lett and his group finally got to rest while others filled their boots at guard patrol. Lett smelled that food again and was amazed to find that it was theirs. He, Jock, and the others were led into one of the Quonset huts, where grilled meats and fresh fruit were laid out on a table along with a macaroni salad.

"The leftovers—compliments of the meeting," a young captain told them before darting out again. "He figured you deserved it and had enough Spam."

They dove in; their filled bellies and the coffee would get them through their next watch. But the meeting must have been coming to an end, because Filipino helpers lugged in a large metal bucket of beers on ice: San Miguels. A craps game broke out. Cards ensued.

Lett shot up with his dose after all, huddling in a far, dark corner like a junkie hopping up, even though he could've just told the rest it was insulin or any matter of regular drug and no one would've cared, all of them having their own particular woe and fix.

Sometime later, he and Jock sat with their second allotted beer in a corner of the hut, their feet up on folding chairs.

"Dugout Doug, right here in the flesh, what do you make of that?" Lett said to Jock.

Jock didn't answer at first. His wet beer label kept sliding off, and he kept sliding it into place with a fingertip. "I ever get close enough, I'd ask him why he left us Marines in the lurch," he said finally. "Plenty of my fellow gyrenes been visiting me at night asking why."

"I would not do that if I were you," Lett said.

Jock grunted.

"Think about this mission," Lett said. "Aren't you wondering about that?"

"In what way?"

"Why they don't use their own troop. They bring us all this way. Lansdale does."

Jock nodded. "Sure, I been wondering. I'm just trying to be on my best behavior."

Lett nodded in turn. "This must be real secretive."

Jock let his label slip off. He snatched it from his thigh and balled it up and tossed it across the floor. "You had that feeling. Before a patrol, say."

"Or before entering a town."

"Wading onto some island."

"Forest."

"Jungle."

"All leads to the same."

"We been through the grinders enough to know the bad feeling coming on."

"That something just ain't right," Lett said.

"Yep," Jock said. "So, why don't neither of us have the feeling right now?"

Lett had to shake his head. "I don't know. I sure hope it's not because we like this too much. That we need it back."

"Maybe that's the angle, Lett. Maybe this is all we know. All that is natural to us."

Lett turned to Jock. "The angle?"

Jock shrugged. "I just mean, that it's part of the treatment they're giving us. That we realize this is natural to us."

They sat a while in silence, looking inside the brown mouths of their beer bottles. Jock added another grunt. "I was thinking, as you know: I figure maybe this is our leg up. Mine, anyways. Like I was saying before. I—"

The young captain rushed back inside, filling the doorway with alarm. Before he could get a word out a tall man pushed him aside and strode inside to them.

They shot up saluting, their folding chairs sliding backward, one tipping over.

"At ease, men." Five-Star General of the Army, Supreme Commander for the Allied Powers, and onetime Field Marshal of the Philippine Army Douglas MacArthur stood before them, hands on his hips.

"Do find your seats, please," General MacArthur added in a soft voice.

The men gathered around the man by forming a three-quarter circle of chairs without anyone prompting it, as if initiating the gesture were whispered to them all. They sat erect; hands flat on their thighs. The general found a chair, and he pulled it around to complete the circle. Facing them, nodding, smiling faintly. Lett found himself two men away from him. MacArthur pulled off his famous stitched cap, pushed his hair down, pulled out a platinum cigarette case, and offered smokes all around. Some accepted, saying thanks.

"Where's the corncob pipe, General?" said one in an upbeat voice worthy of a newsreel.

MacArthur chuckled. "That MacArthur is for the cameras, son."

They laughed. Some lit up, the rest intending to keep the cigs as souvenirs, Lett figured. They were Pall Malls. "This your favorite smoke, General?"

"My preference is whatever they have in the PX, son."

The general was pushing seventy, with sun and age spots and visible veins to show for it, but the sparkle in his eyes was that of an Olympic athlete winning his first medal. This surprised Lett. It wasn't like the man with the hard CO stare in the photos at all. He found all their eyes with his, one at a time, and when he found Lett's, Lett could not look away. The gaze was too warm.

"I just wanted to thank you men for helping out today. I wasn't always *MacArthur*, you know. I was like you. I was up on the line." He spoke, they listened. He didn't talk of his Medal of Honor or the numerous Silver Stars, or Back to Bataan or lording it over the defeated Japs from the heart of their own capital or ruling all of Asia and probably the United States if he wanted it. He talked of being up on the line in WWI, in forests like Lett. The stench of dead in trenches, the bodies above covering no-man's-land like so much underbrush, the cold and wet wanting to crack your bones, the horror sounds of our outgoing versus their incoming. He made mistakes, just like them. One time he couldn't find a gap in the barbed wire for his dear men. Another he forgot to carry his gas mask and got gassed for it. As he spoke, Lett noticed a couple officers poking their heads in the windows. "I well comprehend what the experience brings to a man. What it leaves. I understand that you fine warriors are special. Handpicked. This is because you have endured the grim wonder that is modern warfare. You are never the same upon knowing it so intimately. You know something greater than yourselves. Few will know this, throughout all of man-made history. You may consider yourselves wounded. You are not. You are instilled with a gold that can never be traded or stolen. As such, you offer society a worth that is beyond the comprehension of mere civilians. But I know it, men. MacArthur sees it."

Lett found himself wishing the general would reach over and touch him, and later the thought would make him cringe, like a man holding a sharp kitchen knife and having the overwhelming curiosity to cut himself with it, just to see.

"Well then," the general added, "you good men look like you might wish to know a thing or two about MacArthur, so do feel at ease to—"

The door flung open and Lansdale stepped in. "General, sir, you're required urgently," he said and glared at the men as he did so, his mustache vanishing behind his scowl.

"Well then, duty calls," the general said. He slapped his thighs, stood, and strode past Lansdale and out the door.

Lansdale stood there. He wiped at his mouth and the mustache was back. He added a wide-open smile. "The great man knows no rest, and that's why he's the best!" he chirped and hurried out the door.

The men ignored the Air Force major, laughing and shaking their heads and nodding and recapping the last couple minutes as if it had included a curvy dancer who'd just burst from a birthday cake. They sucked their beers. Lett too had to shake his head in wonder.

Jock said to Lett, "I reckon the ole general ain't half bad for an Army man. And he was a doggie, too." Lett didn't reply so Jock added, scratching his head, "Guess I should stop calling him Dugout Doug, at least until my new posting."

The door flung back open. Air Force Major Lansdale marched back in, but the men only nodded at him, still busy as they were retelling the story of the great visit. It was already gaining embellishments. MacArthur had beers with them, see. MacArthur played craps with the whole crew. Before long, this Quonset hut would become a bordello.

"Attention!" Lansdale roared. "Snap to when I tell you." The men came to, all in a line. The scowl was back. "Do you know who I am?" he said, and it wasn't a question. "I'm Intelligence. So listen, and listen good: You never saw the general here. You yourselves were never here. Understand? This is *top secret*. You peep a word of this and you're right back where you came from."

The men stared back.

"I don't hear you. Do you understand?"

"Understood, sir!"

Lansdale turned on his heels and marched back out, slamming the door behind him.

Lett watched from a window of the Quonset hut. The Japanese men who had arrived in the Dodge trudged out of the building toward their sedan. They looked no happier than when they arrived, unlike most men after a long day of meetings. No slapping of backs, no laughing. Heads down. The sedan sped off. Then the silhouette of one General MacArthur exited through a back door surrounded by staff officers. The helicopter blades turned and whooshed, and soon the general's flying machine was rising into the sky, a glowing light, the dragonfly turning into a firefly as it rose higher, farther, leaving only the detached fronds of palms and even more dust.

The sun had lowered beneath the ridges, dimming all. Lett could barely see the spot where the carabao had vanished. He hoped it was watching from somewhere safe inside the surrounding jungle. What better way to avoid that giant insect?

This is top secret, he recalled. Another top secret mission had once changed him forever, from a hopeful orphan into a paranoid killer. But now he felt something like hope again because this mission was accomplished.

"Where's Lett?" Lett heard. He turned around. Lansdale strode back in with that slight stoop he had, left arm hanging lower than the right, left hand with a slight twist to it. Lett turned and Lansdale found him, Lansdale smiling now.

"You'll come with me," he said.

15.

Lett left that night. Lansdale had picked three others—but not Jock, who pulled a face like the kid not chosen for stickball. The four rode in the two empty heavy trucks that had been parked at the warehouse, two men to each cargo bed. They got a canvas cover, seat cushions, and an aluminum pot of coffee for their trouble. Lett should've felt the old warning signs convulsing him, riding as he was in the back of a truck to who knew where with poor bastards just as unsure as he. Carrying a weapon. Not having a clear identity or mission. And yet, he felt talkative. Maybe it was the beer or coffee or both. Maybe it was simply that stimulating effect of General Douglas MacArthur. Maybe it was that dose he'd done in the Quonset hut, forging steel inside him.

Lett's opposite number in the back of the truck wasn't feeling talkative, however, and only grunted in the affirmative when Lett asked him if he wanted some joe. The man was squat with big ears and hair everywhere, even on his sinewy neck. The coffee braced him just enough for questions. He was a former Navy commando who never returned to the States and didn't see the point, considering. "I got the goddamn malaria, besides," he told Lett, "keeps coming back." Then he clammed up and turned away from Lett, treating him like a new replacement.

The truck ride, the cold shoulder, the imposed silence—it all finally brought a dark mood, becoming one with the night that was sucking all light from under the canvas. Lett lay on his back and stared at the canvas above, dark as pitch, cloaking what had to be a million stars up there, the road jostling him, working away at his back like a thousand hands poking and prodding and none of it like a massage. He was hugging his M1 carbine, he realized. He pushed it aside.

Keep moving. Stop and you're cornered.

"Damn right there, doggie," the commando replied from his dark corner, and Lett realized he'd been muttering to himself, out loud.

They traveled south for two hours, the trucks' headlights finding only green tropical forest, brown streams, and an unending line of steep hills and surely mountains beyond. The last sign of civilization they passed was a village called San Mariel, just a junction of huts, their tires thumping on old cobbled road. They turned down a side road and the softer roll of the tires meant it was all dirt. Then Lett and the former commando were out standing guard with the other two vets. They were still in the Cagayan Valley, but the clarity of the sounds reminded Lett that this area was even more remote. He could hear an occasional wild animal rustle through bushes yards away. One palm frond brushed another—and another, and another—up the hill above. Water ran low and rough nearby, swishing around rocks.

Two hours later, they were still there. Sporadic flashlight beams and a spotlight that was eventually brought out showed a high bank near a river, set back about ten yards, where a tall mango tree stood. Beyond its trunk, at the base of a hill, other men had erected a standard Army wall tent, normally a billet for five to ten men. But this was no billet. Lett and the other three were posted outside in case anyone approached. But no one would approach this place. Who would know how to get here? A native jungle mountain man, maybe, loin cloth and all.

Lansdale arrived by motorcycle, riding in the sidecar. Driving the bike was the Japanese man with dents in his head—and knobby scarred knuckles from fighting, Lett now saw as he stood close, while the man steered the bike to a stop at the pointing beam of a flashlight. The Japanese goon was clearly working with the team, Lett noticed, providing them with info, pointing out this and that. Lett and the commando had been told to meet them, escort them up. Up close, the Japanese also had a blocky jaw, pockmarked cheeks, thick lips, and dark eyes Lett didn't want to look at any longer than he did a dark well. Lansdale was back to wearing khaki without insignia. He wore a holstered pistol now, too, and had a spring in his stoop of a step and a sparkle in his eye that Lett knew all too well. He knew it from wild ones up on the line who couldn't get enough of a firefight and the blood that came with it. He always imagined that those types ended up in a psych ward, if not the electric chair. But here this one was, his beaming mug now making Lett shudder more than the Japanese man's brute face.

When Lansdale headed for the tent, he didn't acknowledge Lett except to bark, "Top secret is top secret, and don't you men forget it," in passing.

And, now, finally, Lett truly had that bad feeling.

Suddenly the truck engines revved up. They had to be reparked because they stood too close to the soft earth of the riverbank—the water here sucked away trucks and houses alike at whim. Lett, left in the dark a moment, used the opportunity to remove the shells from the cartridge of his M1 and slip them into a pocket, leaving the gun looking as lethal as ever.

He'd gotten the urge and simply acted on it. It surprised him. This was the opposite of what the bad feeling usually brought, which was a careful, machinelike preparation of his killing tools. He couldn't explain his impulse. Something deep inside him simply commanded him to respond differently. To resist certainty. Clear the metal chamber. He had been thinking about how relieved he'd felt not having to carry a weapon at first, and how having to carry one now should make him grow ever queasier. In the truck he had pushed his M1 aside on impulse. So why not unload it, too?

Lansdale and his Japanese partner were inside the tent. Soon screams and cries came from another man inside: a mix of Tagalog, English, Japanese, denial, lament. Lett couldn't make it all out. But what sounded like pleading turned to moaning, and yet no promises were made to the target as in a normal interrogation. Some might call this torture. Lett heard water pouring and splashing and gasping at one point. After a pause of quiet, there came the slowly mounting screech of a man having something peeled away.

***

Longer stretches of quiet came. Lett got sandwiches, more coffee. Near dawn, the steep slopes looming around him began to reveal themselves as an ever-higher series of ridges and mountains and the river as mostly mud.

The torture continued, an early morning shift. The conversations Lett heard from inside the tent sounded like monks praying, chanting. Lett heard words carrying a Filipino accent but muffled and wet. Then, silence again.

Lansdale pushed the tent flap open, stepped outside, took a deep breath of air and rubbed at his stomach and stretched as if having had the best nature sleep of his life. His sleeves were rolled up but otherwise he looked the same. He combed his thick dark hair, though it didn't need it, his part still perfect. His eyes still had that sparkle, too, and they caught the first rays of sun shooting up into the sky through gaps in the high ridges—rays that beamed, Lett couldn't help noticing, much like those of the notorious Japanese rising sun.

"Rifles down, men," Lansdale told Lett and the commando a few minutes later. "Grab a shovel." They took turns digging a pit at the base of the large mango tree. At one point, Lett, his arms and thighs burning, had the grim thought that he was digging his own grave, but he only pushed himself harder, letting the sweat roll down him, into his eyes, stinging.

His shovel clanged against metal. Lansdale waved them away, telling them to go rest out of sight.

Lett and the commando sat sucking on canteens under the shade of a neighboring tree. A Plymouth arrived; two white men got out. They looked like adventuring engineers in their civilian khaki, slouch hats, metal-rimmed eyeglasses, and bulging briefcases. They inspected the dig, conferred with Lansdale and others. Steel pipes were laid down. One of the trucks pulled up and its winch deployed.

"Be honest, you thought maybe we were digging our own graves," the commando muttered before spitting out a projectile of tobacco. "Not that we don't deserve it."

"What's that supposed to mean?" Lett shot back, but neither

discussed it. They were too tired, and too busy watching. The huge truck had difficulty dragging out two large boxes from the pit, even when they rolled along the steel pipes other men had laid, but it got them out. Lansdale, the Japanese brute, and the engineering types assembled around the boxes. One of the engineers crouched at a box while the Japanese stood over his shoulder as if coaching him. Lansdale had stepped back a few paces, Lett noticed—curiosity wasn't going to kill a cat like that. But nothing blew, no booby traps triggered. The engineer flipped the box open, the lid blocking Lett's view, and all stepped forward as if gathering around a newborn baby, nodding, and two were smiling. But one engineer looked like a doctor who knew something was wrong with the baby, and Lansdale wasn't smiling, either. He shot a glare across to Lett and the commando, as if something were somehow their fault.

"You two," he barked. "Inside the tent."

***

The face was bloated on one side. Dried blood caked the bulges and filled the cracks and crevices, some of the blood still shining gooey there. It filled an eye socket. The man's clothes were soiled and torn, and most of his fingernails were missing, just tips of coagulating blood.

Inside the wall tent, Lett smelled urine and feces and that unmistakable smell of burnt hair and flesh. The man, slumped in a folding chair, wasn't tied up. But he wasn't going anywhere. Whenever he slumped enough to topple, a man pulled him back up, setting his shoulder straight like a soft pillow that wouldn't stand.

The man propping up their interrogation target was none other than Frankie.

Frankie had arrived in a gleaming coupe after the engineer types left. Lansdale and the Japanese brute called him by name. Frankie loomed even larger inside the tent, his broad shoulders and big paws casting wild shadows on the canvas. His neck was as

thick as two, and Lett saw the pointy tips of another tattoo shooting up that trunk, snaking up inside kinky black hair that was
parted down the middle. His face was a block, with cheekbones so
pronounced Lett could practically see the coarseness of the bone
itself through the skin in the lantern light. His lips were thin and
hard and purplish.

Lett's bad feeling was even worse inside the tent. Lansdale, Lett
figured, had ordered them inside to help keep the pressure on.

Seeing Lett, Frankie's eyes lit up and he wagged a finger. "Mister
Lansdale told me about you," he said, grinning now, giving Lett the
eager once-over. "He told me you something special—special army
guy warrior man."

Lett was beyond any shock at this point. He was only glad that
Kanani didn't have to deal with Frankie. He, this, they, were the dis-
traction she likely needed while she maneuvered away back at The
Preserve. So be it.

Frankie had Filipino blood too, so at first Frankie simply spoke
Tagalog to the man in the folding chair. Lett had heard Lansdale
call the man "de Garza" outside, but he and Frankie used the name
"Reuben" to his face. The Japanese brute meanwhile piled on incom-
prehensible grunts and words that, from the sound and spit, Lett
could only assume were an insult to someone's mother.

Lett and the commando held their M1s unslung as ordered,
but they kept their backs pushed against the forgiving canvas walls
of the tent. Nothing else could forgive here. Reuben's one good eye
widened, and he tried to straighten up. But then he passed out again,
slumping over. Frankie propped Reuben back up. After a couple
rounds of slumping and propping, Frankie stood close to Reuben,
his feet apart. He said things in Tagalog to Reuben. Reuben nodded—or at least tried to nod—and then shook his head, followed
by more Tagalog, then sobbing. Eventually, Frankie said to Reuben,
seemingly for Lansdale's benefit, "This wasn't all of it, Reuben. Not
even close. You are tricking us. There is more."

More head shaking and nodding and Tagalog and sobbing.
Frankie held his ear close to Reuben, who, after several failed starts,

whispered something in his ear before passing out again, his head so far to one side that his neck looked busted.

Frankie nodded. He walked over to Lansdale, whispered to him, and the two strode outside, leaving the Japanese brute confused and then glaring at the floor in something like sadness—as if left out of the ball game once again.

The brute looked up at Lett with as if suddenly realizing he was there. "You. Hello. Do you know how they know?"

"Know what?"

"How Lansdale knows this location. About Reuben! I don't understand how. Only I know it. Tell me how." He added a sickly sneer that not even a bow could've helped.

"Search me, mister, I'm just the help." Lett shrugged.

The Japanese brute stood over Reuben with his arms cocked as if the bloody sandbag of a human in the chair were a boulder that he had to roll away with his bare hands.

Reuben woke again with a start. His surviving eye popped open. He wheezed to the Japanese man, "Why? You promised. You promised your honorable commander. Why do you give it away?"

"You shut up!" the Japanese man barked. His hands kept compacting then springing open; squeezing, opening.

One side of Reuben's face moved to contort into a smile. It had to hurt like hell. "You know what they do to me now. What they must do. It's what you do."

Reuben passed out again. The Japanese man squatted down, his back straight, his wrists fixed atop his knees, staring into space now.

About five minutes later, Lansdale strode back into the tent grinning. "Chop-chop," he said to the Japanese brute, who stared back, not understanding.

"When the work's begun, don't leave it till it's done," Lansdale chirped. "Be the labor great or small, do it well or not at all."

The Japanese man only grimaced, still squatting. Lansdale stood near him and gazed down on him as if about to give his kept thug a kiss on those dents in his skull.

"I'm back, Kodama," Lansdale said. "We will continue. Understand?"

"We continue? So we finish?" the man called Kodama said.

"That's right, kemosabe."

"What mean 'kemosabe'?"

"It means 'trusty scout.'" Lansdale winked at Lett.

"Ah," Kodama said. He muttered in Japanese.

Then Kodama glared at Lett, shot up, and bounded over to Lett. "You!"

Lett straightened up but not too much, the hot ball of disgust in his gut not letting him.

"You shoot man," Kodama barked at him, stabbing a finger at their target passed out in the chair. "You."

A normal man might have blanched, reared up, stormed out. But Lett had been places a normal man would never know. In times like these, just as in his nightmare daydreams and night terrors and blackouts, time did not exist. He was back in all those horrid places at once, all planes converging. It made him calmer somehow.

And there was also the fact that he had emptied his magazine.

He eyed all of them at once. Kodama's scowl. Lansdale's smirk behind Kodama's shoulder. The commando's eyebrows riding high. The target whimpering, trying to keep that one eye open.

"No, you shoot him," Lett replied. "You Japanese started all this."

Kodama growled, stepped closer to Lett.

"All right, all right, take it easy," Lansdale said, moving between Lett and Kodama, "This isn't Lett's responsibility anyway, Kodama . . ."

Just then Frankie pushed through the tent flap and stepped inside holding up a hand like the best boy in class.

"Now that's what I like to see," Lansdale said.

Kodama backed away, nodding. Lansdale rocked on his heels, smiling.

Frankie paced around the chair, each step measured. Calm. He then stood behind the chair. Reuben took a couple deep breaths, closed his one eye, and let out a groan that sounded almost like a death rattle. Frankie crouched, leaning into Reuben's side. He produced locking pliers from one of his pockets. He rammed fingers into Reuben's mouth with the other hand and yanked down Reuben's jaw, then prodded the pliers into Reuben's mouth before he could bite down. Frankie swung Reuben's head around to peer in, jerking Reuben's head side to side, up and down. Reuben's feet pushed out, off the ground, one chair leg rising, then another. Frankie grunting, drooling. Shoving, heaving.

He jerked out the pliers with a jolt. Slings of drool and blood hung from the pliers and Frankie's wrists. The pliers held a white tooth. Frankie wiped at it and turned it their way so they could see its twinkle. It held a gold filling.

Reuben released another slow, deep moan. His arms hung from his sides.

Frankie plunged back into Reuben's mouth for more—five more teeth. Reuben fought it less and less, Frankie grunting and muttering whispers in his ear. When finished, Frankie let out a deep yet satisfied sigh. He set the pliers in Reuben's lap. Frankie looked to Lansdale, who beamed back with that sparkle in his eye and nodded. Frankie wrapped his tattooed arms and hands around Reuben's neck and snapped it with a great crack.

16.

Lansdale finally gave Lett and the commando a break. They didn't even have to clean up the mess that had been Reuben. They dropped down under their tree again, and the commando kept slamming his back against the gnarled trunk. This time he had a few things to say.

"Why?" he said. "Just because they can? And all on account of top secret. Who is going to know? No one."

Lett was the only one within earshot. He didn't respond at first. He was too beat. So much was happening so fast. Sure, he was shocked. Like a man was after any mission. The reasoning would come later, along with the stewing if need be. For now, he would simply cope. Assignments were part of the treatment. Besides, no one said this would be easy. Selfer never promised it. He had taken their cure in exchange for doing a duty. It was keeping him out of a stockade. And, he had to admit, he'd been calmer since the cure had started.

"You stood up back there," the commando said. "To them. Don't think I didn't notice."

"I didn't stand up," Lett said. "I simply don't see why I should do their dirty work, especially not from a former enemy—who started all this. It's not what I'm here for."

The commando laughed. "Don't tell me. They're going to fix you, right? Help you with what's ailing you? What a crock." He spat.

"Why don't you get some shut-eye? You're getting irritable."

The commando's head sank between his knees. Lett hoped to hear snoring. After a couple minutes, the commando popped up and started in again. "Listen. You know what the Nips did? During the war, when they had a tunnel or cave or what have you that they wanted kept secret? They buried the help in there right along with their spoils."

"Like I was saying," Lett said.

The commando grunted. He then muttered that he was going to go take a leak.

Lett considered using the opportunity to get his syringe from his musette bag and give himself a dose. But he didn't. He simply didn't feel the urge. And his body felt too heavy. He was too dazed from all the duty, the intense incidents. He let his eyes lose focus. He embraced the return of the old thousand-yard stare, and part of him even embraced the possibility of his dead friends visiting. But his old ghosts stayed away.

***

The commando didn't return. No one had seen him.

Lansdale sent out men looking for him, but he didn't seem per-turbed when they didn't find him, joking that one day they might discover the fellow up in the hills wearing a loin cloth muttering the "native mumbo-jumbo." He told Lett that it wasn't his fault.

With the commando gone, Lett had less time for rest. He was left to stand guard while others cleaned camp, loaded up. Lansdale, Kodama, Frankie, and the diligent engineers held meetings and pored over maps. They came and went. They seemed to forget about him.

As he used to do up on the line, Lett drifted in and out of sleep while standing and pacing and standing, his eyes seemingly open to an unknowing bystander. He could march like this, they all could, if they had been worn down long enough. Like this, time itself lost measure or meaning. His state only intensified here with the dense jungle and steep hillsides rising all around, another world com-pletely, just as the cold, wet, pine- and fir-choked Ardennes Forest might as well have been the moon to a Pacific grunt like Jock or the commando. Like this, Lett retained a sense of alertness even as he lost any sense of alarm or urgency—and any recognition that he had to flee all of this now.

At one point he heard a series of rustles up in the higher stories

of jungle around them, but one of the Filipino helpers just laughed—
and told him those were only monkeys.

***

They gave Lett a pup tent to himself. He had the first few dark
hours off so he could catch up on sleep finally. They were going to
hit the road first thing. At first Lett couldn't sleep. He kept thinking about his still-unloaded M1, lying next to him. He could hear
Lansdale and Frankie and the rest in their top-notch command tent,
sometimes laughing, sometimes boasting, though he couldn't make
out the words.

Lett realized he was alone for the first time in a good while. He
lay there. Soon his head turned hot and his sinuses swelled like from
instant hay fever. Then the heat moved to his chest and gut.

It was Lansdale there. Inside him. Growing, distending.

His bad feeling about Lansdale was more than just a sense, he
knew. It was stark reality. This third stage of his treatment was confirming it. Lansdale had helped him at first, with stages one and two.
Sure he had. But the man wasn't just ambitious, with a dominating
demeanor. Lett had seen his share of those types both on and off the
front line. No, this was different. He'd just witnessed Lansdale order
the torture and execution of a helpless human being—and grin
about it.

The stark new reality was more than just a breaking sun above
the horizon, casting its rays. More than full sunlight. It was the bright
and glaring white of floodlights right before an overwhelming surprise assault, blinding Lett alone in his forward-operating foxhole.

The truth of such a stark white shock? He was already a dead
man if he didn't act.

Lett pulled his bedroll over him, up to his chin like a boy sleeping outside for the first time. He more than mistrusted Lansdale, he
now realized. He feared him. He feared the very man who was giving him his cure.

He was sweating, but it cooled. Eventually, he dozed off.

Later, he dreamt. Some would call it a nightmare, but to Lett it was the dream he'd always had, the one that woke him alone in his Kona Town billet room and then in Kanani's borrowed bungalow down on Alii Drive . . .

He grabs his own throat, squeezes and squeezes. He peers into his eyes and sees horror in his bulging white eyeballs, his distending pupils. Then it's her. The German girl. He feels her so deep within his chest, wrenching his distended heart, that he tightens his grip on her muffled screams just to make it all stop. This little German girl is no more than eleven and her long dark braided pigtails whip around as he suffocates her, clamping down, his knuckles gone all white. His mouth hangs open, but nothing comes out, like hers now, and his hot tears drop onto her dulling eyes as he hovers over her for leverage, pressing down, compressing, and his heart aches all the more. He can't look at her. He peers around and all he can see is that cold, gray, bombed-out street in Cologne, the scene of his war crime. What could he do? She'd spotted him and his team and she was going to alert the street patrol, was going to give them away in their hiding place, and then they'd be surrounded, no way out . . .

Lett woke in his pup tent, wide awake. He heard rustling in the leaves, from afar, then closer. His head reared up. All was dark. He was all alone. It was a pup tent now, but he might as well be the only man in the forward foxhole, a human tripwire. The rustling came closer.

Attackers! Surprise raid!

He started sweating again, his chest hot, his blood pumping, but it was good. It was his steel and cables and gears and fresh oil.

He must alert the first line and the command post before he's surrounded, but they didn't string comm wire, didn't give him a field phone. It's all up to him.

He felt around in the dark, mechanically, fingered his M1 carbine and cradled it while he fastened his web belt holding his sheathed trench knife. He didn't need his boots. They only made noise, soft ground or no.

He heard whispers. And footsteps now, boots along soft ground and grass.

Always keep moving. Stop and you're cornered. Keep your eyes open.

He slipped out of his pup tent on all fours, his light M1 riding in the bends of his arms, sliding toward the sounds like a snake, his tongue even stretching out, tasting the air.

He followed the silhouettes in the night, and he could see in the pitch dark.

They've passed the first line and are heading for the command post.

There were three of them, crouching, with no gun barrels that he could see, but knives surely. They moved in a triangle pattern, fanning out but not too far, just enough space for him to strike and strike and strike.

He lunged.

He took out the first two in quick order. One now had wet gleaming blood for a face. The other was curled up but with one leg bent forward doll-like, as if he had no knee. He struck the third as he came at him, got on top of the man, digging into him, keeping him down.

Lett was choking the man below him with both hands, pressing down, twisting, making him wheeze.

"Stop, stop," the man wheezed.

"You?" Lett loosened up a little but kept him down.

"Goddamn it, listen to me," the man sputtered, words tumbling out like gravel into water. "We shoulda killed them when we had the chance, killed them in that tent, got me?"

"No. No . . ."

"I know you thought it. They're gonna wreck you. He is. There is no fucking cure—"

"Let him loose, Lett! Stop."

Lights flashed. Hands pulled Lett up. He reared around, but they had him by the arms and he floated. They dropped him down on his rear. Their flashlights shined on the bodies. The two lifeless ones wore small shorts, old boots without socks, burlap. They were dark. Natives. Dead.

"Holy mackerel," someone said. "Man, oh man."

The light shined on the third man. It was the commando. He was still gasping for air, moaning.

Frankie whistled in wonder at Lett's work, and Kodama showed him a bow.

Then Frankie and Kodama carried the commando away, his feet dragging.

"Lett? You hear me in there? Lett?"

The flashlight pointed upward and found a long and delighted face, casting an eerie glow, making him a happy Frankenstein. It was Lansdale.

"Now that was some mighty fine handiwork," he sang.

17.

K anani could not wait. She didn't have a choice. That ringmaster Edward Lansdale wasn't at The Preserve. He seemed to have left and taken that Japanese thug with a thing for geishas with him. And Frankie, she had to assume, could show up any moment even if he had only been spotted once, on the other side of the island. She could've used trusty Wendell Lett here, but he was out on assignment. She wanted to wait for Miss Mae, but the clock was tick-tocking.

She'd been snooping around even more while they were all gone. All the clues, like the ones she wrested from that Japanese thug, always led away from the Territory of Hawaii, to places and possibly players she could not know. She needed clues back here, right here.

The only angle was probing any weak links.

This got her thinking about Lieutenant Colonel Selfer. Charlie Selfer, she was starting to see, might not be anything like the high *makamaka* he appeared to be, let alone the big kahuna he dreamed of becoming. That was the way it looked when she'd spied on the Main House windows with the opera glass that was included in that footlocker of strange toys at her boogie bungalow. She knew body language, all right. The important visitors who'd been here discussed and debated from their sofas and leather armchairs, always led by the one and only Lansdale. Selfer had never led any talks. Selfer barely talked at all. Selfer never got to sit. Selfer smiled and smoothed and was the only one to bring their drinks on a platter like at some catered affair in the Kona Inn. Selfer only hosted. Selfer waited. Selfer ingratiated, sure, but it got him nowhere she could see. Sometimes the important visitors had asked him to leave the room. And sometimes they had snickered after he left the room. Lansdale had snickered.

Selfer appeared to manage The Preserve, and he likely filed a report from time to time, but he might just be a glorified confidential secretary. And he might not like that very much, based on what Wendell Lett told her about how the man made his name during the war.

And so she let Charlie Selfer find her, just strolling through camp that evening after she had a drink in the bar. Selfer had been there holding court with the nurses at their usual table in the corner, and he didn't eye her once—except the one time he strolled over to the men's and shot her a glance out of the corner of his eye. She was, after all, wearing one of those suggestive tropical numbers every haole liked . . .

All she had to do was get close to him. Get her face close to him. No boy could resist a girl with her face close enough to him. Miss Mae had taught her that. A girl had her wiles. Those could be a curse, something every man used and exploited. Or, she could use them to her advantage. Use her sex against them. She thought about how it could shake out. Once she was inside the Main House a few times, she could figure out the lay of the place. Supposing there was some cabinet or safe? Supposing Selfer liked a little strange, or even some opium or other dose with his strange, and then he might well tell her things he didn't mean to and not even remember. She had to try. *Keep moving,* Wendell always said.

So she swung her hips as she walked by him in the bar and had proceeded to let him flirt, and the next morning she found herself riding in Selfer's convertible DeSoto out the front gate. He drove her along the narrow roads that delivered them down the hills heading makai, toward the sea. A road below crossed the old 1871 Trail and led them to the water. They could hear it once Selfer parked the DeSoto and put up the top, and they could smell its salty freshness. They walked a path to a flat open strand punctuated by solitary palm trees and spans of sandy earth and walkable black lava. A cozy inlet had a beach no wider than a football field, framed by short walls of black stones.

"This is a sacred area," Kanani told him as a breeze stroked their foreheads. "The Place of Refuge. In old days, Hawaiians who broke the ancient laws could avoid certain death by gaining entrance to this sacred place. But, you first had to swim across that bay out there called da Shark Den and if you made it without dying, then the kahuna—that's like a priest to you, haole—he had to offer you sanctuary and absolve you of any wrongdoing."

"Now, if I'm not mistaken there's another small bay nearby," Selfer said. "There the explorer Captain Cook got pummeled and dismembered—and baked—by the natives for the 'mana' the priests believed was contained in his bones. Mana, that's like a person's mojo?"

"Ho, that's not bad. Yep, that happened over in Kealakekua Bay."

Selfer thought of everything. His picnic basket contained shrimp-and-cucumber sandwiches, mango salad, and a white wine from France. She spread out the blanket and propped up the large umbrella just so. She sunk her toes in the beach sand and so did he, smiling at her as if being tickled.

"If you don't like the wine? I have rum in the trunk—that or basi."

"Basi?"

"It's Filipino. Wine made from sugar cane. Has bark and leaves in it, can be rather bitter." Selfer added a scrunched-up face.

"Why don't you take your hat off so I can see you?" she said.

He was wearing a white panama hat. He removed it.

"Now you look less like one plantation owner."

"Is that what you all think of me?" he joked.

She shrugged. He also had bags under his eyes. That was new. Maybe he stayed up late burdened by the worries of managing a camp he didn't actually run. Or maybe he'd only had a late night with that fresh nurse he was pursuing.

"Wine sounds good," she said.

He pulled it from the basket. It was still cold, wrapped as it was in a thick hand towel. They drank from paper cone cups. The wine was sharper than she thought it would be, but it went down nice.

"Look out there to the left," she said. Farther out stood what would look to Selfer like a shack but was a rebuilt ancient temple. "Out past that rock wall."

"You mean that shack?"

"That's a temple."

"Ah. Imagine that. Nothing's ever like it seems, this part of the world."

She turned to him. "Plenty stuff is coming in from the Philippines nowadays, yeah?"

"Coming in?"

"Get rum and cigars and trinkets and china and who knows what, and now it's this bisi."

"Basi." He added a shrug. "Well, this is a US territory."

"You don't requisition it yourself, though, do you? You yourself, I mean. But someone has to requisition it, and someone has to send it."

He yanked his toes from the sand, pulled out a pack of Camels. He didn't offer her one.

"Don't get sore," she said. "It's okay if you don't know. You can't know everything. And, everyone has to take orders from someone."

"It's not that, it's just that . . . I can't talk about certain matters." He paused. He put his smile back on. "You know something? Let's just enjoy this lovely island haven for once." He pulled himself up and jogged the few yards to the barely lapping tide, rolled up his white trousers a little higher, and splashed his feet in the water. She had to admit he didn't dress down half bad. His aloha shirt wasn't too gaudy, and it hung off him well.

He strolled back looking looser and plopped down next to her.

"Be more careful," she said. "Coral out there. If coral doesn't cut you then it's lava rock."

"Is anything simply as nice as it looks?" he said, adding that smile again. "Take you, for instance."

She expected a smoother move from the likes of him, but the man had to start somehow. She smiled and buried her cheek in a shoulder. It was easy to blush with this wine.

They sipped, their shoulders touching.

"All that stuff from the Philippines," she said. "Territory of Hawaii doesn't need goods like that from the Philippines, never needed it before. And the US military certainly doesn't."

"What are you getting at?"

"Remember where I come from. Honolulu. Chinatown. Part of rackets and rings your US Military Government helped create. Yeah? So I know one smuggle job when I see it."

Selfer didn't answer. But he didn't laugh in her face, either.

"Crates say 'Wine' or whatever—that's no wine, just bottles on top."

Selfer pulled out a chrome hip flask and sucked on it like a teat and offered her a snort without telling her what it was. She waved it away. Eventually, he nodded. "We require certain funding," he said, "for what it is we do. But I'm already telling you too much."

"Who's we?"

"You know who. The Directorate. Or whatever they're going to call it." He had lowered his voice, although not even the gecko staring at them from a rock three feet away could hear him over the water lapping and the flapping palm leaves.

"You just said *they*, not *we*."

He held out hands. He couldn't tell her.

"No?" she continued. "Then what exactly do you do here, if you don't know a thing?"

Selfer seemed to think about that for a long time. He picked up his hat and stared at it. Set it back down, just so. He stared into the sand, his eyes widening like a kid trying to count all the granules. "It's a valid question," he said.

"You know what this says to me? Look at me. It means that this isn't at all what you thought it would be when you took the job."

He chuckled at that, but it wasn't through a smile.

"Ho, you mainlanders," she said through an equally bitter chuckle, "always trying to trade up for the next best thing."

They heard laughing and tensed up, but it was just island boys far out on the rocks.

Selfer turned to her. "This is how we fund covert ops. All right?"

She stared at him. "Fund in what way?"

"Sometimes, things can't be on paper, say, in reports, or part of a record."

"Ah. Speaking of: I used to have a good friend in Honolulu," she started to say but stopped—she'd almost said Frankie. She choked back the name. "Her name is Mae, Miss Mae to us. She's Chinese. You ever hear of her?"

"No. But everyone has code names, so who knows?" He held up his pack of Camels and offered her one now. She declined. "This Miss Mae where you got that fancy lighter of yours?" he added.

"What lighter is that?"

"Oh, come on." He grinned.

She stared at him, stalling. She held out a hand for his flask and he passed it to her. "Ho bruddah! Dis da basi? More better than French *kine* wine."

"Atta girl," Selfer said, suddenly sounding more like a streetwise sharpie and not the smoothie officer after all.

"Know what I know?" she said. "There are tunnels under here—there under The Preserve, I mean."

"You know, or you hear? Who told you—Wendell Lett?"

"Mister Lansdale," she said. She lied.

Selfer grunted. "It's Major Lansdale."

"He's a major?"

"After a fashion," Selfer muttered.

So he really did take orders from Lansdale, even though he outranked Lansdale—on paper anyway.

"What else did Lansdale tell you?" Selfer added.

"He told me I was to keep a certain important Japanese partner of his company. A thug."

"Kodama. You don't say? And Lansdale, he wanted you to extract information."

"That his name—Kodama?"

"On second thought? No, it isn't. You never heard it from me."

"Okay. So, this Japanese thug, he was too drunk to tell me much. All he did was give me a location."

"Oh? And what might that be?"

"The Philippines!" She pushed at his shoulder. "Why you think I'm asking?"

"Of course. I see, yes. Was that enough for Lansdale?"

"It must have been. Because he ain't here now, is he?"

"No. Right." Selfer sucked on his flask. "Tell me, why do I get the strange feeling you know more than this, or are after more?"

"Girls do strange things to a guy," was all she said.

"Indeed."

Selfer added a smile that should've given her the heebie-jeebies, but somehow it didn't.

She shook her head at that and drank. "I tell you one thing. He's a good man."

"Lansdale?" Selfer snapped.

"Wendell Lett. You better treat him right. He came here thinking this place was gonna heal him somehow."

"Don't you think I know that?" he snapped again. "I'm the one who promised him."

"Okay, okay, sorry," she said. She shifted closer, and his smile came back. "Will you promise me, too?"

He set a hand on hers and caressed it. It warmed her tummy more than that wine or basi. She squirmed to make it go away, but that only made it worse. He kept gazing into her eyes, and those bags underneath were all gone, flushed away by sparkle and the blush of booze and desire.

She yanked her hand away. "You never answered my question."

"What's that?"

"The tunnels."

"Oh, they're here—up there, I mean. But that's all I can say." He made the zippering gesture across his lips.

"All you can say, or all you want to say?"

He held out his hands, palms up. "We shall see, won't we?"

They got to work pulling out the food and setting it out without speaking like a couple together a long while, or at least months. They poured wine, toasted, ate, poured more wine.

"What is this?" he said. "What are we doing here?"

"We have something like a treaty. I only hope it's not like the *kine* you Americans usually come offering. Those are full of tricks."

"*We Americans*, you mean."

"*Me too?* Huh. I sure don't feel like it."

They kept eating, staring out at the ancient Place of Refuge, and drinking, giving each other sidelong glances.

"I won't take your mana, haole," she said. "I promise."

"And in return, I won't make you swim across the shark's den."

"*Deal*," they said at the same time, toasted the wine, and they laughed.

18.

Lett was now the talk of the operation. Lansdale slapped him on the back and stood so close Lett thought he was going to hug him and squeeze him.

"Man oh man, you're making such progress," Lansdale sang.

He walked Lett into his lavish command tent with an arm around his shoulder. Lett was still in fighting mode, and it was all he could do not to repel that arm and snap it. The tent had ground cover and a living area with canvas armchairs. Lansdale stood Lett in the center of the room like he was the unassuming boy who'd fought off the street bully, sizing him up and down, looking for wounds, and Lett didn't know if he was to be punished or praised and he didn't care. It all took him back to the orphanage in Ohio a moment, and that oddly calmed him. Lansdale shouted and his Filipino orderly rushed in with warm water and towels and clean fatigues for Lett. The orderly pulled off Lett's clothes and a medic came in to check him out fully, prodding and tapping him—"breathe in, breathe out, good"—before the orderly wiped Lett down like a prize horse.

Meanwhile, Lansdale talked to Lett, giving him the rundown. The commando had returned from up high in the mountains with two tribal warriors, likely former scouts from the war. But Lett was there to stop them, hunt them down. Lett had foiled what Lansdale called a "venal and deranged incursion to hijack a valuable operation."

"The man obviously wasn't responding to his cure," Lansdale said. "But you? Look at you. You're back to your old self. And how."

Lett could imagine what Frankie and Kodama would do to the commando. He'd seen it for himself. "Where are they taking him?"

"Don't you worry about that." Lansdale sneered but then wiped at his mustache and a full grin appeared, just for Lett. "Look at you, just look at you. You obviously are responding to the cure—with fly-ing colors, I'd say."

Lett was expecting one of Lansdale's trite slogans any moment, but none came. The orderly wrapped Lett in a dark, satiny Chinese robe that Lett shook off, prompting Lansdale to snap his fingers, and then the robe was out of the room completely.

Lansdale planted hands on his hips. "Why, you didn't even need your weaponry."

Lett remembered he'd been carrying his M1 carbine. His knife was still clean in its sheath—the orderly now wrapped a new web belt around his waist and hung the knife off it. "Where's my rifle?" he muttered.

"We have it for you. You left it." Lansdale wagged a finger. "That old Selfer, he had you pegged right indeed," he said. He seemed to have forgotten altogether that Lett had stood up to Kodama and wouldn't do his bidding.

Lansdale gave him his own breakfast of pork chop, soft scram-bled eggs, hash with plenty of onion, toast, coffee, and guava juice. Lett ate in Lansdale's tent at a table with plates and silverware and could feel the curious eyes of those passing the tent flap outside. He shoveled in the food and, since he didn't have to do a sentry shift that morning, or any duty, went back to his pup tent afterward. His M1 carbine had been returned. It lay on his bedroll.

He made straight for his musette bag and prepared his syringe and shot up a double dose.

Not taking his medicine was why that had happened, he told himself. It was why he had that old nightmare again, and why he'd acted so instinctively, so ruthlessly to subdue three attackers. He wondered what Lansdale truly thought about it. Did those actions somehow prove to Lansdale that the treatment was working? Lett sighed at the sick notion and brooded at the thought of Lansdale in general until his chest was so tight his breath came out wheezy, not unlike the commando's. Lansdale had it wrong—that was not his old self. That was a sick person. All he needed was to take his dose.

***

The next morning, Lett and others climbed into two trucks that were still empty. The mango tree dig had yielded little apparently, but the ensuing interrogation surely offered something better. They traveled maybe an hour, tops. It was nearing noon, the sun rising directly above the valley like a glaring light bulb hanging from the very middle of a ceiling.

They drove between two seemingly impassable ridges and arrived at a place not even that sun at its highest point could find. More trucks were waiting here, big six-by-sixes—their power trains running to every wheel. Two more experts were there, Corps of Engineers men. Lansdale and the previous engineers had led the way over in a Plymouth and held another meeting of their minds. It was an All-American confab now. Kodama and Frankie weren't invited. Neither was needed, apparently—they had done their part for the effort.

Poor dead Reuben must have finally told them what he knew.

Lett and the other guards watched the perimeter, which consisted of only the trucks and the narrow, shaded road. As they did so, Lansdale and his cohorts slung their briefcases and disappeared into dense flowering shrubs, passing first between two palms many yards apart, but that could act as a telltale landmark if a person knew what to look for. They knew. They appeared to map out their way, counting footsteps and gauging angles and directions.

And later Lett heard a boom from somewhere inside the hillside, not an explosion, more like a wall falling over.

***

"You, there," a man said to Lett. One of the engineers had found him standing guard and now glared at him impatiently, all metal-framed glasses and civilian job boss haughtiness.

"What do you need?"

"We need a watchman. Lansdale says you're our man."

Just then Lett's insides squeezed up, and his stomach turned from an unholy smell that he recognized all too well. It was worse than rotting meat, or decaying jungle vegetation, or decomposing flesh. It was the gas from corpses left far too long in an enclosed space.

The engineer smelled it too and his already pale face colored green. "You recognize that," he said. Lett nodded. "We're just lucky it's been leaking out for a long time now; else we'd have to wait weeks before we could stand it." The engineer pulled nose plugs from a pocket and shoved them in. "Sorry, I don't have any more."

"You got cigs?"

The engineer handed Lett a pack of Camels. Lett shook out one, tore it in two and placed a half in each nostril. The engineer nodded in appreciation. "Well, if that isn't some GI ingenuity."

He led Lett straight into the side of the hill, through a tall opening that became a cave, then a cavern, then a wide tunnel. He put on a hard hat, although the tunnel was more than high and wide enough here. A couple mining lamps showed the way. Voices echoed from about thirty yards down the tunnel, which curved until the beams of flashlights appeared, then spotlights.

Lansdale and his latest team had gathered around a spot in the floor of the tunnel.

"Here is fine, just keep watch," the engineer told Lett and strode back to his place among the current meeting of the minds. Lett stood at the curve of the tunnel. He crossed his arms and cradled his carbine in them. He kept one eye on the entrance but one on the work at hand, and no one seemed to mind.

They crouched over the spot in the floor, dismayed and enrapt and inspired at once like schoolyard boys poking a downed bird to see if it would wake again. They had shiny prodding tools instead of sticks. Lansdale eventually placed an ear to the ground. After about twenty minutes of this, they marked their spot with a little flag, then they ate Spam sandwiches and drank coffee, the remainders of which they offered Lett. Then they moved on, waving at Lett to follow as if he were a slow-witted dog.

He slung his carbine and followed. He figured the place had been rigged and trip-wired to the hilt—Reuben must have revealed how to enter and avoid any booby traps. The tunnel led to a larger cavern. The rays of their flashlights bounced off walls, revealing angles and crags and hollows that the darkness washed away again like sand under surf, but when their lights combined, they made matters clear enough. The space was reinforced with concrete. Lett saw the remains of a steel wall or door. Beyond he saw rifles, pistols, a radio set, and empty ration boxes all strewn about, the requisite samurai sword, and three skeletons in Japanese uniforms. They wore telltale Japanese rubber-soled shoes with a separated big toe.

The sight had steeled the team, and made them slap one another's backs, and Lett could taste the metallic tang of men on a mission.

Lansdale eyed Lett, smiling. Lett looked away.

Lansdale led them on, the engineers whispering, sharing their findings. A few wooden boxes stood along the way, about the size of milk crates. One of the engineers was marking these with a wax pencil. Farther along, the cavern had partially collapsed, leaving mounds of rubble—Lett guessed this was how the stench had slowly released. Among the rocky debris was the wreckage of tracks and a handcar like miners used, and wiring and cage lights hung along the walls. Other tunnels branched off the cavern, Lett saw. Slabs were built into the floor here and there, some concrete, some steel, and he figured this was what they had been studying out in the entrance tunnel—another slab to break through, but one disguised to look like the earthen and rocky floor.

One of the shafts branching off looked man-made, or at least neatly carved out. This was more like a chamber. The team shined their lights on what had to be hundreds of rectangular wooden boxes, all stacked like ammo in a depot—or gold ingots in a vault, Lett thought. He immediately drove the thought from his mind.

More chambers appeared. The Japanese must have run out of boxes because now Lett saw platinum and gold bars in perfect rows. The flashlight beams on them ignited flashes and sparkles that made

Lett shield his eyes. Then he saw large urns holding gems and jewels and glistening nuggets. These loomed phosphorescent in the darkness when the light beams moved onward. Lansdale approached each find and touched it and spoke to it like a general visiting a field hospital; the engineers stood back like doctors and nurses ready for any urgency.

They trod farther, on the balls of their feet. Lett followed. At this point a red cord hung horizontally along the tunnel wall to guide anyone who might be getting lost in this maze. They saw other shafts blocked off but made to look natural; the engineers chipped away at these to reveal walls of concrete. Lansdale had a map out, Lett saw, and they consulted it more often, stopping to gather around it, leaving Lett in the dark. They hadn't bothered to offer him a flashlight. It made him feel more comfortable somehow.

Eventually they reached another access tunnel like the one they'd entered. Rounding the final bend, the group stopped in their tracks. Lett followed up behind, his eyes widening at what their flashlights revealed.

Piles of skeletons appeared, some wearing nothing but loincloths, but then Lett noticed it was their ragged underwear. Others wore the shreds of dungarees and uniforms. These were POWs—they had to be. Lett could imagine the way it went down. Like slaves had built the pyramids of old, these poor fellows labored to fill this cave for their Japanese masters before being walled inside. Their rags were so worn and meager that he couldn't be certain these were Allied POWs. He thought he saw a Marine cap but didn't want to get close enough to look. They could be Korean, Filipino, Australian, American. He suspected all of the above. Labor was labor.

One of the Corps of Engineers officers was vomiting, which brought more smell.

Lett couldn't stop staring. They must have numbered in the hundreds. Had they been clawing at the wall and gassed somehow? Or had they been left here to run out of air and starve, and here they lay to die? Or had they turned on one another, for the scraps of raw meat that would keep the last of them going?

Lansdale was standing close to Lett, so close Lett felt his breath on his ear. "May they rest in peace," Lansdale said. "This is why we fought."

He looked to Lett for some equally solemn confirmation. Lett could only snort. As victors, the Americans had and might still have all the best reasons for appropriating these spoils, he thought, on account of plenty of crimes. There was what the Japanese did in China, to Nanking alone. How they took no prisoners. The kamikaze terror. Not to mention Pearl Harbor. And there were these poor POWs left to die. Seizing spoils had surely been going on over here since the war, just as in the ETO. But the spoils part of this? No, this was not "why we fought." These so-called spoils belonged to their original owners.

Oddly, the gleam in Lansdale's eye returned. He patted Lett on the shoulder again. It was all Lett could do not to recoil. Then Lansdale stroked Lett's M1 carbine. "You know, you will have to use that thing eventually," he said.

And he strode off, back where they had come, back toward his treasure finds, leaving Lett in the dark. Suddenly, Lett felt so cold, more chilled than in any midnight hole in December in the Ardennes.

***

Lett and the rest of the sentries took turns guarding the perimeter over the next two days while laborers and carabao arrived to do their work inside the tunnels and caverns. Lett never saw Kodama or Frankie after they did their work on Reuben, and Lansdale only showed once or twice to reenter the caves and reemerge smirking. He had the laborers burn away foliage around the entrance, to make room. A few large items came out. A giant gold Buddha required two carabao and ten men moving it along cut logs. Apart from that, Lett heard the occasional booms and cracks, saw the engineers coming and going with their clipboards and briefcases. But most of the find did not come out.

On the third day, a captain Lett had never seen before—a spiffy command-staff type—came and left them new uniforms and gear, still without insignia or even markings but neat and tidy. Lett didn't have to be told to clean his weapon and make things shiny all around, and neither did the others. None of them wanted to catch a holy wrath from a staffer or worse yet, his master. Lansdale made the rounds, telling them to "look sharp, boys," and spewing another of his cheery homilies: "Act the part you play and become the part and the man, too!"

Lett knew why all along, but he hadn't figured on brass as high and as shiny as they got. He heard the roar of the new command car coming up the road. The burnt foliage opening was trimmed back to resemble an arched gateway. They stood at attention along the way. The command car pulled in close enough to brush leaves and fronds.

Army General Douglas MacArthur rose from the backseat followed by two staffers, including that spiffy captain. The general had his pipe in his mouth now, and his mouth scowled slightly like in that famous photo of him wading ashore at Leyte, returning to retake the Philippines just south of here. Or, Lett wondered, was that just a smile the grand leader was stifling? Lett, for one, would have bet that gold Buddha alone on the latter.

Before he strode inside that cave the general slowed half a step, just enough to give Lett a most honorable and respectful nod.

19.

Lett returned on a fast-running cargo ship, reuniting with Jock and others they'd flown over with. Jock sized up the fittings, paint scheme, signs, and sound of the smooth engine and told Lett their vessel had probably been refitted during the war and commissioned to fight as a Q-ship or any manner of disguised, undercover merchant vessel with concealed weaponry. The cargo hold was off limits to them, but Lett figured that some of what was found in those caverns was making its way back to the US Territory of Hawaii, and that they were on board as extra watchmen if needed. Their cramped quarters, with its protruding bolts and bars, stacked bunks, and stale smells of his fellow humans, took Lett back to a wartime hospital ship where he'd despaired so much that he'd wanted to leap into the cold Atlantic and end it all. But this time, inside the head of this cargo boat crossing the postwar Pacific, he shot up his trusty dose—and he swore it was helping.

The men were able to lounge on the top deck of the clandestine trawler, and Lett sprawled in the sun on a pile of netting for the first few hours. The breeze and blue sky and open horizon should've brightened his thoughts. It helped him focus and simplify, like breaking down his M1 carbine did. Again he tried to justify his actions, and even the acts of Lansdale and Frankie, by recalling how understanding General MacArthur had seemed. Winning the war hadn't been pretty and keeping the peace wasn't going to be, either. Thus, men like Lansdale. Someone had to complete that dirty work. He just couldn't be a part of it, not that way. It spooked him too much. He had to get clear of Lansdale somehow. But how?

Jock wasn't helping his mood. Jock sulked. Jock joined him on the pile of netting, tugging on the coarse greasy cords. "I don't know what you done on your special patrol or secret mission or whatever," he said. "But I ended up getting duty. Mine was no joyride."

Lett hadn't told Jock about what he'd done. A grunt always kept things in right after. Maybe a part of him didn't want Jock to know, to be sullied by it. Maybe he didn't want what made him choke the commando or, worse yet, what Lansdale and Frankie had done to start catching like some fast-spreading onboard disease. Scurvy with a death wish, reopening previously healed wounds.

Jock kept opening and squeezing a fist. "They took us to this one hill," he said. "It was green like jungle but only a thin veneer, all rock underneath. There was a cave or a cavern or whatever. We holed up. Tents. Anyways, they must have known I don't do so well with caves and caverns, what have you, so they kept me posted outside. The others went inside that hill. They took a prisoner in there with them. A local. Just a boy."

"Hold on," Lett said. "When was this? How long were you there?"

"No more than a day. They kept us in reserve for a couple days before that. Put us up in some rural inn for the duration, real shit-hole. But I had a suite. Well, you know me—I went on a bender of that rum they got and that basi wine they got or whatever the local hooch is called."

That meant Jock and others were made to wait for his own operation to finish.

"Who was all there?" Lett said.

Jock just shook his head.

"Lansdale there?"

"Early on he was. Right down to that class ring of his and his irritating, peppy slogans."

Lansdale wore a class ring, Lett recalled, a big one. Jock had an eye for things. That meant Lansdale was shuttling between their operations after Reuben.

Jock added, "I already didn't like how that Lansdale was showing off to ol' Dugout Doug back at that special meeting we guarded. But this? This was different. And, there was another one there."

"Describe him."

Jock described Frankie, the tattoos, the hulk of him. "He looked part Flip maybe, hard to tell."

"The one from the Hilo boat?" Lett asked, to confirm. He had to be sure. That meant Frankie was still in country after Reuben. But if Frankie or Lansdale were flying back, they could beat them by days.

"The very one," Jock said.

"I saw him, too. His name is Frankie."

Jock didn't speak a while. Maybe he was waiting for Lett to elaborate. Lett waited it out. They stared out at the shifting, rolling sea.

"Over the course of that day," Jock continued, "I heard screams coming from inside that hill, had to be their prisoner, and sounds that might have been electricity, and others like hammering, but tapping-like, what have you . . ."

"Any engineer types show up, Corps of Engineers, Seabees even?"

"Nope. Not a one."

"Where were you?"

"Not too far from where Dugout Doug had that special meeting. Still Cagayan Valley."

"He ever show up again? The general himself?"

Jock smiled. "You kidding me now or what?"

Lett just shrugged.

"But that Frankie fellow comes strolling out of that hill, big grin, like he just got off a carousel ride. Even patted me on the back. He had that look, Lett. You know the one. The guys on the line who truly don't give a shit anymores. The ones who enjoy it too much, who you'd call a psychopath killer back home and lock him up, throw away the key to the straightjacket. But this Frankie, see, he had all the keys and they were golden. He certainly enjoyed doing what he did to the boy. Now, if that prisoner was some Jap war criminal, what have you, maybe I could see it on account of all the Japanese did to his country—"

"He's Hawaiian," Lett blurted. He couldn't help himself. "Hawaiian Filipino. Kanani knows him, from Honolulu. She says to stay clear."

"Oh. Our Miss Kanani, from camp? Then you got to warn her Lett, you got to. I know it's top secret and all, but—"

"I did." They hadn't seen Frankie yet on The Preserve itself, only on other parts of the island. Lett only hoped it stayed that way. "Though, she can sure take care of herself," he added.

"True. True. I seen that about her."

"So, then, Frankie and company never found what they wanted?" Lett said. "Never got it?"

"How do you figure?"

"No trucks came for hauling away items out of that cave?"

"No. I reckon that poor boy led Frankie on a wild goose chase, meaning that boy never knew, or he never was telling. They got a strong honor system."

Jock fell silent. After a while, his head shot up as if Lett just arrived. "Yours was different, though, wasn't it?" he said.

"My duty? I'm not supposed to talk about it."

"I told you about my shift."

Lett held out hands. "There's nothing to tell. But, okay. There was an interrogation, too. Locals gave us a little trouble but nothing we couldn't handle. That's pretty much it."

"Well, word is, you did all right."

"I just did what I know," Lett said.

Jock didn't push it. He knew the unspoken rule. A grunt only talks if he needs to.

Lett didn't tell him that, on his last day in his own remote stretch of steep hills lining the Cagayan Valley, General MacArthur had stridden into the tunnel with Lansdale and staffers and stayed inside there a good hour or more. A meeting inside Lansdale's tent had lasted another two. After the mighty general sped off, Lett and others were given local rum and San Miguel beers and were told to drink their fill because they were leaving in the morning.

Jock was glaring at Lett. "I don't like an interrogation like that, Lett. It's not right."

"I don't, either."

"Don't tell anyone I told you."

"Of course not. Fuck 'em all."

Jock grinned, sat up. "I'm sorry I got mad about things."

"It's okay. I'm sorry for my next time. Tell you what, let's run a tab."

They laughed, but not even their smiles lasted long. Jock started tugging at the greasy netting again.

"I shouldn't have been talking about that Lansdale," he said eventually. "Me, I just don't want to screw up. I have to get myself back in the regular Corps. I'm a lifer Marine, Lett. Got me? Maybe a Gunner, a Mustang even. I'll do anything to get back in. It's all I have. Otherwise I'm doomed, see. We're all doomed."

***

A week after sailing from the Philippines, Lett was back on the Big Island of the Territory of Hawaii, inside The Preserve. Here he sat again, on the porch of his bungalow. They'd given him a day off. He was nearly halfway through it, the humid afternoon pestering him.

He broke matters down all over, and it didn't end up clean like an M1. His assignment might have been top secret, but they weren't even designated as a unit or even a branch of the military. They might as well have been a mining operation with hired tin badges. Why didn't they just use local muscle? Why drag them all the way to the Philippines? The reasons sent a shudder through him. No unit designation or official postings or trip papers meant that it could all be disproved. No paper trail. No witnesses.

There was top secret, and then there was top secret forever.

Lett got another shudder, left over from being so close to Lansdale for a few days. Lansdale was simply a new incarnation of that same old rear-line player during the war who acted like a daredevil but had the game sewn up so tight he never lost. From his cocky stride to that large class ring he wore, Lansdale reminded Lett of one of those happy-go-lucky college students who belonged to every possible club and one certain revered fraternity, which, Lett suspected, gave the man a secret knowledge about how things worked in the world to benefit only a few. A fortune-favored and in-the-know comer like Lansdale only appeared to care about certain matters that fed his winnings, such as patriotism and the Red Menace and the Good Book, because he knew this was how the deal was sealed. One hell of a sweetheart pact had been struck long ago, by his father's fathers, a backroom handshake passed down to the inheritors, each heir more fortunate. Sure, someday the mojo would run out. But that only made a possible final inheritor like Lansdale all the more reckless.

That thought had launched him out of bed and onto the porch. He simply could not sleep, and lying awake had nearly been worse than the assignment. He'd been stuck there reassessing far too much and wishing he knew more. He'd been with The Preserve a few weeks. It was now March. He was getting his cure as promised, and he couldn't fault Selfer or even Lansdale if it didn't end up working. But this was also some kind of secret base. It held about fifty personnel at any given time as far as he could tell. Some came and went quick, some looking shakier than others. He thought about those tunnels underneath the complex. He wondered if any personnel were down there now. He even wondered if the camp brought in people—prisoners, let's call them what they were—who never left the tunnels, never even knew about a camp above them. The tunnels had to be operating, he figured. He had never again seen the men who had guarded him down below, but why should he? They would be needed down there. That troop might have separate quarters somewhere because of their work and could even get in from some entrance outside of camp. Meanwhile, up above, more were being trained for covert operations as far as Lett could tell. He imagined them helping rebels overthrow the new Communist governments cropping up or looming throughout Southeast Asia. Some of these men were housed in another corner of camp and had already received heaps of instruction, training, drilling. Lett still heard their weapons pop sometimes, and he thanked his dose for not letting that get to him. Here on the other side of the tracks were the hard luck jobs, the fatigue cases, the near mental defectives. Each needed their own particular cure. Each got it different. Certain troubles were avoided, certain tendencies cultivated. But they all had their inclinations. And those could be nurtured, like a noxious weed meant to destroy all.

Like a certain guy who took out a commando and two native scouts with his bare hands.

That final thought made him bring his dose and his whisky out to the porch, keeping both at the ready next to his Adirondack chair. He couldn't help thinking Lansdale was singling him out for something. He had proven, inadvertently, mechanically, that he had special skills, and those skills seemed undeniably tied to his cure. Was that all this was, just a way to make him perform the way he had before he started cracking back at the very end of the war? He wasn't in this for that. No. A robotic killer was never who he wanted to be. He took a deep breath, hoping to catch a scent of those bougainvilleas nearby, got nothing but the dead night air. He sighed, thinking that sometimes it seemed like the dose part of the cure was the only thing keeping him from cracking up altogether and for good.

Lett shot up right there on the porch. He washed it down with a belt of whisky. He didn't care who saw.

Kanani saw. She was standing at a corner of the stairs, eyeing him.

"Welcome back," she said.

"Aloha," he said.

"You okay? You don't look so okay."

What was he supposed to tell her? Kanani wasn't doing much better herself, it seemed. Her shoulders slumped, her dress had a stain on it, and her hair was pinned up sloppily. And her eyes looked puffy.

He waved her up and reached for the whisky bottle. They shared an awkward hug, Lett patting her on the back like a distant relative. Kanani dropped into the Adirondack chair next to his and sighed. They looked out. His lane of bungalows was quieter than usual this morning.

"You're still here," he said. "How goes the recon? Find out anything new?"

Kanani shrugged. Smiled. "We'll see. Getting closer." She looked away.

"Tell me," Lett said.

"Charlie—Colonel Selfer, he's looking for new friends, it seems."

"So now it's 'Charlie'? What sort of looking?"

"We went on an outing. A picnic."

Lett wasn't surprised. He knew what she was getting into. "Just be careful. He came to me once, too."

She stared at him.

"Oh," he said. "You went to him. I see." That stung a little. He drank. He held up the bottle for her, but she waved it away.

"Still no Miss Mae, I take it?" he said.

She shook her head.

"How's the boogie house?"

She shook her head again. "Slow going. I'm starting to wonder how I'm supposed to get ahead, if I ever was supposed to. Like I already did what they needed me for, maybe. Those important visitors left the same time as you."

"Can you tell me about them?"

She held up her hands. "One was Japanese, a real thug. Wouldn't be surprised if he was a war criminal."

Lett sat forward. "What did he look like?"

"Plenty of scars, and hands made for fighting. Dents in his head."

Lett lowered deep into his chair, slowly. *Kodama*, he thought. Lansdale was manipulating even his closest partners in crime.

She cocked her head so sideways that a flower would've fallen from her ear if she'd been wearing one. "Wait, you saw that one, too?"

Lett didn't answer.

"Let me guess—you can't say any more, yeah?"

"Yeah. Top secret. Lansdale's orders." Lett sighed. "All right, look. His name is Kodama. But that's all I can tell you."

Her face opened up, and her eyes widened. "No, there's more. I can tell. I can see it on your face." She shot out of her chair. "You saw Frankie there again?"

He nodded.

"Ho, you saw all of them. All but Mae? Auwe. Shit . . ."

She reached for the whisky. It still had a little left. He twisted off the cap for her. She lowered back with the bottle and muttered something in Pidgin.

"How did you get back here?" she asked him after a while.

"On a boat, into Kona this time. A smaller cargo ship. Fast, too."

"But you don't know where that cargo went?"

"No. They drove us up in that old disguised jalopy of a pickup."

"Okay, all right," she said. "So, we just keep going, right? Me with my cure, and you with yours."

"We go for broke," he said.

"Go for broke." She smiled for him. But her eyes were racing, and she produced a Camel for thinking, which she lit with her gold Chinese lighter, and she never did pass back the bottle.

20.

K anani's head floated and blurred a little from the whisky, but at least it helped her stay calm and think. She had apologized to Wendell for downing the last of his hooch and kissed him on the forehead and promised to bring him back something to eat. First, though, she had ground to cover. She had the afternoon off and a few hours before dark.

She roamed the camp, down the other lane of bungalows, through other clearings, passing by the mess hall and bar, offices, latrines, storeroom, training grounds, working up a sweat under the high sun. She ducked into the forest for shade and marched as far as she could get on the paths, reaching perimeter fences. She encountered few others the whole way. She didn't know if the camp being empty was a good or a bad sign for the future, but it helped her stay discreet.

She had to find a way into those tunnels. She had seen one possibility, just a hatch in a camouflaged outbuilding no bigger than a small shed and locked up tight—that matched what Lett had told her. He must have exited that when he first had his incident. She'd seen other signs, such as concealed housings for ventilation fans and ducts no bigger than chicken coops, and there were hills just up the mountain, but these were outside the perimeter fence, beyond the high forest even. She saw lava-gravel roads leading to them. Lett had mentioned other roads branching off back from Hilo. Maybe the trucks had gone there?

She took more trails and passed through the corners of camp, the bushes and ferns swelling around her. She reached the edge of the thicker tropical forest. The trails only skirted it. She sized up the wall of foliage just as she had the one behind Miss Mae's bungalow that let her and Wendell escape from Frankie. She shot through, kept going, twisting and pushing the branches clear, the fronds and gnarly boughs slapping and scratching at her, and eventually the forest loosened up.

She looked down into a little gully. A narrow road ran down to it, from somewhere outside of camp. A skinny side path was cut out of lava rock. She followed that lower, grasping at rocks and leaves and flowers because her head was floating again from the whisky and humidity. She neared the end of the gully, where she saw a large black hole in the rising rock wall—a lava tube. Ferns grew all around it, wanting to poke their fronds inside, the spiky leaves making the orifice look like a giant green sea anemone about one story high. The road ended there. But there was also that lava tube.

She heard a *clink*, a *clank*.

She shot over to a bush along the path and squatted behind it.

She peered out, focusing on the lava tube hole. The clink-clank must have been a door; a metal door, a lock.

She heard footsteps.

A man emerged from the tunnel. He wore Army coveralls like a mechanic but they were clean as new. A holster and long knife hung off his web belt. His silhouette seemed to grow as he passed her and headed up the road when it should've been getting smaller.

It was no optical illusion. It was Frankie.

Her skin rippled, cold and hot and then colder.

21.

Early the next morning, right before dawn, Lett heard a noise outside. He was already wide-awake, rigid on his bed. He rose mechanically and cracked his door open.

Selfer stood alone out in the lane, in khaki shorts, his white open-collar shirt unbuttoned, hair slicked back. He might have been a statue. His hands were clasped behind his back. Eventually he moved, something sparkled—he'd drawn a chromium flask from his rear pocket and took a long, slow drink. Lett remembered Selfer had the flask during the war. He once offered Lett a drop, but Lett had refused it. Selfer pocketed the flask and his statue-like stance returned. Maybe he was thinking about that con man father of his he was so fixated on, wondering if he'd finally bested the old man yet, or if he ever truly would. That was one thing they shared—deadbeat fathers. Or maybe he was just thinking about another date with Kanani, prime rib and dessert and . . . Lett imagined Kanani at the Main House, sunning by the pool in one of those scanty new two-piece bathing suits in an aloha print, that flower back in her hair now.

He pushed the door open, it banged at the wall.

Selfer swung around. He stepped up onto the porch. "Welcome back," he chirped. "And good luck! You must have done something right, because you're getting your next mission."

Already? "Assignment," Lett said. "They called it an assignment before."

"Well, Lansdale is calling this one a mission, so that's what it is," Selfer muttered, his chirping now stifled. "Look at it this way: You'll never have to do KP again. That part of your duty is over. Isn't that just the best? Congratulations."

Selfer was still trying to sound upbeat, but it came off like a dad telling junior they were going on a fun trip but the truth was they were skipping town and a heap of unpaid tabs.

"When do I go?" Lett said.

"Now."

Something about the way Selfer said it made Lett's leg twitch with bad feeling. And if it was now, why hadn't Selfer just knocked on his door instead of loitering around? And why not just send a runner over? Things were clearly troubling Selfer enough to make the man stall.

Lett had to find out more before he was going anywhere, let alone on a mission. But they couldn't do it here, not where he lived, not out in the open. He ducked inside and pulled on the rest of his khakis, a field cap, and sunglasses. He also grabbed his musette bag with his dose.

"Follow me," he told Selfer and started off.

Selfer shrugged but followed. Lett picked up the pace and followed a trail until they were far into the woods. They assumed patrol distance, single file with Lett five yards ahead of Selfer who had likely never marched like this since boot camp, if then. Craggy bark on knotty trees hung like flaking paint. An insect buzzed like a small electric motor seizing up. Lett eyed the perimeter for sentries. He saw none. Selfer, to his credit, was watching their backs. Lett reached a thicket of flowering shrubs and went down on one knee like a squad leader.

Selfer went down on a knee and tried a smile. "Look at us. Like we're sneaking cigarettes behind the schoolhouse." Lett didn't smile. "All right," Selfer added. "You want the latest score, is that it?"

"What do you know about a Japanese goon named Kodama?"

Selfer started. He shushed Lett, his index finger to his lips.

Lett saw what Selfer had spotted: a camp sentry was passing by some twenty yards away, head down, carbine bobbing on his shoulder, moving away from them.

It was Jock Quinn. They had him doing sentry work, and Jock probably saw it as a feather in his cap. Lett's heart sunk a little.

They waited it out. "Very well," Selfer said. "For your ears only?"

"None other."

"First things first. One Edward Lansdale. I've been looking into him. He used to be attached to SCAP intelligence section, sure, but he was operating out of Manila and he got himself moving up real fast."

"SCAP being MacArthur—"

"Shut it," Selfer hissed. "Do not mention the general's name. They do not get linked, see? Not anymore."

"I see."

"That Lansdale, he's a real conniver. Let's go further back. He wasn't even in the war! Wrote advertising copy for the OSS out of San Francisco. Office of Strategic Services. Probably ran a nice tab at the Top of the Mark. When Washington disbanded the OSS, this conniver Lansdale got himself sent to the Pacific by the head of OSS Donovan, Donovan wanting his own boys in the right places."

"So, just to be sure—Lansdale has never been a doctor."

Selfer sneered. "That's rich. No. He just knows what gets results."

"Top of the Mark?"

"Forget it. Let's just say his spoon is silver and we're not talking plated. Ah, but these days Lansdale is making his own play. SCAP staff never liked him much because he's sharp and slick, yet strange, I tell you, but now he's got his own sponsors and they might have more pull. Hear he's getting a new rank in the new US Air Force branch, just to keep all the players happy."

He already has that, Lett wanted to say.

With a slight speeding of his heart, he realized that Selfer was confiding in him. To Selfer, he might even be something like an ally. And Lett wondered, with a shiver, just how much Selfer really knew about the big picture behind closed doors. The notion tightened his asshole with horror more than anything. What if Selfer was only a shinier version of himself here?

"What you're saying is," Lett said, "that he's landed himself loads more free reign."

"And how." Selfer was holding out the chromium flask. Lett took it and sipped. He was expecting rum but it was Johnnie Walker, the good stuff. It went down all right.

"You've had this hip flask a long time," Lett said, handing it back.

"It was my father's." Selfer shook his head. "I stole it from him."

Saying that made Selfer put a Camel in his mouth that he didn't light.

"Tell me something," Selfer added. "How's the treatment? Are you still feeling better?"

"As long as I take my dose," Lett said.

"I'll take that as a yes."

They shared another slug from the flask.

"What about this goon Kodama?" Lett said.

"The Jap? Strike that—we don't call them 'Japs' anymore, or 'Nips.' Some of them are our friends now."

"He looked like a friend like an SS-Man does a traffic cop."

Selfer just stared at the ground, like a dice player who'd just emptied his pockets.

"But you can't talk about him," Lett added.

"Hands are tied, Wendell. Your turn."

"My turn how?"

"Kanani."

"I wouldn't say she's an equivalent."

"I didn't say that. Have you told her?"

"About where I was? That what you mean? No."

Selfer took a breath, looked around. "And Kanani wasn't asking? Probing?"

"Snooping, you mean?"

"I mean."

"No."

Selfer squatted closer. "Listen. You think she's all right? Someone to trust?"

"I do."

Selfer nodded at that, taking notes in his mind, boxes checked. "Something for you, in any case—consider it a booby prize. I once heard that name Kanani keeps mentioning on the QT."

"What name?"

"Come off it, Lett. Mae. Chinese, right? 'Miss Mae,' she calls her."

"Oh. How? For what?"

"Overheard it in a meeting. Maybe I wasn't supposed to be there. Never heard it again. Okay, learned enough? Good. You two just remember that. Now, time to follow me—I got a mission briefing to get you to."

***

Lett got good steak and fresh eggs. He knew what that meant. Whenever troops got a special hot meal up on the line it meant they were being sent into one hell of a meat grinder. But this time Lett was a troop of one. He ate his special meal alone in a windowless room at the Main House while he was briefed on his assignment. To soften the blow, they threw fresh fruit into the bargain, mango and pineapple. Lett hadn't touched the aromatic coffee, but when the dirty lowdown started to sink in, he gulped down the fine stuff to look alive and sharpen up and absorb each and every detail that may save him or fuck him.

Selfer himself led the briefing at first, just like old times. Selfer didn't bother with upbeat now. Over the bamboo wallpaper hung maps of Honolulu on the island of Oahu. Lett was to enter the city and bring back someone Selfer called a "target person."

Then Lansdale strode in, and Selfer stepped aside. That old boiling heat swelled inside Lett again, but he kept a lid on it. Lansdale's jovial way cloaked what was an iron glove. Peppering his instructions with his upbeat sayings, Lansdale told Lett that if his target wasn't cooperating, then Lett was to eliminate with the "merry utmost of unholy bias," grinning all the while as if delivering an original limerick. This, Lansdale added, was the least they could do for all the civilians their target had helped the Japanese kill—for Lett's target had sold out hundreds if not thousands of civilians in China and later in the Philippines. "They severed the heads of children," Lansdale reminded Lett. But he sounded as if he were selling detergent on a radio show. On top of that, Lansdale was telling him to be prepared to kill someone for reasons that Lansdale, and only Lansdale, gave him—reasons Lett was to take as simple facts.

Selfer, meanwhile, played the diligent boy scout to Lansdale the frisky scoutmaster. It made Lett's stomach turn, but he shoveled the eggs in anyhow. His gut only turned further when he realized he felt something like empathy for Selfer, who kept his head lowered and his hands clasped in front of him like Lett imagined a man about to be beheaded by a samurai sword-wielding Japanese officer might do—all he had to do was kneel down and it was done. Lett listened to Lansdale, nodded, and glared at Selfer when he had the slightest chance, but Selfer wouldn't return the gaze.

"Good luck, hero," Lansdale said.

After he strode out, Lett glared all he wanted.

Selfer waited a moment before stepping over to him. "This will get you cured," he said through clenched teeth. "It'll be the test of your treatment. Your final stage. You succeed, you're home free."

"That's good. You memorize that?"

"This is no time for jokes," Selfer said.

"Who's joking? You don't like the sound of this, I can tell."

"Just do it," Selfer snapped, "and get back safe."

"It all sounds so familiar. Sir."

Lett expected a dressing-down, spiteful words, something. But Selfer only dragged in a deep breath and sighed. He handed Lett a wallet with civilian ID in the name of one Wendell Lett, which Lett didn't like, not at all, and he imagined it was their way of keeping him honest. But whose fault was that? After all, he had chosen all of this.

The next hour was filled with rushed preparations. Lett was sure to take his dose. A clerk in the quartermaster's Quonset hut issued him his civilian clothes: linen trousers, rubber-soled sneakers for quiet, a lightweight driver's cap and sunglasses for hiding his face, and a muted aloha shirt loose enough to conceal a holster. He got a Colt pistol, this one brand-new, feeling lighter somehow than the ones he'd held during the war. He knew Colts. He'd carried one on night patrols especially. Despite that, they had him report to an instructor on the training ground.

It was Jock Quinn. Lett almost didn't recognize Jock striding up, his posture straighter than a flagpole and a voice like a snare drum in a way that could only be a Marine's.

"Good morning," Lett said.

"Morning," Jock said. "Let's get to it."

Lett spared Jock the sick wisecracks. And Jock didn't make small talk, joke, or even cuss. He made sure Lett remembered the weapon, had him take it apart, load it, arm it. Next Jock handed Lett a suppressor, which civilians called "silencers" in crime pictures. Lett didn't know the suppressor. It was as long as the gun itself and not all that silent. It made a sharp crack, like branches being snapped, which sounded to Lett too much like trees busting. The suppressor was strapped to his leg, where it would stay. He told himself he wouldn't have to use that piece any more than he would the gun.

"Get back safe, wherever they're sending you," Jock said.

"Amen to that," Lett said.

22.

Late that afternoon, Lett entered Honolulu harbor on a fishing boat from the Big Island. They passed a clock tower bearing the word ALOHA. Once docked, Lett walked out to the main road as instructed and met a cab. The cabbie asked, "Where to, buddy?" and Lett replied, "Pacific Heights, friend."

The cabbie had red hair under his cap and more eyes on Lett in the rearview mirror than on the road ahead. Lett happened to ask him where the red-light district was and cabbie said they already drove past it, down Hotel Street to the left—thus the neon lights Lett had seen out of the corner of his eye. That had once been Kanani's world, Lett recalled, and her stepping-stone to The Preserve.

They drove down a street named Bishop and then up a road called Pali heading inland, the hills above town looming before them. Lett saw signs for grocers and drug stores, bars and churches, in Chinese and Japanese. Palm trees leaned his way as if to greet him, and they passed a cop wearing oversize white gloves directing traffic in the middle of the street from a booth topped with an umbrella. And yet, if Lett squinted, he could imagine his surroundings to be those of any small American city, something nearly foreign to him these days.

The cabbie was eyeing him through the rearview mirror. "You all right, Mac?"

"Sure I am. Sure."

The cabbie drove him up a road that narrowed as it wound up into the hills, lined in stretches by black lava stones or overhanging ferns or both. Pacific Heights. It would have been expensive real estate in any mainland American city, but here many houses looked modest. After a couple bends the cabbie delivered Lett right to the address Lett had never uttered—that they never actually gave him.

The cabbie passed slow, kept going, and dropped Lett off around the next bend up. He tipped his hat. "So long," was all he said.

From the road, Lett had an expansive view of the city along the water far below, and beyond it a stretch of ocean beach named Waikiki and that giant volcanic rock of a hill—Diamond Head, it was called.

The target location was a modest stucco house with a flat roof. It sat atop an open carport that housed a nondescript Ford and was inundated with palms and long-leaf bushes as if the jungle were growing right over it, though Lett imagined it was intentional on a property like this. The lot was set into the hill and, sitting as it did on a turn, had no direct neighbors. Most blinds were shut, but the ones in the window next to the front door were cracked, just barely.

Lett walked up the steps and knocked. No one answered.

The target was supposed to be here. It was supposed to be a woman. She was supposed to be alone. Lansdale gave her the code-name of Jade. She would answer to that.

Maybe she was sleeping? Lett knocked again, got nothing. He went around back, through a snug backyard that was secluded like a jungle ridge. He stood at the rear door to the kitchen. The blinds were shut.

The door opened. Lett recognized Jade from the photo Lansdale showed him. She looked Chinese, about forty, thick mop of black hair, wide shiny cheeks. She could've been anything from a school-teacher to a simple, happy merchant. She wore blue pajamas.

"Jade," Lett stated.

Her eyes drooped a split second. "Please, enter."

She walked Lett through the kitchen into a front room, Lett eyeing a hallway but hearing nothing, seeing nothing. It smelled like nothing apart from a whiff of something fried hours ago. Shadows filled the room, sliced by orange rays of light coming through the barely open blinds. Inside, even in the front room, no one could see them from the street. It was too high up.

Lett had his Colt pistol out.

"Do not worry," she said. "No one else here."

Lett held the pistol at his hip, pointed down, finger off the trigger and on the slide for the woman to see. He wouldn't bother with the suppressor.

"There's a boat waiting for us," he said. "I'm to bring you back." He spoke his words slowly in case she didn't understand. He sounded motorized this way, like some movie hit man; it couldn't be helped.

"Oh," she said, "I see." Her face had hardened. She spoke good enough English. "They tell you what I did?" she said. "I do many bad thing, many, many. But not what they tell you."

"They don't tell me anything. They tell me to do a job." Lett thought of the tunnels below camp now as he spoke.

"Sure, Joe. You their messenger man."

"Don't call me Joe."

"I didn't kill people. I was liaison for them. Middleman, you call it. Drugs. Treasures."

"For who?" Lett blurted. Of course, he wasn't supposed to ask questions.

"The Japanese. Imperial Army. You ever hear of Golden Lily?"

"No, and I don't want to. Let's go. Get a robe on or your clothes, your choice."

"Wait. Please . . ." She lowered to her knees.

"Don't do that. You won't like where it leads." Lett stood inside a shadow. From there he tried to sound tough, but his voice creaked.

"I won't go with you," she said. "They send you here to kill me. Yes? If I don't go?"

"You got about one minute."

Lett's instructions were to make her drive the two of them down to the harbor in her car, the modest two-door Ford in the carport. But his stomach prickled, as if threads were being yanked through it by needles. Finally, he said, "We go in your car. We get your car keys."

"You hear of the name Kodama?"

"No."

"Lansdale?"

"No."

"Frankie Baptiste?"

"Shut up. Shut your trap, will you?" Lett bounded out of the shadow and towered over her, again acting just like a hit man.

"They send you here to kill me, only kill me. Because they know I won't go. They give you order. I no come, so I die. So kill." She gritted her teeth and bared them to Lett.

Lett took a deep breath. He put on a grimace, tried to make it form a smile. "You're stalling. You're good, but you're stalling all the same. It's not going to work."

"They don't need me," she muttered. "Why go through middleman when they can get direct from source? That sounds like Lansdale, does it not?"

"It's not going to work," Lett repeated.

"Just listen. You know why? Why they send you?"

He lied: "Here's what I do know: If I don't bring you back, I don't get paid. I like to get paid."

"What you don't know? The men who own you, they have their own intelligence plan, they worse than any OSS or what come next now. Secret fund. You know about it?" She was the one grimacing now.

Lett glared. He heard himself say, "What do you know about it?"

"Too much. There is a certain person they want to die. They plan to assassinate."

"Stop it. You're stalling again. Get up off your knees."

"Please, listen. They plan to assassinate . . . one very important man. I cannot say his name." She gasped as if she'd just uttered the name by accident.

"And then what?" Lett said.

"What else? Big confusion. They use the chaos. The people weak. They take over." She was whispering now.

"Take over what?"

She held up a finger. "No. I tell too much." She jumped up, but Lett waved his gun and she stayed in her spot.

She looked him up and down. "What's your name?" she said.

"It isn't. It isn't anything."

"I know a journalist. That is why I here. I will leave for mainland. I will tell him many things. That's why they send you. So I don't do something like tell a journalist."

Her eyes glazed, all wet. Maybe she was sad. She might be on opium. Maybe she was crazy. Then again, she might be mad with despair from the things she'd done and seen. Lett and Jock and the rest of them, they certainly understood that.

Yet Lett didn't so much as blink. He didn't forget what Selfer had told him. Maybe this really was his big chance. Maybe this woman was the consummate operator, and she was just reeling him in. She could have a weapon, or close access to one.

He gripped the Colt with both hands and trained it on her. He pushed off the safety with his thumb.

Her eyes flashed seeing it—she'd probably assumed he already had the safety off. The hammer was cocked, after all. But now Lett meant it. The shine in her eyes went dark.

"Very well," she said.

And then it hit Lett. Her looks were so nondescript that he hadn't realized who this Jade might be. He would've expected a lissome younger woman in a slinky red dress with Chinese dragons, a cigarette holder, a knowing smile. He'd seen too many movies. They all had.

A shiver shot through him.

"Miss Mae?" he said. "You're Miss Mae?"

Her eyes widened, shined again. "Why, yes. It is I. Who—"

Footsteps. The whoosh of a car, pulling away. Miss Mae listened, then hissed something in Chinese and "shhhh" to Lett.

They stepped over to the front window together, Lett touching the barrel of the Colt to Mae's ribs. The sun was only an ember left on the horizon, casting all in silhouette.

Figures were coming up the stairs, a man, two smaller figures—children.

Mae swallowed a gasp. "They are not supposed to come back," she muttered to Lett, "they stay with a friend—"

"Who wasn't?

"My husband. Children."

"Jesus. Okay. Open it."

Lett slid the pistol back inside his shirt as Mae opened the door smiling. She and the man she called her husband exchanged words in Chinese, which made the man search the louvered sundown light for Lett, who was standing back. Lett held up his left hand, smiled. The children rushed into the room, a boy and girl of no more than ten wearing matching outfits with aloha print, but the boy had short pants, the girl a skirt. They only glanced at Lett before rushing by, and Lett figured they were used to visitors. The husband was small and wore a threadbare suit of gray that made him look older than Jade. He was already trembling, sweating.

Mae kept talking to her husband and rapidly, the husband eyeing Lett with widening whites of his eyes, nodding along.

Lett felt like someone had poured sand down his throat. He felt at his shirt for his pistol.

The children chased each other around the sofa, the boy reached for a light switch. The husband barked at him in Chinese. The boy stopped, dead still, and the girl did the same, like recruits on maneuvers.

Lett kept close to the front door. Inside him, the old gears kicked into position. He would have to do them all in, the gears confirmed. These people had seen his face. He had killed a girl before. Of course he would do it. It was logical in the moment. What came later didn't factor into it. He had the machinery already working inside him to do it. The whole apparatus was pumping away now, numbing his nerves and calming his blood. It sent signals of that pure cold reason to his brain. And all nagging emotion drained away, pushed out through valves that opened only for situations like this.

The husband wasn't a threat, but he would have to be the first one—to shock them, and then Mae, and then . . . He might even use that suppressor, just in case.

"Keep them all in this room," he said to Mae. "No one leaves it."

The children stared, not knowing English apparently. Mae spoke to them, and they sat on the sofa and chatted casually. The husband joined them. Mae must've lied to them in Chinese. Maybe she promised a presentation from Lett. Maybe she said he was here to save them.

Mae turned to him. "Keep smiling," she said in English. "They think you're a friend."

"None of them understand us?"

"None of them," Mae muttered, losing her put-on face. "They are innocent."

"Just, keep it together," Lett said through his smile.

He couldn't look at the sofa. If he did, he would see the boy kicking his legs that didn't quite reach the floor, something Lett always did in the orphanage and got in trouble for. He would see that the girl had her black hair in long braided pigtails, just like the German girl he had to kill on that snafu mission in enemy-occupied Cologne—it was that or be found out.

Mae's face reflected the last flash of sundown. In a moment, it would go dim.

A burn of vomit rose up his throat and he tried to swallow it, and the machinery inside him barely kept it down.

Everyone fell silent. Time seemed to stop a moment. Lett wasn't sure how long. His gears weren't working.

"What options do you have?" he heard himself say to Mae.

"Options? Yes! I have one," Mae replied, the words popping out as if she'd been holding her breath, "just one, please, I can tell you, please."

"Why didn't you tell me before?"

Mae uttered a bitter laugh. She threw a glance at her family. "You never ask."

"All right, all right," Lett said.

"I have a way off the island. No one knows. The family won't know. About you here, with me? Husband will never tell. The children never tell. The war taught them silence. They know what happens. They have seen it."

"What's your play?"

"I go through the kitchen and out the backyard and go. As soon as they in bed, or sooner. Gone forever. I know how. I send for family later. Much later. When safe. I have means."

"What about the reporter?"

"He doesn't get to see me. I don't tell. I disappear. Forever."

"Why should I trust you?"

"It's my family's life now. Everything change. You can trust that."

Lett stared a long while. Miss Mae babbled in English to fill the silence for her family's benefit and even laughed, but still Lett didn't speak. He might have nodded along.

"I never saw you," he said finally. "Here's what I'm going to do. I go out the back. Your family came home but never saw me. Ever. Keep it together, will you? Just listen. Tell them to turn on a light or two right after I go. It looks natural."

Mae nodded. "Of course."

"I just saved your life."

"No," Mae said. "You just save theirs. Yes? My life mean nothing. Not now."

"Forget it. One more thing. Once I'm gone, and they don't know? You disappear like you say. Or else."

Lett started for the kitchen. Miss Mae touched him by the elbow. "You came from there, didn't you?"

"Where's that?" Lett grunted.

She smiled now, and Lett saw her real smile, full of teeth and happy creases.

"Is Kanani there? She is! Ah, I see it on your face." Mae clasped hands, held her chin high. Lett could see the mama-san now.

"Pipe down, will you . . . geez."

But Mae's eyes dimmed again. She glanced back at her family, then whispered to Lett. "Is Frankie there yet, Frankie Baptiste?"

"Yet?"

"You must watch Kanani. She gets in over her head, that one."

"She can hold her own."

"No. Not for long. Oh, oh. This is my fault. The Preserve, it's not what I thought."

"You ain't the only one, Miss Mae."

"Go," Mae said, pushing at his back with both hands. "Go!"

"Okay, okay," Lett mumbled and marched past the sofa without looking and went through that kitchen and he was gone, through the backyard and around the side, out onto the road.

Twenty minutes later, he was walking back down toward the harbor, keeping his eye on the light of that Aloha tower. It was dark now. The boat would be there as planned.

It occurred to him that he could've asked Miss Mae if he could flee with her. But he had no moves after that. There was also the looming proposition that his life could prove to be worth less to them than Miss Mae's, and at any moment. As he walked, the anger boiled in him so hot and his arms cocked and his hands clawed so tight, that it felt as if he could reach out and grab and crush one of the city buildings down below like some giant lizard unleashed from the depths of the ocean.

He had tried walking away before. It would all catch up with him wherever he ran, hid, fled, landed.

For now, he was better off on The Preserve. At least there he had Kanani. At least there he had his dose.

Maybe he would pass through Hotel Street on the way to the boat, drink himself into a stupor before he boarded. It would certainly fit the lie.

Down around another curve, headlights found him from behind. A cab passed and pulled over in front of him. The same cab. Lett dropped into the back.

"What happened?" the cabbie said as he pulled away.

"Jade wasn't there," Lett said. "I was waiting for her, all good and ready, then her damn family shows up. I guess it was family. No one told me about that possibility. Why didn't you? What a goddamn snafu." He added a kick to the front seats.

"Easy. Mistakes happen. What then? Did you . . .?"

"No. Didn't need to. Why should I? No one saw me. I slipped out the back just fine."

The cabbie handed Lett a flask. It was rye. It burned away the sand in his throat.

"I got to tell you," Lett said, wiping his mouth, "I don't think your target is there anymore. Or here in Honolulu for that matter. I think your target fled the coop, see."

"That was a safe house."

"Which is my very point. You leave a safe house? It's a one-way ticket."

Lett took another long drink, and any machinery left inside him disengaged for good, and all his emotion came surging back through the valves, rushing his whole body and brain like a stray fast wave, and he had to gasp from it, as if choking, and the cabbie said, "You want I pull over?"

"I'll be all right. Just, get me back."

"You did good," the cabbie said, but the only thing that let Lett breathe again was when he yanked out the Colt and thumbed the safety back on and uncocked that hammer.

23.

Kanani holed up in her boogie house preparing for the worst, starting with a hard rap on the door from Frankie. Frankie hadn't spotted her watching him exit that lava tube tunnel secured with a metal door. But she'd always known he would show up here, ever since Lett saw him on Hilo Side, ever since he appeared in that Packard Clipper down on Alii Drive, probably. Still, nothing transpired. She holed up overnight, eyes fixed on the sheer lace curtains. Still nothing. In the morning, she found the courage to venture out into camp. She went to the laundry and helped fold clothes like she did when she needed to think. Frankie never showed, not anywhere.

She took a ham sandwich to Wendell Lett, but he wasn't there— his bungalow all locked up. He wasn't on duty in camp, she found out. Then she heard they'd sent him to weapons training first thing in the morning. But he wasn't there, either. She only hoped it had nothing to do with Frankie. And she thought about the tunnels running under the camp like so many lava tubes, and that brought shivers to the ache in her heart and the unease in her gut.

She started coming to her senses. The daylight helped. Maybe Frankie was only visiting that part of camp she saw, and would never be back? Even if he did, she might have time.

She knew what to do. It had always been her only angle. That afternoon, she cased the Main House from her bungalow with the opera glass. They had no visitors, all quiet. Colonel Selfer's car was there, that was it. When it was pushing evening, the setting sun just a glowing cinder, she strode over to the front door of the Main House. The little local old lady opened, Yoshiko. Yoshiko gave her the stink eye and told her that she "gotta wait cause she get no appointment." She led Kanani to a living room and down into a sunken area she called a "conversation pit," obviously not her word for it, and again Kanani couldn't help being reminded of an imu for a kālua pig roast. She sat alone down there, in a rattan chair. On shelves in the living room she saw more little treasure objects and figurines with plenty of golden glimmer to them, buddhas and temples and bowls. The bar had Philippine rum and more bottles of that basi rotgut.

Five minutes passed. Still no one came. She plopped her feet on the coffee table. It had been a week since she and Charlie Selfer had returned from their jaunt down to the coast. They could have reached first, second, third base, and wherever else it led. But she'd played it cool. The home run would come. Let him come to her, let him think it was his doing.

There was no time for that now. Frankie had been looking for Miss Mae at her bungalow near Kona Town. And if he saw her here? He'd know that she knew. She and Frankie both had cooperated with the Military Government during the war. Frankie was even on the payroll of Police Chief Gabrielson when he wasn't in bed with US intelligence. Playing all sides. Informing. He was smuggling too, because he knew when they would and would not be watching. Cooperating with their clampdown only made things like prostitution and gambling easier on the sly, as long as you pretended to go along with their hard set of rules in Chinatown, that was. When Chief Gabrielson found out she and Miss Mae were trying to open a boogie house outside of their red-light district, the chief threatened to beat her good once martial law was done with her. It was always easier for men. Frankie meanwhile helped run the sailors' favorite cockfighting ring on the south shore of Oahu and made even more dollars that way despite the cops' hefty take. Cockfighting wasn't illegal before the war, but martial law changed that, too. Now it wasn't a crime unless the police chief didn't get his cut. The bare truth was, the Territory was learning how to deal and operate like the mainland and there was no turning back. She and Frankie had teamed up at one point for this and that racket. He liked her. He made his play for her, he wanted his hands on her. But she had kept him at bay. Then Miss Mae told her about The Preserve.

For a moment last night, her night terrors had intensified and a kind of delirium set in—and she considered the prospect of join-ing with Frankie for good. She shook it off. Not a chance, she told herself. It would be going backward. Sure, it sounded like a prime opportunity for a secret pact between locals, but it really, truly was nothing of the sort. Frankie's showing up here could easily backfire. Frankie was too close to them. Who knew what he was promising them? What they were guaranteeing him? The *moke* was smart but even he had no idea what he was getting into. This wasn't Police Chief Gabrielson, not even Military Government. This was some-thing bigger and darker, from that same mainland ambition that grabbed the land with a promise then tore up the guarantee, laugh-ing and spitting in your sorry brown colonial face.

Gotta keep moving, was what Wendell always said.

She threw back her whisky down in that living room pit.

She heard someone talking. She sat up in her rattan chair. Set her glass down on that barrel of a table.

Charlie Selfer strode in. He wore another handsome aloha shirt, pressed trousers, those white leather sandals of his.

She smiled.

Selfer rushed down to her, his face flushed. He wasn't smiling. "What are you doing here?"

She wiggled her empty glass. "I ran out," she said, "whisky, neat."

"Right." He fixed her one and one for him in seconds flat. He lit two Camels and bounded down to her, gulped, set a lit cigarette in her hand, sucked on his. Gulped.

"You okay? You not sleeping very well?" she said.

"I'm not sleeping at all." He rubbed at his temple.

Kanani couldn't believe her eyes, ears, nose. In a mere few weeks, Lieutenant Colonel Charles Selfer had declined from one of the smoothest haoles she ever met to someone more like a rattled old gentleman from another era adrift in a new age where smoothness and subtlety played no part. It was such a contrast to Lansdale with his cockamamie sayings and that crazy look in his eye. If Selfer was the suave poet, Lansdale was the brash advertising man, and all knew who would win that day.

"I'm just . . . preoccupied, dear," Selfer added. He flicked his already half-sucked Camel into the ashtray, a polished coconut shell. He set a hand on her wrist. "I'm sorry."

"Don't worry about it. Where's Wendell?" she said. She hadn't planned to ask this first. It just came out.

Selfer stared a moment as if trying to recall the name. "Lett, Wendell, he is . . . on a mission. That's all I know."

"So now it's a 'mission,' is it?"

Selfer put on a smile finally and poured them another and swooped back down with two more lit Camels. His hair seemed more in place somehow, and his face relaxing. This was more like it. He crossed his legs, showing off his smooth, nearly feminine ankles, and brushed ash off his knee, though there wasn't one speck.

"So, you hear about the recent arrival?" she said.

"There's a recent arrival?"

"Francisco Baptiste."

Selfer's leg dropped. "How do you know about him?"

"I saw him. Accidently. Passing through camp."

"Oh. Oh, I see," Selfer said, his eyes darting around but they couldn't keep up with his mind, which was apparently racing. A single bead of sweat appeared on his forehead, and he pushed it back up under his hair with a manicured fingertip. This wasn't a good sign. She was hoping to find that Selfer was helping to control Frankie somehow. But someone else was clearly running Frankie. Selfer might not even know who or why.

"I knew him from Honolulu," she said. "Everyone called him Frankie. Not sure what he goes by here."

"Ah, yes, of course you would know him." Selfer nodded like a person pretending to still know the score. "What do you make of him?"

"He's all business. But he can bust 'em up if he needs to."

"Bust 'em up?"

"He uses his muscle if a certain situation isn't working. That's sort of his specialty."

"Ever work with him?"

"Sure. US dollars, for example. During the war, the Territory treasury stamped them with 'Hawaii' so they couldn't be used by invaders, fifth columns, what have you. But ho, we laundered them through the haoles themselves—the same guys who were stamping them."

"Sure, sure, I get you. Ever see him get rough?"

"Of course. One time, Frankie beat up a rival wanting to take over a boogie house. That rival *moke*, he never walked again. Never remembered his own name, neither."

"He ever get rough with you?"

"No. And I hope he never tries."

Selfer drank. He stared into his whisky, still swirling. "Know what I think? This must be Lansdale bringing in his own man. To watch over things . . ."

She'd told herself she wasn't going to come begging. But an angle was an angle. She leaned closer to him, ever so slowly, her body moving almost imperceptibly as if she were about to swat a fly. She opened her face to him. "Please, Charlie. Please keep him away from me. Could you?"

"Ah, dear. Don't worry," Selfer said, uncrossing his legs.

She pouted.

And Selfer's head was lowering her way.

"You have to protect me," she said, her face hovering just under his. "You must."

Selfer kissed her. He held her by the shoulders, gazed into her face, kissed her again, and then pulled her onto his lap with a strength that his arms did not show, and the next thing she knew she was kissing him back with all she had.

24.

Despite his smooth way, Charlie Selfer didn't make love like a smooth guy. Kanani had expected lots of flourish, showing off even, telling her how much he cherished her like one of those men bringing flowers and showering gifts on the second date. Men like that were only in love with the thought of themselves courting a girl. Yuck. Her fear was that she'd like Selfer just as well as she'd imagined herself liking Wendell in bed, and then she would have a problem. That wasn't the case, either. Selfer made love mechanically, but it wasn't like those low-grade psychopaths she knew from the boogie houses. His grip on her shoulders—nice enough in itself—soon became a series of controlled maneuvers he used to carry her into the bedroom. Set her on bed. Remove clothes. Place her in position. Assume his place. Adjust accordingly. Never looking her in the eyes the whole time. These weren't even gestures. He was on top of her and inside her, yet nothing but his male member touched her, which was something of a feat, she had to admit.

She should've been offended. She wasn't just a glory hole. The strange thing was that it wasn't half-bad. The sad part was that the man probably couldn't enjoy intimacy. He couldn't give it. Maybe he feared that he might not get it back? So he couldn't risk it. She stared up into his eyes and couldn't help squirming a little but still he didn't touch her. His eyes looked just above her forehead. He even kept his orgasm under control, even when her insides went all warm and expanding and she couldn't help but let loose. Again, not what she expected from this. What plenty of guys in the boogie houses could not understand, or any man for that matter, was that a certain kind of sex was so often a transaction. A girl did it to get something, or because she had no other choice. It gave her time, a home, a break from a beating. But this? She didn't know what this was.

They lay on the large bed in the master bedroom, both on their backs. Selfer had the covers pulled up to his throat like a virgin who had just lost it. His eyes searching the ceiling. He told her about his upbringing, his father a con man. He never had any love, so he didn't see any in the world. He didn't know how to find any, and he wouldn't know it if it lay right under his nose.

"I know my rambling on like this is pitiful," he muttered, "I don't know what's gotten into me." Then he fell asleep.

Kanani felt sorry for him. All he knew was how to get a leg up and climb a ladder. She told herself, staring up at that ceiling, that she herself was nothing like him. She had to tell herself this at least three times. And then she let out a bitter chuckle. What else was she doing here but getting her mitts on gold or whatever treasure she could find and abscond with forever? She'd told herself that she'd use it to help out her mother. She'd told herself she'd create a new life. But what then? She knew what her faddah would have told her if he were still alive: she could never be happy this way.

Selfer snorted awake. He rolled off the bed, tossing covers, and stumbled across the room.

"What you doing?" she whispered.

"Can't sleep," he muttered. He went into the master bathroom, flipped on the light and pushed the door shut, but it bounced back open a crack. She could see his reflection in the mirror, pale, a gelatin. He kept staring into that mirror. Then he opened the mirror and pulled down a bottle of pills and threw a couple back and drank a glass of water.

Sleeping pills, she hoped.

He came back to bed. He patted her on the knee, lay on his back. She waited for his breathing to calm. She waited a long time after that, too, until a person wouldn't even know he was lying there, he was sleeping so still.

She slid off the bed, inches at a time, rechecking that he was asleep. Once up, she went over to the bathroom, turned on the light, and pulled the door shut so that a line of light showed under the door so he might think, if he woke at all, that she was only in the bathroom. She went back to the middle of the room. He still hadn't moved.

She tiptoed out of the room.

His office was two doors down the hallway. Luckily an outdoor perimeter light reached into the room, just enough to lighten the edges and shapes and show her around. A teletype machine stood on a side table, the trash can below it empty. His desk had no photos of family and certainly not of a girl. She picked up papers in the inbox and under a paperweight of the Eiffel Tower and peered at them, finding only boring regular reports and ledgers, all befitting a glorified head clerk. She slid open drawers but only found pens and unused notebooks and lighters and more packs of Camels. The desk had a leather pad topping it. She lifted it, a paper slid out. She raised it to her eyes.

It was a map. Tiptoeing, she walked it over near the window for light. It was a type of surveyor's map of the island, probably one used to build this camp. It bore no official military source such as Corps of Engineers and yet it read TOP SECRET in one corner and OFFICIAL USE ONLY in another. She located the up mountain forest where they were, and southeast of there where the volcano rose, and east where the landscape was just fields of lava rock for miles and miles, so barren that the US military had used some of that land for target practice during the war. The only route traversing the island's desolate interior, Saddle Road, was mostly gravel.

The map was marked with little triangles. These appeared just inland from their camp, but close. Each triangle had a few numbers and letters, drawn precisely. But these markings had the same dark purple color as the lines of the map—meaning this was a copy, a mimeograph.

She studied the map as long as she dared, concentrating only on the triangles closest to camp, and then she slid the thing back under the blotter.

***

She stepped back into the bedroom. A jolt traveled through her. The sliver of light was gone from the bathroom door. She looked to the bed. Empty.

"You're not going to find a thing," Selfer said. "Not in my office, you won't."

He was sitting in a chair, in the corner. His head hung and he stared between his white knees, into darkness.

She didn't answer. She moved closer, but there wasn't another chair. She sat on the edge of the bed.

"You didn't find anything, did you?" he said.

She shook her head.

"See there? You want to know more about what's been transported here, is that it?"

She didn't reply.

Selfer sighed. "You ever hear the name Yamashita?"

"He one local boy? Plenty guys with that name."

"He was one of the Japanese Imperial Army's top generals. Responsible for their last stand in the Philippines. Back in '45, General MacArthur put Yamashita on trial in Manila, first time in history that the US of A tried a defeated enemy general for war crimes. He was charged with massacres committed by Japanese sailors and marines in Manila, even though some of this happened against Yamashita's own explicit orders or outside his command. The defense had a case, at least. Yet Yamashita was found guilty—and all appeals declined. He was promptly hanged. MacArthur, you see, was getting his old nemesis out of the way as swiftly as the rules allowed. Many thought MacArthur was just taking his revenge, the general making it personal because the Philippines had always been his claim. Oh, he was probably doing that, too—two birds with one stone, as it were."

"In that trial, they didn't mention . . . ?"

"Mention what, Kanani? Get to the point, please."

She couldn't say it.

"Then bear with me," Selfer continued. "Meanwhile, members of Yamashita's staff were interrogated on the sly, to put it mildly. Especially those serving with him in the Philippines."

"By who?"

"Ah. That depends. I can't say, but you can probably guess."

General Macarthur. His intelligence section in Tokyo. Later, other intelligence operators unspoken. Miss Mae had told her some of this, but Selfer didn't need to know that. "This was where Mister Lansdale washes ashore. What about that Japanese thug, Kodama?"

Selfer nodded. "Officially, Yoshio Kodama is supposed to be in a high security prison in Tokyo—awaiting trial. He's heading back now. Certain players were giving the man a secret little prison leave."

Kanani grabbed the covers and pulled them around her, even though she was hot. "Now it's a gold rush," she said.

"Correction: It's a *secret* gold rush. Full-scale retrieval, to be even more precise. Way I hear it, it lasted into 1947 at the least."

"But this is now 1948, the last I checked." So that meant it was starting all over again, based on new intelligence.

"That's right." Selfer swallowed a gulp of air, as if holding his breath, and fell silent for a good few minutes.

The revelations were over, Kanani realized. But she tried anyway. "You once mentioned something called 'The Directorate.'"

"No, I did not. Never say that again."

"Okay. Calm down."

Selfer muttered something under his breath. He let out a long sigh. "There is something new going on, yes," he said. "I'm afraid that things have changed. Just in the last week or so."

Kanani had a hand up. "How you know all this if you're so in the dark, eh?"

Selfer touched an ear. "Loose lips." He added a bitter smirk. "I told you. I listen. That's what a host does. I'm headwaiter and a maître d' all in one. The host staff in the secret clubs know all the secrets of the world, I expect. And they're trusted to keep quiet. And, sometimes maybe I do see papers, reports, not many."

"What does Golden Lily mean?"

"Oh, you are a good listener too, aren't you?" He stared at her a moment. "I heard the name you mentioned. Miss Mae."

"You did? Where is she?"

"Overheard, I should say. All I heard is that she's still in Hawaii. But she's been given travel papers."

Kanani clapped, bobbed on the bed.

"She's where you first heard about all this, isn't it?" Selfer said. "From Chinatown."

"Yes."

"And you must have gotten that other tidbit from Kodama when you slipped him the Mickey? Yes? That's what I thought. So, yes, Golden Lily. Kodama was once Japan's top gangster. Then the Imperial Japanese Army calls him to China after they invaded. They need a man who can deal with the local gangsters there. Golden Lily was the program for moving all the loot, the plunder. Sometimes it involved gangster measures like swapping for drugs. So Kodama was Golden Lily's number one negotiator with gangsters in all of Southeast Asia, Indochina, Siam, Malaya, Burma, the Philippines, and Indonesia, doing whatever it took to get them to play along. Damn clever of the Japanese, really. Why not simply commission a gangster as an army officer?"

Selfer fell silent a while after that.

"You said something has changed," Kanani said.

"Yes. Lansdale, this whole camp, it's under new ownership." Selfer wiped at his mouth as if he'd just spat.

"Who's the kahuna?"

"Ah, you want the big kahuna. At the very top? I don't know. I'm not supposed to."

"General MacArthur?"

Selfer shrugged. "I doubt that. Not directly at any rate. The generalissimo would have it arranged just so, so that he could deny anything if he needs to. No, it's bigger."

"What's bigger than MacArthur?"

"Indeed. Deeper, anyway. Some of it's surely out of DC. And Lansdale knows just the right angle. It's the American Way: enterprise, capitalism wrapped in the flag, all that business." Selfer spoke rapidly, gasping words, flinging his arms around in the darkness. "Now Lansdale's spewing this and that about America's great mission to reform Asia, all richly frosted with his hokey homilies. I'm sure he was a big hit in his secret meetings back home. They don't know from Asia. Only Lansdale knows. Lansdale! He can do whatever he wants." He let his arms drop.

"People get secret money, people can do secret deeds," Kanani said.

"That's right." Selfer snorted, then went quiet again. Eventually he said, "You know that novel *It Can't Happen Here?*"

Kanani shook her head.

"Ever hear of a Marine General Smedley Butler?"

"Don't know him, either."

"Well, he wrote a book, a pamphlet really, titled *War Is a Racket* . . . You know something? Forget about it." Selfer came over and sat next to Kanani on the edge of the bed, lit a Camel, and offered one to her.

He smoked and sneered at her. "So, how did you like my office?"

"Your office is boring." Except for a certain mimeographed map, which she wasn't telling him about.

"That's because I'm just a manager. I take and give the most common of orders. That's it."

"You feel like you're missing out," Kanani said. "I know the feeling."

Selfer held out his hands as if ready to catch something heavy. "They have their great cause now. Their crusade. It's the war against Communism. Not just in Asia, but worldwide. Some actually believe in it. They actually believe Lansdale."

"We don't," Kanani said.

Selfer stared back, holding up his cigarette between thumb and forefinger. "No. But the problem for us is, they now have Frankie Baptiste, too."

25.

L ett returned in the middle of the night, the boat dropping him off in a snug little cove. A jeep was waiting in the dark, the headlights blinding him. Lett climbed in back. "Where are we?" was all he said.

"Place of Refuge," the driver said and shifted and sped off, driving fast inland up the hills. Lett slumped dead tired in the backseat, his head bobbing. Then he noticed the driver, a big man.

Frankie. Francisco Baptiste. Lett hadn't seen his tattooed hands in the dark. He wore coveralls like the men in The Preserve tunnels wore, and a holster. Lett sat up and grabbed at handles for the rest of the ride.

He should have been terrified. But he stayed calm, unlike on the boat coming back, where he'd vomited his guts out overboard until it was just slimy strings hanging off the railing at the visions of him murdering father, son, and daughter in front of Miss Mae before doing her in. That done, he shot himself in the forehead. He had never envisioned that before, and didn't ever want to again. He knew he had no choice, letting Miss Mae and her family live. He could never have lived with the alternative. He ended up taking his dose twice on the boat, and luckily it helped. But he would still have to live with a new terror—that his masters here would find out. They could do anything to him, with him, in his name.

The front gate of The Preserve opened for Frankie as if he'd pressed a button in the jeep, and he sped them on through. He drove Lett right up to his bungalow and cut the engine.

He turned in his seat—the movement rocking the jeep that was still creaking and pinging and hissing from the fast, rough ride—and stared at Lett, his chunky brow accentuated by a faraway camp light. Lett stared back.

"What happened?" Frankie said, and Lett heard his local Hawaiian cadence.

"She must have gotten away," Lett said. He added a shrug and told Frankie what he told the cabbie. He lied through his teeth, just as he had told Miss Mae he would. That camp light shadowed Frankie's eyes the whole time as he listened, and Lett wasn't sure if that had helped him tell the lie or not. "Maybe someone tipped her off," he added.

"Maybe," Frankie grunted.

"Anything else?" Lett said.

"Rest up. We're going to train you for your next mission, so stay sharp."

"All right." Lett climbed out.

"Leave the gun."

"Oh, right." Lett placed the Colt, holster, and suppressor on the front seat. Frankie watched him. Lett added the wallet with civilian ID of one Wendell Lett.

"Keep dem clothes," Frankie added with a grin.

Lett smiled back, but Frankie's grin had already dropped.

"You saved your ass back in da Philippines," Frankie said. "Don't think I don't notice."

Lett winced inside. He didn't know if Frankie's response was good or bad, but he guessed the latter so he wasn't about to say thanks. "Well, good night," he said.

Frankie only nodded. He watched Lett go.

Congrats, Lett thought as he trudged up his steps. *You're officially a traitor here, too. But, maybe it's just as well. Because maybe their savagery and subterfuge and soul-selling changed what it meant to be a traitor. So, in the words of any GI or Marine worth his salt: fuck 'em all.*

***

He passed Kanani in camp the next morning. They didn't stop long to talk. Her eyes were puffy again and she kept her head down. Their mannerisms reminded Lett of two inmates in a stockade yard passing a secret, and the shapeless twill fatigues he was wearing for training certainly fit the notion.

"I should warn you," he began.

Kanani formed fists and her face screwed up.

"You already know," he added. "Frankie."

She nodded.

"He gave me a ride up in a jeep. Seems to have some pull. Have you seen him?"

"Once, briefly. Two days ago. He was coming up from underground. I haven't seen him since." Kanani was peering around as if just mentioning the big man's name would make him pop up from some hatch in the earth. "Please, stay clear of him."

"I'm trying."

He didn't have the heart to tell her about Miss Mae, not yet, not here.

"What does Selfer know about him?" he added.

"Not much more than us, I'm afraid."

"Oh." Lett took a look around, if only to make her feel safer. "You doing okay?"

"I am. I don't know why, but I am."

"Maybe it's the calm after the storm," he said, thinking of his own ordeal.

"That or the calm before." She took another look around. "Let's keep it moving. I'll be in touch," she whispered, and she headed off down a trail, marching along with her head still down.

***

On paper—if there was any—Lett seemed to be responding to his treatment with flying colors. He seemed the model recruit incapable of anything deceitful, and certainly of anything unsound. In training, his new weapons instructor Jock Quinn seemed to want to confirm Lett's elevated status—as well as his own. They had likely given Jock the duty because they considered him close to cured. So Lett did his pal Jock a favor and played it straight, ever the good recruit. Jock was playing his own role to the hilt, with his flagpole posture and staccato snare drum delivery and ball bearings for eyes. He even had a crew cut now despite his balding head, like a bird's nest pared down by a windstorm. At the same time, Lett never stood at attention because Jock had never called on him to. He certainly didn't call Jock "sir."

Jock had his instructions. He was training Lett individually, to *ascertain* (Jock's new word) what sort of sharpshooter Lett was. Lett could choose between an M1 Garand, an M1 carbine, or a Springfield rife. Lett chose his trusty light and compact M1 carbine. He checked the cartridge in the chamber, five in the magazine. He harnessed his weapon, using his strap as a sling to steady his upper arm, tightened just so, all the loops and hooks and buckles in harmony. He lost himself in it and forgot Jock was there standing over him until he commented on the ease in which Lett used the rifle sling like it was second nature to him.

On the third day of their one-on-one training, Jock brought Lett something new—a huge grin. Jock's gapped teeth were like polished dominoes before the spots went on.

"Excellent work," Jock said. "You get a reward."

Jock handed him a sniper version of the M1 carbine, with a telescopic sight.

"You should be proud," Jock said. "Used one of these myself."

Lett felt its weight using both hands. "I didn't know you were a sniper."

"I was a lot of things, Lett, and so were you."

Jock had him shoot round after round, into the hundreds. As sniper instructor, Jock didn't instruct much. He made sure Lett squeezed the trigger with the ball of his finger so he didn't jolt the weapon firing. He reminded Lett that the most accurate position was prone, with something supporting the stock, with the side of the stock against his cheek. Lett kept using his sling, but Jock also introduced a bipod. Using such a crutch didn't feel natural to Lett any more than did using a bridge to a pool shark, and there was a certain pride factor, but his accuracy did improve. Lett of course knew about breathing deeply before firing, about firing between heartbeats for utmost stillness. He let Jock tell him anyway. Jock nodded a lot, checking off boxes in his head.

Jock told Lett what their superiors needed from him. They could find expert sharpshooters and cold-blooded killers anywhere. Instead they wanted a man who could always make the right decision, who could keep a cool and level head. They wanted someone who could work alone, on his own.

"You are independent," Jock reminded him. "You make sound decisions without relying on orders."

I sure am, Lett thought. He had shown it in spades by deserting a suicidal if not criminal mission during the war and then by making a go of it on the lam despite his terrors, and then by deciding to come here for a cure, where he'd just recently defied their clear orders to kill, and for good reason. He was sound as hell, just not in the ways they knew.

Lett spat out a bitter laugh. He hadn't meant to. It was out there before he got his lips back around it.

"Look," Jock added. "I know you were a deserter. And I don't care. Plenty good men were. This is your chance to make up for that, too."

During a break, Lett asked Jock, "Why are you training me? What for?"

Jock started, his head rearing back. It was such a simple question, but Jock eyed Lett as if he'd just landed in a rocket ship. "For any situation we put you in, we will assure that you have a clean head shot," he sputtered, as if reciting a manual he couldn't quite recall.

"What's the situation?"

Jock looked around as if someone had sidled up to listen. "Well, any situation involving security, or surveillance."

"So, nothing aggressive. Nothing where I was making the first move."

Jock stared a moment. "A capable sniper," he recited, "must possess the ability to control varying factors involving trajectory, point of impact, accuracy estimation. You have distance to the target to consider, wind direction and speed, altitude and elevation of both sniper and target and—"

"Stop. You're saying that I have a lot to worry about?"

Jock nodded. "I guess I am, yes."

"I noticed you never trained me much on camouflage, or concealment. If I'm going to provide security, surveillance."

"I can't speak to that. It's not my orders." Jock added, in a whisper, "don't push me, Lett, all right? I'm just getting my points in."

"Okay, Jock. Fine. You don't have to worry about your end."

Jock hung his head after that, just went through the motions. At the end of that session, Jock told him he was to wait in the camp briefing room.

"What for?" Lett said.

"How should I know?" Jock said, "I'm just—"

"You're just getting your points in. I know, I know."

26.

Lett sat alone in the camp briefing room, waiting. He was brought lunch. It was a nice pork chop with a macaroni salad and a side of fresh pineapple. He got coffee and a slice of apple pie. And he waited. The briefing room was just a hut of its own, just bare plywood like a giant chicken coop. He heard something booming outside. He told himself it was just thunder, another afternoon rain front. But soon the room seemed to shrink around him. Then it was massive, the ceiling taller than the sky. Then the metal roof pinged, then pitter-patter, then . . . He wanted to keep moving but he couldn't leave. His head spun, he squeezed his eyes shut. Now it was rat-a-tat and it turned into the staccato metal punch press of machine guns. He grabbed at the desk. His leg started bouncing. He pushed it down.

He needed his dose. He didn't have his dose. His bag was in his bungalow.

The door opened. Lansdale strode inside. He was wet on the shoulders and he shook the water out of his thick hair.

Lett sat up straight, refocused, made himself look shipshape. Hell, he even smiled.

"It's been too long, Doc," he said.

"Indeed it has." Lansdale wasn't wearing a white doctor's coat of course, just khakis as always but without the holster. He tossed the wet stub of his cigar in the trash can. "How you faring, hero?"

"Fine. Say, could I pop out a minute?"

"No. You have a briefing coming. There's the latrine." Lansdale wagged a thumb at the door to the toilet, the only other room attached to the briefing hut.

"No, it's . . ." His leg started bouncing, he leaned on it. "I need my dose," he blurted.

Lansdale stared a moment. "You know what I think? I think it's finally time you go without. I mean, you've been performing so well—you're further along than you think. You're well into the third stage."

"I don't know . . . not unless, maybe you got something else to replace it?"

Lansdale held up a finger, and his giant class ring flashed. "See now. Such a thing is exactly what I do have." He spun on his long feet and picked up a piece of chalk from the empty chalkboard on the bare plywood wall.

Lansdale, his hands dusted pale with chalk and his face streaked with it like some cuckoo witch doctor, lectured Lett on the marching legions of Communists taking over Eastern Europe, now poised to overrun Asia and the Pacific and soon America itself. They had to be faced. They must be stopped. Defeating Hitler was only the first step. Millions might be enslaved. Standing up to Joe Stalin and his Chinese henchman Mao Tse-tung was the true end goal. Bold deeds were required, but steely men like Lett were the very men for the great task at hand! The lecture reminded Lett of those films they were shown in boot camp, *Why We Fight*, but this was more cheerful, oddly, accompanied by positive yet hollow slogans that Lansdale kept writing on the board and erasing.

To succeed, we must first believe that we can!

Nothing tames the old worries quicker than pure action!

And on and on it went, for an hour, for the rest of the afternoon.

It submerged Lett in a grinding, thrashing blur of panic. He tried to keep it together, but his cruel old monkey was creeping back on top of him, clawing at his temples and the top of his skull.

Lansdale finished scribbling another silly homily, turned around to Lett, and started. "What is it? You're sweating something awful."

Lett unbolted a smile like a hatch falling open. He couldn't appear too weakened, not now. Maybe the point of this was to see if he could forgo his dose? "I'm trying, I really am," he said.

Lansdale, eyes narrowing, turned to the board and drew more figures on the matte blackness, the chalk tapping, dragging, screaking.

Lett tensed up. He felt others at his shoulders. The whole crew sat here with him, now, finally, every dead GI he'd known in their bloody rags with their grimy grim mugs, an auditorium full and a line out the door. Then Lieutenant Tom Godfrey pulled up a seat next to him. Tom was Lett's favorite old ghost. Tom's face was scorched, and he was covered in steaming blood and entrails from the bullets in his back that exploded his chest. Tom Godfrey was the best looie Lett ever had. Tom was killed in action on December 18, 1945, at the height of the Battle of the Bulge. Lett had tried to save Tom but couldn't.

Be careful out there, Wendell, Tom said now. *It's all I've ever asked of you.*

Lett nodded along, and to all his other dead buddies going way back, all the way to his first, Sheridan, right after D-Day, Sheridan with a hole where his nose had been and the pink and gray insides of his head still decorating his collar like the truest insignia ever known to an army.

Every time Lansdale turned around, Lett showed a happy open face. It shut down as soon as Lansdale's back turned, Lansdale drawing crude maps of Asia and Eastern Europe with arrows depicting armies swooping onto cities, nations, peoples. He broke chalk, picked up another, kept scribbling, screeching. Hammer and Sickle. Red Stars. Red White and Blues. The Cross!

Lett was like a wrathful boy sticking his tongue out at a violent father behind his back. He rapped at the table to make the monologue of a lesson stop, but he disguised it as a happy drumbeat to Lansdale's paean to the American Way when the man whipped around again. But the folds in Lansdale's brow were stacking up. Lett pressed his hands to his ears. If he didn't do something soon he wasn't going to be able to follow Lansdale's epic razzle-dazzle at all.

Lett started rambling and couldn't stop. "I'm just an ant and I'm done for, see. We are all ants and done for. All out of change. Back against the wall! Under the heel of the iron boot!"

He'd interrupted Lansdale midsentence. Lansdale pivoted as if on a revolving pedestal, his face looking as if someone had squirted water on it or something worse.

"You cannot let down your guard," Lett went on, "even when you think you are dreaming. Because you're dreaming. Then you're dead. Dead!"

He shot up and paced around the table, rambling on, all his dead buddies following like in some ghastly conga, Lett slapping at the table and then he was pounding on it.

"Stop! Sit the hell down," Lansdale shouted.

Listen to the man, Wendell. Just sit and can it for a second. This is not what we meant.

Lett stopped, took a deep breath, sat back down on his chair.

Lansdale took a deep breath, too. He set down the chalk.

"You usually give me an injection when I do this," Lett said. "Just do it. Please."

"All right, just, hold tight."

Lett planted his elbows on the table, folded his arms, and set his face into the dark little cabin of his arms. He felt his buddies there, but only as a presence, watching over. He didn't know how long this went on. He might have slept a moment, a minute, more.

He hadn't expected a relapse such as this. He told himself it had just been the weather.

Lansdale came striding back in. He had a case that looked like a house call bag.

"Sit up, please."

Lansdale delivered Lett the good old shot. It stung a little at first. Then Lett leaned back, let it flow through him.

He believed that it was helping immediately. His face felt like it was opening like a flower, like he was yawning wide yet not moving his face. He blinked any remaining tenseness away. His limbs unlocked and his muscles loosened and he let his arms hang off his sides.

His friends were gone. The room was normal size.

"All right? Fine? You happy *now*?" Lansdale said.

"Sure am. Thanks, Doc."

"Good. So don't screw this up. Not now."

***

Lansdale left him there, told him to wait. Lett had his dose, but the fire inside him still wouldn't douse. The heat found his head again, boiling his blood, and it filled his fists. To hell with Lansdale and his positive sayings. Fuck them all. War and death and tortures and all that came with them were never something to be enjoyed, savored, promoted like some newfangled toothpaste. He hated Lansdale. He hated himself for hating. Then he started speculating, anticipating, preparing. What were they going to throw at him next?

About thirty minutes later, Selfer came striding in. He wore his fatigues, but they were uncharacteristically wrinkled and his shirt barely tucked. His eyes darted around. He carried a slim map case on one shoulder.

"Just what are you trying to pull?" Selfer said.

"I needed my dose. Weather can cause it. Or maybe it was the Worldwide Red Scare routine?"

Selfer ignored the comment. He pulled out what Lett first thought was a map, but once Selfer rolled it out flat Lett saw that it was a blueprint-style sketch of a series of buildings. They were simple and squared in their arrangement with a gap in the center like locations around an airfield or a city square. No locations were marked. Selfer spread his hands across the paper, smoothing it, eyes searching for something he could show Lett, apparently.

Lett stopped looking at the paper. "Why isn't Lansdale briefing me?"

Selfer didn't answer.

"Because Lansdale told you to," Lett added.

"Lansdale's higher level now," Selfer snapped. "That's the word."

"So there really are changes being made around here. I've noticed it."

Again Selfer didn't answer. His eyes kept searching the paper diagram. As soon as he opened his mouth again, Lett interrupted him.

"Where are *they* sending me?"

"I can't tell you that," Selfer said to the paper.

"Why not?"

Selfer banged on the table. He shoved the paper off the table. He stepped over it and stomped around the room. "Because it's not for you to know," he barked.

"Says you."

"Don't get smart."

"Then, show me on a map."

Selfer glared at him. "Whatever you're doing? You do not want to do it, believe me."

"Don't just dump me on a seaplane again without a clue. Please. I might as well have blindfolds on. I'm not a prisoner."

"Does this look like a prison? Maybe you should be in a stockade, like you should've been in the first place."

Lett let the comment ride. Selfer sighed at his own words. He turned away a moment, deep in thought. He bounded over to the chalkboard. It slid on a track. He pushed it aside to reveal a map of the Pacific Theater on another track. He pointed at spots in the Pacific Ocean.

"Territory of Hawaii," Selfer said.

"That's us, yes," Lett said. "What is this, a guessing game?"

Selfer glared again.

"Okay, okay." It was a guessing game.

Lett expected Selfer's finger to move to Oahu again, or across the ocean to Wake Island or Guam or even the Philippines or, conceivably, Japan. Australia maybe. But Selfer's finger moved rightward, to the eastern edge of the map, where the coastline of the western United States would have begun if the map didn't end there. His finger stopped just off the map, pressing into the plywood, and he gazed over his shoulder at Lett with wide eyes as if to say, *If it's not on the map, I'm not actually showing you.*

The mainland?

"Los Angeles," Lett said.

Selfer shook his head.

"San Francisco."

Selfer yanked his finger away as if he'd burned it, still glaring at Lett.

There it was. San Francisco.

Lett felt the same burn in the tips of all his fingers, then it was shooting through him as a shudder. If Selfer was confiding in him like this, Selfer must truly be worried.

"Now, the why?" Lett added.

"Why?" Selfer rushed over to Lett. "All right, fine. It's an important meeting," he hissed. "A secret meeting."

"So. A mission to the mainland, to San Francisco. An important meeting. Security and surveillance. All right. Now, who?"

At first, Selfer didn't answer. He stared into Lett. He stared back at the map. Eventually he spoke, slowly, deliberately. "Listen. If I could call Lansdale back in here to answer your questions, I would—or to address my questions, for that matter . . ."

Then Selfer lurched, took a step back. His heel knocked at the plywood.

Lett had never seen Selfer taken aback. He looked as if molten solder and melting ice were surging through his veins at once, a horrid paradox of a surge. Lett thought the man might be sick. Selfer pressed his hands and back to the plywood.

"What? What is it?" Lett said.

Selfer looked down, as if to locate his feet there, like Lett had seen Joes do up on the line who had body parts blown off and searched the ground for them, picking them up before falling over dead. Selfer's feet stepped and they moved him, but gently, mechanically; he picked up the paper on the floor, rolled it up, set it inside his briefcase; he pulled the chalkboard back across the map; he stood at the table and slung his briefcase.

"I'm leaving now," he said. "You better, uh, return to your billet and wait for any . . . instructions." From the doorway, Selfer stared at him one last moment. "Good Lord," he muttered.

27.

As Lett watched Selfer back out of the briefing room, he saw a man so very different from the intelligence staff captain leading a certain premission briefing well rear of the front lines in a lush Belgian villa in '44—the charmer in a pressed tunic who worked the room like a politician mingling with donors, shaking hands, smiling, offering cigarettes, thoroughly unruffled by the naked terror on the faces of these GIs he'd called up for his special mission.

What made Selfer freeze up like that, made him back out of that briefing room like . . . well, there wasn't any other word for it—like he'd seen a ghost? Had he just realized something about the mission now at hand? Or had he realized something worse, something deep and dark? Maybe he sensed that horror that Lett always had, that was now returning full force—that incessant dread he had understood even when V-E Day and the so-called peace came. V-E Day was just a fine party for the rear and the home front. "For the duration" was finally over, they'd thought. But there was no duration. This was beyond death. This was eternity. The iron boot would grind them down eternally. The wearer might change, but he always had an aching and unquenchable lust for power and riches and they were the fodder and the fertilizer. He didn't need an official war, or medals or even insignia on his chest, and he certainly didn't need official orders. In secret was far better. Peacetime would do just fine. All the wearer needed was the money.

Lett went back to his bungalow, just as Selfer ordered. He kept off his porch. He waited for instructions, as instructed. He hunkered down there with a bottle of Johnnie Walker, but it only made his head spin and his thoughts tumble around again. He tried coffee. That only made his body heat up and sweat and his thoughts collide and ricochet. He paced the bungalow. He looked out windows.

His dead friends appeared, one friend for each window, then it was all of them at every window he approached. There they stood like a group photo of a squad after taking a town. He yanked all the blinds shut, but now they sat on the bed, all piled on there like in the bed of a troop truck. They spoke to him, individually yet all at the same time; a grim chorus.

You need your dose again, Wendell. That's what you need.

"I already got my dose," Lett muttered, "he gave it to me."

You need it again. You need to see Lansdale. He's the key. His dose is the key, Tom Godfrey told him.

Then his kindred spirit appeared. Holger Frings. Lett had met the German deserter when he himself deserted, deep in the dark Ardennes. Frings had vowed to help Lett return to Heloise, whom he'd met on leave in Belgium. But American MPs spotted them—they fled but not before the MPs fired. Lett got a bullet in the back. Frings saved Lett's life, and he then vanished. Lett had always held out hope Frings was still alive. But Frings was dead. Because only the dead spoke to him.

You must listen to them, Frings said in German. *Listen to your good old friends.*

Lett kicked at the bed. But he had to listen. He'd named his son after Holger and Tom.

Go find Lansdale, they told him. *Go demand your dose.*

"No!"

Trust us. Because the dose, it's not what you think it is. Not even close.

Lett kept kicking, stomping. His friends left the bed. It was empty. He'd kicked it so hard the mattress hung off it. It was just him now.

I'll take the damn thing myself. He found his musette bag with his dose. He pulled out the vial, but he fumbled it in his sweating fingers and the already loose rubber stopper popped off. Some of the clear liquid dripped onto the crook of his thumb and forefinger. He stared at the clear drops. He'd expected it to sting, turn color, something. He smelled the vial. He tried again, breathing deep. Nothing. He smelled his skin. Still nothing. He was tempted to lick it but recoiled instead. "What the hell?" he muttered, glaring around the room as if anyone else were there.

He kicked at the bed again. He pulled on his shoes and shot out the front door.

***

Lansdale never stayed at the Main House—he had his own bunga-low just beyond the infirmary, but it wasn't visible from there owing to a strategically placed high picket fence. It wasn't any nicer than the other bungalows, but it had its own clearing with a hammock and a little lawn Lansdale used to putt golf balls.

Lett had always believed what his good old friends told him, because the dead knew truth. But he had to see for himself, feel for himself.

Dusk had passed and the clearing was submerged in darkness. The open front door was a rectangle of light. Lett kept moving, past the fence and into the clearing and up the steps. He hit the screen door, kept going right through its feeble pine frame.

Lansdale was sitting in a rattan easy chair with his bare feet up on a matching ottoman. He wore short white pajama bottoms and a white tank top. His skin was nearly as white, his shoulders bony.

Lett stood in the middle of the room, catching his breath, his shirt unbuttoned and hanging out on one side, trousers stained and wrinkled, hair a greasy yarn mop.

Lansdale eyed him. "What are you doing here?" he said.

"Inject me," Lett said, "give me another dose."

Lansdale showed Lett his sneer of a grin. He snatched a robe from the neighboring coat rack and wrapped that around him. "What makes you think I should? You coming here like this."

"Just give me the dose," Lett repeated. "And I'll be on my merry goddamn way."

The sneer stuck to one side of Lansdale's face. He eyed his tele-phone, on a side table by the doorway to the kitchen, just steps away.

Lett stood between Lansdale and the phone. Lansdale's eyes

darted. Lett stepped toward him. Lansdale tightened the belt of his robe.

"You have no idea what you're doing to yourself," Lansdale growled, leaning in close, and Lett smelled the stench of stale cigar ash.

"Give me the dose," he said.

Lansdale's eyes twinkled. "Yes! Right, all right. Let's do that." He stepped around the room until he found his bag. He pulled out a syringe ready to go, and he held it up.

"You first," Lett said.

"What?" Lansdale laughed.

Lett came at him and Lansdale stabbed at him with the syringe. Lett was faster. He ducked and propelled Lansdale against the wall, Lansdale's head knocking against it. It stunned him. His eyes rolled around. He let the syringe drop into Lett's hand.

"Open your mouth," Lett said.

Lansdale laughed again, this time loud and resounding, releasing more tobacco stench. "Open your own!" he chirped. "Go on. Have at it."

Lett just stood there. "Don't you think I've had enough already?"

Lansdale bared slimy yellow teeth at Lett. He snatched the syringe from Lett's hand and squirted half the liquid into his own mouth. He glared at Lett, wiping at his mustache.

Lett waited a moment. Nothing happened. Lansdale just smiled away.

Lett grabbed the syringe. He squirted into his own mouth.

The clear solution tasted of nothing. "It tastes like water," he muttered.

"That's because it is water," Lansdale sang. "Sterile water! That's all it ever was."

"A placebo."

"The very same. You got duped, friend. Good and duped by the dose."

"There's no medicine involved," Lett stammered, "no real science at all." The blood drained from his face. He backed up. "That means . . ."

Lansdale came at him. "That there is no cure. There is no cure!"

"But, it was the only part I thought was working. The only one." Lett felt so cold suddenly. He had so wanted it to work, and Lansdale, that relentless psychological trickster, he had always seen that in him. Lett backed up a step, then another.

Lansdale raised his chin in pride. "It was just another angle, see, to get funded. All part of the pitch."

"The pitch?"

"To prove our value. Show how we're different. Didn't you know? I'm a former ad man—"

"Con man, you mean." Lett's arms lowered. His feet shuffled, his legs so heavy.

Lansdale grinned. "However you like it." He pushed at Lett's chest, sliding him back to the door. "Now you get the hell out of my house. Get some sleep. If you're lucky? Maybe I'll forget this ever happened."

"But, why?"

"Why you? GI, you sure got a numb skull. Isn't it painfully obvious?" Lansdale snarled. "It's because you wanted it. You wanted it bad. Bad enough to prove yourself."

28.

Lett rushed across the compound. He'd buttoned up and tucked in his shirt and pushed back his hair to approximate a fellow on an evening stroll. Except he was walking too fast. Except his thoughts and fears rode heavy on his back like a pack full of river stones and his old friends would not return to help him, guide him, save him. He wanted to ask them:

Why am I the only one left? Like this. Why me?

He headed down a forest path. At this hour, no one was around. He thought he kept hearing a guard coming his way, and halted to listen, but then he realized it was just the underbrush making that crazed whisper it always did. Any sentries would be farther out along the perimeter, where a fence stood and then nothing but lava fields for miles inland. He found the wide main trail, out in the open. A breeze picked up. The few lights in camp filtered through curled fronds and contorted branches to create fantastical shadows that swooped and barbed yet showed the way to him.

He found the boogie house bungalow but it was all dark, locked up. The Main House had lights on inside. Lett rushed through the trees and up the driveway and hugged the front door to stay in shadow on the porch. All clear. He gently knocked on the door with his knuckles, so as not to alert any possible sentry. He stopped, placed his ear to the door and listened, the sweat making his ear a suction cup.

The door pulled away from his ear with the slightest wet smack.

Kanani stood before him. She wore a robe too big for her. Her hair was up. She hadn't turned a light on. "He's not here," she said from the dimness.

"I'm not looking for Selfer." Lett stepped inside, pulling the door shut. "Is it safe?"

"I'm the only one here. They laid off old Yoshiko, she went home—"

"There is no cure," Lett blurted.

"What?"

"My dose. It's bogus. It's all a sham. Lansdale . . ."

Kanani's eyes widened. She pulled him into the sunken living room area without turning on a light. She sat him down and sat facing him.

He told her about confronting Lansdale.

"You what?" She pulled back. "Oh, no . . ."

She moved to punch him in the arm but he snatched her wrist.

"My treatment, it makes me even worse than I was," he told her. "Corrupts me all the way. Early on, 'Doctor' Lansdale told me treatment has three stages: talk, medication, training. He said treatment involves the full confrontation of what's troubling a guy. First, I talk it out, then I get a 'revolutionary' new medication, then I 'replace' my toughest issues with new assignments that rebuild my ability to cope, all by reinforcing my latest actions. Lansdale claimed I would own my trouble this way and thereby destroy it. 'Rebuild,' he called it. The mission makes the man—"

"You're hurting me."

Lett was squeezing her wrist. He kept squeezing. "Treatment turns me into a man who doesn't feel the combat fatigue, the terrors. That makes me a psychopath. A guy who likes it. And who doesn't need his dose after that. But I was fighting it. I kept needing my dose. Even though it was a placebo. See? I was fighting it inside and didn't even know it at first."

"Let go."

Lett released her. "The end stage of the cure—it's killing. The cure is the cause."

Kanani, rubbing her wrist, stared above his head, into darkness. Thinking.

"Finally using a gun? That's the clincher," he added.

"Your next mission," she said.

"Who's at this important meeting?" Kanani said.

"I don't know. Has Selfer told you anything? Confided in you?"

"No, not like that," Kanani muttered. She wiped at her face, pushing the last of her sleep off it. "He just said things are changing and changing fast."

"Frankie. You seen him here again? Anywhere?"

"Not yet. Just that once coming out of that tunnel. But I can feel him."

Kanani rocked in place, hugging herself, still thinking. He let her think.

"Selfer did say there are new bosses, big kahunas, more secret," she said eventually. "Sounds to me like some *kine* transaction happened."

A transaction. That made Lett think of Lansdale's big haul in the Cagayan Valley, visited by MacArthur, like an inspection. A new arrangement. Old deals nullified.

He remembered what Miss Mae had told him. She knew things. She'd learned they planned to assassinate someone so important she could not say his name. Then? *Big confusion. They use the chaos. The people feel weak. They take over.*

His chest ran hot, a bed of coals, his heart the fire.

"What's wrong?" she said.

"Miss Mae," he blurted. "I saw her."

Kanani's face lit up in a smile, but he doused it fast enough. He told her about his mission to Honolulu. He even told her what he had done. "I think she ended up knowing too much for her own good," he said.

"You're an angel," Kanani said. Her eyes welled up, and she touched at one with her index finger to keep the tears in. "I owe you even more, Wendell Lett. You always help me."

"You want to repay it? Save yourself. Drop this gold hunt. Get Selfer to transfer you somehow, if he even can. Or just run. You're playing with fire."

"Haven't you heard? We're surrounded by live volcanoes," she muttered. "Madame Pele."

"Who?"

"Hawaiian fire goddess. No mess with Pele. She mess with you."

He shook her, gently. "Listen to me. If they find out? They're gonna do to you what they were gonna inflict on Miss Mae—and she thought she had a deal."

Her face hardened, and she raised her chin. "Frankie must've cut a better deal," she said. "More money." But her voice creaked. Her chin gave in. The tears pushed out and rolled down her face, bright lines in the dim light.

Lett brushed her hair with his fingers. He set an imaginary red plumeria behind an ear. She chuckled through sniffles.

Lett said, "I tell you one thing, right here and now: I will not complete the treatment."

"What does that mean? Speak English."

"I won't do their dirty work for them. Get blood on my hands when it's really on theirs. I will never use violence again. Ever. I will never fire their weapons. I vowed that to Heloise a long time ago. I owe it to Holger Thomas." And to all of them, to all his friends who had helped him. To her, the little German girl. If he only knew her name, he thought, and now the tears welled around his eyeballs, heating them up, too.

"Oh. Now you are really talking *lolo*," Kanani said.

"Call me crazy. I don't care."

"Don't do anything stupid. Not till I can catch up. What about Jock Quinn?"

"Unknown quantity. He's conflicted. He wants to believe in something. I don't want to make him choose—it might just break him. Besides, there's no time. I probably ruined my chance already by confronting Lansdale like that."

"But, what if you haven't? What if the mission really is just for security, surveillance? Like they tell you."

"It's not. I can feel it. A dogface, he knows . . ."

Kanani closed her eyes, and the room seemed to darken even more. When she opened them again, her tears were gone. "They will do whatever they want to you. Take it from one islander. Cause you don't have the mojo. They have all the mojo and they're gonna keep it every time."

"Mojo funded by gold," Lett said. "Gold that you want."

"How else I gonna make my own way. Eh? They only gave me one assignment—get that Kodama to talk nice. That was it. There's no moving up here."

"That's what they do. They zero in on what makes a person tick. Exploit it. Bang."

She drew her gold Chinese lighter from her robe pocket and turned it in her hand like a talisman.

Then she took his hands in hers, the lighter between their fingers. Their knees were touching.

She sighed, and she growled, "We shoulda made love when we had the chance."

"I imagine you are probably right. I thought about it, you know, what it would be like."

"Me too, Wendell. Me too."

Lett stood.

"Go for broke," he said.

"Go for broke."

Kanani grinned at him. Lett made himself grin back. His shoulders felt heavy. He shrugged them to lose some of the ballast.

She let him go and find his way out. He entered the nearest tree line. He didn't take a trail. He moved through the underbrush crouching low, using tree trunks for cover. He was on night patrol in the Hürtgen again. He was sneaking over the German border into Belgium and again across the American lines after that senseless mission that had finally wrecked him.

As he moved through the trees, he peered back over his shoulder and thought he saw a figure sticking to a corner of the boogie house, watching him go. He told himself it was just another illusion. He kept moving, kept his eyes open. Stop, and he was cornered.

29.

After Wendell Lett snuck away, Kanani, keeping the lights off, changed into her dark denim overalls and sneakers. Charlie Selfer was still in the bar, and the camp was emptier by the day. It was high time to try looking at night again. She could only keep notes about Selfer's mimeographed map so long, let alone keep it memorized, especially since Selfer had moved the map from its hiding place under the leather blotter on his desktop. She folded up her faint penciled notes into a pointy wad, slid that deep in her long front thigh pocket, slipped out the back and moved through the forest like a crab on the lookout for feral beach cats.

She first needed to get inside her boogie house bungalow. There was a baby revolver in there, from before the first World War most likely, but a gat was a gat. It came with the footlocker they'd provided for any eventuality, tucked in next to that opium pipe.

On the lanai, a sharp chill hit her, and she hoped she wasn't getting a fever. She unlocked the door and moved through the main room in the dark.

The light clicked on, she screamed.

"Try stay calm, yeah?"

Frankie. He was lying on the chaise with the gold legs, his own legs hanging off one side and end like logs, his thick head and neck upright on the raised part. He wore those Army coveralls, still clean, and holster and knife on a web belt.

Her blood was pumping, sweat running down inside her overalls already. Stay calm, she told herself, stay calm. "You went scare me," she said.

"No make ass, wahine," Frankie said and smiled. The lamplight on his face reminded her how long and fair his eyelashes were compared to his kinky black hair, which he parted down the middle.

She tried a smile. It felt okay. "Ho, you making that chaise look like one baby bed," she said. "You always big for one Philippine boy."

"I'm Hawaiian. Just like you."

"What you doing here?" She found the armchair, lowered herself into it.

Frankie didn't answer. His slim purplish lips pressed together. He rose and moved around her, the floorboards creaking. When he was behind her he said, "Got one light?"

She shook her head.

"What in your pocket den?"

"Oh, right . . ." She pulled out the gold lighter, held it out.

"Who give you dat?"

She turned to him, scowling. "Miss Mae. Remember her? Den she went scram and I never see her no more. Dat no-good bitch owe me money."

Frankie shrugged.

"You see her around?" she said.

"Nope." He took her lighter, eyed it and weighed it in his hand, fired it up and lit a fat rolled cigarette.

Kanani smelled *pakalolo*, what haoles liked to call reefer, muggles, pot, anything but its actual name. Locals had always chuckled at that. From the plantations to the towns, no one had minded a little *paka*—until the Military Government decided otherwise.

"Who the *lolo* that stole my *pakalolo*?" she joked. It was a favorite local saying.

Frankie laughed. He still had that strange chuckle, high-pitched and strangled as if he'd stuffed a little funny man down inside his throat.

"How you went get in here?" she said.

"I could say the same."

"My house, I mean. All locked up."

Frankie shook his belt and it jangled. He had a pouch holding a ring of keys, as well. "Miss Mae tell you about dis place?"

"Among others." She looked around, as if someone else were in the room. "Dem army guys," she whispered. "Hotel Street."

"Okay." Frankie turned on the radio, found a station playing hao-leized Hawaiian melodies, probably KIPA out of Hilo Side.

"I was looking for you," he said, losing his Pidgin suddenly.

"Yeah?"

"Yeah," Frankie said. "You want some?" He offered her his *pak-alolo*. She took it and smoked. Coughed.

"What's in your other pocket?" he said.

"Huh?" She glared downward as if discovering her pants down. "Oh, dat . . ."

She pulled out the pointy wad of pink paper, stood it on the little lamp table, and straightened out the spikey parts.

Frankie cocked his head. "An elephant?"

"Not! Dat one nēnē bird. Come on."

"I guess I can see it. You Japanese always were *lolo* about paper."

"Origami, da name. And I Hawaiian, just like you. Hey, why you no talk like one island boy no more?"

"You know why," he said. "Same as you." His face hardened now.

"All right, fine," she said, dropping her Pidgin.

He sat back down, facing her, and blocked all light in the half of the room beyond. It made her want to stand up, but that wouldn't look too good. She had to give him something or he wouldn't leave.

"I came here looking for it," she added.

"We are talking about gold, yeah? Yamashita *kine*. Golden Lily, all that."

"Yep. Just like you. Why else would you be here?"

"Huh," was all he said. But her confession seemed fine to him, especially with Miss Mae out of the picture. He didn't say anything else for a while, though, and that started to worry her. He hummed a song but it wasn't the one on the radio.

"I won't lie," she added. "I thought maybe I could get my little fill, and I'm on my way."

"Where? The mainland? You? Don't make me laugh." Frankie added his strange chuckle.

She laughed back. "Stick out like one Molokai leper. You're no better."

"How you think you gonna get any booty out of here anyways? You need a truck. You need manpower. That takes arranging."

"I know. You don't think I know that?"

Frankie sucked on the *paka* and handed it back to her.

"Where you think you're going?" she said. "Somewhere they don't own you? Pshaw." She waved at smoke.

Frankie leaned forward. "They don't own me."

"That's what you think."

"I have things they need. I always have. You just have things that they use."

"Such as?"

"One washout by the name of Charlie Selfer."

She flinched but kept it inside. Frankie was just trying to spook her. That was his game, how he found out things—start a fire and see who and what came running out.

"Maybe I'm only hunting," she said. "Maybe I'm the one doing the using."

"Maybe."

They eyed each other.

Frankie lay back on the chaise again. He folded his arms behind his head, his elbows knocking against the wall. "By the way," he said, "it's 'Francisco' now."

She pretended to fight a chuckle.

"Laugh all you want. But listen up too and good." His arm was so long, he reached over and touched her chin from there. "It's not for the taking," he said.

"What's not?"

"What we just talked about. What's being stored here." He pointed downward, underground. "Not any of it."

She sat up. "You mean, you're here to protect it? Not to take it?"

"That's what I mean."

She wanted to spit at him, but she swallowed it back down.

"Yep, that Selfer's a loser of a haole," he said. "Mister Lansdale, now he's the future."

All she could do was growl. She snatched up the origami and lighter off the little table and shoved them into her pockets.

"And stay clear of that Wendell Lett," Frankie added. "That one's on thinner ice. His days are numbered. Maybe he gonna get dirty lickens."

Lickens was a beating. Dirty was worse. Her stomach tightened up, that sharp chill bit her again. She could only shake her head. "Numbered?"

"*Tita*, you better stick with me," he told her. "I gonna give you this one chance. You're smart. I see that. You show me that."

She eyed him, sideways, adding the slightest roll of her eyes.

"Me, I'm gonna make the right *kine* moves," Frankie said. "*Uku* plenty."

"How so?"

"One day, they're gonna leave this place. They'll give it back to us. And that leaves me in charge."

He was holding the last of that *pakalolo* reefer pinched between thumb and forefinger. He handed it over.

Kanani's throat filled with the *paka* smoke and this time she didn't cough. She let it burn. "Bruddah," she said, "I got one story for you. They never give back what they take. Not ever."

30.

Lett had expected immediate retribution from the likes of Lansdale. But none came, which worried him even more. The next morning, he got a visit from Jock Quinn, Jock's face long from frowning. Jock wouldn't take coffee, not even cold. He told Lett to report to the training ground in one hour but wouldn't tell Lett why. Lett wolfed down an early lunch of cold Spam and rice and colder coffee. He had no choice but to report. When he'd left the Main House last night, he'd made it to the perimeter and saw no chance of bolting anywhere. The compound still had sentries, and just beyond them stood a high fence expertly camouflaged, topped with barbed wire, and probably electrified. As he suspected. He didn't even want to fathom mines or other silent, Asian-style traps he could not anticipate. So he had trudged back to his bungalow along the usual trails and tried to get some sleep for what was to come. It was just as well. He couldn't bear leaving Kanani here.

On the training ground, Jock had a new exercise for Lett. He would have Lett fire his carbine with scope from a rise of about one story, a situation they would approximate by having Lett shoot from atop the weapons shed—Jock had instructed two men to build a compact platform up there. Lett was to fire standing and lying. Out on the range, a jeep would tow another jeep, slowly. In the rear seat of the towed trailing jeep sat what looked like a tailor's dummy, a bald, cream-colored figure with fatigues pulled over it.

Jock handed Lett his carbine with scope. Lett checked the safety lever. He slung the rifle on his shoulder. Jock walked Lett over to the ladder standing behind the shed, explaining that a head shot was the goal but not to worry about missing. They had plenty more dummies. Lett didn't answer, which only made Jock look more nervous. He tried to joke, "They're dummies, they won't know what hit 'em," but his voice strained.

Lett cut off Jock right there. "You told me this was for security."

Jock shrugged. "I said what I said."

"Surveillance, you said."

Jock held out his hands. "I tell you what I'm told."

"Ordered."

"Yes. Damn right. What do you think this is?"

Lett unslung his rifle. He held it out for Jock.

Jock stared at it. "What?"

"It's all yours."

"I don't follow," Jock said, his voice lowering.

"Oh, yes you do."

Lett was still holding out the weapon for Jock. Jock wouldn't look at it. He kept his stare on Lett. Something flickered in his eyes a moment.

Lett stood the rifle against the shed. "I'm done," he said, and he walked off.

"Done for, more like," he heard Jock grumble.

But then Jock shuffled after him. "Don't do it," he whispered.

"Stay out of it. You've done nothing wrong."

They were marching along with Jock pressing into his shoulder, and it looked routine enough from afar, the instructor giving trainee the earful.

"It ain't about me. They are going to crush you. This ain't some front line gone all snafu. You can't just grab a truck back to your unit once you done your bender, changed your mind. Oh, I know how you doggies did that in the ETO. Well, we didn't have the luxury stuck on some rock, some beach hotter than fugging embers."

"Listen to me: I'm not changing my mind."

"Goddamn, Lett, don't make me have to save you from this."

Lett halted, Jock with him.

"Do not do that," Lett snapped. "Don't."

Both were hissing now, all whispers. Each took a step back, looking around, making sure it didn't look too personal.

"Do not do that," Lett repeated. "Not for me. I'm not your crew. We were never in the grinder together."

"No? Then what the hell you think this here is, huh?"

"I want you to make it out of here. Please do that," Lett said, and he marched off.

Jock didn't follow. Lett felt the man's eyes on his back. They might as well have been a sniper sight. But from whose side?

On his way Lett passed the two men waiting at the jeeps with the dummy, young goon types with greased hair, smoking out of the side of their mouths. One cackled and said, "Get a load of him." "Whatsa matter, bub?" the other shouted to Lett. "You prefer the real McCoy?"

Lett kept going.

He thought about heading over to the Main House again and appealing to Selfer somehow. He considered walking straight to the front gate and seeing if he could just walk out. Maybe that would send a message to Lansdale, Frankie, whoever would deal with him. He strode back toward his bungalow instead. Down the midway he felt all the eyes on him. A couple people might have stopped and watched him, or so he imagined. He kept his head down, made no eye contact. He thought he heard a walkie-talkie rasping somewhere, the voices muffled but urgent. The sweat rolled down his face. He let it.

He strode right up into his bungalow, nearly hyperventilating now. He lay on his bed. He closed his eyes. He might have slept. Something made his eyes pop open, a creak maybe, but he didn't know if it was in his dreams or the reality of this room that had never been his, a reality that wanted to boil his very marrow with shock. The sweat beaded on him again.

He closed his eyes.

He felt a prick, in his neck. He slapped it. Hoping it was a mosquito or even a shit-craving horse fly. The prick became a sting and it spread fast, expanding like a brush fire, so he kept slapping at it. By the time his arm came back down, he couldn't feel his arm anymore. He moved to get up but nothing moved except inside his brain—his body refused to listen to his brain. He hoped this was a nightmare. Of course it wasn't. He couldn't feel the bed under him. He floated, but not in a comforting way. It was as if he were being held over a deep and gaping crevice. He wanted to scream but his mouth wouldn't move. Then his thoughts were fading, as if far away, as if he were hearing them from some faraway walkie-talkie himself, all tinny, and thinner, and then his thoughts were miles away like storm clouds on the horizon and he wondered if this was what dying was like. But there was no light. He didn't see himself outside his body.

All just went still, and dark, like a switch had been flipped. Into nothingness. And then even the oblivion was no more.

31.

The darkness returned, from beyond oblivion. It had a coarse texture, and it itched, and it carried the odor of saliva. A burlap hood was roped around Lett's neck. Through the black fabric Lett felt a chill he knew from foxholes and trench huts and bunkers. This absence of warmth was uniform, lacking any breeze, as if he were now underground. His eyes sensed a pale light beaming from above. His cramped butt confirmed that he was sitting on a concrete floor with his back against a wall, leaning on one shoulder so as not to squash his arms, which were in handcuffs behind him. He knew this place. All the concrete was painted gray, he recalled. But the air here was now stale, from sweat and blood and a sour reek like urine.

He was in a cell, probably in the same corridor where they first brought him when he arrived. No windows. Ventilation was controlled through a square grate up high. Doors were like submarine hatches with a wheel handle on the outside. Before, the other rooms in his corridor were empty. Now Lett doubted that very much. That smell came not only from him.

So be it. He expected nothing less from them.

A sharp spasm of fear and guilt seized his brain, pressing at his eyeballs like thumbs. He realized, yet again, that he was putting people at risk with his defiance. Kanani. Jock. Possibly even Selfer, and that made him sadder than it should have.

The air thickened under the hood. Lett bit at the coarse fabric and tugged on it, to adjust the airflow.

He heard something scraping. Scratching. From no more than twenty feet away. A cockroach? He would crush it. But a cockroach made more of a soft clatter. This was fingernails maybe. Toenails?

"Who's there?" Lett wheezed.

He heard nothing.

A rat? He pulled in his legs and bent over, ramming his head between his legs to help protect his genitals. Listening.

The scraping was repeating a pattern—four dots together and two spaced out, like Morse code. Lett kept listening, nodding along, recalling his code alphabet. Four dots together, two spaced out . . . Was it the start of a Hello?

A pause. Lett tapped and scraped Hello with his right big toe.

He paused. In return he got what sounded like: No . . . Hell Now.

A giggle rippled from across the room. Then came a piercing wail. Lett sunk his head between his legs again and pressed his thighs against his ears, waiting, hoping for it to die out. It took a while, and the echoing prolonged it, but silence found them again.

"Are you hurt?" Lett said eventually.

No response.

"Who are you?"

A gagging sound came, and another, like someone who had to sneeze. And then, sobs.

Lett's heart thumped. Cold strips of sweat drenched his forehead, his upper lip. "Kanani? Is it you? Oh, please, no." It couldn't be. It was the wail of a man.

"No," grunted the voice. And the voice went silent again.

Don't let it be you, Jock, Lett thought.

***

Hours passed. The other prisoner never spoke again. The man had long stopped sobbing. It might have been night or day up above, but Lett could not know, and that was the very point.

Lett heard muffled laughing and footsteps, from outside in the corridor. Dogs barked. Lett's cellmate moaned hearing it. Then the footsteps and laughter stopped, the barks hushed. The clank of a lock sounded and the squeal of a wheel handle spun. The door flung open, clanged against the wall. Lett heard the footfalls of four or five guards scuffling in and their dogs panting, their long claws scraping at the concrete.

Lett pulled his legs in tight, bent over. A dog sniffed and licked at his knee.

"Ah, reeks something awful," one guard muttered. "Shut your pie-hole," grunted another.

Strong hands yanked Lett up and dragged him out. He ended up down the corridor, dropped into a chair. They untied his rope and yanked his hood off, and Lett gasped to take in new air. He blinked and squinted at the light from above. His eyes adjusted. He was sitting at a metal table. Nothing lay on it.

Across from him sat Lansdale. He wore a crumpled beige linen suit with pale blue tie, looking like a country lawyer. Lett felt breath on the top of his head, looked around. Frankie loomed over him, larger than ever. The Army coveralls he wore didn't help matters.

"I think you know Francisco," Lansdale said. "Francisco is in training. He will be running the show here. Because soon I'll be on my merry, merry way."

Frankie and Lansdale shared a laugh. Lett wanted to ask where that put Selfer, but then Lansdale set a doctor's bag on the table. He pulled out a glass syringe. This one was wider and ringed with a dull metal around the nozzle and piston and bulb, like a device from the previous century. The liquid inside wasn't clear this time, but yellow—like urine, Lett thought. The needle had a girth to it that he did not like, not at all. Frankie moved in, held him in place. Lansdale, humming a tune now, squirted the yellow fluid and came around the table. Frankie pushed up Lett's sleeve. Lett gritted his teeth and pressed his bare toes to the floor, but Frankie tipped the chair back and Lett's toes dangled.

The prick didn't hurt. Lansdale knew how to find a vein.

What came after was no placebo. A warmth surged through Lett. He floated. He loosened up. He grinned. This darn cell was an amusement ride, that was all, a happy Tilt-A-Whirl, and all Lett had to do was ride it out.

"Rock it, keep that chair arockin'!" he shouted at the big ride jockey, and Frankie did so grinning.

After a while, the ride slowed. Stopped. But Lett couldn't get off.

It was like before. His limbs wouldn't work. No one needed to hold him down.

"No need," he muttered. "So don't you even try . . ."

The room spun now instead of him in the chair and the light whipped around and Lett squeezed his eyes shut and his stomach whipped in the other direction and he leaned forward to throw up, but banged his head on the table. Then a bucket was between his legs, and he let it rip, emptied his gut whole until it was just bile and saliva hanging off his lips.

After a while, Lett came to again. Lansdale was still with him. Frankie was gone. Lett remembered Lansdale telling his goon at one point that he wouldn't be required for a while.

Lansdale pulled his chair around backward and sat on it and pushed up his suit sleeves and grinned. "Ready?" he chirped.

He started talking a mile a minute like a carnival barker and he plied Lett with more of his anti-Commie Red Scare routine all wrapped in the red, white, and blue and bearing a golden cross. And, eventually, it started to make a lot of sense to Lett. That horrified him so much, like a child left in the dark, and he screamed to make the reason go away. Was Lansdale right? Was it the yellow liquid? Lett nodded along to Lansdale's words and cheery appeals, but inside he fought it. He kept moving his true thoughts and shifting them around hoping to hide them; to himself he repeated reality and possible outcomes as he knew them . . .

The cure was the cause was the cure. The end stage of the cure was killing.

They might know that he'd let Miss Mae escape in Honolulu. That, or she was a test. He had tried. Maybe he'd failed. But he'd stayed true to himself.

They were training him to be an assassin and wanted him to possess a modicum of anti-Red sentiment. His mission might involve San Francisco. That crude map Selfer had showed him could've been buildings and streets around a city square.

Selfer might not know the whole story. He might only fear it.

Kanani might survive, if she knew the truth. She might even help him, but he couldn't count on that. He couldn't count on anyone but his dead friends.

He had Lansdale wondering something, because Lansdale was now pacing the room and studying him, tapping a finger to his chin.

"What was that you gave me?" Lett said. "You're testing it out on me, that it? It's part of your next pitch? That it, ad man?"

Lansdale grinned. He held up the finger, long and bony with that chunky class ring. "Look at the smart kid." He dropped the grin and snorted at Lett. "You refuse to fight for the American Way?" he said. "Is that it?"

They might be recording him somehow. He couldn't know. He tried to speak but his mouth was so dry. He swallowed and flexed his mouth to get some last saliva going.

"I fought for my buddies. I killed for them. But they're all dead now."

"Oh? Then what about Colonel Selfer?"

Lett spat. He didn't have much saliva left so his mouth just popped.

"He brought you here," Lansdale said. "He gave you one last chance. That sounds like a friend to me."

Lett snorted. "Brother, you don't know from Adam."

"Fine. What about Jock Quinn?"

"You kidding now or what?" Lett snickered, shrugged. "You can't figure a Marine. He hates dogfaces. Wants nothing to do with the likes of me."

"Maybe. Then what about our Miss Kanani?"

Lett sneered now, rocking his head back, laughing. "What about her? You fucking idiot. You really thought I'd fall for that old trick? The honey pot? She's working for you! She was playing me for the fool. She's nothing but a whore native and a hustler and a viper to boot."

32.

Lett woke up in his cell, his hood back on. Maybe an hour had passed since he had to face Lansdale, hopefully for the last time. Maybe it had been a day, considering how thirsty he was. He couldn't remember things. He might've said or done something expedient, though, because his cuffs were off. And they left him alone for now. He tried to piece the episode together. That thug Frankie was there. He had said things about Kanani and Jock to divert attention from them, to ward off Frankie.

He felt a chill all over himself, persistent, in his every fold and crevice. He was naked, he realized. Stripped naked. He curled up, but that only made his shoulders and buttocks feel colder, more exposed. He sensed his cellmate over in the other corner.

"Are you there?"

His cellmate grunted.

"Who are you?"

His cellmate snickered.

***

Footsteps. The wheel spun, the door flew open.

"Where's Lansdale?" Lett shouted. "Get Colonel Selfer. I demand to speak to them. It's my right!"

"Shut up," Frankie shouted back. "What's a haole know about rights, eh?"

"Go to hell," Lett said.

"Get up," Frankie said. "Both of you."

Lett heaved himself up, his head whirled inside the hood and he swayed; he used the wall to steady himself. But he was up.

"Why aren't you up?" two others were screaming at his cellmate, "Get the hell up," but the cellmate only laughed a sickly cackle.

Thuds sounded, groans. They were kicking at him. The cellmate laughed harder. The dogs growled, moving in.

"Wait!" Lett shouted. "Please. Let me help him . . ."

They paused, stood back. Lett felt his way over using his toes as feelers, the dogs nudging at them with cold noses. His shin found his cellmate's chest. The cellmate held Lett's ankle with both hands, grasping it like a child on a bottle.

Lett crouched down. "Just do as they say. All right? Can you understand? I'm with you."

The cellmate rose from the floor along with him, holding on, hanging on his shoulder. They stood side by side, their shoulders pressed together.

"Move out," barked a guard, and each of them got a stiff jab in the side.

No cane or bat jabbed like that, Lett knew. That was cold steel.

***

They were led along, prodded if they slowed. Lett's hood was still on. Doors opened, shut, opened. They never exited outside yet the air had changed, and Lett's breathing seemed to create a faint echo. It was as if he'd been led into a giant bucket standing on its side.

Jagged, hard ground poked at his bare feet and he had to keep repositioning them, like a kneading old cat. They left him to stand in one spot. He heard the crunch of footsteps and talking that echoed.

A light clinked on—bright white through the hood. "Stay still," barked a voice. It was Frankie. Lett's hood came off. He folded forward, shielding his eyes from the light. Spotlights. He let his eyes adjust, peering around. He was standing in what seemed to be a clearing, though he could make out no trees or bushes. About fifty feet away, at the other end of the clearing, a man was curled up on the ground, also naked, his skin glowing fluorescent in the harsh light.

His cellmate.

A guard bounded out and kicked at him, yelling, "Stand the hell up!"

The cellmate rose, pushing up from all fours. His hood was off, too. His face was puffy and splotched with dried blood. He held his bound hands over his genitals. His squinting, blinking eyes stopped on Lett and kept blinking, as if hoping to make Lett's image go away.

It was the commando.

They must've shipped him back, shackled down in the cargo hold, on the very same boat that he and Jock returned on.

"I won't hurt you," Lett said to him. "Just do as they say."

The commando nodded back. A sick laugh rose out of him and drool hung from his mouth, swinging in the light.

It seemed like they were outside, but . . . Lett looked up. The sky was pitch black. Too black. No stars? How could that be? He stepped forward.

"Stay put," someone yelled at him, and that echoed, too.

And Lett understood why.

They were in a cave—a lava tube, they called them here. These were all over the island. No one knew how many there were. Some were massive. They stretched far and deep into the land, into the earth, and within their cores the ancients had hidden from foreign invaders. It was just like in the Philippines. But the tunnels under The Preserve had led to it.

Lett now made out silhouettes along the lava rock walls—men in those belted coveralls. Lansdale wasn't among them. Lett recognized none and imagined they were Frankie's handpicked crew, though none looked Hawaiian. He could see Frankie too, relaxed, rocking on his heels.

His crew had machine guns and pistols, pointing at him and the commando.

The commando's eyes had gone glossy with sadness. He sucked up the drool.

A guard strode over to Lett and the commando and handed each a Colt pistol. Lett held his by the end of the butt, letting it hang as if it had been dragged in shit.

"Better grab onto that," the guard said, backing up.

"Nothing doing," Lett muttered.

Lett and the commando stared at each other, the guns dangling at their sides.

"It's duel time," Frankie said. "Raise your weapons."

The grip safety was off, the safety lock off, and the hammer cocked. Keeping his finger off the trigger, Lett eased the butt upright, into the crook of his thumb and forefinger, and he raised his gun halfway so that it aimed at just before the commando's feet. The man was doing the same, nodding along to Lett's moves.

"No way to hold a weapon, soldier," someone said. Jeers followed. Chuckles.

Lett spoke to the commando, soft yet firm, his head craning forward. "Listen to me. Don't do it. Don't let them make you. Okay? Can you?"

The commando nodded.

"Take aim," Frankie shouted. Someone giggled.

The commando was shaking his head now. Good man.

"Take aim or we fire," Frankie shouted.

Lett glanced sideways. Their machine guns and pistols were trained on them. They'd have to be good shots or they'd strike the lava rock, and no one wanted ricochets in here.

"Last chance. Take aim!"

"Don't do it," Lett repeated to the commando.

But the commando aimed his Colt with both hands. He leaned forward, knees bent.

"Goddamn you," Lett muttered. He raised his gun with both hands but kept his index finger off the trigger, resting it along the barrel.

"All right, that's it. You get a five count," shouted a guard. "Five . . ."

The commando's eyes bulged but his arms steadied and his finger found the trigger cage.

"Four . . . Three . . ."

"Aw, hell." Lett's finger found the trigger. The commando's pale chest was easy to see.

"Two . . ."

Then, Lett took his finger off the trigger. He stood up straight, chest out, not caring that he was naked. His heart had suddenly calmed.

"One . . ."

Nice and steady. Hit me right in the heart, please.

"Fire!"

The commando swung his gun around and rammed it into his mouth and fired.

It clicked. No round.

The commando squeezed the trigger. Still no round. He squeezed again, stumbling backward. Nothing, nothing. He landed on his back and kept squeezing, his legs kicking.

Lett aimed down at the lava rock earth and squeezed his trigger, again and again. Nothing. No rounds in the chamber or in the magazine, none at all.

They were laughing at the commando, howling and pointing, gasping from the hilarity. "Ha, my sides are splittin'," someone said. "Shoulda gone with the bullets," said another.

Frankie was just shrugging, shaking his head, like a parent who doesn't quite get why children love a playground so.

Lett should've known that he had no ammo, just by the lighter weight of the weapon. That riled him more than anything. He glared at the guards. Sweat ran down his forearms in long hot slivers. "Did I pass?" he barked.

No one replied. They were surrounding the commando. Two guards held the commando by the arms. Laughing, howling, they thrust him up by his wrists as if he were the prizefighter who just KO'd to win the title belt. Others yowled and cheered, some raising bottles of Primo beer, cigarettes shooting sparks. The dogs rushed in past Lett and barked and jumped around the commando, growling and showing fangs and snapping at his feet. The commando danced for them with his mouth hung wide open like he wanted to cry or scream, but no sound came out.

Lett's shoulders felt heavy, as if he were loaded down with gear. He slumped and lowered himself to his knees, letting the jagged rock cut into his kneecaps.

I should've killed the man when I had the chance, he thought, *put him out of his misery.*

Frankie ordered the dogs off. His guards turned the commando around, facing away from Lett. The commando's arms found his sides, and his shoulders squared. And they marched him off, leading him into the blackest, darkest reach of the cave. And onward, and onward.

A guard bounded over to Lett with a black hood. The last thing Lett saw before they pulled the hood on was the commando's white back fading into that pitch-black darkness, like a bag of concrete sinking into a deep lake at night, sinking down, under it went and deeper still until it would find the bottom of everything, and nothing at all.

33.

When Kanani didn't know where to turn, she always found a banyan tree. The Preserve had one, near a trail far off in a corner of the camp perimeter. She went back to it the morning after she found Frankie waiting for her at the boogie house bungalow.

A banyan tree was special. A craggy and curvy web of roots wove its way vertically along the outside of a central trunk and horizontally along branches where they then hung, some eventually reaching earth again, intertwining, recombining. A banyan, her faddah had told her, was an interweaving of many lean roots that once began as a single seed attaching itself to some unassuming tree—and had taken over. They had moved plenty when she was a girl, but there was always a banyan tree to be found. On the plantation, and later, her faddah had always located the banyan with the tree fort, and if there was no fort, he would build her one.

What would Faddah do in her place? Well, he wouldn't have been going for gold in the first place. He would have stood up instead. Faced these bastards. And he had paid dearly for that, she reminded herself.

For all she knew it was Frankie Baptiste himself who made sure Faddah got crushed by crates so that he couldn't organize the union. Frankie had done some nasty work for the union busters too, after all.

She stood among the hanging roots and gazed mauka, inland and upland, through a break in the forest. Farther up mountain, the forest gave way to desiccated thickets and knotty shrubs as lava earth and old flows reclaimed the terra and turned it scrubby then bare. In the southeast this naked land rose steeply, ever higher to Mauna Loa. In the northeast it rose before mighty Mauna Kea. And straight ahead, in the arid and jagged center of the island, that exposed saddle of vast lava fields stretched between the two volcanoes, on and on until the green earth was reborn near Hilo Side.

She touched a large green oval banyan leaf, like a glossy piece of thin leather, and followed the path up its root and more roots, like a gargantuan ivy. Some haoles liked to figure this was all just ivy gone out of control and immediately conceived ways of cutting it back. How dare they.

They too were getting cut back, each got shafted in their own way. Wendell Lett thought he was coming here to get cured, but they were only using his combat fatigue to remake him into the type of man who didn't require a conscience. A psychopath. The end stage was killing, he'd told her. The cure is the cause. Wendell had told her about Miss Mae, about the bad things they were training him for. It didn't surprise her, not after what happened to Faddah.

As for her? They never were going to give her a chance. It was all lip service as usual, just like on Oahu. She could get them something they needed, and they got it. So be it. But she still had her shot at that gold. And then Francisco appeared. He was their new man. It changed everything. Now she had to find a way to neutralize him.

Even Charlie Selfer the climber was getting the shaft. Someone had promised him a big shortcut up the ladder of success, but now he was getting left behind and fast. A bait and switch, the haoles called it—Selfer's dear old deadbeat for a dad was probably real good at that move. How humiliating for Selfer. He was feeling a grudge at first, but now it was one hell of a panic because the new owners had installed Francisco and for the duration.

Maybe ex-Marine Jock Quinn was the smartest of all, she thought. He had kept his head down. They couldn't find a way to use him for their own ends—and destroy him in the process.

The banyan roots, her faddah had told her, eventually envelop the tree supporting it, killing off its trunk, and when the trunk rots away there remains a hollow center. Natives used to live and meet and hide in them. If only this one held such a refuge inside, she thought. She could hide in there indefinitely. Meanwhile those roots could keep spreading and spreading, seeded by birds she commanded, and she imagined her web of roots taking over this whole damn evil camp. If she could only give the order. Strangle Lansdale! Strangle Frankie!

It only made her sigh. This banyan wasn't developed enough or old or strong enough for strangling or even for hiding, and it might just be too high up mountain to survive forever.

Still, Frankie would get his comeuppance. Because that *moke* was getting suckered into the oldest con: the ones in power lead you to believe that you really could become like them, all so that you avoid thinking what was best for you and your own.

She wondered, again, if this was what was happening to her too, and then she pushed the thought from her mind by pulling binoculars from her bag. She looked toward the perimeter fence, topped with barbed wire. Just beyond this stretch of the fence, maybe a half mile mauka, was supposed to be one of those markings on the map she remembered. She'd nabbed the binoculars from the Main House. She lifted them to her eyes.

The clouds were low but she could still make out a hill, and what might be a lava tube entrance, but the rise of land obscured it. A two-rut road led up to it.

She had given up trying from inside The Preserve. Frankie lurking above and below made it too risky, especially without help. She had finally considered enlisting Wendell Lett, but then she couldn't find Wendell and she could only hope he wasn't on his next mission already. This location outside of camp was one close enough that she remembered from the map markings. But how to get there? If she exited camp toward the interior, there might be no returning to this side of the island. She would be fleeing alone in the rugged and unforgiving saddle, exposed between the two volcanoes.

She heard crunching. She turned to see Jock Quinn coming her way. He carried no sentry gun and had his shirt unbuttoned. His sleeves were rolled up like a sailor spoiling for a fight after losing a game of craps.

She lowered her binoculars into her bag, stepped out from the hanging roots, and waved.

He didn't wave back. By the look on his face she thought he was going to bust her up. She pegged him for drunk, maybe.

"What are you doing?" she said, putting a smile on.

One side of his mouth turned up but it was no smile. "I should be asking the same of you," he snarled as he bounded up to her.

"Can't an island girl take a stroll? I love banyan trees, see, my faddah, he—"

"I haven't seen him," Jock said and stopped before her. "He's just vanished like."

Her gut twitched with uneasy feeling. "Wendell, you mean? Maybe they sent him on assignment."

"He's not. I got it on authority. I'm worried. I'm worried he might've told them where to get off instead."

"Get off? Oh. Instead of what?"

"Instead of just getting his damn points and peace of mind and cure and getting posted the hell out of here."

She nodded, glaring at the ground. It was clear to her now. They must be holding Wendell underground, below The Preserve. But no one went down there. Only Selfer could probably get her down there, but he refused to discuss the subject.

"What are you doing with those binoculars?" Jock said.

She winced and he could probably tell he'd caught her off guard. He certainly wasn't drunk. Now she wondered if he'd been tracking her out here. He was a Marine guy after all.

She patted the binoculars inside her bag. "Just . . . taking in the volcanoes," she said. "I was hoping there might be a way to climb up these roots for a better look."

Jock nodded up at the roots. "Might be better if it was hollowed, then you make your way up without being exposed, but you'd still need a good perch with leafage for, uh . . ."

"For a sniper?"

"For the OP," Jock insisted. "Observation post. It's not always about killing."

"No," she muttered. "I guess not."

This was an awkward moment for them. Neither had gotten too

close to each other, even though each had to realize that the other knew a special side of Wendell Lett. Jock fell silent a moment. He kept facing her as if pretending to chat, should anyone be watching. But he peered side to side from the corners of his eyes.

"No one's behind you, either," she whispered.

"Let's assume they're holding him underground," Jock said out one side of his mouth. "You think you could get to him?"

"Get to him how?"

"You know, with your contacts." Charlie Selfer, he meant. Tricking him if she could.

"What then?"

"I'm not going to let the man rot, even if he is a doggie."

She fought an urge to look around her now.

"No one behind you, either," Jock added. "Just outback."

"What's that supposed to mean?"

Jock glanced in the direction of the lava tube. She held out her hands, shrugged.

"Just, let's keep this between us," Jock said. "Wendell's life might depend on it."

"I will let you know. Okay?"

"Roger," Jock said. "You know where to find me. But don't make it obvious-like."

"Like you coming here was?"

Now Jock glared at the ground, his boots digging into it. "I had no one else to try. I know he trusted you."

"You got a plan for it?" she blurted.

"I might. But I don't have much time. You?"

"Maybe. But what if we made our plans one and the same?"

"That could work. And then? It's gung-ho time," Jock said, and he stomped off glaring over his shoulders.

**

On the way back, Kanani felt like some small jungle animal about to be swooped up by a giant bird. Exposed, no armor, claws too small to pierce. Or maybe a snake could snatch her and eat her whole at any moment.

They had Wendell somewhere. What had he done now? What would they do to him?

She had lied to Jock—she didn't have a plan. Not yet. But she knew how she would do it. It was how the smaller animals did it. Like her faddah had told her. Scrawny boxers. Artful boogie house bouncers. Even Frankie probably.

You had to react first and keep bobbing and weaving on your toes giving no one time to think let alone recover. You didn't use your own fists. You only needed to make it work.

34.

There is no cure, Lett reminded himself, again and again. *There never was a cure.*

They had locked him back in the same cell underground where he'd been reunited with the commando—where the commando spent the last days of his life.

That man was dead now.

I'm dead soon.

Lett accepted this. They had pulled his hood off when they returned him to his cell, obviously not caring anymore what he saw or didn't see. Because he was a goner. The one caged light bulb wanted to blind him, so he stayed to the farthest corner of the cell, sitting, letting his spine firm up against the hard wall. They'd given him a tattered and filthy T-shirt, Army-green boxer shorts. Then they threw him a raspy, soiled wool blanket so grimy it was greasy, and he drew that over his head to shield the light. He slept on his side, knees to his chest.

He looked forward to seeing his friends again. Tom Godfrey, and Holger Frings, his foxhole buddies. He expected them to visit him now, in here. But they never came, even when he begged out loud for them to come. This made him feel colder and more horrified than that image stamped on his eyeballs of the commando descending naked into that dark cavern forever.

He soon realized why his friends had mostly stayed away before. It wasn't because Lansdale and his fake dose had led him to think he was getting cured. His friends didn't visit him here for one simple fact: he was in hell. Not even they could reach him in hell. He was back in the shit, was what he was. When a certain brand of GI went back up on the line, getting his hands bloody and his brain blackened all over again, his troubles would recede. That was why certain GIs needed to be back in combat so bad—until it became a death wish.

"Come and get it over with," he shouted into the blanket only to inhale the sour air of the untold numbers who wore this grisly shroud before him.

Another hour passed. Hours? He was losing sense of time. He flung the damn blanket off and paced the room, the harsh light glaring down on him as he shielded his eyes with a hand like some sickly catatonic salute. Soon his stomach rumbled and he had a dry, metallic taste in his mouth. He had to urinate so he yelled, "Hey! Gotta piss here. Got a bucket? Hey!"

No one came. He urinated into the drain in the floor, and the translucent yellow of his stream told him he still had nutrients in him. "Lucky man," he muttered.

He paced the room again—five steps one way, then the other, back and forth, gotta keep moving, always keep moving, stop and he was cornered. But he was fully cornered now. They were training him as an assassin. Some might call it a hit man, others an insurgent, and some a hero. No matter the name, history told that an assassin was used for all manner of power politics, good and bad and every credo in between. Often a lowly assassin such as he was presumed to be acting alone if not crazed, especially at first, but history often proved that certain forces were at least influencing the assassin if not ordering him directly. The targets varied. Regicides. Czars killed. Among the US presidential shootings, there was John Wilkes Booth and Lincoln. The assassination of Archduke Ferdinand was used by the powerful as a pretext to set in motion the mobilizations that began the first World War. And not twenty years later, the Nazis used assassination attempts and bombings real and invented to begin dismantling democracy for one final Teutonic cataclysm.

He wondered if Lansdale's genuine dose of dope had made him tell them things when he thought he was out cold. But he hadn't known anything to tell. What if they told him things instead? What if they suggested things to him under that dose that he would eventually come to believe? Lansdale had spoken the language of the Red Scare. What if that became natural to him later, his native language? A way of life. A belief. Faith. What if they had put their own lever inside his brain that could be flipped on at any point, quicker than a knee jerk? He couldn't rule it out. Injecting him with various radical thoughts, just enough to leave him babbling when he was apprehended. He could be portrayed as anything from an anarchist to a Communist, a reactionary to a fascist. He was already cracked from the war, that much was proven. And a dirty deserter to boot. He was one bad apple.

If all else failed, they were going to use him as their scapegoat. They had tried and tried to save him—tried to cure him—but it just didn't take. He was acting on his own, they would say. Another GI that was "all out of change," as it was called—the good soldier who lost his way and his mind. After all, hadn't Selfer himself told him that there had been reports of him voicing threats to important persons; that he'd declared he'd wanted to kill Ike, President Truman even? He still didn't remember ever doing that, but it didn't matter because it was in a report somewhere.

They didn't even need him alive for it. It was surely cleaner for them that way, all tied up neatly, just the corpse of a cracked and spent vet with the sniper rifle that he worshipped. Someone would clean up the blood.

All the more reason to die, and real damn soon.

He crawled under his blanket but the greasy shroud stuck to his skin, and he couldn't breathe through it, so he clawed at it and rolled out of it kicking. He lay on the floor, splayed on his back, glaring into the harsh white bulb, panting, drooling.

He was their man, no matter what he did. History proved that much.

He wanted to laugh, but only tears came out.

***

Lett reckoned that another day had passed in his cell. Maybe one and a half. He noted the footsteps of guards passing and didn't recognize any pattern or schedule. What was more, they passed more infrequently, maybe once or twice a day and no more than one or two men at a time. He wondered if he was the only one left down here, underground. That chilled him, and he pulled the grimy blanket over him and under him to keep his hips from bruising on the concrete.

When the door opened, Lett was expecting Frankie. Charlie Selfer came to him. Selfer was alone. He stepped inside the cell and then checked the corridor. He was back to wearing summer khaki without insignia, but it didn't fit as if tailored anymore. A button in the center of his shirt front was missing, and one sleeve was partly rolled up while the other wasn't and it hung there flapping unbuttoned at the cuff. His hair fell in his eyes; dry, no tonic—a sight new to Lett, and Selfer kept pushing it away as if it were a fly buzzing around him.

Lett was sitting on the floor with his back slumped against the wall. He said nothing. What could he say? He wouldn't bother standing until Selfer was forced to make him.

"Good Lord," Selfer muttered. He had bags under his eyes so distended they looked ready to burst. He'd lost weight, too, his trousers cinched up under his web belt, his cheeks hollow. He was panting a little, and Lett suspected he'd jogged all the way here in a panicked lather. An unknowing stranger might have mistaken Selfer for an escaping cellmate.

From his pocket Selfer produced a bread roll, wrapped in a white napkin, still warm.

"You better devour that, while you can."

Lett nodded. He unwrapped the napkin. The roll had fresh butter and salami inside. Glorious.

"Well? Eat."

He sunk his teeth in, inhaling it, and finished off the roll.

Then Lett noticed Selfer wore the strangest thing—he had a holster on his belt, and it held a Colt pistol. Lett couldn't remember seeing the man wear a gun, not even during the war.

"I can show you how to use that," Lett said.

"That's not funny."

"I'm not trying to be."

"I don't have time, Lett. I need to think . . ."

Selfer was grousing like a man twice his age. Yet Lett noticed a softness in his eye. And Lett wondered if the man had children, a boy he once put to bed and watched like this before turning the lights off. A wife? He always assumed not. Now he wasn't so sure.

He can go right to hell with me, Lett reminded himself. Selfer was the reason he was here. It all started with him.

"Why do I get the feeling," Lett said, "that you're not supposed to be down here?"

"Shhh." Selfer listened again.

"Let's hope they don't pass by for a while," Lett said.

"I spotted them going off on a break." Selfer crouched next to Lett. "Listen. I've been doing some figuring. I still do have some wits left in my noodle, I can tell you, and I'm using them. Now, you're going to think I'm half-cocked if not a little cuckoo, but . . ." Selfer spoke lower. "Have you ever heard of something called the Business Plot?"

"I think so," Lett said.

"You do? Even better."

"But I don't know the details."

Selfer smiled, held up his index finger. "It was 1933, to be exact. A cabal of top businessmen wanted to overthrow Franklin Delano Roosevelt and establish a fascist-style dictatorship of America." He spoke fast, like an auctioneer, getting it all out. "The Business Plot conspirators weren't simply angered because FDR was striving to help the common man with his New Deal programs, which big money simply could not allow. It wasn't even their fear of any senti-ment they could brand as Communism, socialism. No, the scheme was cheaper and meaner than that. The business barons were angry because FDR had taken the dollar off the gold standard. This meant they might lose a smidgen of their vast money, on paper, which was far too great a loss for them, and for this alone they were ready, willing, and able to topple American democracy while pretending to be the only ones patriotically American. For their figurehead, they wooed a maverick Marine general named Smedley Darlington Butler."

"I've heard of him," Lett said.

"Good, okay. Now, they tried to trick the proud Marine into playing along," Selfer continued, "assuming as they were that he would hunger for the same unchecked power and riches they craved, all he needed was a taste of it. But Butler felt more in common with everyday people, you see, born as he was to a Quaker family, and the fellow loathed the idea of a single gilded room of the richest men pulling all the strings. So Butler blew the lid off the plan. It first broke in the *Philadelphia Record* and *New York Post*, I believe, and some were calling it the Business Plot and others the White House Coup."

Selfer listened to the corridor again, then grimaced at Lett, letting his hair hang in his eyes. "Now get this. You might not know of this part. After the hearings and news stories, hushed and sanitized though they were, it was revealed that the cabal's first choice for their fascist strong leader wasn't Butler, but none other than . . ." Selfer thrust out his hands like a desperate vaudeville comedian low on laughs. "Guess who?"

"General Douglas MacArthur."

"The very same. At the time, Chief of Staff of the United States Army. Well, MacArthur certainly has the pedigree and connections and certainly the perfectly aggrandizing nature. Yet MacArthur proves too extreme a choice. Even for them. In 1932, MacArthur had led a crackdown on the famous 'Bonus Army'—WWI military vets who converged on Washington, there to protest nonpayment of their bonuses long overdue. They and their families were going to starve without the reward they'd earned through so much blood and sacrifice to the nation. Ah, but the great General MacArthur sees things otherwise. He orders in troops and tanks and rides at the head of the charge, his men attacking with fixed bayonets and sabers drawn, and when that isn't brutal enough, our grand general deploys tear gas—goddamn tear gas, Lett—just as the enemy did to these heroic vets in the Great War."

"I don't think it sounds cuckoo, not at all," Lett said.

"No? It's documented, too. There were hearings in Congress, on 'Un-American Activities,' they called it—to investigate Nazi propaganda and other schemes. Though you wouldn't find much in the big newspapers and magazines except the briefest mention and those, well, they're dismissive at best. Sanitized, like I said."

"How do you know so much about it?"

"That General Smedley Butler wrote a book about it."

"*War Is a Racket*," Lett said. "I remember that now."

"Correct," Selfer said. But this time he only sighed. He sat and pulled his knees up like a GI still rattled after a long firefight. "Then, there was my father. It doesn't hurt to tell you. He did some small-time hustling for those bastards behind the Business Plot, basically playing their messenger boy. Shameful. He probably thought he could finally get a leg up. Finally. And you want to know the real tearjerker? Back in '32 he should've been in the Bonus Army, standing up to them strong and tall. That's right. He was a WWI vet, Lett. In the dark woods like you. The Argonne. But, no. He was too damn busy running penny-ante numbers rackets. So I know. And meanwhile my dear mother and me were always wondering where and how and when the milk would come, stolen or no."

Lett only glared at Selfer. "You're a lackey here. Their tool. You make your dad look good."

Selfer recoiled. "I should slap you for that, seeing how you're so weak, but I'm afraid you might be right."

"You know where I was in the Philippines, and what I saw?"

"I didn't even know it was the Philippines." Selfer added a bitter chuckle. "Of course."

Lett told Selfer that he had seen and even met MacArthur.

Selfer lost color in his face, and the bare light bulb wasn't helping.

"That's more like it," Lett said.

"You know what they're going to do exactly?" Selfer said. "Do you?"

"I thought you might."

"I only got the theory, Lett. Look at history. A bastard like Hitler and the forces behind him, funding him, they failed with their Beer Hall Putsch a good ten years before Hitler got into power. Sure. But they did not fail the second time."

Lett grunted. "America loves a winner."

"And no one in our history is more popular than General Douglas MacArthur at this very moment. Maybe Ike. But President Truman? Couldn't be weaker . . ." Selfer let the words trail off. He stared between his legs, his hands hanging off his knees.

"I should've brought you water," he added. "What the hell is wrong with me?"

"You've had the rug pulled out. You're spooked."

"That bastard Lansdale," Selfer said, shaking his head. "The man is so damn crude in his opportunism, it grates. He's like some cheap carnival barker." He muttered something, his eyes rolling around. Then he was itching at the one sleeve hanging over his lower arm. Lett hoped it was only whisky causing his bender and not something stronger. Even so, this had to be the moment. He might not find Selfer in a more compromised and vulnerable state.

"I'm going to tell you something," Lett said. "Remember when they sent me to Honolulu? Do you know why?"

"How should I know what happened there? They don't tell me what your missions are. I just see regular teletypes, and everyday report requests, and the usual approval forms—"

"Listen. The person I met was named Mae. She was Chinese. She told me she knew things no one else knew. About something called Golden Lily. The other thing was, she was fixing to meet with a reporter."

Selfer's head had reared back, his eyes wide. "Spit it out."

"She knew that this place, The Preserve, was training an assassin."

"Say it. Just say it."

"This assassin, he kills a very important man. This, in turn, will spark a take-over. A coup. Just like you told me about."

Selfer's arms had lowered to his sides. His hands lay on the cold floor, knuckles down, palms up. His head swiveled to Lett, his face on a flat track, eyes gliding with it. "So it is true."

"It's just what you were afraid of, wasn't it? About San Francisco. When you backed out of that briefing room? Thus your figuring. Thus the history lesson you're telling me."

Selfer stared at Lett for a long time. Lett stared back.

"Stand up," Lett said finally. "For once. Stand up to them."

"Like you did, during the war? Or here? Yeah, and look what happens."

"Well, at least I'm not you."

"Don't tell me. I know what I'm doing. Sure, maybe I never fought up on the line, rear-line staffer like me, but . . . You know something? Maybe it is about time I do get in a fight." Selfer shot up, adjusting his holster, pushing back his hair.

"Can you get me out of here or not?" Lett said.

"What?" Selfer whipped around. "How can I? I don't know the score. I need to know the score, see."

"Can Kanani help? Tell me she's still up there."

"She is, but, I don't know. I just can't trust her. It's too risky. And now there's that heavy Francisco to worry about, and I can't know if those two Hawaiians will stick together or not."

"Lansdale?"

Selfer laughed. "Oh, Lansdale's out, gone, scot-free. On to the next con. It's that Francisco I have to worry about now. He makes Lansdale look like a file clerk."

Selfer felt at his holster again, and he stepped back, out of Lett's cell, into the corridor.

"Water," Lett said after him, but Selfer didn't respond.

35.

Kanani didn't like returning to the boogie house bungalow, not after Frankie had found her there. She couldn't get it out of her mind. He had made her slide her chair closer to him on the gold chaise. Then his eyes went narrow and dark inside. He warned her never to run from him again when she had a secret that he also knew. Because he would be right behind her, again and again.

"Promise me," he'd said, "that you tell me, and only me, if that fool Selfer or anyone else makes any moves that could endanger the pact I made with Lansdale and those head haoles who run Lansdale."

"Who runs Lansdale?" she had dared to ask.

Frankie's face went hard and crimson, and he admitted that he didn't know. "Has to be big kahunas from the mainland," he said. "Who else?"

So she promised Frankie, she had to. Charlie Selfer certainly wasn't a man she could stay loyal to, she told him—if she were playing that quaint old sort of loyalty game she wouldn't have left the likes of Wendell Lett to his own sorry devices.

Frankie laughed at that.

"Besides, we Hawaiians gonna stick together," she added. She didn't elaborate that Frankie himself was practicing about as much loyalty to his fellow Hawaiian as the imperialists who first came bearing their power and greed, as the colonialists, as the so-called democratic Americans with their shameless and manifest land grabs.

At the same time, she fought the realization swelling inside her that she was making her own play from a position of unrepentant greed. A person could argue that against her. Her own faddah certainly could. He might even claim she would never live it down.

But, there was another problem. Frankie had held her hand and told her, in the kindest way he knew, that she should take things further. She should hitch herself to his star. She could tell by that twinkle in his dark eyes that he would demand sex with her eventually. He once made a move for her when he was a boxer in Honolulu, the country kid going for broke in the territorial finals. She had somehow evaded him. But soon she might have to give it to him. It might be the only way.

Then her stomach flushed with warmth and her brain with the relief of clarity. She recognized: There might be a way to get all of what she wanted. She could get at the gold and get Wendell out, too. Just maybe. If Jock Quinn truly was as gung-ho as he said.

She was holing up at the Main House instead of her bungalow for now. But she needed Charlie Selfer to come back. She hadn't been able to keep track of Selfer the last couple days. He had been rushing around camp on his own when he wasn't disappearing possibly underground or locking himself in his office, always having just left the last place she tried. He could only keep moving so long. She waited for him in his bedroom, hunkered on his bed in his terry cloth robe.

The front door slammed shut. "Where is she?" Selfer shouted, even though old Yoshiko had been sent home long ago. The bedroom door flew open, and Selfer bounded in as if he'd just leapt from a sinking canoe onto the beach. He looked it, too. His khaki shirt was unbuttoned and his tank top underneath sweat-soiled, his hair in his face. To her surprise he was wearing a holstered Colt—yet this suited her plan well. Afternoon light from the louvered glass window illuminated a splotch on his neck. As he came closer she saw it was a bug, so smashed she couldn't tell what kind—probably a mosquito, yet another plague the haoles had brought to the islands, from the bilge water in their whaling ships.

"What? What are you looking at?" he said.

"One bug on your neck all slimy."

Selfer slapped at his neck and wiped, leaving a track of red. He landed on the wicker chair nearest the bed with a great creak and a sigh. She moved to the edge of the bed closest to him, braving a reek of stale sweat and whisky. He lit a cigarette, handed her one. And then she saw it. He had needle tracks on his forearm, close to his elbow.

"Where you get those? *Doctor* Lansdale?"

Selfer stared at his arm as if he'd never seen veins before. He waved away the notion. "Lansdale's no doctor. This here? Just a little something to keep me calm."

"I can see that."

"Look. What do you want me to say?"

"You tell me."

"Well, I can tell you I've found out some things. Lansdale is long gone, for one."

"The Directorate is no more."

"Right. It's something else now." Selfer sipped from his flask, then offered her a tug but she declined. "I thought I was one of them. But I'm not. I just get orders by goddamn teletype."

"From those machines in your office."

Selfer shook his head, and the veins on his temples swelled. "There's no record of any so-called Directorate. Of Lansdale even. Only of us. Me. You. Lett."

"Where's Wendell?"

Selfer jumped up. He paced the room, looked out the window. He glared at her through smoke. "Wouldn't you like to know?" he said.

She didn't answer. She let him calm down.

"Where's Wendell?" she repeated.

Selfer didn't seem to hear. A sickly chuckle puttered out of him. "Do you know that President Truman's approval numbers are plummeting? Look at him. He's weak. Desegregating the military, wavering on other issues. And then, there's General Douglas MacArthur."

"Charlie . . ."

"The big man doesn't even have to know about it, and he probably doesn't, not the details. They simply prepare the throne for him and he strides up and he assumes. He never got the respect he deserved, and now by God he will."

"Oh. Maybe I do see where you're going with this. Who's *they?*"

"Who do you think? Old money, new power; new money, old power. It's a revolving door, all the same players. Damnit to hell." Selfer formed a fist and pounded on his knee.

"Calm down."

"Easy for you to say. You're just a native."

Kanani jerked back, raised a hand. She could've slapped him. "You got no idea, mister."

"Well, maybe I'm starting to get an idea. I bought into this deal hook, line, and sinker. I had no idea missions were going to fund something like this. A coup?"

"Hold up, bruddah. A *coup?*"

"You heard me." Selfer fell silent a moment. "San Francisco," he muttered. "The president will be there soon, it's on his schedule. All right, sure, supposing it's a lesser important person. Only they make it look like a grave threat. It could even be a foreign leader, one not playing along. Or this could simply be a test run. But the havoc it might create? A vacuum for a strong man? What if it's a first step?"

Kanani let her robe drop. She yanked her denim overalls off the chair. She put them on.

Selfer just glared into the carpet, didn't look at her bare flesh. "All they have to do is say Lett did it. They could even deliver him to the very spot. By then it's too late. It doesn't matter what he says or claims to be."

Kanani placed a hand on Selfer's knee. "I hate to sound cruel here, but you're not gonna end up much better."

Selfer placed his hand over hers. It pulsed hot and small and wet, as if he were clutching his own heart. "My dear," he said, "don't you think I know that? Don't you?" He then held his hand to his heart as if replacing the organ.

"So do something about it."

He snorted. "Me, their head paper-pusher. Head lackey. There's no one to call. That was always the deal. We are on our own. Secret operation. They tell me. Us. It's a one-way street, a dead end."

"So stand up to them. Here."

"Well, I'd need to know when, wouldn't I? And how. Problem

is, I'm not in the know. Never was. The only loophole I'm seeing is a noose. If even a sense of what I or Wendell Lett suspects is true? They're leaving me to hang. We're all hanging. There are so few left in camp, more leaving every day. Lansdale can deny it all. And this goon Frankie, he is their new man."

"Do you know where Wendell is?"

Selfer looked away, side-eyeing her.

"Look at me. You do!"

"You can't—"

"Where's the map?"

Selfer grimaced at her. "So you did find it, that time in my office. Well, I burned it."

"You what? Shit." She buttoned up and slid into her slippahs.

"Can't have any evidence, dear, or they might pin it all on me."

She grabbed her purse and slung it.

Selfer stood. "Where you going?"

"Where you think? I'm going find a way to get us all out of this trap."

Selfer stared, his lower lip hanging. "How?"

"Tell me where they have Wendell. Stop glaring at me. Listen to me."

"You can't visit him. It's not possible now."

"Then just tell me where. Answer me, dammit."

Selfer kept glaring. He wiped at his neck.

36.

K anani returned to the boogie house bungalow, she had to. The baby revolver was there, in the footlocker. She cased the place first. Luckily Frankie wasn't inside. She kicked off her slippahs and pulled on her army boots and a good broad hat, slid the revolver into her purse, and moved to leave. At the mirror, she stopped. Her eyes looked drawn, the skin of her face loose. It could've used makeup but she didn't have the time.

Moving through camp, Kanani noticed that something was fishier than spoiled poke. The personnel in The Preserve had been steadily dwindling, but today almost no one was left. Before she knew it, this would be a haunted place, a prospect that made her take deep breaths as she strode across the grounds. She didn't want to be a ghost, and surely not the last phantom out to close the door. Adding to the spookiness was the sky entombed by low clouds, sheets of battered lead pushing in from the sea and going ever higher up mountain, dragging over. The palms shuddered from it, and the eerie quiet gave her a chill. She wished she had a rain poncho, a tarp, anything.

She entered the command office. No one was on duty, but she spotted a chalkboard on a back wall that listed the day's sentry assignments—she didn't see Jock's name there.

Next stop was the training ground where Jock had trained Wendell and others on various weapons. That, too, was empty, as was the laundry hut, and even the bar. She fast-walked it over to Jock's bungalow. She knocked, no one answered. His screen door was shut but wasn't locked. She went inside, calling his name, got no response. His small bungalow was sparse and spic-and-span like a barracks, bedcover taut, all stowed away. He even had a stand-up locker. No padlock, so she pulled it open. His fatigues hung neatly there. She checked his bathroom, saw his toiletries arranged just so. Same for the kitchenette, the washed dishes drying on the counter.

On the way out she noticed a small photo on his nightstand. It was a girl no more than twenty-five, modestly pretty, dishwater blonde hair, angular jaw and nose and something feisty in the eyes.

Jock was still here, she assured herself.

She roamed the compound using secondary trails. Inside the woods it turned darker than dusk with the low clouds still pressing down, and the wind picked up, making the palms slap around. She saw the mess hall and realized she hadn't checked it.

The place was dead, the tables unoccupied. A young busboy in cook whites was clearing a table. On the other side of the room, in a corner, sat Jock Quinn. He wore civilian clothes—a cheap rayon aloha shirt of muted coconuts and palms, brown cotton trousers, and those strange green USMC jungle boots with canvas uppers and rubber toes and soles, like high-top basketball sneakers. Even in haole civvies he resembled a Marine in camo. She watched him from the side. He sat over a plate of rice stacked with Spam and brown gravy. A coffee mug stood at his one hand out on the table. Dim light from the window illuminated the top of his wispy crew cut.

She stepped inside. Jock also had aviator sunglasses on, so it was hard to gauge his feeling. But this was as good a place as any. They'd have a buffer of four empty tables around them, and it might even look natural. He hadn't looked up. She stepped toward him.

"You found me," he said to his plate.

She sat across from him. "It wasn't easy," she said.

They spoke in staccato, like sentry and encroacher confirming a password. She now saw his eyes behind his sunglasses because of the light from his window view. His position, she also saw, gave him a wide sightline of the main way through camp. This would do even better. From here, she could see if Frankie was coming. Though anyone could be on their payroll. Even a busboy in cook whites. Even Jock Quinn. But she had already decided. It was all worth the risk.

No steam came off his food; he'd been letting it sit. "That's better with a hamburger patty," she told him. "Locals Hilo Side call that the Loco Moco."

Jock made a face at his plate. "You can have it."

"I don't want it."

"We shouldn't be talking here," he said. He lifted his coffee mug, to look natural.

"Who's the girl?" she said.

His eyes fixed on her. "I told her I was never coming back. I never thought I was, either. Not then."

"What did she tell you?"

"Told me nuthin'. Just left me. Not even a Dear John. Nothing." He shrugged. "What was she supposed to do?"

"You gonna try and find her?"

He shrugged again. "Now they inform me that the Marines should take me back. Now they tell me. I'm cured, they say. Selfer told me that. Lansdale had given his okay, apparently. Some of the guys are off the hook. No strings attached."

"So you're a regular joe again, eh?"

"Gyrene, ma'am. No. I'll never be a regular joe again."

"No strings attached—that means what?"

"They don't require my duty for any more of their special assignments. I can leave. Reenlist. Their rosters are set. Certain men passed, others did not."

"It sounds like you're the one who passed."

"You could put it that way." Jock looked around. "I was never here, they tell me. No one was. Top secret. I can't speak of it, not ever. Remains classified. Me, I was just lying on some remote beach this whole time, feet up in a hammock, stoned on rum, and maybe I had me a native girl to boot."

"When do you leave?"

"My last shift is done. Selfer says I need to go. I can head on down the hill. The new goons will let me out of this cage."

"Congratulations."

"Uh-huh."

"You packed?"

"I got my sea bag."

"For where?"

"They gave me enough pay for a one-way passage to the mainland, if I want it."

"What do you want?"

"I'm thinking interisland steamer, Kona to Oahu." Jock lifted his mug again. "I cool my heels on Oahu a while, make sure I don't crack up again. Then I reenlist. In Honolulu."

The busboy got closer, so Kanani ranted about Jock owing her money and whisky, putting on a big act with her hands and bared teeth. Busboy snatched up silverware and scattered.

"Why aren't you eating your food?" she said, still baring teeth.

"I can't. I'm a wreck, see."

"Eat it, Marine."

He picked up his fork as if he'd never seen one before, cut at the Spam, scooped up a piece along with some rice and gravy, opened his mouth, and dumped it in. He chewed, staring at her.

"Good. Try eating again in one minute. Look natural."

Jock nodded. "I just can't leave. Not yet."

"You thinking what I thinking?" she said.

"They have Lett."

"So what are we are going do about it?"

"Supposing you tell me."

"I got a plan," Kanani said.

"And I'm listening."

"I'm not talking about some secret sneak-away out the gate, down mountain. He won't get out that way and I won't, either."

"Good. That's just for yellow bellies anyway."

"Me, I'm talking about burning down the house."

"Now you're talking."

"You'd be putting plenty on the line," Kanani said.

"If they don't know it was me, who's the wiser outside? No one even knows this place exists. You just let me shove off for Honolulu in one piece when it's done. Can you do that?"

"You'll have to leave Hilo Side. Maybe it's not an official berth on a steamer."

"A ship is a ship." Jock shoveled in another forkful, added a lift of his coffee mug. "Like I said—I been holed up on North Shore with my rum ration for all the enlistment office knows."

"Good, okay." Kanani eyed the room. "Now. Can you get us below?"

Jock nodded. "I've done sentry duty down there."

"You ever see Wendell down there?"

"Not personally. But he has to be there. They have cells down below. I even have a map."

"Oh. Even better."

"They don't know it, but I do," Jock added.

A silence crept in. Both listened to the room, and to outside, looking around. Things were just too quiet. They heard taps, then tapping. Kanani peered outside. The first drops of rain were splashing on the dirt, fluttering the grass.

"Hate the fuggin rain," Jock muttered. "Even when it's warm."

Kanani picked up Jock's fork and took a bite. The meat was tough, the rice mushy, the gravy bitter, all of it overcooked. She made a face. "Folks make this better Hilo Side."

"So I'll have to go try it there."

"First, we go for broke. Eh, gyrene?"

"Yep. We bust 'em up."

"Ho, not bad for a haole. You're gung-ho."

"Mahalo." Jock pushed his coffee over to her.

"Why are you doing this with me?" she said.

Jock smiled. He shook his head. He eyed her and the grayest slivers of his irises shined like metal. "What the brass and the con men and the rich suits never will get is that we don't do it because they order us to. We do what we do for each other. And that's that."

37.

Lett lay in the dark, so pitch-black he could hold his hand before his face and see nothing. In one respect, it was as if he didn't exist anymore. He couldn't see himself. At times he couldn't feel himself, so he would pinch his ribs or unwrap the greasy blanket to feel the brunt of the cold on his skin like a dunk in a winter stream. It was getting colder. His light bulb had gone out so long ago. He had screamed for a guard then, but no one came.

Sometimes he would wake and panic that he wasn't even in the cell anymore, that he was down inside an abyss they'd dumped him in. Other times he was underwater, a casualty from a ship torpedoed, or he was floating beyond the earth in a black space, like man would someday but in control of it, unlike he. Not like this. Not held in suspension. This must've been what it was like for the commando deep in that lava tube, with nothing, no one, only the beating of his heart and gasps choking his throat. Giving up all hope. To quell the panic, he clawed at his blanket and felt the concrete to confirm that he was still in the cell. Then, through the cold, he could smell his shit bucket. It was half full now.

He craved light more than warmth. He had to see something. He would stare and stare, hoping his eyes would adjust, but they never did. Such was the seal on that cell door. The Seabees or whoever built this had done a hell of a job, for the war effort. To contain the Japanese. To preserve democracy. Good for them.

Death for him.

And yet they had brought him food, a metal dog bowl of mixed slimy scraps, stringy meat and gristle and mushy rice or tapioca mixed in, all in a gelatinous pap that could be anything from raw egg to the guards' saliva. He couldn't see it. He tried not to smell it because it had a foul tang a little too close to the reek of bodies rotting in front-line mud. At one point he wondered if the meat wasn't the commando himself. He then realized that they didn't necessarily want him to starve in case they needed him half coherent and strong enough for whatever they were to do with him—even if it was just a vile setup to frame him as the fall guy.

No guards had passed by out in the corridor for what felt like a day or more. What if they just left him here? Packed up and went. He would go mad even without their needles and guinea-pig drugs. Someone else might find him. He would wake up in a VA nutcase ward, if he was lucky—though it might just be the electric chair. He wouldn't put that past the America of today, let alone in the iron-fisted leviathan that the cabal coveted and was sure to get, those mongers of the insidious plot. The way forward wasn't what anyone expected. We had forged our past and won the present but we would lose the future.

They will see, he thought, and laughed. But it will be too late by then, the seeds already long sown. No one will see.

He imagined himself as a corpse in here. He wondered if the cold would stave off decomposition and preserve his body for a time, like a pig carcass hanging in a butcher's cold storage. He figured his soul or whatever a person wanted to call it would exit well before then. But where would it go? Would it hover in here until his body reached a certain state, until his body spasmed and clenched up as he'd seen bodies do from violent death on the line? Or would his body relax, all flaccid, and then only harden up with rigor mortis many hours later? He told himself he would close his eyes and mouth upon dying, and willed himself to do it, chanting it even. "Close eyes, close mouth . . . mouth closed, eyes closed." More than anything, he hated the thought of something crawling in his mouth, or of his eyeballs decomposing bared to the air.

His stomach clenched up and his head spun and he clambered over to the drain and vomited into it. But only bile came up now, bitterly sour like apple vinegar.

He could try to kill himself, but even then, they had him. They will let him be found however they want him to be found.

Supposing it's a building in, say, San Francisco, or some other major US city he had never seen and never will, six stories up, situated by a window, overlooking a plaza where an important person or even the president might have been shot, his rifle still beside him. Maybe he'd used it to blow his brains out, though he wouldn't know about that. He would never get to be present at that meeting where his death is staged and he thereby gains a certain notoriety in that dark pantheon of assassins.

He laughed out loud at that. He rolled backward and kept going, kept rolling, kept moving, and rolled into the blanket as he went; rolling wrapped up, telling himself, *Gotta keep moving. Always keep moving, don't bunch up. Stop and you're cornered. Keep your eyes open.* His knees and elbows clattered against the concrete wall so hard that he might've broken skin if he wasn't blanketed up. He rolled the other way, chanting, "keep moving, always keep moving, eyes open, stop and you're cornered . . ."

He kept at it, working up a sweat, not caring if he struck the shit bucket. Maybe he could go out this way, in pure and utter exhaustion, no fluids left, the only man ever to do so, simply expire from motion, just a wool sack, twitching and quivering, until the final spasm and he'd flame out, one last spark in his brain to turn out the lights.

He panted and moaned as he rolled, finding the opposing walls again and again, itching from sweating, so hot now he let the blanket fall away, his limbs gathering scrapes and bruises as he went.

"Keep moving, eyes open . . . stop and you're cornered . . ."

38

K anani trotted through the driving rain after leaving the mess hall. She tried the cover of a forest trail, but the drops only struck bigger and faster there, propelled downward by sagging palm fronds and pointed ferns and slick leaves. Back out on the main path she dodged the forming puddles, telling herself that the rain made her running around camp look less conspicuous and hoping that she wasn't being followed by one of the few left here.

She headed over to the main gate, keeping to eaves and covered porches when she could, and checked the guard shack at the front gate. The half-asleep guard who normally had this shift was long gone. The new guard looked like a *moke* she knew from Honolulu. It was the same all over camp. Francisco was bringing in all his goons, posting them at the gates, using them for random sentry duty, and the ones who weren't his presumably shared the same enforcer mindset of the low-grade psychopath.

She headed back to the Main House as the sun went down, the last light fading from high inside the low clouds. She shook the wet off her like an island cat. She passed the bathroom, grabbed a towel and wiped herself down.

She found Selfer in his office. He was passed out at his desk, face down in crossed arms like a schoolboy taking a nap—except this boy had a bottle of Filipino rum in his outstretched right hand. He wore the same outfit—he probably hadn't bathed. As she stepped into the dim room, she felt cobwebs at her feet. No, it was teletype ticker tape. The floor of his office looked like the VJ-Day parade down King Street in Honolulu. A metal garbage can stood over in a corner, overflowing with more of that ticker tape and papers of all sizes.

She approached the desk, dragging along ticker tape and papers stuck to her damp feet and ankles.

Selfer twitched and sat up, his hair whipping back. He blinked at her. "What, what's happened?"

"You tell me."

"You got caught in the rain."

"You can see—that's a start. Tell me, goddamn you."

He held up his hands. "Tell you what? What do I know?"

She sighed and wrapped the towel around her hair and made it a big production like she was about to stomp out of the room.

"Just, let's take it easy," he said. He frowned at the rum bottle.

"I demand to know what they're gonna do with me," she said.

His eyes widened as he rediscovered the room. "Look at this paper trail. I've always gotten certain directives via teletype, sure I have. Plenty of it's been routine stuff, most recently about closing down this command post, handing it over to you know who."

"Frankie Baptiste."

"He goes by Francisco," Selfer growled. "But now? Just look. More of it keeps coming and coming and piling up. I don't know what to do with it all."

"Why all the paper?"

"I don't know. But it's directed at me, names me by name. Don't know what they want, can't make heads nor tails of it. It's all code mostly. Ordering me to implement this or that or ordering me to relent from performing deeds I'm not capable of anyway and I don't even understand their code words anyhow. It's like there's a madman on the other end."

She blew air out one side of her mouth. "Auwe."

"Ow? What's that mean?"

"You got instructions for what to do with me or not?"

Selfer pressed both hands to the desktop. He glanced around at all the ticker tape as if her orders were in there somewhere. "Right. The orders for you are clear. They want you in Honolulu. You're to report to a new special office there, another new agency, what they're calling the CIA—Central Intelligence Agency."

"They're sending me back, you mean."

"That's all I know."

"It's just going in a circle." She kicked at the ticker tape. "Back where I came from. All I am to them is their goddamn honey pot."

"Their what?"

She glared at him, baring all her teeth.

"Okay, okay, take it easy. I get you: it's back to the boogie house for you."

She flung the soggy towel across the floor, it gathered paper. She turned to leave.

He shot up and came around the desk, grabbed her elbow. "Wait, where you going?"

"Leaving. Getting the hell out of here. I'm not sticking around for Frankie and his boys to complete his assignment, uh-uh, no way."

"Assignment?"

"Sure. Why you think they brought him in, him and his goons?"

"Enforcement? I don't know. It's not . . . in the paper trail. He takes orders from others. Lansdale maybe. It's—"

"I tried to tell you. They brought him in to clean things up."

"You sure? Oh, God. Of course."

"He's known for that. Has the knack."

"Who's he going to clean up?"

"Everyone. Everyone left, that is."

Selfer pressed a hand to his chest. "Including me."

"Especially you. And that paper trail, it incriminates you."

"In what?"

"In whatever they decide—whatever fits. Just in case. That's my guess."

Selfer turned away. He muttered, "This is what those German leaders must've felt in those final days, with us closing in from all sides. You know? The last man standing, you're Hitler's best friend."

"Or Tojo's. We in Asia, bruddah."

Selfer kicked at the ticker tape and papers and scooped it up and dumped it in the garbage can. He patted his pockets and peered around the desk, pushing papers and folders off it.

"Lighter?" he barked at her. "Give me that lighter of yours."

"No."

He grabbed the rum bottle and took a long swig, then poured the rest on the paper in the garbage can. He wobbled a moment. It made him lean on the can's edge, clenching it with both hands, his knuckles white. He vomited into the can and half the stream shot over the opposite edge. A stench of stomach juices and rum hit Kanani, parching her skin like a vapor, and she turned away holding her nose.

"For God's sake, get ahold yourself," she told him.

He nodded, wiping away dribbles of vomit hanging from his lips, leaving them on his trousers. "Oh, if only dear old dad could see me now." Something made him grin at her.

She only glared back at him.

His grin dropped with a jolt. "What?"

"That's why you wouldn't tell me my new post right away—you want me to help you."

He rushed over to her, his hands clasped in deference. "Can you? What do you want? You know I can't help you get Wendell free."

"It's too late to help Wendell. That would only give Frankie his big excuse to break you."

"Break me?"

"In two."

Selfer clawed at a cheek. "How do you know? How're you so sure?"

Now, finally, Kanani smiled. She was waiting for this moment. She smoothed out her overalls on her hips, puckered her lips. "Because he told me. Frankie, that is. We go way back."

Selfer stepped away from the garbage can. "Then get your own damn keys to the tunnels," he snarled. "If that's what you want. Because you're not getting mine—"

"It's not what I want, Charlie. I'm telling you this to help you."

"Sure, sure." Selfer threw open his desk drawer and pulled out his Colt pistol and fumbled with it.

"You like I show you how to load that?" she said.

"Shut up," he muttered under his breath, turning the gun in his hand.

She stepped close to him and caressed his shoulder, her red fingernails on his chest, his cheek, the gun. "You have to make the big move. Yes, you. It's the only one that's gonna save you."

Selfer cocked his head at her. "Why are you helping me? Frankie's from Hawaii."

She pulled her hand away, bowed her head. "Frankie, he . . . probably killed my father. Maybe it wasn't his own hand. I can't know for sure. But it was his *kine*. Bad people."

Selfer choked on a nervous laugh. "Hell, you're not messing around, are you? Is that why you came here, really? To avenge him?"

Her head flushed hot, maybe from surprise, maybe pride. She'd never looked at it that way. Selfer could be plenty perceptive when he had a death sentence. "Maybe. Maybe it is. Now listen. You can't just go and eliminate him just anywhere up here. He's gonna expect that. He's gonna see you coming. You're gonna have to wait for just the right *kine* moment."

"How will I know?" Selfer said and stared at his gun again.

Kanani waited a beat. Pretended to think. Nodded at a thought. "I will tell you when."

"Okay." Selfer nodded, then shook his head. "No, I mean, how?"

"I know a guard," she whispered.

"One of the new ones? No. Wendell's friend—Jock Quinn?"

"Yes. Keep it down."

"But, he didn't want to get involved," Selfer whispered back. "He made it out. He got papers back to the regular world. Wants to rotate back in. One of the few."

"He's still here. Lying low. I'm only gonna have him tip you off. He won't know why. Then he's gone for good."

"So he won't know from Adam—okay, okay," Selfer said, sliding the Colt into his front pocket. "It's the funniest thing. I can't find my holster in all this mess."

You're not gonna need that, Kanani thought. *Only the ammo.*

39.

Kanani undressed and dried herself off again, powdered her face and put on makeup. She found her bright red lipstick and applied it to her chapped lips with care, taking as much time as she needed, making the cleanest line she'd ever painted. She pinned up her hair on one side and set a pink-orange hibiscus behind her ear. She wore the sort of wraparound floral dress that made a haole woman look sweet and cute and a Hawaiian *tita* a whore in the eyes of a mainland sailor. She pulled on a rubber raincoat and galoshes and carried her bright red Mary Jane shoes in the same hand as her shiny black purse that concealed the baby revolver, just in case.

Frankie had his own bungalow, Jock had told her, not far from Lansdale's before he left. Frankie wasn't in, but a gang of the new guards, all of them demons with leering oily faces, were there having a little party, with dice and dirty magazines and Johnnie Walker hosting. They were the wrecking crew and the cleanup detail all in one. She insisted on waiting there for Frankie to come back, so they started to wind things down. A couple *mokes* she knew from Honolulu were the first to go, setting the example.

Waiting for Frankie gave her time to dry the last damp ends of her hair and put herself in order. She didn't need rouge. The adrenalin had flushed her cheeks good. She poured a Scotch neat in a short glass and settled on the sofa with her legs crossed just so. She didn't clean the place up—she'd let Frankie see how his pals disrespected him. The last *moke* to shuffle out didn't even close the door behind him.

The rain rattled the roof like a chain across railing. It found the doorway and drenched the threshold.

His footsteps were so deep and resounding she heard them over the rain and practically felt them in the sofa cushion. They bounded up the steps. He leapt through the wet doorway as if through a ring of fire, pressed the door firmly shut, both screen and front door, then peered around with his shoulders jacked up as if someone were waiting to jump him from a corner. He wore the coveralls the guards used down below. They were smudged with something dark around the cuffs, and she didn't want to know what. At least he'd washed it off his hands. He also had his holster and a combat knife hanging off his belt and, slung on his shoulder, one of those little M3 machine guns Marines called "the greaser." He scrunched up his chin at the mess his pals had made. But then he saw it was only her here now, and he loosened up.

"Aloha," she said.

"Aloha. Make yourself at home." He held out his tattooed hands as if to ask: What was she doing here?

"Dat Charlie Selfer, he going make plenty big play," she told him. "He try for save himself before too late. Before busted up already."

Frankie grunted. "How he going save himself?"

"He going try bust you up before you get him. Maybe he kill you, Frankie."

"Yeah? How you know?"

Kanani smiled. She crossed her legs the other way. "I went sleep with him."

Frankie didn't smile. He dropped the Pidgin. "Well. Look who's the sly gal. Can't say I'm surprised—"

"Shut up. So? What are you gonna do about it?"

"I'm gonna take care of it, that's what."

"Looks like you're ready for it already."

Frankie patted his combat knife. "Just part of the job, sistah. Orders are orders."

"Orders from who?" Kanani said.

"I told you. Men plenty higher than Selfer. Than Lansdale even."

"Wendell Lett in those orders?" she said. She couldn't help it. She made a face as soon as she said it.

"What do you care about him? I thought you didn't."

"I don't. I just like to know all the angles, how the loose ends get tied."

"Ah." Frankie showed her a grin. "Soon Lett, he's gonna get sent. . .

let's call it 'reassigned.'" He whispered, "Lansdale, he's gonna set that up plenty good."

"Oh. Fine. That serves him right, I suppose."

"Why?"

"For not playing along."

"I thought maybe you liked him."

Kanani shrugged. "Nah. He's just another dumb army guy."

"That's the truth. Anyway. Mahalo."

"For?"

"For sticking with me. Gold or no gold." Frankie straightened his belt and turned on his heels.

"Wait. Where you going?"

"I'm gonna go pay that Selfer a visit—"

"No. You have to wait."

"How come?"

"Timing. You need to wait till he makes his big move. Think about it. That way you got the reason why if they ever come asking why you didn't do it exactly their way. Maybe they wanted him in a stockade instead, or the looney bin. But he attacked you, see."

"Ah. Okay. How will I know when?"

"Me. I'll tell you when." Kanani stood, smoothing her skirt, and stepped around Frankie while showing him her flower and a smile. "You rest up. Try make yourself at home. I'll be back. I'm the one who goes now. This has to look natural."

"Then what happens?" He leered now, just like the rest of them did.

She giggled and tapped him on the tip of the nose. "Why, that's easy. I'll send a messenger."

"There's no one left. The last left by trucks, down mountain."

"I have someone."

"He better not be trouble. I got work to do."

"He's not. He'll give you the word, tell you where. You stay ready, yeah bruddah? Because it's coming tonight."

"And after?"

"After I come see you," Kanani cooed. "Come see you for good."

40.

Wendell Lett lay still in the dark, wedged in the angle where concrete wall and floor met. Cornered. It might as well have been the jaws of a vice. Rolling against the opposing walls again and again had not worn him out, so he had flung himself at the door, again and again and again. That only bruised him, then injured his shoulder—one arm might have come clean out of its socket, such was the searing pain, and he instinctively jammed it back in, gritting his teeth, only to hate himself for acting as if he would survive any of this.

The frantic activity hadn't worked. He'd simply run out of gas, yet his mind was still going. He lay there, blind, searching the darkness, looking for any way to kill himself. He thought of forming his blanket into a fat noose but had nothing to hang it on; and he couldn't reach the light bulb up above even if he stood on the shit bucket, and even then, it wouldn't hold him. What if he drank his own shit, right out of the bucket? He longed for any feeling of weakening, for that damning sickness people felt when facing a flu or some harmful virus—a disease, hopefully one that was a quick killer. But it hadn't been near long enough for weakening.

He heard the softest clatter and lay still, waiting. "Who's there?" he muttered, but of course he was alone. For a moment he thought it was an inmate in a neighboring cell scratching or tapping a signal, but such noises had stopped long ago, well before the screaming had stopped. He set his ear to the floor. It was a small animal or insect, roaming in circles from the sound of it and probably just as desperate as he. A rat maybe. A cockroach? Finally, a creature had come. He wondered what drove it here. Was there inclement weather up above? Fire? A battle? But how had it gotten here? Up through the drain, surely. It must not be very big to do that. He wanted it big, and contagious, with long sharp teeth or claws. His survival instinct urged him to catch it and eat it, and he suppressed the thought by biting into the inside of his cheek. His only hope was that this rodent-roach was only the first of a great wave that would flow into the dark room and consume him.

The soft clattering became a scuffing scratching, and then it was gone. Nothing to be had here, not even for a cockroach.

He moaned now. He felt such a failure. He wanted to be able to say it with assurance: *See you soon, Holger Frings, and Tom Godfrey,* though he doubted they would be heading his way. As for his Heloise, he didn't expect to see his only love anymore, not ever again. She was far too good and pure for where he was surely heading. At least there he could finally proclaim to Selfer and hopefully even to Lansdale one day and, if there were any justice, to all the power mongers who ran them: *You see. You've never done a thing for the human race except destroy and profit at others' expense. This is your reward. I hope you all burn down here with me, because you truly deserve it . . .*

He was about to drag himself over to that bucket of shit and drink it down whole. His mind was ready. But his body wouldn't move. So he muttered, before he passed out, "Good-bye, Heloise . . . goodbye, Holger Thomas, my good boy."

41.

Kanani waited in the unoccupied bungalow, in the dark. She sat on a metal folding chair at the little dining table, her hands pressed to her knees. She had told Frankie it would likely be tonight, and now she knew it had to be tonight, what with all of Frankie's *mokes* getting so drunk. Like local boys guzzling rum before a cock-fight, they were juicing up for a big bloody *kine* bust 'em up, and soon. But it had to be Frankie alone. Adding to that was Frankie telling her that Wendell Lett was about to be shipped off to who knew where and used for who knew what. Her nerves ran hot and buzzed, like charges of electricity on a ranch fence.

She had tried empty bungalows and had located this one with the door unlocked. She then found Jock in his own bungalow, sitting on a chair in his tidy room, the pack with his few belongings at his feet. It included anything from the room that could identify him. He had the small photo of his girl in there, his travel papers, letters from his mother. She'd told him it was time to start doing what they had to do. What he had to do. He'd nodded, didn't ask questions.

She had told him to meet her here in this unoccupied bungalow afterward. She chewed at her nails, caught herself, pressed her hands back to her knees. It just seemed like Jock was taking too long. But she wouldn't let herself open the blinds to look. The one nearby light outside on a log pole lent the contours of the room a dim yellow glow. The rain came back. Broad spurts lashed against the window and dragged along the metal roof like sand, in and out with the wind like sweeps of a huge wet broom, irritating her nerves even more. She had her denim overalls on, and jungle boots she'd nabbed from the now–near empty quartermaster's hut. She had the baby revolver in her hip pocket. Jock had no gun out there—he'd given his up because he was rotating out. She was expecting him to carry at least a fighting knife. They would just have to risk it.

The door banged and she shot up. Had someone knocked? Before she could get to a window the back door flung open and Jock rushed through the kitchenette to her, all wet and panting, his breaths controlled like a man climbing a long rope with much length and height yet to cover.

"It's done," he said.

"Tell me."

"Selfer was first. Main House. Rear entry so as to stress secrecy. He opened the door for me, he's the only person there. I tell him. He goes pale, wants to shit his drawers. He didn't want to go down there, but I convinced him. If he doesn't get Frankie alone down below and now, all alone in that break room, then it'll be too late. He got quiet a moment. I tell him it's the only way to fix what he helped create. He nodded at that, gained a little color in his face, asks me what comes next. I told him to give it one hour, until Frankie was sure to be in position. By then Frankie will have relieved the only guard down there."

"You sure there are no other guards?"

"Yes. I checked it again. We can't be sure about a random sentry, though."

"Then what?"

"I went to Frankie. This one's not so easy. His bungalow was all fouled up. Quite a card game they had going. The rest, his skeleton crew, they're all there throwing one hell of a wingding like before shoving off for combat detail, some passed out already or on their way."

"So?"

"I told him. Gave him the lowdown, what Selfer was planning, and it wasn't no scuttlebutt, I got it on good authority—because Selfer himself came to me with it."

"Why would Selfer do that?"

"That's what Frankie asked. I told him that Selfer was trying to recruit me. I'd been hanging around on a bender, in no big hurry to shove off down to Kona Town. So Selfer found me. He needed someone to get his back, see. Nothing doing, I says, to Frankie. I'm rotating out and anyways I seen enough blood for my kids' lifetimes."

"That's a nice angle. You don't have kids."

"Who's counting? So, I get to the gist of it. Selfer will be heading underground, and soon, and on no one's orders but his own. I think he's after a little of that gold, I also tell Frankie."

"Good. Okay."

"And I tell Frankie, Selfer's aiming to release Wendell while he's at it, let him run free and clear. But, and here's the thing: Frankie would have to face Selfer on his own. He brings that reckless blotto crew of his, then Selfer's going to hear them coming. Well, Frankie just smiled at that and said he wanted to do this one himself anyways."

"Frankie believe you?"

"He asked me why I'm doing this. I told him I got no orders for what Selfer wants. I only follow orders. But I do report any transgressions I see to the highest authority—meaning Frankie. That got Frankie smiling too but it wasn't a smile you'd want to see twice."

"I don't want to see it once. What then?"

"I asked Frankie how he's going to handle it. He wasn't going to tell me, but he couldn't resist, not with that smile. He told me he would simply be lying in wait for Selfer down there."

"All right. Well, let's see who gets there first."

"What now?"

"We wait a bit. Hopefully this rain will stick around. You all ready?"

Jock had his combat knife on his web belt. He patted the sheath. Then he lifted his pack, to show her. It was much smaller now. Three canteens hung off it. He pulled a small map from the front pocket. He unfolded it, turned it to her. It was a map to the underground tunnel system. Kanani's eyes scanned it, and she recorded locations in her head, making sure to focus on the break room, and on Wendell's cell, and especially on certain storage chambers farther out, these on the way to the exits beyond the perimeter and possibly to lava tubes at the base of the volcano. She couldn't help that last part. She could not rule it out no matter what her faddah would have done or told her. She didn't let her eyes stop long though in case Jock saw it.

She heard jangling. Jock was holding up a ring of keys.

"We gonna do this, let's do it," he said. "Keep this moving."

"Not yet. This might look like the front line to you, but this isn't that *kine* war. This here is a knock-down bust-up in a back alley."

"Hey. War is war."

Kanani had to nod at that. "We still have to wait. We can't be seen out there, just hanging around. Why don't you sit? It won't take long to get this cockfight up and running. Our two cocks, they have to want it and bad. And when they do? Ho ka, bruddah, dey all buckaloose."

42.

Kanani and Jock moved along through the bushes, fern to palm to shrub, squatting and crossing the paths only at their darkest stretches. The rain had let up but still soaked them, trickling off their hats like a gutter leaking. Two guards approached. Kanani and Jock hunkered down behind a wall of impatiens. The guards passed and were staggering drunk.

They pushed on. They saw a figure at the next tree line. They crouched behind a palm trunk. The silhouette moved from bungalow to bungalow for cover. Both recognized that stride with the slightest stoop, his left arm tending to dangle, left hand twisting slightly.

"That rat bastard," Jock grunted.

It was Lansdale. They followed him as he kept moving along trails. He was heading for the rear gate where Kanani and Wendell first arrived in the disguised jalopy pickup. The gate was now fenced, barbwired, and guarded. A DeSoto convertible waited for Lansdale there, complete with driver. He was taking Selfer's personal car. One of the gate lights illuminated him, revealing the briefcases and bags he was clutching tighter than his holstered gun.

"He never left," Kanani muttered. "That or he came back for more."

"Well, he's leaving now. Unless I can help it." Jock crept forward, drawing his combat knife with its jagged edge out.

"No," Kanani whispered. She crept after Jock, tugged at his web belt. "Don't . . ."

Jock halted. He pivoted slowly, and his eyes took her in whole as if he'd never seen another human being in all of his existence. She shuddered.

"Please, Jock," she said.

He blew air out his nostrils and slumped, making his knife disappear.

They watched Lansdale go. One bag hung low and he dragged it along. Kanani knew what was inside that one. With her heightened alertness, she thought she'd heard keys jangling on him and wondered if he'd paid one last visit to Wendell Lett. Maybe she should go take out Lansdale herself, jam her revolver right down his sneering mouth.

Jock was eyeing her in a new way. "We need to let him go," she said, reminding herself.

Jock led from here, back onto trails. Flowery bushes and spiky shrubs began to thicken and swell among the wild palms and vine-tangled trees. They had reached the edge of the more tropical reaches of the forest—and that tight little gully where Kanani had first spotted Frankie here.

They peered down into the gully. Kanani nodded at Jock. He was going to lead them into the tunnel system using the special entrance that normal staff didn't know about—it was also Frankie's and Selfer's route inside. A narrow road ran down, bordered by a skinny side path cut out of the lava rock. They took the path, slippery from the rain, grasping at the rock wall as leaves and flowers and veins grazed their cheeks. Halfway down the growth thickened, giving good cover. They crawled up under a bush for shelter from the rain and surveyed the end of the gully, where all that remained was the black hole of a lava tube.

Kanani shook the water off her hat. Jock pressed fingers into her arm with one hand, one finger to his lips with the other.

Someone was approaching. They crouched lower.

Frankie was striding down the road, wearing holster and knife, speed increasing. He disappeared inside the lava tube.

"He took longer than we reckoned," Jock whispered.

"Good. That'll make Selfer sweat all the more inside there."

"Let's give it five minutes."

They waited it out. Kanani shifted her weight, wiggled her toes. Worst thing was to have a foot go asleep. Jock pivoted and peed on the spot, into the trunk of the bush for quiet.

Soon Jock showed her his watch: five minutes gone by. He'd stopped blinking. He gazed as if watching all things at once, as if able to look through the lava rock with X-ray vision.

He held up a hand. "Did you hear that?"

She hadn't. She shook her head.

He nodded anyway, to himself. This made her start to worry. She touched him on the shoulder but he didn't react. He felt as rigid as the rock before them, all around them, one with it.

"You okay?" she said.

"I'm okay. I just . . . I don't always love tunnels."

"Oh." He didn't look okay. She knew locals who feared the lava tubes, and nothing a person could say would get them to think otherwise. So she hugged him instead, on pure instinct, and that seemed to scare the ghost. He grimaced at her, still from somewhere else, neither smile nor scowl but an otherworldly sort of wonder. It chilled her again. She only smiled back.

"Zero hour," he said.

"Yep. Go for broke."

He grasped her hand. He led her into the lava tube. He didn't need his flashlight. She trusted that. His breathing deepened and strained and it wasn't from the exertion.

About fifteen yards inside they reached a concrete wall, which held a gray metal door. Jock had the right key out, fisting the rest for silence, and inserted the key in one fluid motion and turned it. He pulled the door open, into near darkness, the only light coming from far down the slightly bending corridor.

Down concrete corridors they moved. They reached a mess strewn about the main corridor floor—cigarette packs, pouches and bags, a towel, a watch, a phone receiver and cord as if ripped from a wall, a notebook, map, a bashed walkie-talkie; two drawers of silverware and kitchen utensils; a bloody knife; and a set of keys, dark with the blood. The blood was inky red and sticky along the keys and knife and floor. Kanani gasped under her breath, but seeing the fresh living blood seemed to bring a calmness to Jock, she saw, regulating his panting, and she felt the bloodlust coming off him like steam.

Jock gazed up from the mess and locked his stare on the shut door just beyond, on which a sign read, AUTHORIZED PERSONNEL ONLY. He nodded at the door. This was the break room.

"Give me your revolver," he whispered.

She hadn't told him about it, but of course he would know. She handed it to him. He grinned at how small it was in his fist.

He fingered the keys inside his other fist until he found the right one. He turned the lock, and twisted the knob, and parted the door open.

***

They heard heavy breathing, and a hissing whir.

They heard a grunt. And a gurgle.

Jock shouldered the door open, aiming the revolver into the room with both hands. Kanani peered inside the room from behind him.

One light bulb was on, flickering from above. This had once been a nice break room, with a new icebox and cupboards, a Formica table, and a spartan but roomy sofa. A phone housing was mounted to the wall, the remains of a severed cord hanging from it—belonging to that handset out in the corridor.

Charlie Selfer lay on the floor, his back slumped sideways against the sofa as if he'd been trying to heave himself up. One arm was stretched out, looking twice as long as the other, which had curled up in his lap, the hand clawed. His face was battered, misshapen, bloodied, one eye a clot of black and blue and syrupy blood. His other eye stared at them. A bubble of blood expanded at a nostril, rising and falling. The crotch of his khaki trousers was seeping with blood. His right leg was bent back, but in the wrong direction as if the knee had been broken.

His Colt lay on the floor, just out of his reach.

Frankie sat at a table with blood sprayed on him from head to toe. He was pale, his skin a mustard. Under his chair a pool of blood was widening out from a trickle that rolled off his left arm, down and off the chair. He held the left arm tight with his right hand, but blood was oozing out through his whitening fingers.

Kanani tried to piece it together. Selfer must have been hiding and ambushed Frankie and got a shot off before Frankie lunged. Then . . .

Three other chairs were upended about the room along with more debris—shards of plates and mugs, magazines, wrappers and greasy wax paper and meat and vegetable scraps—the contents of the garbage can. This nasty fight had either started or continued out in the hall, but it had ended here. The reek was bitter and sour and yet fresh, like a compost pile just stirred. And that overhead bulb kept flickering and buzzing like an electric ranch fence shorting out.

Kanani blew air out of her mouth. She couldn't look at Selfer, even though his dull one eye had set on her. Jock had eased a bit, his feet taking a wider stance. There wasn't much work left for the bloodlust here, he must've realized.

Frankie grunted something. He raised a foot and his boot slid right off, into the slimy muck of the debris.

"We need all the keys," Jock said to both men, keeping to the doorway to avoid slipping on the muck.

Frankie shook his head. His toes felt around in the blood, hoping to find the boot.

Selfer opened his mouth, but a gurgle sputtered and sank in his throat and he had to cough to bring it back up. "You . . . have them," he rasped, his throat whistling.

Jock shook his keys at Selfer. "All on here? Each one. How do I know?"

"You have . . . to trust me." His eyes found Kanani. "I trusted you." He added a sick grin that must've hurt like hell, his head wobbling from it.

Kanani's face burned. Tears rolled down it, off her chin.

"Help me," Selfer said.

"Too late," Jock said. "Now you know what it's like. Up on the line."

"What Wendell knew," Kanani added.

Selfer nodded, once. "Tell Lett . . ." His head slumped to the side.

Frankie growled but it ended in a groan. Blood squirted out from the grip on his arm.

Kanani instinctively moved to help him, an island bruddah. Jock blocked her. She turned away and stepped out the door. Jock backed out into the corridor.

Frankie gasped and clucked but couldn't get words out.

Kanani kicked the door shut.

Jock tried keys until finding one that fit. "Locks from the outside," he said.

He held the towel from the floor up to the nearest light bulb and smashed the bulb with the butt of the revolver, the sound muffled. He hugged the wall, aiming the gun.

Kanani crouched behind him, both listening. They heard nothing. No one.

"Should've put down that rat bastard Lansdale when I had the chance," Jock whispered. "How's that for your cure?"

He waved them onward, farther down the corridor. As they trotted along, they heard a muted scream from that room behind them, but Kanani couldn't tell if it was Selfer or Frankie. Not knowing comforted her oddly, pumping her legs with a fresh power, assuring her that it did not matter. Not now. Not anymore.

43.

Kanani led down the corridor but Jock steered her along, right behind her, watching their backs. Her tears had stopped coming, but they left her cheeks moist and she didn't bother wiping them. They turned down the next corridor. She halted. They listened a moment, heard nothing, no one.

"That was tidy work back there," Jock whispered.

"I only got them both there," Kanani replied. "They did the rest to themselves."

They spoke like they moved, with a determined efficiency lacking snags of emotion.

"How did you figure they'd do each other in like that?"

"They're just scared little boys," Kanani said. "That's what you all are."

"Amen to that. Didn't hurt that it was a gal such as yourself telling them. With all your wiles. You played them off each other like—"

"Wait," Kanani said. They paused to listen again. If any guards came down here now, they'd be cornered. Yet only the caged light bulbs hummed above, and the screams from the break room had faded and ceased. Coast clear. They continued on, the corridors longer and colder than she imagined. The route turned, reached a fork. A right corridor had stairs at the end, leading up at a sharp grade. Jock pointed them left. The left corridor ended at a large door with a wheel-like handle, like on a ship. The wheel's hub had a lock. Jock spread the keys out in his palm and tried a few in the lock while Kanani stood back as if Jock were defusing a bomb.

The seventh key released the wheel. Jock spun it; the door popped open. Stale and sour air hissed out, warm on Kanani's face, making her squint. The cell was dark inside. Jock drew his flashlight. He pointed the light in. The beam hit the scarred, stained concrete wall opposite, no more than ten feet away. A rusty drain in the middle of the floor. This was surely a cell. It smelled like an outhouse. In the near right corner stood a latrine bucket. A dull metal dog bowl sat empty. In the far left corner was a lump, under a dark blanket.

"Wendell?" Jock said.

Kanani rushed into the doorway, then stopped.

No answer.

Jock went inside on the balls of his feet, careful not to step on anything. The dark lump had legs and toes sticking out. Jock tore off the blanket.

It was Wendell Lett. He was facing the wall. He wore a torn and soiled white T-shirt, Army-green boxer shorts. He lay curled up as if to shield himself. His hands were pressed flat to his ears so that he couldn't hear whatever was invading his dark cell.

Kanani had frozen just inside the doorway with a hand outstretched, as if begging.

"Lett. Wendell," Jock said. He tugged at Wendell's elbows and barked, "Lett, Lett," but Wendell only recoiled. Jock hooked his fingers around Wendell's and pried half a hand off an ear. "Wendell, it's me, Jock," he repeated. "The Marine."

Wendell loosened. He looked up at Jock.

It was the blankest look Kanani ever saw on a face that wasn't dead.

They pulled Wendell out into the corridor, and the gamy reek of the cell came with him. They stood him up, but he stumbled as if his legs were asleep, and his head wobbled. He looked to each of them, squinting, blinking. They sat him on the floor, his back against the wall. He was covered in purple-and-blue bruises, scrapes and crimson marks, the stains of excrement. Jock checked him out like a medic would, feeling here and tugging there. Wendell let him, his arms out like a baby boy hoping for a piggyback ride. Meanwhile Kanani peeled a smashed cockroach off his ribs. She stroked his upper arm, kissed his head, his greasy hair.

Jock nodded at her that Wendell was fit enough to move.

"I'll live," Lett grunted.

"We came for you," Kanani said, "we gonna get you out."

"We're a team," Jock said, "me and her and you. Can't just go and leave you here."

Wendell raised a hand to shield his eyes and they widened, bloodshot but aware, adjusting to the caged light bulbs above. A smile spread across his face. Kanani grinned, gasped. Jock laughed. And Wendell laughed, his voice cracking.

***

Kanani and Jock carried Wendell between them on their shoulders and hurtled him down the corridor, his feet dragging but doing their best to help push himself along. They turned back, passed the stairs leading up, and slowed as they neared the first corridor.

Kanani propped Wendell against the wall. Jock pulled out the small revolver and peered around the corner. The corridor was empty and the debris still there, the door to the room closed.

Kanani saw Jock's lungs heaving, pumping. She knew what he was feeling. A heat kept surging through her chest and up her neck. It was the bloodlust, and it was transforming her, too. Now it became a revenge lust, that marauder of the aftermath. A plunderer. Dark thoughts filled her mind. They were going to finish off those two vile fuckers in that room, make damn sure they were goners. She and Jock were gonna carve them up for what they did to Wendell and plenty, too, just like a kālua pig for roasting in a pit but without the care and good cheer. "You better believe it," Jock muttered as if reading her thoughts, a sick smile spreading on his face. *Let it happen*, a snarling sweet voice told her. Let it feel powerful. The Marine was nineteen again, and she one tough *tita*.

They reached the break room door, Jock's shoulder gliding along the wall, the revolver an extension of his fist. He waved Kanani over to him. She brought Wendell, who stared at the blood-splattered debris, his hands balled at his chest as if he'd done all this himself and it was only now coming back to him.

Kanani grinned at Jock grinning at her, and she nodded, yes, yes. He nodded at the blood mess of silverware and she picked up a steak knife, and a butter knife, one in each hand. For Wendell. Dinner time! They were gonna finish this thing like nothing had ever been finished. You want gung-ho, you want go for broke? *We bust 'em up forever.*

Wendell saw the door. "Selfer in there?" he said to them.

Jock nodded. "And Frankie," he said. "Two birds, Wendell."

And Kanani nodded along. They were going to separate the two limb from limb until you couldn't tell who was who. They might as well be Captain Cook. Maybe they'd even bake their remains. Aloha! Close your eyes, boys, because here we come . . .

But Wendell wasn't smiling. "Both of them are in there?" he said.

"Yep. Oh, yeah."

"We need them quiet," Kanani said. "Never talk no more."

Wendell glared at the revolver in Jock's hands. His own hands clamped to his waist. "They in bad shape?" he said.

"You bet. Frankie might be done fer."

"They deserve it," Kanani added.

"No doubt. That's the Golden Rule."

Jock's head cocked at Wendell and Kanani's cocked at Jock. "Come again?" Jock said.

"And now you plan to finish them off," Wendell said, his shoulders filling out. "That about right?"

"You look disappointed," Jock said, his grin fading.

"I'm not. I just want to know—did you use that? That gun?"

"This? No," Jock said. He looked to Kanani.

Kanani shook her head. She lowered the knives. "They did all this to each other."

"We only helped them along," Jock said. "Got them in the ring, see."

"It was gonna happen sooner or later," Kanani added.

"Lansdale?"

"Gone," Kanani said.

"Though he could always come back with a crew," Jock said.

"I see. Which is exactly why we need to keep moving," Wendell said.

Kanani and Jock had crouched to the wall, looking up at him. Jock said, "But . . ."

"I don't know how to thank you two." Wendell paused to clear his throat. "But, no more blood. All right? Just leave those two in there."

"Let them rot. Like they did to you. In their cell. Yeah," Jock said.

The revolver went into his pocket. The heat had cooled in Kanani's chest. Wendell reached down to her and touched her face, and she leaned her head into his hand, smiling.

Jock nodded at Wendell. "I bet you were one hell of a patrol leader. Okay, Lett. Thanks."

"Don't thank me yet," Wendell said, "because we're not out of this. Are we?"

"I know my way around the tunnel parts," Jock said. "But after that?"

They looked to Kanani.

"Let's go," was all she said.

44.

Kanani, Jock, and Wendell moved down more corridors, through doors the keys unlocked.

They smelled the cigarette first. Then they heard the footsteps.

They huddled as one, pressed into the dark depression of a doorway at another fork in the tunnels. It was one guard, no, two. Then the two guards were talking, jawing on about making it with island girls, souping up a coupe, busting skulls.

The two passed right by, took a turn, and their drunken babble faded.

"They're heading away from the break room," Jock said. "Come on, let's go."

They moved on. Wendell didn't want food yet, not until they were safer. He hobbled but kept up with help from their shoulders. A break every few minutes, more water from a canteen. It gave them time to listen to the tunnels. Wendell smiled at Kanani again. It calmed her deep and warm in her belly and she grinned back, wondering just what Wendell had experienced in that cell, all alone, in total darkness. She'd never seen a man more ready for what came next.

They were heading up mountain, reaching the part of the map from Selfer's office that she'd memorized. She couldn't help but think of all that treasure.

Jock said he knew of a locker room. It was vacated. Jock grabbed coveralls and rubber-soled jungle boots for Wendell, both the boots and suit too big but they would have to do. It kept the fabric from rubbing at his wounds, Wendell told them, thanking them again.

They moved on, passing through a larger sealed door that a jeep could drive through. Here the tunnel was rougher on the sides, like in a mineshaft, the lights few and far between. They'd reached lava rock.

Jock had slowed his pace, slower than Wendell. They waited for him. He tried but had to lean against the jagged wall. He touched it, then yanked his fingers away like it was hot and took a step back from, turning to them with his arms hanging, his face glowing pale green.

Kanani left Wendell to rest on a stray empty crate and walked back to Jock. His breathing was labored, a low pant.

"Those tunnels back there?" Jock said. "I could deal with those, they're man-made, by Seabees most likely, and I was loaded for bear to rescue Wendell. But these caverns, these lava tubes you call them? We had these in the Pacific. Saipan. Some lead right to those cliffs."

"Cliffs? No cliffs here."

"No? Okay, okay. But . . . So they strung some light bulbs in here. So? They could shut them down anytime. So I don't know. I don't . . ."

Kanani didn't know what to say. Maybe Jock had a pint of booze in his pack—maybe that would help. Or supposing it only made him more spooked?

"I don't know, either," they heard.

It was Wendell. He had heard them. He stood and walked over to Jock. "I don't care for them much, either. Tunnels, I mean. Any kind of hole. Not where I've been. Come to think of it, I don't care for jeeps much, or brass who never been on the front line, or truck beds, or these goddamn coverall fatigues. It's all a damn prison cell. So let's just get through this, me and you. Just like up on the line. So? What do you say?"

Kanani looked back to Jock and saw his face shining and his teeth sparkling, finding the dim light. He nodded at Wendell. "Fuck 'em all," he said.

"That's right. So buck up, gyrene."

"All right, dogface," Jock said. "We go."

And on they went.

They came to a second lava tube tunnel, branching off theirs.

Now Kanani slowed. The map came rushing back to her, plastered onto her eyeballs like a View-Master. Her heart squeezed up, restricting the blood in her legs, and they felt so heavy.

Jock came over to her, letting Wendell rest with his canteen. "You know the way. What's wrong? You can't remember it?"

"No, I can."

"So?"

"That new tunnel doesn't go far. It's one way. A storage cave."

"For what?"

She shook her head.

"Listen. Whatever it is that's eating at you, you have to face it."

"He's right," Wendell added from over at his spot.

Kanani whipped around to him. "They go and replace your ears or what?" she snapped. "Give you supersonic hearing?"

"You have to see it," Wendell said, "so you can choose."

Kanani growled at him and grabbed Jock's flashlight from his hand. She marched off into the connecting tunnel.

***

Wendell and Jock followed her, with Jock on his tiptoes now because of the near darkness—only Kanani's narrow flashlight ahead and one dim bulb above offering any light. It wasn't far. The tunnel was just a cave. They found her at the end, staring at a boarded-up narrow opening. She was shaking her head at it.

"I don't want to see," she muttered.

"Yes, you do," Jock said.

"You have to," Wendell added.

She glared at them, her hands on her hips. She handed the flashlight back to Jock. "You're the big strong Marine guy. Pull one of those boards back."

Jock nodded, and at Wendell. The opening was no taller than Jock. He stepped up to the boards, just thin slats hammered to a frame like a standing pallet, the wood still new. He reached up and pulled away a slat, bringing a creak of nails coming out. He straightened his shoulders, took a deep breath, and shined the light in. He stole a glance back at Kanani and pulled away a couple more slats, faster each time.

He shined the light in again. He leaned forward, his head inside, the light dancing around.

He whistled.

Kanani stepped his way but stopped herself from going any farther.

Jock turned sideways and squeezed through. They heard more creaking, whistling. He stepped back out with something behind his back. He clicked the flashlight off, which should have rattled him to no end.

He clicked the flashlight back on. Kanani started. Jock held a bright golden flash on the upright palm of his other hand. She stepped forward holding a hand to her eyes, squinting. Jock was grinning, his teeth reflecting golden light.

She first felt a warmth down low, then in her chest, and it spread throughout her in waves, so that she had to shift her feet in place to keep the feeling moving around, it was so intense in one spot. Too intense.

Jock kept grinning, his teeth illuminating as if plated with the gold and then greased as if the gold lacquered his fangs. He seemed to have gained half a foot yet shrunk at the same time, such was his obsequious stance, like the proudest butler there ever was.

Wendell meanwhile seemed to be looking at nothing at all. His face had slackened, and his eyes went dim despite twinkling too, and he released a couple sighs from deep within him, like a man exhaling the finest cigar available on this earth to go with that award-winning aureate cognac he was now licking his lips wet with. Wendell whistled.

Wendell, too? Kanani glared at him. The warmth inside her had retreated to just her gut and to her head, where it burned itself out behind her eyes, leaving her legs and limbs so cold. This chill scared her. If her head went cold too, she was done for. What was happening to her? She felt such deep sadness, the kind that made locals leap to their deaths into canyons.

"We take what we can carry," Jock said.

She shook her head.

"You earned it," Jock said, "here, just touch it."

She stepped back to avoid him. She pushed at his chest.

"What's wrong with you?" Jock said.

She shook Wendell, who blinked and blinked until his eyes were his own once more.

"We don't got all day," Jock was saying, "there must be fifty boxes to choose from, there must be other caves of them, ooh, sure, I can just taste it—"

"No," Kanani snapped. "We can't move them. Not one."

"What?" Jock said.

"They're tainted—they could be marked, I mean," she tried, "and who's gonna move goods that are marked?"

"Goods? This ain't just goods. Well, if you don't then I sure will."

"No!"

Kanani hadn't yelled it this time. It was Wendell again.

"She's right," he told Jock. "In a manner of speaking. She touches that, takes it, then she's marked, too. Cursed. We're all cursed."

Jock sighed. He stared at the ingot of gold, a compact brick. It had Japanese symbols on it, maybe Chinese, Kanani wasn't sure from here. He lowered the gold bar, his teeth recovering from their sham gilding. He lowered his flashlight, stepped backward, and without looking tossed the gold bar behind him, back through the opening where it landed with a tumbling thud, like a tree falling in a forest that no one ever hears.

45.

Wendell Lett had been returned to the world and felt it. He felt every ache, breeze, smell, pain, light, but his stamina and energy surprised him. As a GI, he'd slogged, starved, and battered for days, and it was apparently like riding a bicycle. He, Kanani, and Jock marched along a lava tube tunnel. They passed the last dim light bulb, and full darkness loomed ahead.

Jock already had his flashlight on. He aimed it with both hands like a gun, sweeping the beam back and forth before them. Lett and Kanani walked along either side of him, patting his shoulders for encouragement.

The lava tube was sloping upward, toward the surface.

Lett assumed Kanani would grow worried and angry after what she'd just turned her back on, but she was smiling now, lighter on her toes. "Morning's coming soon," she told them.

The lave tube widened into a cave. Kanani reminded them that their location was up mountain and well outside the underground complex. Selfer might've been the only one who knew about it apart from a few others, none of whom appeared to be at The Preserve anymore—not alive, anyway. Lansdale remained the only wild card. "The fugging Joker," Jock called him. They grew quiet and eased their steps, careful not to turn any rocks with their soles.

Darkness hit them. Jock's flashlight had gone out. He gasped, froze. He kept clicking and clicking the switch. He started hyperventilating, lowering down, crouching. Lett's lungs tightened, too, and he squatted with Jock, taking deep breaths, one arm around his back. Jock banged the flashlight with his hand. He moaned and patted his pockets.

Light came. A flame flickered. Kanani stood before them holding up her lighter, all of it gold, etched with Chinese characters and that angry dragon spitting fire.

Jock sighed with relief. He slapped Lett on the shoulder.

The cave ended at a concrete wall, with a rolling metal door big enough to fit a light truck. Next to that was a standard door. It had a peephole, covered with a metal disc. Kanani held up her flame. Jock swung the disc with a finger and put an eye to the peephole. He jerked back.

"What?"

"Nothing. That's the problem. It's all dark. Just like this damn cave."

"It's not daylight yet, that's all," Kanani said. "The opening must be yards away."

"Oh. All right." Jock tried the door handle but it didn't budge so he brought out his keys and tried them finding one that worked. "You two stay here," he said. He handed the dead flashlight to Lett. He set down his pack. Crouching, he turned the handle and cracked the door open, looked out. Then he went, careful to pull the door shut behind him.

Lett banged on the flashlight, but nothing happened. Kanani stood at the door on tiptoes so she could look out the peephole. Soon she opened the door. Jock was already back, with beads of sweat on his forehead.

"The opening checks out," he reported. "There's no one. Nothing. Barely a bush," he added to Kanani, who nodded gravely.

They headed out into the cave entrance and continued outside, crouching at first, peering around like small desert animals. They soon saw they had no reason to fear, not out here, not yet. Facing east, Kanani stood tall and eyed the vast open plain with hands on her hips like a prospector. "Boys, you two take a good look at that no-man's-land. 'Cause with any luck, that's what's gonna save our lives."

***

Five o'clock. They fled across the barren landscape, the wind cool and whipping at them. Lett finally let himself eat. Jock opened him a can of C-ration, what Jock called "C-rat," but to Lett the lukewarm beef and vegetable stew was Thanksgiving dinner and dessert, too. He ate as they marched and hummed as he chewed, even though his knees and ankles ached and his thighs burned and his lungs wheezed. At least they had boots for him. And he couldn't help smiling, grinning. They had fled only a few miles inland, yet he could see every star in the sky, it seemed, more stars than he'd seen in any desert or forest he'd ever known. Theirs was a new world—the Big Island's high outland interior. And Kanani and Jock were there for him, believing in him. Whenever he stumbled or stopped to pant, leaning on his creaking knees, they would stop and huddle with him, their hands on his shoulders. Along with those C-rats, Jock's pack had D-ration tropical bars and the three canteens of water hanging off it. Lett had only emptied one canteen. They would ration the rest, obeying a cardinal rule of outdoors survival, as Jock reminded them—hydrate in the cool of the evening or morning to regulate sweat, thereby saving water.

They took a break. Jock insisted that Lett eat a tropical bar from his pack.

"If you do me one favor," Lett said.

"Name it."

"You'll have to lose the revolver. You'll have to lose it for good."

Jock stared, his elbows bent. He turned to Kanani. She stared.

"Don't you two look at me like that," Lett said. "Hear me out. We can maneuver smarter without it. We won't make our moves based on firing back. We'll base them on avoidance. Less the lumbering bear, more the wily fox."

Jock said to Kanani, "I think maybe they did something to his noodle."

Kanani's face screwed up as if she'd sucked on lemon.

"Supposing the local authorities happen to find us?" Lett said. "It's far better we're not packing a loaded revolver. And if someone starts pointing fingers? It wasn't us, we're not the guilty party. We're not even armed."

Jock rubbed at his temples. Like Lett, he knew this was about smarts, but also about faith in the others' ability in the field—as whispered by Jock and his fellow Marines in dark island huts riddled with bullet holes, as chanted by Lett and his dogface buddies in French farmhouses scarred with shrapnel. They would honor one another's madness so that they might reach what came after.

"Maybe it makes sense," Kanani said finally. "We no have gold bars, and we no have guns, either. We're pure like a newborn babe."

Jock snorted. But he already had the revolver out. Jagged lava rock piles and ragged crannies waited on either side of them. He stepped around and over them, looking for a good spot. He stood over a dark crevice. He dropped the revolver, and the abyss proved so deep they didn't hear the gun hit bottom. He pulled his tunnel map from his pocket, crumpled it, and tossed that down, too.

"Well done," Lett said. "I know that wasn't easy."

"Your turn," Jock said and broke up the tropical bar for Lett. The chunks tasted like a cross between potato and stale chocolate and Lett choked them down.

Jock marched them onward, pushing the pace, his pack bobbing between his shoulders as if empty. They had a long way to go. They were crossing the island over its unforgiving volcanic center, a gritty and grim gauntlet of lava rock fields. Heading northeasterly, it was roughly fifty miles in a straight line to the opposite coast, about a day's journey if they could cover a mile every half hour or so.

As they marched on, the sun rose and bloomed pink and orange. Then it emerged golden round and white in its heart, and their black moonscape turned mustard and olive from the dry grass that covered the rolling outback as far as the eye could see. The terrain looked like a vast cracking tarmac carpeted with khaki. But it was no carpet. Up close the grass was thin and sparse, its soil just another variant of the black lava rock.

Steep vast slopes rose to the left and right, dwarfing all. To their hard left, which was northwest, stood Hualalai, the island's third largest volcano. On the horizon loomed the two mighty volcanoes, just as Kanani promised—to the right Mauna Loa and ahead on the left Mauna Kea, their gradual high peaks masked by dense cloud banks in the otherwise clear sky. Linking the two mauna farther ahead was a lava-laden funnel of a basin, only a few miles wide at its lowest stretch. Kanani called this the Saddle.

The Saddle was their passage through to the other side.

Eight o'clock. Full daylight. "Sun's up—heads covered," Jock barked, and Kanani pulled her khaki bucket hat on. She handed Lett one from Jock's pack. Almost no trees or bushes remained. The wind carried some warmth but still it ripped at them. They trudged on, their feet pounding at the hard earth that was turning so creviced and jagged that they couldn't take their eyes off it. A half hour for every mile had seemed conservative. Now it was looking optimistic.

Jock waved them down into a shallow gully. They lay on flat lava and looked out, catching their breath, the grass poking and itching. Behind them, the tropical forest holding The Preserve was only a green line along the blue horizon. Jock got binoculars out.

"It's too quiet back there," Kanani groaned.

She didn't need to say it. They had to expect a mighty wrath.

Jock rolled around and peered ahead at the looming basin between Mauna Kea and Mauna Loa. Somewhere along the Saddle, a narrow and dipping and choppy road had been blasted out of the lava. Saddle Road locals called it—the only vehicular route through the middle of the island. "They could take Saddle Road," Jock commented, and no one disputed him.

They took bites from a tropical bar, sipped water, pushed on. By noon they'd gone twenty miles. It was only about sixty degrees out, but they could feel their rubber soles growing warmer.

Kanani slowed. She kept looking back over her shoulder. She stopped. She grabbed and pulled at them and they crouched down. "Look, back there. What is that thing?"

***

A giant beast rose into the sky, far behind them but ever higher. They scrambled into a trench for better cover, lying in a row. Lett and Jock tore at grass and laid it over Kanani and then covered each other as best as they could. Kanani muttered something in Hawaiian.

"*Helicopter*," Lett and Jock blurted at the same time.

The small helicopter rose fast, its nose down as it roared up. It hovered over The Preserve, then over the open plain just beyond the tropical forest, passing back and forth. Jock clamped the binoculars onto his eyes, focused.

"Markings?" Lett said.

"Don't make out any, but it's Army green. Shit."

"What?"

"Jeeps. Motorbikes. Combing the plain beyond the forest. Can't get far with those. Looks like guys on foot, though, too."

"We're miles ahead," Kanani said. "Hours."

"Right now we are."

"You think they know we're crazy enough to cross the island?" she said.

"Maybe, maybe not. They're covering all their bases. Kona Town, the port, probably got so many of their boys snooping around you'd think it was Hotel Street. But then again, we were crazy enough to take out two birds with one stone, weren't we?"

"It's Lansdale," Lett said.

"If it's him, they'll head this way," Kanani said. "It's only a matter of time."

***

An immense slab, purplish black in the sun, its plateau as high as their heads, its width at least a couple miles, its length that of a great river. They had come to a massive lava flow formation, more than a century old but looking as if it had only just cooled. No grass, no weeds up there. Jock was up above climbing around, crouching with the binoculars.

It had been a half hour since they'd spotted the helicopter. The adrenaline of freedom had helped Lett tame his aches and pains, but now the fatigue of full flight was setting in. His throat was dry, his hungry stomach a throbbing hollow, his muscles shaky and his nerves prickly.

Jock waved them up.

"This is one of the main lava flows," Kanani said, sounding proud as if she were guiding tourists. "But this isn't the worst rock," she added as they climbed. "You get two *kine* lava on Big Island—*pahoehoe* and *'a'a*. Pahoehoe flow, that's your smooth and wavy surface, like this. Ho, but the *'a'a*? It's all broken up. Jagged, loose, rocky piles of hell. No good, bruddah."

"I thought we already passed that."

"Oh, no. This flow will have plenty of *'a'a*. I can almost see it up ahead."

Jock led them along. "It's like a goddamn obstacle course up here," he panted, "so be careful. Man, do I hate fuggin islands. Just rocks, all of them."

He had a raw red scrape on his elbow. Kanani made a clicking sound at it.

"Look at it this way," Lett offered. "No scout bike could traverse this, certainly no jeep, not with this busted-up lava."

"True," Jock said. "But that helicopter decides to head this way now with us out in the open? We're fucked beyond all recognition, I tell you."

They scrambled across the black river of slabs, zigzagging to avoid the spans of *'a'a* rock, and then came gaping crevices. Their usual half-hour-a-mile pace slowed, each mile taking closer to an hour. Then it was all *'a'a*, and it was like hiking across a bed of coral. The brittle sharp chunks wobbled and shattered and shifted under their feet. Ankles nearly rolled, palms scraped. After an hour of it they could finally smell the dry brown grass of the Saddle. Almost there.

Behind them the helicopter hovered nearer, high in the sky.

"Why are they staying away?" Kanani asked Jock.

"If they got good sighting gear? It don't matter—they could probably see us from there."

"Oh."

They rushed on, tiptoeing and skidding and kicking up rocks.

The lava flow ended as it began—with a sudden drop-off. They had to navigate it like a rocky cliff, grasping at one another's hands and elbows. Back down on the scrubby grass, about a quarter mile to the north, they came to a white sign, black letters on a white background:

OFF LIMITS
AUTHORIZED MILITARY PERSONNEL ONLY

46.

Seeing the off-limits sign made all of Wendell Lett's aches and pains return throbbing. His head spun. "This is no good, no good at all," he blurted as he backed up, intent on heading back to the lava flow. A rock and a hard place was safer than this.

"Maintain calm," Jock said, "we're all right."

"Yeah? Says who?"

"The Preserve wasn't a military camp. Lett, stop. Listen to me."

"I don't see any *kine* barb wire," Kanani said.

"They don't need any," Lett snapped, "not in a no-man's-land like this." He rushed up to Kanani. "You knew. You knew we'd need to pass through a military zone. Didn't you? You knew all along."

Kanani was shaking her head. But she held up a hand. "Okay, okay—I did think it was possible. I'm sorry."

Lett faced Jock.

"Does look like the only way out, Lett. Or through."

"All right." He grabbed at the canteen. He passed it around. Jock and Kanani avoided each other's glances. Kanani was eyeing Jock as she sipped water. She kept eyeing him.

"What?" Jock barked at her. "You're the one. You said you had it all figured out."

"I got us out of there. I had that part figured. The rest was just . . . hoping."

Jock lapsed into silence, sorting things out in his head. "Look at it this way," he said eventually, "if this area is official military, then Lansdale's helicopter won't dare get too close. That's my guess. They must need to keep a low profile. So that's something."

"Not exactly a silver lining," Lett said.

"We still need to cross Saddle Road at some point," Kanani said.

"Yeah, that's still a major obstacle," Jock said. "Lansdale could have a crew waiting there. Like I was saying before."

"Saddle Road isn't military land itself—it's open to anyone," Kanani said. "Maybe Lansdale goes to the police even?"

"Nah. Police take too long here. You know that. And want nothing to do with this."

They gnawed on tropical bars and shared a can of C-rat, each deep in thought and worry.

They headed onward, across more of those high plains of brown grass and lava earth like they had traversed before the lava flow. The gradually rolling plains stretched for miles and miles, and they made better time. Mauna Loa stood behind their right shoulders now, while Mauna Kea waited before them, ahead on their left. They heard nothing, saw little but brown grass and the occasional bunch of scrawny short trees. They fell silent for whole miles at a time, each pondering what brought them to this and what lay in wait. Even if they cleared the military zone, Lett imagined, they still might encounter an army of Frankie clones lining Saddle Road with shotguns as a grinning Lansdale stood ready holding a black hood and the fattest glass-and-iron syringe known to veterinary science.

Four o'clock. Two more hours had passed. The wind let up, the sun blazed. Lett was drenched with sweat. Almost twelve hours into this. Up ahead another lava flow slab came into view, ever thicker and higher. They reached another warning sign:

FIRING RANGE
BEWARE LIVE ORDINANCE

A cinder cone loomed ahead, slightly to their right. Halfway up the dark and barren hill, white target boards gleamed.

Kanani looked to Lett and Jock.

"Not a good idea crossing that direction," Jock said.

"Might as well be a minefield," Lett added.

"Then we got no choice but to keep heading left," Kanani said and led them due northeast, straight toward Mauna Kea, a massive slope of a horizon rising into the sky, its peak still concealed by a solitary cloud bank that never seemed to clear. "We're in the Saddle now. No other way. Saddle Road will be straight ahead."

Jock reached a lone tangle of ragged trees that were more like diseased bushes. Lett and Kanani joined him. Jock crouched within the tangle, pushing away dry scrawny branches, and raised the binoculars. Lett didn't like how quiet Jock got. He grunted once, twice.

Jock handed Lett the binoculars. "Ten o'clock," he said.

Lett shifted his view slightly to the left. At the base of Mauna Kea's slope, he made out a cluster of short long buildings of corrugated metal. Quonset huts.

His throat went dry, his stomach wanted to seize up. He handed Kanani the binoculars.

"Auwe," she said and muttered similar thoughts.

Jock added a heavy sigh. "Way I see it? Must only be a small troop posted to those Quonset huts. Supposing they're Marines. They could take care of us."

"*Could. Might*," Kanani said. "No, nothing doing. It's too risky."

Jock didn't respond.

"And what if they're Army?" Lett added.

But Jock just growled.

***

Half an hour later—pushing 5:30 p.m. They had pressed forward, but it was slow going and they needed a break. They found a gully. It held a small cave, surely the entrance to another lava tube. Lett faced the hole, took a deep breath, and waved them down in.

The cave held the three of them standing and little more. Any farther and they would have to crouch and crawl. Their shoulders rubbed at rock and one another. They sipped more water rations, two swallows each. Something other than the cave was nagging at Jock. He kicked at pebbles like a kid left alone too long in a sandbox.

"What is it?" Lett said.

"Look. I done some thinking." Jock lifted his arms, let them slap at his hips. "I'll go there. Me only. Go it alone. Tell them I was hiking around and got lost. 'Cause I'm just this cuckoo gyrene still fouled up by the war and it's the only way to get some peace, see. Hawaii's just full of us." He held up a finger. "But. Some crazy types were coming after me. Don't know who they are. They followed me onto the firing range. My fellow Marines won't like that."

"You're a decoy," Kanani said.

"Let's call it a diversion. Might be the only way to get you through this gauntlet."

"If they are Marines," Lett said.

"We'll just have to take the chance. I won't muck things up. I got my papers all squared. I never was on The Preserve, remember? No one's to talk of it ever. Top secret." As he spoke, Jock couldn't look at Lett.

"Tell me something," Lett said. "Are you really aiming to reenlist?"

Jock's eyelids hung, making him look more sad than tired. "Look, don't ask questions. Don't worry about me. Just go along with it. It's the best plan and you know it. Maybe I even persuade them to head off Lansdale's posse? They're probably bored to tears out here. They'd love the action. Track down some deadbeats. What I'd really like to do is tell 'em Dugout Doug himself is involved somehow. But that's only asking for the stockade—for you and for me."

"Fuck 'em all," Lett said.

"Fuck 'em all," Jock responded. He sang a few lines of the old song. Lett joined in.

"*The long and the short and the tall . . . Fuck all the generals and above all fuck you! . . . So we're saying good-bye to them all . . .*"

They laughed. Kanani clapped.

Lett's laugh sputtered out. He stared at Jock. "Stay with us instead," he said. He didn't have to spell out what it meant. They could be on the lam quite a while.

"It's not my style," Jock muttered.

"Then, don't reenlist. Promise me that much."

"Too late. My mind's made up."

Lett's chest tightened and grew hot, as if he were smoking and holding it all in.

"I am what I am," Jock said. "They drilled it into me. And, hell,

I'm practically an Asiatic anyways. What am I supposed to do back there, home sweet home? Become a Pinkerton man? Busting strikes? Cracking down on the next wave of vets with a valid beef?" He spat.

Lett only now noticed that Kanani had left them alone. She was crawling out into the daylight with the binoculars. Jock was watching her, too, and an incredulous smile spread across his face as if he were watching some rare bird in a zoo. "One hell of a dame," he said.

"Ain't she, though?"

"She did what she had to do."

Jock went through his pack with Lett, separating items. He handed Lett one canteen, a can of C-rat, a spoon. Lett handed back the can. Where would he put it? Jock gave him the last tropical bar instead. He slung his pack back on.

"Keep your head down, gyrene," Lett said.

"You do the same, dogface."

"I don't know how to thank you," Lett said.

He saw the glint of tears in Jock's eyes. Jock must've seen Lett's own tears welling.

"Give me an hour," Jock said.

"Will do. Give 'em hell."

Jock squeezed Lett's shoulders. "You just make it out, will you? And some day? I hope you will know where to find me," he said, and he was off, scampering out the cave on his haunches like he was playing crab.

Lett, his eyes blurring wet, watched as Jock and Kanani shared gentle words and a hug out in the gully. Kanani pushed the binoculars into Jock's hands. He forced them back on her. She took them, pressed them to her chest like a teddy bear. Jock kissed her cheek. And he was away again and out into the blazing daylight. So fast had he passed through Lett's strange life that Lett wasn't sure if his soldier friend was an angel or a ghost.

47.

L ett and Kanani stayed in the cave a little while, listening to the
wind, crouching, debating their chances, hoping. They splashed
drops of water on their faces. They crept out of the cave; the sun
hung low on the horizon. They were a quarter mile south of Saddle
Road. The lava rock on this south side of the road stretched on for a
few miles to the east. They hiked northeast, heading straight for the
road, mighty Mauna Kea a brown monolith before them. Their plan
was to cross Saddle Road where the lava ended. The grassy slope
plains around the volcano would eventually lead them to the island's
lush and remote eastern coast.

They trudged on. They skirted the jagged 'a'a lava and flanked
the wavy slabs of *pahoehoe*—this wild mix of lava-lands was a laby-
rinth with no solution. The wind had picked up, flinging dust and
grit.

About ninety yards from Saddle Road, they hunkered behind a
mound. Lett drew the binoculars. The military encampment, well
behind them now to the northwest, looked as dead as ever, just
drab squares and rectangles. Closer to them he could see the road,
a winding strip of mottled gray cut out of the purple-black, a gravel
route packed down from use but so narrow and uneven that locals
warned visitors never to drive it.

Lett watched a truck approach. It was black, a panel truck, and
unmarked. It passed by.

Then another unmarked black panel truck passed.

Lett refocused; Kanani tugged at him; he kept watching. The
two black panel trucks kept passing, back and forth, east and west,
so much so that the gravel loosened and dust billowed.

Kanani squatted closer, whispering. "It's them."

"Lansdale's men," Lett said. "We have to assume it."

One of the panel trucks parked halfway between the encampment and their spot behind the mound. Two broad-shouldered men in dark gear exited the truck's rear, raised binoculars, and scanned the landscape.

Lett pulled behind the cover of the mound. He checked his watch: 6:30 p.m. The sky was dimming fast. Far west, over Kona, pink-and-orange streaks of clouds painted the sky. Soon the sun would be down and the lava would turn as black as night, impossible to cross without a flashlight. Even with their eyes adjusted to the dark they could bust an ankle or land facedown in the jagged stuff. And their pursuers had to know it.

The second black panel truck was still roaming the road, back and forth, west and east. Lett dared another look. The parked truck was there still, but the men weren't visible. Were they back inside it? Could he be sure? Or were they now out roaming the land?

The sun set, Mauna Kea blending into evening sky, their skin losing glow, going blue.

"They're trying to lock us in, get our exact coordinates," Lett told Kanani.

"What about those Quonset huts? See anything? Any *kine* activity?"

Lett shook his head. "Too far off. Soon it'll be like being in a cave, but outside."

Their pursuers could even be using the new night vision glasses. Lett didn't tell Kanani that. He didn't have to.

"We gonna cross that damn road," she said, "and we're going soon."

***

It was pushing seven o'clock; darkness was falling. The wind had calmed, bringing an eerie void of sound, like in a tunnel. The temperature was sinking faster, causing their sweat to cool clammy on their skin. They waited behind the mound, going over the plan, letting their eyes adjust. The sole good news was that the moon was out, only half a sphere, yet it would help light the terrain.

"It's shorter distance than a football field," Lett told Kanani. They would stay close, holding hands, and would have no choice but to take their time or they might trip. Lett would lead and Kanani would step where he stepped, like in a minefield.

They took deep breaths. They grasped hands and squeezed.

They scrambled out from the mound, crouching. The moonlight did help. Lett stepped here and there, bounding forward, and Kanani followed, lunging and wobbling, in what must have looked like two winos doing the bunny dance.

"Wait. What's that?"

Shouting sounded, from west of them. They lowered onto all fours, the lava poking at their stomachs. Lett fumbled for the binoculars.

More sights, sounds. Lights were flashing, then came what sounded like someone on a bullhorn. But this was from farther off.

Kanani planted the binoculars on Lett's eye sockets. "Some kind of alert," Lett said.

Beams of light shot into the sky.

They pushed on, scrambling along like spooked lizards. Lett banged his shin. Kanani tore her overalls.

Headlights glared along Saddle Road, coming their way. The black panel truck. Flashlights flickered on then off, from the lava just west of them.

"That's Lansdale's crew, getting on top of us. Keep going."

Lett stumbled. Kanani landed on him, but they rose as one and kept moving.

More headlights were coming up the road, pursuing the panel truck's headlights. A spotlight arced around.

"That's louder than a truck," Lett shouted. "A big scout car maybe."

They hit a stretch of flat ground and sprinted.

It was a big military scout car, armored, six wheels, mounted machine gun. The scout car gained on the panel truck.

"Look, look!" Kanani panted.

More headlights, a spotlight. A military jeep was coming from the other direction—from the east. It crossed Kanani and Lett's path and soon halted sideways, filling the narrow road.

Cutting off the panel truck.

Lett and Kanani were less than fifty yards from Saddle Road. Dust from the churned gravel made a fog, but Lett could see the flat and brown opposite side, where the lava ended, glowing blue in moonlight.

On they went, scrambling, one eye on the cluster of headlights. The scout car had pulled up behind the black panel truck to box it in—blocking its escape with a roadblock. The truck slowed, stopped in the road. Men jumped out of the scout car and from the jeep. From the headlights, Lett could make out their utility uniforms with USMC markings.

"Go, Marines, go," Lett blurted, and Kanani squeezed him as they hurried along.

The Marines surrounded the panel truck, creeping toward it, crouching. Men exited the truck's rear, their arms up high. They wore dark gear. Then the sideways jeep's lights illuminated the land where, Lett could see it now, other Marines were marching back other men in black, their arms up.

Another mound of rock, then the road. They hurried on and huddled at the mound, catching their breath, peering out. "Jock there?" Kanani gasped.

"Don't know. Can't tell."

"Lansdale?"

"Nope. Don't see him."

The Marines lined up their prisoners along the side of the road. Flashlights illuminated their faces white and Lett recognized some from the lava tube, from what they did to the commando. From his cell. Gear was at their feet, goggles and small packs, and grease guns and pistols. The Marines had their weapons aimed. Thompson guns.

"Saw some of them at Frankie's," Kanani said, squeezing Lett's hand, their hot sweat flowing as if from one.

"Go."

Out over the road they rushed, as low as they could, their thighs pumping. A narrow stretch of the lava field lined the other side—the smooth, ropy *pahoehoe*, so flat it shined in the moonlight. They crossed it and their feet hit the grass and it was like carpet. Sprinting now. They were heading toward a dark line, what had to be a gully. Kanani was leading.

Lett had to look, one more time. "Wait . . ."

He pulled at her, and they turned and crouched.

At the rear end of the jeep nearest them stood a silhouette, glowing red from the taillights. Only ten, fifteen yards away. The silhouette wore no USMC gear except for a bucket hat.

It was Jock. Jock was watching the Marines frisking the pursuers in the road. And he was watching for Lett and Kanani, making sure their route was secure.

For a moment, Jock turned to them. Their eyes met, locked. He waved them on, pointing, directing them onward. *Go, go,* he was saying. All clear. Now or never.

Lett nodded. Jock nodded.

Off they ran. Kanani pulled at Lett's loose coveralls and they made it to the gully where they dropped and turned to the road, lying with arms and legs intertwined, panting and wheezing, sweat splashing on their hands.

Lett drew the binoculars. Down at the roadblock, their pursuers were squatting in a circle out on the gravel, the other Marines guarding them. But Jock? He was nowhere to be seen.

Had they really seen him? It didn't matter. Lett now knew that his soldier friend was both a ghost and an angel.

48.

L ett could not think of a more wonderful spot to contemplate how far he'd come—yet still had to go. His open lanai looked out over a sparkling gurgling stream that ran down to him from a spring far away and high up on Mauna Kea. Beyond lay a field of tall, moist, and thick grass that was lined on either side by lush tropical forest. Like all the few structures here, his simple shack was built from debris. Planks and beams and corrugated metal made up his lanai and one-room domain. Thick vines cascaded down on all sides, helping to conceal the rust and graying wood.

The soft, lush basin around him had to be the most remote valley on the island. It ran along the bottom of a steep gorge that plummeted thousands of feet from the fertile plains above. Up there along the Hamakua Coast, the sugar plantations still held onto their iron rule. Up there might as well be Alaska. Inland from Lett's shack, the canyon stretched and snaked and narrowed for a couple miles at least, as far as he knew. No matter the spot, the summits and cliffs high above basked in sun long after the shade and dusk had cloaked them down below. In the other direction from Lett's shack lay a stretch of new taro crops and palm trees, then a compact beach of black lava sand, and finally, the vast Pacific Ocean, the sea softly lapping up.

Only one road led down into this valley, a twisting, rutted, plunging track that few jeeps or their drivers could handle. At first Lett feared one of those four-by-four vehicles would bring Lansdale, or a team of sunburned CIC men, or even CID detectives grouchy from a long journey. But they never did come. He got used to seeing the occasional local or rare haole adventurer. He hadn't gotten used to witnessing the wild horses cross his stream now and then, and he hoped he never would. Same went for the mango and avocado trees and especially the secluded waterfalls he heard. On the whole, it was like the Earth before man, the child before the disease.

Lett and Kanani had reached this valley two days after fleeing The Preserve. After Jock saved their lives, they had marched around Mauna Kea. In the dark, the scrubby grass had given way to shrubs and then a ragged forest of short dry mamane trees. Lett's hand was cut from the loose jagged 'a'a lava, and Kanani cleaned and bandaged it. It grew cool and they could've used a fire, but Lett didn't want to risk the smoke and light and Kanani agreed, adding that mamane were rare Hawaiian floras. They slept on soft underbrush, spooning. Too tired to talk, too relieved to worry.

In the morning, low fog cloaked all within yards. But as they moved on, it lifted, and bright green fern-like plants soon began to replace the mamane trees, filling every gap in the forest, perky and shiny like children come to play. Reddish-pink clover spread over the black gravel like the brightest area rugs. So near a volcano, this was the Earth itself starting over again—what the whole planet must've looked like, Lett thought, before even the first wiggling creatures began to rise up from the water and the soft mud.

They hiked north toward the Hamakua Coast. They passed through rain forest and navigated many streams. They saw waterfalls. They crossed plantation lands, including one Kanani had lived on as a girl. They passed through a couple small junctions with mom-and-pop stores offering homemade dried fish, fruit turnovers, and ice shaves. Kanani went into one for water and food, and Lett meanwhile spied a family of touring mainlanders staring at her, as if to say, *just look at that dirty island woman.*

She then led him north along the coast. She knew the exact way now. They followed a winding road and she stopped at a hillside cemetery. She went quiet and walked away from him, passing among the tombstones. Most were sooty and crumbling, but one was a glossy new gray. She stood before it, hands clasped at her waist, head bowed. Lett thought he heard her speaking and moved to her, but she waved him away.

"My faddah," she said afterward.

And they had marched on, following the coast road.

It seemed like he'd been in this valley much longer than two weeks. It took him the first week just to get his strength back, recovering while holed up in this shack that Kanani's people had given him. Like everyone down here, he had no electricity or mail service. No addresses existed. He boiled or purified his water, and his light was candles. The first couple days, the valley dwellers had passed to stare at this outlandish haole with his pink skin and sandy blond hair wanting to curl after an afternoon rain. Old Samoans, the skin hanging off their once-corpulent bodies. Wiry Asians in cast-off plantation work clothes. Dark-skinned paniolos in worn riding hats. Even a white couple with leathered faces, salt-and-pepper longish hair, and knives on their belts. Some must've wondered if he wasn't plainly *lolo*, or worse yet, dangerous.

He didn't know where Kanani was living down here. She had shepherded him into the valley and this shack, and then left him on his own. She said it had to be that way. He smelled barbecues and imagined that most all the people of the valley often gathered to eat together. He saw smoke coming from the black beach and heard drums at night and pictured a community luau with ukuleles and song and succulent roasted pig. But that was all right by him. The originals tolerated him but wanted no contact. He might be a danger to them, after all. He understood that. After those first couple days, no one appeared to stop and stare. He could sit for hours on this simple lanai and reflect and begin to understand.

This was his decontamination period. It was his purgatory and his purification. They had a tradition for it, he remembered—a place of refuge.

Kanani had visited him only a few times in those first two weeks, to check on him and to make sure that he had enough candles and was keeping his water fresh. She brought him food—pork wrapped in leaves, and poi made from the taro fields. A mango turnover pastry.

Each time Kanani came, she fed him more information, reporting in the measured tones of a sharp young sergeant returned to the CP after leading a critical patrol. She now wore thick old boots, threadbare denim trousers, and had a knife on her belt, too. She sat with him on the lanai, on one of his two mismatched wooden chairs.

"This is called the Valley of the Kings," she told him. "The high ridges around us hold the mana of ancient Hawaiian rulers. But a great tsunami came and destroyed this valley. It was the bad one of '46. Same one hit Hilo. Had one village down here, schoolhouse, post office, but the big water took the whole works. Ancient temples. Graves."

"Did they all work for the plantations down here?" Lett asked.

"Many, yes. Before the plantations came, they had a mission church here. And those missionaries, they brought the plantation owners, and the plantation owners brought your military. That land grab of theirs needed defending after all." Kanani shrugged. "Many native islanders above are scared of this valley. Oh—my grandmother grew up here, did I tell you? Tutu wahine. On my faddah side. Tutu wahine always said the tsunami was the gods' anger at us, for what we were becoming."

"You have family down here now?"

Kanani nodded. She fell silent. The shack creaked in the breeze.

"You never see the Territory of Hawaii flag down here," she said. "That Union Jack, the red, white, and blue—that's a flag of occupation, yeah? Many believe in restoring the Hawaiian nation, want to break off from being owned by the USA. Then we reestablish the sovereignty the haole plantation barons and politicians stole from us."

Two wild horses emerged from the forest and drank from the stream, their hooves kneading at the mossy rocks. Lett loved how shiny their brown coats were in the wild. Kanani smiled at them.

"You're not going back, are you?" he said.

"No. I had orders to join a new intelligence office of theirs, in Honolulu. Never again. I learned that from you."

***

As Lett sat on his lanai one evening, watching the stars, Kanani appeared on the other side of the stream. She crossed the water and took her chair on the lanai, and they looked out. For minutes they sat, saying nothing. When he'd arrived in Kona Town, he could've never sat like this. So damn patient.

"At first, the others left me alone down here, too," she said. "They left me to think about what I had done and want to do."

"Place of Refuge," Lett said.

"*Pu'uhonua*, yes. That's exactly right."

High in the black sky, the lights of an airplane passed, a comet in slow motion.

"We're gonna get you back home," Kanani said.

"To Heloise? To my boy?"

"Yes. We're gonna find a way. When you're ready."

"Thank you. Wait—you said *we*."

"Yes. *We*."

***

One afternoon in the Valley of the Kings, Kanani burst out of the forest and marched across the stream and found Lett up on the lanai. Her hair was down and wet in her face. She pushed it away. She looked as white as he. Her eyes were red. Tears.

"I was up above, in a store." She handed him a rolled-up *Honolulu Star-Bulletin*.

On the bottom of the front page was a headline: MURDER BURSTS KONA RACKET. According to the brief story, former US Army Lieutenant Colonel and reputed AWOL Charles Selfer had survived a violent encounter with known Honolulu gangster Francisco "Frankie" Baptiste. Lieutenant Colonel Selfer was allegedly running a smuggling ring for high-priced valuables plundered from Asia during the war, with Baptiste as his partner. They had a dispute. Selfer killed Baptiste in the fight and was in serious condition. Local police had handed Selfer over to US military authorities, who transferred Selfer to a high-security prison on the mainland.

Lett saw no mention of Jock Quinn, of course. He could assume Jock had already returned to his beloved Marines on Oahu. The Corps had surely taken him back, another troubled wayward son, and hopefully given him a nice promotion. And Jock, for his part, wouldn't want to risk any further exposure—to himself or to Lett.

Lett should've felt something for Charles Selfer but nothing came to him—no remorse, no sadness, no maxims about reaping and sowing. He felt about the same as one did seeing an ant unlucky enough to scurry into the path of a boot heel. He asked Kanani to keep checking the papers and radio, but the story never returned. He didn't expect it to. He imagined Selfer in a cell, possibly a psych ward, raving about a secret camp for which he was only a tool, and no one would believe him. They might brand him a dipsomaniac, a Commie, an assassin, anything that suited their machinations. Perhaps they'd experiment on him with their new drugs. The new agency called the CIA would certainly need fresh guinea pigs.

***

Another afternoon, Lett jolted awake on his cot in his shack and feared his nightmares had returned. But it was something outside. He shuffled out to his lanai. Across the stream, between two bushes flowering red, stood a Chinese woman. Kanani stood behind her. They pulled back when he looked their way.

Lett was sure it was Miss Mae. But Kanani wouldn't admit it. She'd surely made a vow.

***

The next time Kanani reported to him, she told him the camp compound they'd known as The Preserve was completely cleared away. She'd had locals she could trust check it out. The front gate was still locked but had no guard, only an older wartime off-limits sign. They'd spied on the place from the perimeter fence. Eventually they found a way in and walked through the compound. It was a ghost camp, like so many on islands here and throughout the Pacific after the war. It was as if none of them were ever there.

***

The last time she came, she had another flower in her hair, this one pink with long petals.

"You're ready," she told him. "It's time you go back to your wife."

Lett nodded. "How?"

"We'll send you there. I told you."

"It's Miss Mae, isn't it? Miss Mae is arranging this. Don't tell me she's not because I saw her, and don't tell me I didn't see her because I did."

Kanani lowered her head. "Okay. Yes. She was here."

"Why? I understand why Miss Mae would. But why would you help me like this?"

"You saved my behind back there in Kona Town, Wendell Lett. I never forgot that. But that was just the start, wasn't it? And, maybe I might have fallen for you one lili bit meanwhile. So you go. I'm helping you go. That's how much I care for you."

She hugged him a long time, then she turned and disappeared inside the lush greenery.

Kanani's fellow valley dwellers came for him the next day and led him up the old steep road and out of the valley. They put him in the back of a pickup truck for Hilo. From there they would put him on an interisland steamer and then a sea-bound merchant ship, all with full papers in his name, since it was certain he would never be exposed for what he'd endured at The Preserve.

No one would ever believe it. No one would believe him if he talked about it. That alone made him no threat. Talking about it would only prove him insane.

On his long journey back by ship and then by rail and thumb, his dead old friends never visited him, nor did his nightmares. Lett wondered if this meant the war was finally over for him. Could it mean that his troubles were healed, that he finally had his cure?

Sometimes this worried him more than anything. Yet his lovely vision of Heloise waiting restored him, just as it once had when he was on the front line. And only then did he realize just how much he had truly missed his Heloise. Seeing her again was like discovering something elementary to existence, as if a whole color had vanished from the spectrum of light yet had now returned.

EPILOGUE

Jock Quinn was killed in 1950, one of the early American casualties of the Korean War. He wasn't a Marine then, for his beloved Corps would not take him back. But General MacArthur's US Army had. An initial brief obituary labeled Jock a hero for storming an enemy Communist stronghold to save the lives of his fellow soldiers. The truth came out years later, once the records were finally declassified under pressure from journalists and victims' families. Jock had seen US air strikes using napalm incendiary bombs on innocent Korean refugees. He had witnessed US troops being ordered to gun down civilians. He couldn't take it anymore. During an air raid he entered a cave and attempted to pull out the civilians inside being asphyxiated by the fumes. Women and children. His fellow GIs, green and rattled and ready to crack, were shooting them dead when they exited the tunnels. Friendly fire caught Jock. Or, maybe he was just in the way.

AFTERWORD

The story of Wendell Lett is fictional, as is The Preserve itself, but I have plucked certain characters and events from established historical record.

The Imperial Japanese Army and its various confederates did plunder hordes of gold and treasure and goods from Asia. Whether they moved the spoils to the Philippines and buried them in underground caves and shelters is disputed. The topic has become known as "Yamashita's Gold," named after the top Japanese general defending the isles from General Douglas MacArthur's storied return. The clearest and strongest substantiation of the plundering and how it was used once in American hands comes from historians Sterling and Peggy Seagrave, who wrote two books that ask many good questions: *The Yamato Dynasty: The Secret History of Japan's Imperial Family* (2000); and *Gold Warriors: America's Secret Recovery of Yamashita's Gold* (2003). My portrayal of the Japanese Golden Lily program comes mostly from these works.

The ensuing mystery of how the loot has been both exploited and hunted is a compelling story in itself. The Seagraves connect real-life persons to the liberation and commandeering of the plunder. Among them are Japanese gangster Yoshio Kodama and shadowy American intelligence operative Edward G. Lansdale, both of whom appear in this novel.

Edward Lansdale was an enterprising and legendary figure who firmly believed in American exceptionalism and was supposedly the model for Graham Greene's *The Quiet American*. Lansdale has been described as being responsible for everything from America's involvement in the Vietnam War to the Kennedy assassination, depending on the angle. While operating in the Philippines, Lansdale worked to prop up his own man for president, one Ramon Magsaysay, whom Lansdale and the CIA helped in defeating opposing Communist rebels. In the mid-1950s, Lansdale took his road show to Vietnam, and on and on.

I portray these players filtered through a writer's lens, of course. Where I put them in this book is purely notional. Kodama was in a US military prison during much of the period in this novel—I let him out briefly so he could do what my schemers needed him to do.

As for General Douglas MacArthur, the Seagraves contend that the general visited treasure sites in the Philippines after Lansdale reported them to MacArthur's Tokyo HQ.

In the postwar years, General MacArthur remained all-powerful in Asia, much like an aspiring emperor who once ruled and consolidated vast regions of the Roman Empire. MacArthur's power wouldn't hold, however, as President Truman dismissed the popular commander in 1951 at the height of the Korean War. In this novel, I propose, however, that there never was a problem that powerful money could not fix. And as the Seagraves argue, the plundered Japanese treasure would go on to outlive MacArthur by decades, its profits creating one unassailable legacy after another. It went on to fund CIA missions, and black ops, and on and on, right down to the Nixon administration's dirty tricks. We see the fingerprints of such machinations on all of our transgressions right through to the debacle that was the 2003 invasion of Iraq. And onward today. When, upon leaving office in 1961, celebrated former WWII commander and then-President Dwight D. Eisenhower warned of the dangers of the Military Industrial Complex, he well knew what he was predicting, warning, and deploring.

After the war, the early days of a reborn US intelligence system constituted a type of Wild West prompted by postwar musical chairs, power plays, and the seminal National Security Act of 1947 that ultimately created the CIA. From this font of intrigues arose the true and disputed existence of clandestine rogue operations and camps, classified psychological drug programs, and even plots against major figures, including assassination. I'm no conspiracy theorist, but there's enough historical record already released to show such things went on. General MacArthur's power struggle with President Truman of course existed, made no better by an awkward and brief attempt at reconciliation in the middle of the Pacific Ocean at Wake Island in 1950. It came to a head with Truman's dismissal of MacArthur. Like Lansdale, MacArthur remains a controversial lightning rod for the issue of American might. This stretches back to the 1930s, to MacArthur's involvement leading the brutal clampdown of the Bonus Army as well as to his courting by right-wing interests scheming to overthrow FDR in the Business Plot—both of which are fact (see *The Plot to Seize the White House*, 2015, by Jules Archer). As with Lansdale, many either love or hate MacArthur depending on allegiances. I find both characters to be those larger-than-life types that a writer simply can't resist fictionalizing. So here they roam. Some may not like my depiction of MacArthur's realm or even of the man himself, but there exists more than enough complimentary nonfiction to offset any concerns. Other true events and characters in this story include Marine General Smedley Darlington Butler (and his *War Is a Racket*, 1935), US Military Government in Hawaii, Hotel Street in Honolulu, the wartime tragedy on Saipan, early atrocities in the Korean War, and many additional details large and small.

Other characters are completely notional. Kanani Alana didn't exist, but how I wish that she had. I like to imagine Hawaii celebrating her as a national hero. For her self-styled Hawaiian Pidgin English, I relied on novels by Milton Murayama, *All I Asking for Is My Body* (1975) and *Plantation Boy* (1998), as well as on the Internet, but especially on the dedicated work of Kent Sakoda (see *Pidgin Grammar: An Introduction to the Creole Language of Hawaii*, 2003). Previous versions of the manuscript had Kanani speaking hardcore Pidgin throughout—in the end, Kent Sakoda and other wise folks helped me realize that I should ease up on the Pidgin because it might distract the reader. The language dork and literary translator in me resisted, but common sense won out. In any case, all mistakes are my own.

Jock Quinn is also fictional, though millions of sincere yet troubled vets just like him served back then and continue to serve today. Surely, many traumatized vets like Wendell Lett existed, nabbed or not, tens of thousands of them having deserted during WWII and a number never returning. Where did they all go? A few were certainly pressured into severe and damning duties they found themselves all too suited for.

What was often called "combat fatigue" in the postwar years is unfortunately all too real. It has had many names and will remain with us as long as we kill our fellow human beings. Today we know it as PTSD, of course. For research, I'm grateful for *The Evil Hours: A Biography of Post-Traumatic Stress Disorder* (2015) by David J. Morris as well as countless other sources, including a moving 1946 documentary by John Huston, *Let There Be Light*. The Army commissioned the film but tried banning it because the truths within were deemed too "demoralizing." Find it if you can to gain a uniquely disturbing sense of the postwar period.

ACKNOWLEDGMENTS

In addition to Kent Sakoda at the University of Hawaii at Manoa, I'd like to thank the countless kind people who assisted me with research in Hawaii. They include Ermile Hargrove, Brandy Field, The Great Barusky, and so many others whose names I didn't get.

I'm also deeply grateful to the perceptive test readers who slogged through earlier versions of this story and shared their thoughts—thank you a ton Dave Anderson; Gary Cruiser (whereabouts unknown); the crack team of Molly Holsapple, Sherry Cronin, and Lynn Greenwood; and to Mary Bisbee-Beek for her always wise advice. Special thanks to Beth Canova and Kim Lim at Skyhorse Publishing for their keen and invaluable guidance and to Peter Riva for suggesting General MacArthur's postwar Pacific realm as Wendell Lett's next destination.

As always, I thank my wife René for all her support and belief in me—and for introducing me to the amazing world of Hawaii.

***

Wendell Lett's nightmarish experience in WWII is told in my novel *Under False Flags* (2014).